LONG LIVE THE SOULLESS

Dark Maji Book 5

KEL CARPENTER

Long Live the Soulless

Published by Kel Carpenter LLC

Copyright © 2020, Kel Carpenter

Edited by Analisa Denny

Proofread by Dominique Laura

Cover Art by Trif

Map and Graphic Designed by Zenta Brice

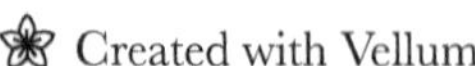 Created with Vellum

"There are different kinds of darkness," Rhys said. I kept my eyes shut. "There is the darkness that frightens, the darkness that soothes, the darkness that is restful." I pictured each. "There is the darkness of lovers, and the darkness of assassins. It becomes what the bearer wishes it to be, needs it to be. It is not wholly bad or good."

Sarah J. Maas, *A Court of Mist and Fury*

The Sirian Continent
N
THE CRYSTAL CONTINENT
TRITOL
LIPH
N'SKARA
JIBREAL
ILVAS
VUSUT
CISEA
CISEAN MOUNTAINS
BANGRATAS
DUMAS
ZYBURN
NORCASTA
SARI SARI ISLANDS
TRIENE
LEONE
IAMONT

CHAPTER 1
WHERE IT BEGAN

*"When it is fear itself you are chasing, neither the past nor the
future can scare you away."*
— *Mariska "Risk" Darkova, beast tamer*

Her sister climbed these steps once.

All one thousand of them.

Now it was Risk's turn to do it for Quinn.

Alpis perched on her shoulder. Her ever-present companion. Leaving the palace hadn't been so difficult when the person anchoring her to that place was no longer there. Just as coming back to where it all began was not as hard as she thought it would be.

While the journey was long, she had the only thing she needed to keep her going.

Hope.

1

Hope that she could do it.

Hope that she would be enough.

Hope . . . it was a terrible thing. Her heart pattered in her chest as she approached the decaying statues of the ancient gods. Mazzulah seemed to stare at her. Those dark eyes watching her movements.

Risk stood at the base of the pedestal and looked up to her patron god.

Mazzulah of the dark realm.

God of beasts.

All her life, she'd run from it. From this dark god and the power they bestowed on her. She believed what the N'skari had said when they called her evil and unnatural. A beast herself. A creature to be broken and tamed.

But Quinn came for her. She showed her that she was not evil, despite being unnatural to this world all the same. She trained her to be strong of body and mind. She gave her everything . . . and Risk ruined it. She killed that noble, and Quinn died because of her actions.

No more, she chastised herself. No more would she live in fear of the dark.

She was not a creature of the light. She never had been.

"I'm coming for you," Risk whispered.

The statue stared down at her, as if in challenge for her to do just that.

Risk walked into the temple.

It smelled acrid. The stench of death and decay and mold conjuring old memories. She closed her eyes against the onslaught.

Breathe, she commanded herself.

Risk parted her lips and ignored the scents of her shadowed past. She refused to look down the long hall toward the cage where she was kept.

No, for this she needed to go to the place where it truly began.

"*The dark realm awaits you,*" Alpis told her.

"I know," she whispered back as she approached the very slab of stone that they'd tied her down on that first time. It was here that any innocence she'd clung to was stripped away. Men of the Council, of the People, of her own household . . .

They raped her.

Taking turns even when her blood ran freely across the stone.

Blood and seed.

From that seed, her nightmares were born.

Risk lifted a tentative hand and brushed it over the place she'd lain against her will. Held down as they forced themselves on her and then had the audacity to blame her for it.

For so long, she believed them true. That something about her had caused it.

That the evil in her incited the worst in them.

Even when she told herself it wasn't, that they

were simply monsters, some part of her still believed it.

Quinn freed her of that too.

Now it was her turn to do the same.

Risk stepped around the cold slab, toward the doors.

They were nearly as tall as the ceiling. Built from some black stone that shined iridescently. They had no handles. No markings. If not for their prominent placement in the temple, they'd likely be overlooked.

As long as she'd been kept here, she'd never seen them opened.

Not once.

"Those of the light cannot see them. Those of the gray cannot open them. Only those born of the dark realm can enter of their own will." Alpis spoke in her mind with complete assurance.

She took a step toward them, her heart beating wildly in her chest.

Sweat slicked her palms as she lifted her hands.

"For Quinn," she whispered, setting them upon the stone.

It was cold to the touch.

She pushed, using all her strength to open them.

A shrill creak of the hinges trilled through the air, but no one answered.

She blinked into the darkness.

Open air surrounded her. A dark sky with violet clouds that drifted on a frozen wind. The marble flooring continued forward in front of her, turning to stairs that ascended so high she could not see where they stopped.

"Quinn?" she called out, softly at first. A hint of something familiar brushed against her, but her sister was not there.

"Quinn?" she yelled this time.

A dark, lovely chuckle was her answer. It seemed to come from everywhere and nowhere at once.

"What was that?" she asked the bird on her shoulder.

"*Your invitation*," he answered.

"Where is my sister?" she asked him. "You told me I could save her. That this was the way. Where is she?"

Alpis stretched his wings. She noticed then that they were darker. Closer to that of a shadow. Where the night could be seen through, he was but a void of darkness with two glowing golden eyes.

Alpis launched into the sky and flew toward the staircase.

"*There*," he whispered in her mind, flying upwards.

Risk swallowed hard on the lump in her throat.

She lifted her eyes; steps as far as she could see.

Somewhere up there was Quinn.

"I'm going to bring you back," she promised into the emptiness.

Then Risk Darkova started to climb.

"An honorable man robbed of all he owns still has honor. A kind man can lose everything and still have kindness. But a soulless man who has lost all that he is and was—has nothing. For nothing was what he came from, so to it he shall return."
— Draeven Adelmar, rage thief, left-hand to the King of Norcasta

S ilence. It permeated the palace like the graveyard it was.

Norcasta had been rid of near all its lords and ladies that fateful night.

The few that remained were smart enough to not ask for an audience. Not anymore, and certainly not with the king.

A month had passed since Quinn Darkova's

massacre and consequent death. A month since Risk Darkova fled into the night, never to be seen or heard from again.

A month since he had lost his king and his friend to the souls that plagued him for so long.

Draeven did not understand what it was Lazarus went through. He couldn't comprehend the strain that the souls put on him. All he knew was that when Lazarus learned of Quinn's death, and his hand in it, the battle that had been waging within finally broke. He lost to his demons, and no one had dared enter that wing of the palace since.

Footsteps echoed in the empty corridor, drawing his attention from the throne room and the memories that accompanied it.

"Dominicus," Draeven greeted, his tone not as pleasant as it once was. The stress of running a kingdom without a king had taken its toll.

"I've received word from one of my spies. Amelia Reinhart is headed to Triene."

Draeven cursed under his breath. He feared this. The truth.

If it was as Dominicus said, there was only one outcome, and her actions had guaranteed it.

"Can your spies intercept her?" Draeven asked.

"No," Dominicus said. "She is too powerful. The few that have tried wound up dead by their own volition. I've told the one's reporting to keep their distance and make me aware if there's any new developments."

Draeven nodded. It was all they could do. If Amelia was in bed with Triene, it explained a great deal. It also meant there was no taking her out. Not until she left their territory.

"And Lord Northcott?" Draeven prompted, as he started to walk down the empty hallway. Dominicus fell in step.

"Settling in the North. Dissension from the locals has lessened over his rule. He's not kind, but neither is he cruel. He's working to build businesses up and increase trade. He wants Dumas to rival Leone for trade, and his ambition is working in our favor for the moment."

That was better than Draeven expected. He'd let the wealthy lord leave with his life and promise of more power should he fall in line. It pleased him that it seems Northcott did just that.

Draeven detested having to kill men because their flaws got the better of them, and frankly, he couldn't afford to after the massacre. The other regions were already struggling enough with their lords disposed. Norcasta was in a state of turmoil that he desperately needed to stabilize if what Dominicus said about Amelia Reinhart was true.

"Has Lazarus resurfaced?"

Draeven tensed at the question.

"No," his answer was curt.

"It's been a month," Dominicus said.

"I know."

"Norcasta is not secure. We took this country, and the heirs are nearly gone. Slavery is ending because of him and the people rejoice in the streets because their old masters are dead. This is when we should be creating our houses to ensure the peace—"

"I know," Draeven said again, then sighed.

"How long is he going to grieve her?" There was an edge of frustration in his tone that Draeven understood well.

"I'm not sure grieving is all he's doing."

Dominicus narrowed his gaze. "What do you mean?"

"While I don't understand it, I think that Lazarus loved her more than he knew. More than he should have. When I told him what happened to her, I saw the change. I think the souls are in control, and I think they want blood for what's been done."

"If he wanted blood, why has he stayed away?" Dominicus asked.

The problem was that Draeven did not know.

He wasn't sure himself, and yet he couldn't shake the feeling that there was more. He could not convince himself this was simply grief—or that this was the worst of what would come from it.

"I can't answer that," Draeven said quietly. "I wish I could."

Dominicus looked away, his lips pressing together in a tight line.

"How do we expect people to fall in line when their king is nowhere to be found?"

"We show them that House Fierté is strong," came another voice. Higher pitched and chiding in a way that only one person could be.

Both Draeven and Dominicus turned to the stewardess of the palace.

"Lorraine," Dominicus said, his tone changing instantly. "We were just—" A softness entered it, followed by a note of apology. It was no secret that Lorraine struggled with Quinn's death. Like Lazarus, she didn't want to believe it. Unlike him, she helped burn the other woman's remains on a pyre, held vigil from sundown to sunup, and kept going.

"I know what you were discussing," Lorraine said, her own voice terse. While she'd moved on physically, Draeven suspected the dark circles beneath her eyes had more to do with the girl's loss than her duties in the palace. "Our king will return when he is well and ready. Meanwhile, that bitch is going to cause a problem. It is *our* job to ensure that House Fierté remains strong. The best way to do that is to show the people we are." Draeven could believe it; the way she spoke and the harsh lines of her face. Her brown and gray hair was pulled back in a tight braid. She might be struggling the same as all of them, but she was resilient. "Lazarus is indisposed, but that doesn't mean that his left-hand can't begin assigning lordship. I will write the letters myself if I must, and if our king is angry with the decision, he can take it up with me when he is back."

"I think you're right," Draeven said slowly. "We've given him time and all we can do until he's ready is hold together his empire. Dominicus, I want a list of recommendations from you by the end of day. It's time we start filling positions. Quinn might be gone, but House Fierté will survive."

Lorraine's eyes were hard as she nodded. "The palace will need to reopen to visitors. I'll make arrangements once the appointments are done."

And with that, Lorraine left, leaving them to their work.

"She's a strong woman," Draeven remarked when she was far enough away that he was sure he wouldn't have burned supper for the comment.

"She has to be to put up with us," Dominicus said.

Draeven cracked a grin, but it felt hollow even as he did it.

He'd said that House Fierté would survive. He meant it, but he didn't say in what state it would be when all was said and done.

As much as he had feared who Lazarus was becoming with her, Draeven now feared what he would become without her.

CHAPTER 3
THE BARGAIN

"Nothing is ever truly free, for freedom is an illusion unto itself."
— *Quinn Darkova, fear twister, dead*

Many days had passed since that first whisper of her name on the wind.

The dark sun rose and fell in the midnight sky.

The blood moon waxed and waned.

Quinn sat atop the dais beside the dark god, Mazzulah, waiting for her sister to finish the climb. It was a long way from the realm of the living to that of the dead, and only those strong enough would survive it without dying themselves.

"She draws near," Mazzulah said in his male form. His voice was the embers of flame. It felt like cold whispers across heated skin. Silk and seduction and, above all, darkness.

Lovely. Everything about the dark god was as lovely as it was cruel.

"You say she's returned for me, but I've never heard of a dead man rising." She didn't ask a question outwardly, but the god's plum-colored lips still curled in a smile.

"You are no man, and the dead do not rise." It was all Mazzulah said. The god loved to play in words, just as Lazarus had, and as Quinn had learned to.

The sound of breathing and the broken whisper of her name drew both their attention.

"Quinn," her sister said as she heaved herself over the last step and onto the dais. To her credit, she did not collapse to her knees, though they shook violently.

"You came for me," Quinn said, moving like she was going to stand. Her body dissipated into shadows and smoke, reforming in front of Risk.

Her sister reached for her, as if she could not believe her eyes.

Chilled hands touched Quinn's cheeks, but they felt warm on the dead woman's skin. When she'd died, her soul had come here, and the cold that she'd always clung to became all there was. All she was.

For so long she'd believed the winter was something the N'skari had created. That the goddess Skadi was responsible for its eternalness.

She now knew the truth.

That the desecrated temple of Mazzulah was the only entry into the dark realm that existed on the Sirian continent, and its cold depths could not truly be contained behind two doors.

"I will always come for you," Risk whispered. Her lips were chapped and cracked. Her skin drawn tight from exhaustion and lack of sleep. A great black bird of prey sat on her shoulder, its golden eyes staring at Quinn shrewdly.

Neiss descended from the twin throne Quinn had sat upon and slithered across the cold stone. Risk lowered her hands from Quinn to the snake at their feet. He lifted his head in greeting to Risk, and she lowered her face, resting her forehead to his.

"Hello, old friend," she said to him, speaking fondly. The emotion that coated her tone was different from what she used with Quinn.

After a moment, she raised her head once more.

There was a sadness in her eyes. A sorrow.

"I'm not sure you should have," Quinn whispered. She felt it the moment the dark god rose from his throne. The very air changed, and the creatures that cried out from below quieted. Cold winds settled in the sky where they stood, overlooking all.

"Mariska Darkova," the god said. His voice wrapping around the syllables of her sister's name. Turning it into something more by simply speaking it.

"Mazzulah," her sister uttered his name as a curse and a prayer.

The dark chuckle the god gave revealed what he thought of that.

"Are you angry with me, child?" he asked her.

Her sister's white eyebrows drew together. "N-no."

"Then what has brought you home?" the god asked, looming closer. Her cold fingers burned as they brushed Quinn's bare arm. She stepped back, obliging to the god's silent command.

"I have come for my sister," Risk said, lifting her chin. To her credit, her voice did not quiver again.

Mazzulah never stopped smiling throughout their exchange.

Quinn looked away. She was torn between the feelings in her chest; such immense gratitude for what Risk meant to do, and such horror for what it would cost her.

Mazzulah didn't tell Quinn his plans, but she'd watched him long enough. Knew him well enough to know that her sister should never have set foot in the dark realm.

"Which one?" he asked. Risk frowned, and then it occurred to her. She was half-raksasa, after all. And the raksasa were Mazzulah's children.

"Quinn," she said, speaking harsher again. "I have come for Quinn."

"Hmm," the god hummed.

A cold hand wrapped around Quinn's waist, pulling her into his side.

Like him, she wore two strips of dark fabric. One over each shoulder that extended the full length of her body. A silver chain around her hips kept the cloth in place.

His clawed nails pressed into flesh as his dark bicep curled around her. Lips trailed from her jaw to her temple.

Risk's eyebrows drew together once more, and Quinn knew she both understood and didn't. That her innocence, and lack thereof, kept her from fully grasping this situation.

"Quinn died, and because the darkness of her soul, she was mine to claim," Mazzulah murmured.

"She shouldn't have died," Risk said. "It was my fault."

"Perhaps," Mazzulah mused, his eyes sweeping Quinn's face. Watching her reaction to Risk's words. "But she did, and now she's mine."

Her sister's hands clenched into fists.

"Alpis brought me here. He said that there is a way for me to bring her back." Her tone was desperate now, and Quinn closed her eyes against it because she could not interfere. The god was not wrong that her soul was as dark as they came. He was owed that. Owed her.

But if this Alpis brought Risk here, Quinn could

only take that to mean that Mazzulah sent Alpis to her sister himself.

She wondered if Risk realized it yet.

"There is," Mazzulah said, pulling away and turning back for his throne. The god of the dark realm was a fickle creature. Mercurial as they came. Possessive in a way that rivalled even Lazarus. "But you see, I've grown quite fond of Quinn. Her darkness . . . it's beautiful. Neiss went above and beyond with her. The greatest of his heirs. The worst of his heirs . . ." he murmured, and she recognized the signs of him getting lost in that maze of an immortal mind of his.

Quinn could see it then, that her sister was starting to understand.

"I will not give her up for nothing, child. In fact, I will only give her up for *everything.*"

While she was dead, she was still fear. Her magic was her soul, and she did not lose that in death. She simply became it in a way that she couldn't with a flesh body tying her to the realm of men.

Quinn did not feel fear at Mazzulah's words.

But Risk did. Still, she stepped forward with her head held high and said, "What is the price?"

At once his golden eyes flicked up, regarding Risk once more.

"War is coming to your world. The war to end all wars. The final fight. You will need her to win."

"I . . . I don't understand," Risk said. "You want us to win a war?"

Mazzulah didn't hesitate as he regarded the half-raksasa.

"Yes," the god said. "But that is not all."

Risk looked between Quinn and Mazzulah, as if her sister could say or do anything to explain what the deity was asking. She shook her head, and Risk's lips pressed together.

"What else do you want?" Risk asked, both her fear and her ire with men was rising. Quinn could see it as surely as she saw the dark sun.

"You," Mazzulah said. "I will release Quinn from this realm, but you will stay."

"I—" Risk started, her indignation giving way to panic.

"I don't want *you*," he said. "Not as I want *her*. I need you. To train you. You will stay until you reach ascension. Because as surely as my lovely little fear twister will be needed for this win, so too will my own heir be needed."

"Heir?" Risk said. Quinn noted it too. She noted many things in Mazzulah's ramblings and meanderings and violent delights. She didn't know how long she'd been here. Only that it seemed like a very long time and yet no time at all.

"Yes," the dark god purred. He motioned with his hand for Quinn to join him. His golden eyes the only warmth in the realm of beasts and death. The intensity with which he stared at her set her blood aflame.

But Quinn didn't act on it. Not yet.

Something held her back, or rather, someone.

Much as Mazzulah made his interest in her clear, he never pushed beyond what she'd offer. He wanted her to want him of her own will. By her own choice. Sometimes she wanted to as well. In this cold realm of misery, who wouldn't?

But she couldn't forget *him*. The man with dark eyes and calloused hands.

The Maji that found her and molded her and then unleashed her upon the world.

She couldn't forget Lazarus. She couldn't move on.

Even in death.

Still, Quinn liked games as much as the dark god. She strode over and placed herself on his lap. He slipped his left knee between her thighs and one muscled arm came to wrap around her torso.

"Every god has an heir. One from your realm who represents them in power and soul. They are our chosen champions. The people we have chosen to guide and shape for the games we play. You are mine. Just as Quinn is Neiss'."

"What is the point of an heir if you're undying and immortal?" Risk asked, carefully treading around his demand.

"To play the game, of course."

"The game to end all games," Quinn whispered as the pieces of what she'd heard over her time there slowly started to click together.

"The game to end all games?" Risk repeated.

Chilled fingertips grazed her cheek, turning her face toward his.

Mazzulah smiled, and it was beautiful, if not terrible.

Man or woman, both his forms were a sight to behold. They were alluring and enticing in such a way that you didn't see how utterly devastating the god was until it was too late.

"My beauty listens," he murmured.

"I'm so much more than my pretty face," Quinn replied just as softly.

"I know. I wouldn't want you if you weren't."

Quinn scoffed and shook her head, which only made the god laugh. He liked her because she was cruel. He took her disinterest as a game itself, though he didn't seem to realize the reason for it. Or perhaps he did and simply thought that death was a long time —and permanent enough to make her reconsider.

"Once upon a time when the world was new, Mazzulah was not the dark god, but the *king*," Quinn said. The god himself leaned back, making no move to stop her. He seemed interested in how she would tell the story. "The other gods thought this unfair. Why should he be king? Was his power truly so great?" Quinn looked from him to her sister as she continued. "So, they devised a game. One where our world was the board and the Maji they created were the pieces. The heirs that were chosen were powerful beyond compare. They were as close to the gods as one could come because the gods wanted to see who truly deserved to be king—or queen. The light gods won."

"We were cheated," Mazzulah corrected. The first hint of his temper showing as his onyx horns straightened and the golden insignia upon his forehead began to shine.

"Cheated or not, you were exiled here—along with the other dark gods."

"How were you cheated?" Risk asked.

He cast her a calculated glance before saying, "Children of the dark are always more powerful. Most were too weak to contain the darkness. Few lived to maturity. Even fewer survive their ascension. How can we play a game when our side has almost no picces?"

"Let me get this straight. You want me to stay here and train with you until my ascension, and then Quinn and I are to win this war?" Risk asked.

"The other heirs of the dark gods will help."

"There was no war when I left Norcasta," she pointed out.

Mazzulah smiled darkly. "But there is now. Or rather, there will be when the king's present arrives."

"Whose heir is Lazarus?" Quinn asked.

Mazzulah didn't answer her immediately. When she turned to see why, he seemed contemplative. "Beliphor. His heirs are the only Maji by nature that possesses the power to defy death. As they devour creatures of magic and steal their essence by force, in turn, the creatures devour them. Should they not die . . . they would live as we gods do. But when they do, nothing remains. For there is no soul to pass on."

Quinn shivered. If he died, there would be no going to the dark realm.

He would simply be gone.

"You're saying there will be war, and Lazarus will be the cause of it?" Risk asked.

Mazzulah lifted his eyes from Quinn to her sister. "I'm saying that there must be war. If I allow Quinn to return to the plane of men, you must fight, and you must win—because that's the only way to free me."

Risk froze, but Quinn, she did not react as people did. She did not understand fear the same.

"You wish to be freed from the dark realm?" Quinn asked.

"I wish to return to *my* realm. Ramiel and the other gods of light stole it from me and locked us away here. The only way to reclaim my home and my place as king and queen—is for you to win." He paused in speaking, and Quinn could have sworn that the winds changed. The dark sun fell below the horizon and the blood moon rose. With it, he shifted from a man to a woman, and she held Quinn all the same. "This is what I ask of both of you, and for nothing less will I part with you." She pet Quinn's side, making it clear who she meant.

Mazzulah, indeed, wanted everything.

"I'll do it," Risk said in a rush of breath.

Quinn quirked an eyebrow. "You should consider this, sister. The dark realm is—"

"You gave me everything," Risk said. Her blue eyes seemed brighter against her pale ashen face and the sable skies. "I will not leave you here. Haspati said my ascension nears. I will not be here for so long before I return. Trust me to do this. Let me win your freedom as you won mine. We will have this war—and for you—we will win it."

Quinn's throat felt thick as she swallowed.

The arm around her waist lifted, silent permission for her to go to Risk.

She rose and padded from the throne to the other end of the dais.

"I did not deserve you," Quinn whispered as she wrapped her arms around Risk. Her sister's form was thin and tiny by comparison. She desperately hoped that Risk knew what she was doing because she hated leaving her here. Mazzulah had promised to release her once she ascended, and Quinn was not a good enough person to pass up a second chance at life. Not when there was still so much to do . . .

"No, sister, it is I who didn't deserve you," Risk said into her chest. "But I will."

She hugged her tight. Tighter than she ever dared to in life.

"It is time," Mazzulah said, moving from her throne to stand beside them.

Quinn released her, and for a moment, she felt despair.

For the sister she had only just got back.

For the sister that she gave everything not to lose.

Quinn turned to the god of the dark realm and pressed her lips against hers.

Mazzulah purred in delight. Her cold hands grasped Quinn by the waist as she pulled away.

"There are two things you must know before I let you leave."

Quinn lifted her chin because freedom was in her sights. She was close. So close . . . and if she did this right, she could have everything.

"Tell me," Quinn said.

"The first is that you will not return as you were, but as you are. As a fear twister you are used to walking between realms. Now you will walk all of them and only take the form of the flesh if you choose. But if you die again, there will not be a second chance. Just as the soul eater will turn to nothing, so will you."

Quinn nodded. That was better than she'd expected. To return as she was, she would not be bound in the same form that brought her to death the first time. She would be stronger.

She would be . . . invincible.

"And the second?"

"If you fail and lose the war, your king will not have to worry—for I will be coming for you and sending death for them. Provided that you're not all dead to begin with."

Her lips parted.

That was what she was waiting for. The catch.

Before Quinn could say anything, Mazzulah brushed the back of her knuckles to Quinn's cheek.

"Good luck, my beauty. I hope this is goodbye, for both our sakes. I fear I now understand the king. To love you is to love destruction. But I cannot have you and my kingdom. Just as you do not have it in you to love me while he still exists. Return to him, Quinn. Return, and set us both free."

Darkness closed in around her. Black spots in her visions.

Tendrils of power that were not her own wrapped around Quinn.

But they were loving and cold all the same.

As she lost consciousness for the first and last time in her dead immortality, Quinn didn't think of Risk. She didn't think of the coming war she would face. She didn't even think of the king she'd be returning to, though it was not far in her mind.

She thought of Mazzulah's parting words.

And vowed to set them both free.

CHAPTER 4
SHATTERED CAGE

"Grief and revenge are not so different. For they both bring out the worst in a man."
— *Lazarus Fierté, soul eater, the mad King of Norcasta*

Lazarus lifted his head. The fogginess that had filled his mind slowly drained away as he focused on his surroundings. His quarters were decrepit. The bed posts were broken. The windows shattered. The table had been overturned. Bits of feathers and fabric and wood and glass littered the floor.

He sat in the only wingback chair that was still usable. Before him, Leviticus' eye was setting, making room for Leviathan to rise.

Blood painted the horizon.

And for the first time in he wasn't sure how long, whispers from the palace reached him.

He heard music and laughter and joy.

Lazarus spent so long in the dark confines of his quarters that silence began to scream. He hadn't heard true sound. Only *them*.

The souls within.

All his life they'd been at war. Him and his monsters. The master and the beasts.

Not anymore.

When he'd remembered the truth of that night, it hadn't merely broken him; it had shattered him. The man that used his body as a cage lost all control.

But in doing so, Lazarus learned that he and his beasts were not all that different.

Lazarus wasn't sure if this was simply another trick of his mind, or reality as it was.

The scent of fresh snow and midnight weeds hit him.

Her magic. Her fear. He wasn't sure if it was trying to pull him under once more or urging him on. To do as she would bid of him.

While he didn't know how long had passed, what he did know was that it was time. The game had begun. The game to end all games.

Lazarus stood and stared at the dying sun.

For what had been done, he didn't simply intend to go to war.

He planned to cleave this continent in two.

He'd done things the nice way. The way his left-hand had wanted.

And it cost him his right.

It cost him saevyana.

She'd gone to a place where not even death would allow him to follow. It was a cruel end. The gods had brought him the one woman that could make him feel —that could make him live. And then they stole her away again.

Part of him still couldn't believe it. Every now and then he scented damp petals in the breeze. He felt some echo of fear calling out to him like a beacon.

It was there now.

Everywhere and nowhere at once.

But Lazarus knew it wasn't possible. It was simply his memories. Those sharp fragments of life that could not be contained. So vibrant compared to what he lived now. Past and present mixed together. He felt as if he were living in a pocket of time where everything existed at once and not at all.

Those parallels shook him to his core. He knew that he wasn't simply dancing with Mazzulah. He'd lost the fight against his inner madness.

But even a mad king was still a king.

And there was work to be done.

He'd mourned for her, and he would continue to until the day that he truly ceased to exist. But the Quinn he knew, she wouldn't simply want him to mourn.

No. She'd want revenge.

His cruel woman . . . she couldn't take it for herself.

But he and the souls, they could. They would.

Lazarus turned his back on the place of his vigil. It pained him in a way that he couldn't have understood before. He'd exiled himself to this place because she was the only one he'd shared it with. He stayed there because the anger was too great to contain, and he needed to hone it to a fine point that would be used when the time came.

Lazarus hated this place for what it represented, and yet he coveted it all the same.

But it was time to move on.

He walked out of his quarters and didn't turn back.

The souls within urged him onward as he trailed down the halls of his palace, following the sounds of music. People passed him by, but he paid them no mind. Lazarus was done concerning himself with the desires of lesser men.

Something had called him from the fog, and he was going to find out what.

Lazarus stopped at the double doors that opened up to his throne room.

Inside it was filled with lords and ladies, though he was certain Quinn had killed them all. The scents of roasted meats and rare fruit and sweet delicacies washed over him . . . and something else.

Something rotten.

He stepped through the entrance and approached his throne. Unoccupied, it loomed above them all.

The music trilled out as people took notice. There were whispered words. They talked of him as if they hadn't seen him in a very long time, which meant that this wasn't simply in his head.

He'd wondered, though he'd never admit it.

At the base of his throne, his left-hand, stewardess, and sword master all stood.

Their eyes locked on him as he continued walking past. He didn't stop, though the music and the murmurs did.

Silence greeted him once more by the time he reached the top.

He turned to his people and seated himself on the throne of oak and iron.

They kneeled at once, and he liked that. The souls liked that. Subservience was all he would tolerate now.

The clomp of hooves drew his attention. He appreciated the quiet. It made it easier to hear that which was important. Without turning to the souls within, he knew that this was what had called him.

The rotten scent grew.

There was a ruckus at the door. It didn't last but a moment, and Draeven had only been able to take two steps when a boy appeared in the doorway. Two of his own guards stood on either side.

Dressed in purple and silver.

He wore Trienian colors and carried a box.

"Your Grace," one of the soldiers began.

Lazarus lifted a hand to silence him and then beckoned the boy forward.

"Come to me," he ordered. The child bordered on becoming a man, but his lips still quivered, and his hands shook as he approached the steps.

His court had the good sense to not speak as the messenger climbed the stairs. Beneath his skin, the souls started to stir.

Lazarus held up a hand to stop him only three steps from the raised dais.

Sweat gathered on the boy's brow as he halted where he stood.

"I come bearing a message and a gift for King Lazarus Fierté."

"I am he," Lazarus said, his voice gruff from the time in disuse. "Tell me who has sent you."

"Your brother, Emperor Nero XX, first of his name, commander of the Trienian militia, savior of the sick, defender of the poor, and god among men."

God among men, Lazarus thought. If those were the titles Nero chose, he was right to believe that nothing had changed.

That was good. It would make this easier for him.

"And what is it that my brother has sent all the way from the Empire of Triene?" Lazarus asked.

The boy shifted to hold the box with his forearm so that he could lift the lid with the other hand.

That rotten scent washed over him. He knew what it was before the boy spoke. After all, he'd been given a gift like this before.

"The head of the traitor, Amelia Reinhart, Your Grace."

Despite his youth, he did not appear all that bothered by the decapitated head he lifted from the box. Long dark hair hung in greasy clumps. Her face that had once been beautiful no longer showed what she truly was. Bits of bone and blood and pus stuck out from the stump that dripped of wretchedness.

His court gave an audible gasp, and it didn't miss Lazarus' notice when both Draeven and Dominicus exchanged a glance.

Interesting . . .

"And my message?" Lazarus asked softly.

The boy began to shake again, and the souls grew excited. They sensed what was coming.

"An eye for an eye."

Lazarus exhaled softly.

Nero had taken Quinn from him, and so he gave Amelia in return.

Some might think it an apology. Others an olive branch. And even still, there were the fools that would not see the treachery in his words.

"Is that all?" Lazarus said, his voice colored with midnight and shadows and death.

"I-it is," the boy stammered. He took a step back and bowed his head.

"Very well," Lazarus murmured. "I shall send him an invitation, then."

"Your Grace?" the messenger asked, not understanding.

Lazarus lowered his hand to the side of the throne.

From his skin, the kuras came forth.

Its form was twice the size of a wolf but coated in light gray feathers instead of fur. The animal lifted its head and snarled once. Icy blue eyes zeroed in on its dinner.

The court didn't even have time to react as it leapt at the boy.

"Leave his head," Lazarus commanded the creature. A slight rumble was the answer he received, but he knew it would obey. Crimson coated the steps and Amelia's horrendous head went tumbling down. "I'll be sending that to my brother."

Nero thought he could take Quinn.

He sent the head of Amelia to challenge Lazarus.

In turn, he was going to receive an invitation of war.

"Loyalty given is the greatest of gifts. Loyalty taken is the worst of crimes. For it isn't loyalty at all, but slavery by another name."
— *Quinn Darkova, fear twister, walker of realms*

T he sound of doors hitting stone startled her into awareness.

Quinn opened her eyes and immediately knew that this was not the dark realm, but the plane of the living. A cold wind slapped her in the face as if reminding her of her senses and self.

Quinn looked down at her form as it drifted between intangible black wisps and flesh. Mazzulah had told her the truth. In coming back, she would not be as she was. Quinn liked that. For all that she gave up, she had gained so much more in death.

Scales slithered along her side, mauve in color.

The god of the dark realm hadn't just allowed her to return, but the beast of her soul as well.

A cruel smile curved her lips as she extended a hand. The snake lifted his head to her fingertips.

"We have much to do," Quinn whispered to him. Neiss bobbed his head before slithering beneath her skin. His presence comforted her.

Quinn sat up and then pushed herself to her feet. Bare as they were, the stone wasn't so cold as she remembered it. She'd existed in the dark realm for so long that she'd become a part of it and grown accustomed. Even the frozen winds couldn't bother her now.

Dressed in only the two swaths of black fabric and a silver chain around her waist, Quinn walked out of the desecrated temple. The statues of the dark gods stood on their crumbling pedestals as she continued past them without looking back.

Eyes followed her, and she could sense those very gods watching as she started to descend the steps that would lead her back to N'skara. She didn't intend to stay for long, but if she were to return to Lazarus, she was going to need a few things for the journey.

It occurred to her that the last time she walked this path, she carried her sister. Risk had climbed these steps again for her, but she was not returning with her.

Quinn pressed her lips together as she thought about that.

Risk had done the impossible. What no one else could do. She ventured into the dark realm for Quinn, and then chose to stay so that she could leave. Quinn wasn't sure how long she'd been gone, but her sister had changed yet again in that time.

She'd grown stronger. If not more sure of herself, then more certain of her decisions.

Quinn didn't like leaving her there, but if her time in the dark realm had taught her anything, it was that Mazzulah would keep her word. She would train Risk into her ascension and then release her. And whether Quinn wanted it or not, the truth of the matter was that Risk's fate was sealed the moment she opened those doors. Even if she hadn't agreed to stay, Quinn had a feeling Mazzulah wouldn't have let her leave.

It was better to have her there by choice, however, than against her will.

Quinn reached the bottom of the steps. Whether it was morning or afternoon, she couldn't tell beneath the gray sky. The clouds were so thick and the snow falling so heavily it was impossible to tell.

At the end of the staircase, the lantern that had once signaled its whereabouts lay broken in pieces. Quinn stepped around them and continued on, her footprints disappearing beneath the next layer of snow.

She trailed through the old parts of Liph. The streets here were cracked. The buildings nearly as decrepit as the ancient temple she'd woken in. These things were normal. They were as she remembered.

The thing she didn't recall, however, was the laughter.

Hearty chuckles that could only come from men chased her as she walked through the alleyways.

How long have I been gone?

Quinn wasn't sure, but the answer to that question was becoming more important with every step. Footprints from heavy boots indented the snow in these parts. Sections had turned to slush, despite the constant downpour.

As she neared the edge of the ghettos where it bordered the main city of Liph, Quinn paused. Two men had walked into the alley and stopped dead. Their eyes roamed her cream-colored skin, drinking in the flesh on display.

Quinn was unbothered by their attention. That wasn't what made her stop.

It was *their* appearance.

Black hair and brown skin. They dressed in thick coats of fur and carried weapons at their waist. Boots that were heavier than that made in N'skara covered their feet.

These men . . . they were outsiders.

Yet they walked through the N'skaran slums as if they owned them. They were not escorted by guards, as all outsiders were. They were free to laugh and jest openly.

Perhaps the most alarming part of this all was that they spoke a language she did not know.

Quinn was fluent in N'skaran, Norcastan, and even Ilvan. She was sufficient in Cisean, Jibrealic, and Bangrati.

There was only one language from her continent that she did not speak but had heard.

"Who are you?" she asked softly in her mother tongue. Out of all of them, she gave it decent odds they'd understand her if they were this familiar with Liph. It meant they'd been here a while.

"Soldiers," one of them said in butchered N'skaran.

"Sailors," the other supplied, his accent was better.

"Which is it?" she asked.

They looked at each other, and then the one that spoke more clearly said, "Both."

Quinn smoothed her features and took a step forward. "What are you doing here?"

They were distracted again by her lack of clothing. The one that spoke poorly swallowed hard. The other had a wicked glint enter his eye. Quinn smiled.

She recognized his kind. Men that thought women were their prey.

"We're from the ships," the better speaker said. "We were just heading back for the night. Would you like to join us? You look so cold . . ."

Yes, cold is what you meant, wasn't it? She wanted to laugh at his poor attempt at manipulating her.

Boys. Children playing at men.

Quinn had lain with a king.

She'd kissed a god.

They were *nothing*.

But at the moment, they were useful.

"I am cold," Quinn said. The better speaker took a step toward her. Their breath mingled. He reached for her, not seeing the wickedness that lived beneath the surface. "But not in the way you think."

"What—" He didn't get to finish his sentence.

Quinn lifted a hand to his face. She cupped his cheek, and he didn't see the black wisps that wafted to it.

All it took was a single caress of those black strands for his eyes to roll back in his head. His arms began to twitch, and his legs shook. Quinn peered into his mind, harvesting his fear for her own reserves.

What she saw . . . it confirmed her worst suspicions.

The other soldier yelled. A flick of Quinn's wrist and the one she'd touched toppled sideways into the alley. Catatonic.

"You-you're the one . . . the-they whisper about. The white raksasa."

Quinn found it interesting that her own people regarded her that way. It was fitting. They'd treated Risk as a raksasa, and she was more human than Quinn could ever be. It seemed they finally realized that. It was just too late.

The soldier looked between his fallen comrade and the woman standing unaffected.

Like all men before him, save one, he gave way from anger to panic to fear.

Delicious, tantalizing fear.

She did miss this. Mazzulah did not fear her, and that was appealing in its own way. But Quinn . . . she thrived on fear.

He turned to run, and Quinn tsked. Extending her hand outwardly, Neiss slithered forth.

"*Snack?*" the great serpent asked her.

"*Snack,*" Quinn confirmed. She sensed his approval as he grew in size over the span of seconds. Quinn didn't look away as the soldier continued to run. Neiss barely had to try to catch him. He struck with a single snap of his jaws and swallowed half the man. The muscles in his body contracted as he threw his head back and swallowed a second time.

The soldier went down easily.

"You're going to need to let that digest before you shrink again," Quinn said, striding forward. She ran her hand over his scales.

"*'Twas worth it.*"

She snorted.

"*I'm sure it was,*" she replied mentally.

Neiss slithered alongside her as they walked out of the lowborn part of town and into a more prominent section of Liph. Here the seashell and sand mortar was laid with precision and cleaned regularly. The houses, while plain for the most part, were also uniform in their quality. The joyous sounds that had bled through the thin walls in the poorer district were absent here, instead favoring the silence she remembered.

"Curious," she muttered under her breath.

She was mildly surprised by the time they reached the temple that no one had entered the street and seen her or Neiss, nor were there shouts coming from where she'd left the pig soldier. While she'd cleaved the information she needed from his memory, thoughts of what he planned to do to her once he had her on the ship were also on the surface. Willing or not, he would have taken her and then let his *brothers*, as he called them, have their way with her.

Quinn reached the bottom of the steps.

Lined up in front of them were the gods of light, in contrast to those of the dark.

She peered up at each of them, recalling the stories Mazzulah had told her about each of them. When she was a child, the statues had intimidated her.

When she was a grown woman, they still impressed her, even if they did not inspire anything.

But now . . . she found them lacking.

Quinn strolled past and then climbed the steps to the temple where the Council met. By the time she reached the top of the staircase, the evening light peeked out from the clouds. It reflected the white stone beneath her feet, casting the place in an eerie glow.

She looked up at the temple. There was a time she'd never thought she'd see this place again. For so long it had been the source of her inner torment, and then the fire that burned with hatred. After endless days that passed in the dark realm, Quinn was almost disappointed by the lack of emotion it invoked in her.

She walked into the temple. The door creaked as she opened it and a plume of dust billowed when it swung closed behind her without prompting.

Her brow furrowed at the absence of torches lit. While the darkness was home, this temple was never meant to be cast in shadow. The N'skari were adamant in their ways. They always had been.

Clearly something had changed.

When she stepped into the Council chambers, she was not surprised to see the pedestals empty. However, as Leviathan's eye peered through the glass ceiling, she noticed another clue.

The floors that were always a pristine white were now covered in a layer of grime.

Wherever the N'skaran Council was, they weren't here, and they hadn't been here in a very long time.

Which begged the question, where were they?

And more importantly, why were Trienian soldiers in N'skara?

"*Never question if a situation could be worse. It could, and to anger Lady Luck is to feel her wrath.*"
— *Draeven Adelmar, rage thief, left-hand to the mad King of Norcasta*

Draeven didn't look away when the kuras began to devour the boy.

He wanted to. But guilt rendered him unable.

Draeven had advised that Amelia and her brothers be invited. He had pushed Lazarus for peace. He'd asked a man whose heart belonged to fear to show mercy.

And now he was paying the price.

A month ago, he thought that Lazarus had lost himself to the souls. He'd been right, and yet not.

Lazarus hadn't simply been lost to them, he embraced them. He became the worst of them.

The man that currently sat on the throne was dancing with Mazzulah because Quinn was gone, and Draeven could not stop the guilt from eating at him. For what was to come was as much his fault as it was the mad king's, and the boy now being eaten alive paid the consequence.

"He's going to bring Triene down on us," Dominicus hissed between his teeth.

"I'm fairly certain that's his intention," Draeven replied, equally hushed. In the silent throne room, only the sound of flesh being stripped from bone and the screams of a young man could be heard. The new court that he and Draeven had formed were in shock.

Lorraine had spent the month arranging this party.

He knew this wasn't the way they'd been planning to welcome them.

Then again, no one had seen or heard from Lazarus in two months.

Autumn was nearly upon them when the king barged through the throne room and finally took his place once more. Only to show them what kind of king he intended to be.

When the screams faded, the kuras dragged the boy's body back up the steps and sat down beside its master, eating the messenger as if it were a dog with a bone. Blood dripped down the marble steps, pooling around his boots.

Draeven swallowed, and Dominicus cursed beneath his breath.

"This is madness," the master of swords said.

"This is consequence," Lorraine said, her voice hard. They both looked to the stewardess of the palace. Unlike the ladies of the court, she hadn't shielded her eyes. Back stiff and posture straight, she stared at the corpse without emotion, and didn't fidget as blood soaked her sandaled feet. "A foreign nation aided our enemies. They were the cause of the right-hand's death. For him to not respond would make him look weak. They decided their fate when they killed her. Lazarus is simply showing them and the rest of his new court what happens when you betray him."

"You can't be okay with this—" Dominicus started.

"It doesn't matter if I am or not," Lorraine replied, her voice like the crack of a whip. Draeven had never heard her speak so harshly to the man he was fairly certain she loved. "I am loyal to Lazarus above all, just as I was loyal to Quinn. Triene took one of our own. For what he asks of each of us, I'd expect nothing less than him waging a war when someone means to ruin his house. He wouldn't be worthy of the loyalty we give if he didn't."

Dominicus seemed to be struck speechless as

Lorraine turned and walked out of the throne room. Only when she was gone did he speak again.

"I didn't realize . . ."

"How hard she took Quinn's death?" Draeven supplied.

"I knew she grieved for the girl, but this . . . she sounded like she wants blood as much as Lazarus."

"She was the daughter she never had. When Quinn killed Lord Callis, Lorraine cleaned her up. When she murdered and schemed in N'skara, Lorraine covered it up. Never in the ten years I've followed Lazarus have I seen Lorraine go against his wishes, but I think if it ever came down to it, she would have for Quinn."

Dominicus grew quiet—they both did—as Lazarus stood once more.

The head of the messenger was in his right hand, while the left pet the creature beside him. He wondered whether Lazarus knew that even subconsciously it was always the left that feeds, and the right that strikes.

"My lords, my ladies, Triene has aided my enemies and brought death to our door." When he spoke, it was the voice of the king he'd always followed. Strength and might pervaded it. Despite the dark circles that lined his eyes and the way his tunic was loose whereas before it had been taut, Lazarus gave the impression that he was king in power, even if that were far from the truth. "They insult me with the head of their puppet," he continued, the first hint of his ire showing. Dark shadows peeked out of his sleeves and a red glint entered his eyes. "We cannot stand for this. The Trienian Empire may be strong, but we and our allies are stronger. Rally your bannermen. Tell them to prepare. We are going to war."

Lazarus did not wait for them to respond. He didn't give them a chance.

As fast as he'd come, he walked back down the stairs with the beast at his side and left the throne room.

Dominicus turned to Draeven, his expression somber.

"Someone needs to talk to him."

"He won't be dissuaded," Draeven sighed. "And even if he was, it's no use. After what he just did . . . Lorraine is right. War will be our only option. What's important now is that our allies will indeed join us."

Dominicus snorted derisively. "As soon as Imogen sees what's become of him, she will chew him up and spit him out. The Ciseans might be brutes, but they won't follow us to their deaths."

"There's a contract," Draeven reminded him, though he worried Dominicus was right.

"Contracts won't mean a damn when the emperor's army comes for us. You've heard the whispers just as I have. Nero has gone to great lengths to make himself untouchable, and we will need more than just Norcasta if we are to survive this."

Draeven looked away. Whispers had broken out in the throne room, but after the show the king had put on, there was little good in quelling them.

"I'll talk to him, but I'm not making any promises."

"I'd be questioning your sanity if you did," Dominicus answered.

Draeven left the throne room in search of his king. As he walked down the halls toward Lazarus' wing, silence crept in. The shadows took on a more menacing form. He sensed rage and knew that the kuras wasn't the only beast Lazarus had unleashed. As he rounded the corner to the study, the dark void of the wraith came forward.

He didn't try to fight it. Nor did he step around it.

"Tell your master I've come to speak to him," Draeven said lightly, clasping his hands behind his back.

The creature had no face that he could see, but it turned and disappeared through the wall.

He took that as a good sign.

A moment later, the door opened.

Draeven stepped forward. Tentatively, he reached for the gold handle and swung it open the rest of the way. Lazarus stood with his back to Draeven, examining the spines of books along the wall. On the corner of his desk, Amelia's head sat. Juices dripped from it. Her sallow skin resembling a melted candle. Draeven's lips pinched together.

"How long has it been?" the king asked. Of all the things Draeven expected him to say, that wasn't one of them. He closed the door behind him, his eyes going to the spot where he'd slain two of the three lords on Lazarus' previous Council. Even after multiple cleanings, red still clung to the ornate rug.

"Two months, give or take a few days."

"Hmm," was the only answer he gave.

Draeven frowned, not sure what to make of that.

"Lazarus," Draeven started, coming to stand behind one of the two chairs on his side of his desk. He rested one hand on the back of it. "What happened in the throne room . . ."

"Needed to happen," Lazarus said, leaving no room for discussion.

"Perhaps, but in declaring it, we only have so much time to prepare. Our allies must be called on, and while I can write the letters—I cannot be the one to ask them to take their people to war. That has to be you—"

"Do you think I am dumb, Lord Adelmar?"

Draeven paused. Never, not once in all their time together, had Lazarus called him by his surname. "No," Draeven said slowly, trying to predict where the situation was going.

"Then why are you giving me advice? I am king. I did not ask you." Lazarus still hadn't turned around, but the tone in his voice left no room for discussion.

Draeven's hand clenched the back of the chair, his

nails digging into the plush cushion and wooden frame. For so long he'd followed this man because he knew he would be king. He knew he would change the world . . . and that by following him, Draeven could change it too. For the better.

That was before Quinn. Before Lazarus' infatuation that turned to obsession and then became something more. Before Quinn had changed the course of their plans, both making those plans a reality and simultaneously setting them up for destruction altogether. They won allies because of her. They survived battles that Draeven doubted anyone but Lazarus would have walked away from.

Draeven owed her his life as much as he did Lazarus, to an extent . . .

But it was because of her that the king changed.

No, Draeven shook his head. *Not her.*

Nero and Amelia. It was because of them that she had died, and it was her death that changed his friend. The man that wouldn't even look at him had irrevocably changed in the two months of self-imposed exile.

"You are a king that's been gone, consumed by your grief," Draeven said, trying to reason with him. "I know that Quinn was—"

"Do not speak her name in these halls again if you wish to live," Lazarus said, his voice dropping to a whisper. "It is only because of what we were that the souls have not killed you where you stand, but do not mistake that mercy for friendship. I listened to you once, and I lost a woman worth more than this entire country and all the gold in it. I will not listen to you again as I avenge her death."

Draeven's lips parted before closing firmly. His jaw tensed as he weighed his response.

While it was Nero and Amelia that killed her, both he and Lazarus—and even Quinn herself—all aided in sending her to the dark realm. Not for the first time, he wondered where Risk had gone that night. She'd disappeared, and not even his spies could find her. It was like she all but vanished. Then again, without Quinn, there was nothing to hold her here. He had played a role in that too.

In the end, it was his own guilt that led him to say, "What do you wish for me to do, Your Majesty?"

"Have the carriage readied and word sent ahead to my residence in Dumas for it to be prepared. I'll be holding a summit there one month from today. Ravens will be sent tonight to bring word to my allies, as well as Bangratas and Jibreal. My right-hand had secured an envoy from them, and unless it arrived without my knowing, I should follow up."

"No envoy from either country came," Draeven said stiffly.

Lazarus didn't respond, and when the silence ticked by long enough it was clear he wasn't going to, Draeven asked, "Is that all, Your Grace?"

"That is all," the man he'd once considered his closest friend said.

Draeven turned on his heel to leave and then paused.

He knew he should keep his mouth shut. That he should not push, certainly when he'd lost all favor that he ever had with Lazarus. Yet . . . this was at least partially on him. He had to try. Just one more time.

"I followed you when we were sellswords, and I follow you now. When you're ready to talk—if you're ever ready to talk—I'll be here."

And then he let himself out.

The silence that answered was all Draeven needed to hear to know that whatever friendship they'd had also died that night.

It was yet another thing he had to blame himself for because he had no way to fix it.

Unless he could summon the dead, the redemption that he'd been chasing for a decade as he followed Lazarus was not just gone, but dead as well.

CHAPTER 7
LETTERS FROM THE DEAD
"TRUE LOYALTY CANNOT DIE."

— Quinn Darkova, fear twister, walker of realms

Taverns hadn't existed in N'skara. Until now.

After searching the temple for hours, she'd turned to searching the homes of the councillors. Only to turn up empty. Just like the meeting chambers, a layer of dust and grime had collected. Unlike the temple, it was clear that homes had been ransacked.

The peculiar part was that she searched other homes in the highborn section, and they were empty as well—but not ransacked.

It didn't make sense. Somehow, Triene had gained a foothold, and she needed to find out how.

Which is why after a night of searching, she

turned to the fragmented memories from the soldier's mind she'd broken. While she couldn't understand most of the words in them, she could see places. Quinn may have been gone a long time, but the buildings hadn't changed, and neither had their placement.

She followed them to the square in the lowborn section. This had been someone's home before. Now it was where soldiers went to drink and pick up N'skari women who were willing to whore themselves for the right price.

Clothed only in her makeshift dress from Mazzulah and an illusion of a cloak, Quinn approached the door. The walls were made of plaster and stone. Hairline cracks ran through them. The single door was made of gray ashwood, the same wood used for everything else to those without fortune in N'skara. There were no windows, and the lone chimney puffed black smoke beneath the snowing sky.

Quinn pushed the door open and stepped inside.

It was early afternoon, and before most of the festivities.

With only a few soldiers, several lowborn serving ale behind a makeshift bar, and herself—Quinn took a seat at a table in the back corner of the room. If the people noticed her otherness, they didn't show it. In true N'skaran fashion, they barely looked her way before returning to work. Using her bare toe, she nudged the wooden chair backwards. It groaned in protest against the slightly rough texture of the crushed seashell flooring.

Quinn took a seat and leaned forward into the rickety table. She braced her arms and clasped her hands together, keeping an eye on the door, the bar, and the soldiers all in one.

"Can I get anything for you?" an older man with white hair, a balding head, and tired blue eyes said softly. He walked even softer. His actions were those of someone timid, but not weak.

"Water," Quinn said. "If you have it."

He nodded once and backed away.

Across the room, Trienian soldiers dressed in purple and gold spoke in hushed tones. Quinn angled her head, listening in with hearing they didn't know she possessed.

The only problem was they spoke their language.

Not any one of the six she knew.

Still, she caught a few words.

Captain. Maji. South.

There was one word that perked her ears more than anything.

A name. One she'd only heard Lazarus speak in his sleep, and only once.

Nero.

Quinn frowned, sensing the shift in nervousness as the N'skaran man scuttled back to her table with a cup of water.

"Will that be all?" he asked. His voice was steady,

but his emotions were not. In the time she'd been here, he'd grown subtly unsettled. Suspicious.

Quinn took a drink from the cup. Crisp water touched her dry throat. She swallowed three times and then clapped the wooden cup back on the table when she was finished.

The man narrowed his gaze.

"Tell me," she started. "Where have all the highborn gone?"

She had a feeling. An inkling in her gut. Quinn was rarely wrong when it came to these things, but the game . . . playing it was just as important as who won in the end.

His eyes widened, not expecting that question. The moment of shock passed quickly.

"You speak N'skaran well," he said, instead of answering her. "Draw back your hood."

Quinn's lips curved upward. She pushed the hood covering her, but in place of her lavender hair, it appeared silver—the same as all N'skari.

She looked up at him, and again surprise shone in his expression. He covered it faster this time.

"That's because I am N'skari," Quinn replied. "Are you going to answer my question?"

"Forgive me," he said, lowering his head once. "Your question is just odd, given the change in times. Surely, you know. There's no way you couldn't. Unless . . ."

Wheels were turning in his mind. He looked her

over, indecision clouding his judgement. He didn't understand the fear response he was eliciting by simply being in her presence. Men never did. While subconsciously they sensed what she was, it was hard for them to grasp what and who they were dealing with.

And yet, as that indecision slowly cleared, she could see that he was coming to the same conclusion as the soldiers last night.

"Darkova," he spat the name.

It appeared that at least this N'skaran was better informed on the specifics of who and what she was. Quinn dropped her illusions and leaned back almost flippantly.

"Such a pity," she sighed. "I was giving you the easy way out, old man."

"This is all on you," the man's voice rose with his ire. Spittle flying from his thin lips. "You and your lord—you ruined us—you've destroyed our culture—"

The soldiers quieted, and Quinn sensed them listening in.

If the night before was anything to go on, they knew enough N'skaran to piece together who she was as well. In truth, she was already tired of her homeland. Quinn came back for multiple reasons, but none of them were these people.

No, the only reason she was still here was her own curiosity.

That and Lazarus. While she was no longer bound by an oath, she chose to serve him in life and held to her vows in death. A foreign country invading a land under his treaty . . . that meant war.

But first, Quinn needed the facts.

She lifted a hand and tendrils of fear shot forward. The old man dropped to his knees as she wormed her way into his mind.

"Now, let's try this again. Where are all the highborn?"

The soldiers across the room all stood and unsheathed their swords. There were six in total. Quinn smiled.

"South," the N'skaran called Isiah said. He clutched his head, his short nails digging into the skin. No matter how hard he tried, there was no way to break her hold unless she chose to break it. Or he died.

Every person that had been forced under it before preferred death.

She had that effect on people.

"Where south?" Quinn asked, a hint of announce entering her tone. "Norcasta? Ilvas? The Cisean Mountains—"

"Triene!" he declared, the single word a sobbing cry.

The soldiers crossed the room quickly. Efficient, given the way red tinged the whites of their eyes.

Quinn could smell the liquor on them, and they were still feet away.

"Why?" she continued. Without losing her grip on Isiah's mind, she sent a tendril of power at them. It hit the first square in his chest, and he stopped dead in his tracks. Fear fed on the negativity inside him. Black filled his veins and his eyes darkened.

Quinn was not a passion cleaver. She could not control all emotions on the spectrum.

Only one. But she only needed one.

"Kill them," she commanded in Trienian—one of the few phrases she'd learned from Lazarus.

The soldier turned on his brothers. It was one against five, but they did not want to kill him, and he was her puppet.

Steel met bone as he beheaded the first who did not raise his sword when he should have.

When the real fighting began, Quinn focused once more on the server at her feet.

"As I was saying, why did the highborn go to Triene?"

"Magic," Isiah answered through gritted teeth. "Revenge," he spat.

"Revenge?" she prompted, tightening her hold around his mind. If she had claws, the feeling would have been akin to her running them over his skin.

"The southern lord took everything from us. *You* took everything from us. The Council pledged its loyalty, and as soon as you were all gone, they ordered us to execute them so that he wouldn't sense their treason. He wasn't the only lord looking for allies, though." He started to laugh, and it had an unhinged, painful sound. "Triene came to *us*, but we accepted them because of what you did. The emperor needs Maji in his war. The armada needs ports. You and *your* king crippled us, but we found a new king."

Quinn wanted to be surprised, but in truth, she should have expected this. The only thing she felt was disappointment in herself for not ensuring Lazarus set stricter binds on the councillors. Then again, no matter how hard you bind a snake, they always find a way free. She'd wiped out half the Council in a night. The other half chose death, and then the people chose revenge.

Perhaps she and her people were not so different after all.

Either way, they made a mistake.

Before she had been questioning if Triene took them by force. Now . . . she knew it was treason.

Which meant that she wouldn't be returning to her king just yet.

However, that didn't mean she couldn't send him a message.

"Stop," she commanded her soldier.

Quinn didn't even stand. She simply vanished. Her body entered the spirit realm, turning to black smoke in the mortal one. The strips of fabric fell onto the empty chair and the metal chain around her waist clanged as it slid over the side and hit the ground.

With only a thought, she reappeared in the middle of the four soldiers still standing.

Wisps drifted off her skin, drawn to them.

And just like with the first, they slipped past the armor and beneath the skin, burrowing inside as Neiss burrowed in her.

They staggered, arms jerking at their sides as their bodies tried and failed to fight off her magic.

They wouldn't have had any hope of surviving her power before she died. Now?

She might not be a god, but she was the closest to one that walked this realm.

When the fear had settled in each of their hearts, they parted for her, obedient soldiers awaiting commands.

"Go back to your ships and gather your brothers," she said in N'skari. "Bring them to me."

One by one they turned and walked out the door.

While they were gone, she turned back to the server who was still lost in his own mind where she'd left him—and the young serving girl that stayed huddled behind the bar throughout the entire encounter.

Quinn chose to walk, letting her bare feet slap against the floor as she strode around the side. A girl no more than ten crouched beneath the counter. She wore torn gray robes that looked like they hadn't been washed in months.

"What is your name?"

The girl blinked, her wide blue eyes glassy with unshed tears.

"Trissa," she whispered.

Quinn approached, watching as the girl's eyes dropped to her naked form and widened further. "Do you have any family, Trissa?"

Her eyes darted over to the man who even if Quinn tried, there would be no piecing back together again. Then she shook her head.

"What about friends?"

The girl seemed to think, and then nodded tentatively.

"Do your friends have family?"

She shook her head again.

Quinn sighed. She had few boundaries she wouldn't cross. Killing children was one of them. The N'skari might have brought this down on themselves, as had Triene—but this girl—she didn't choose this.

Quinn wouldn't punish those who didn't know better.

"I want you to gather your friends that have no family and bring them here. Can you do that?" Quinn would not compel her to do this. She wouldn't use fear or magic.

She gave her a choice, one that if the child chose

right, would likely mean the difference between surviving and not.

"Will you hurt them, like you hurt the other men?"

Quinn tilted her head. "Will they try to hurt me?"

Trissa squinted. Her eyebrows drew together in confusion. "N-no," she whispered, shaking her head.

"Then I won't hurt them," Quinn said.

The girl seemed to think, and then she nodded.

Quinn stepped back, letting her come out of her hiding spot. She climbed to her feet and then started for the door. Her eyes drifted to Isiah's form, but instead of watering more, they dried, and her lips tensed. She continued on and the door swung shut behind her. Quinn wasn't sure if she would come back or not. That was up to the girl.

In the meantime, while Quinn waited for the soldiers to return, she climbed the decrepit stairs in search of parchment and a quill. The house was small, but the basics were there. Beds, dressers, a desk with the things she needed.

Quinn took a seat and picked up the quill, but paused when she brought the tip to the paper.

N'skara had turned on them.

The king needed to know, but she couldn't be the one to tell him.

Lazarus might have sent her to the dark realm once, but it wasn't of his own volition. If he learned that she found a way back and didn't return to him immediately . . .

Quinn shook her head because she was doing what she always did.

She was doing what needed to be done. Quinn made a deal with a god, and if she wanted to stay, she had to keep it. Lazarus had to go to war. He couldn't be concerned with finding her. He couldn't be distracted.

With that in mind, she began to write.

CHAPTER 8
DARK CRAVINGS

"Strength and power are two sides of the same coin."
— *Mariska "Risk" Darkova, beast tamer, Mazzulah's heir*

Her chest heaved. The air was entering and leaving her lungs at such a fast rate, it burned. The exertion of breathing seemed to tire her more. But she knew she couldn't stop.

Risk lifted her boot and put it down on the step above her. Her muscles protested, shaking violently as if with rage. She was beyond rage, though. So far gone in exhaustion that all she had was a singular purpose.

To climb.

The days had blurred together. She wasn't sure if

it were weeks or months or even years that had passed. She was starving, and yet her body hadn't given out. Risk hadn't fallen prey to hunger, nor had she withered to bones as she once was. Her muscles were simultaneously stronger and weaker than ever.

It wasn't natural how she could go so long without food or water . . . and yet she did.

Somehow.

Risk climbed higher and higher and higher until she could no longer use her feet. Instead, she climbed with her hands and knees.

It was on all four limbs that she finally reached the top and could climb no more.

A lovely voice rang out; the first she'd heard in what felt like ages. Time was lost to her.

"Is it done?" Mazzulah asked her.

"It is," she whispered back between cracked lips. She tasted blood on her tongue, and she wasn't sure if it were her mouth or her lungs bleeding. Perhaps both.

She'd climbed the stairway to the dark realm twice now.

The first time for Quinn.

The second for Mazzulah, who said that if she wished to release Quinn from this realm, she had to carry her back. Risk did just that.

She carried her sister in her arms for endless days, back to the realm of the living. She left her outside the door and walked away, but Risk knew that Quinn would be okay. If there were ever a creature that was meant to not just survive this harsh world but *own it*— it was her sister.

"Good," Mazzulah said, drawing Risk's attention once more. She lifted her head from the stone slab where she'd rested it. To another, it might look as if she were bowing down or praying.

In truth, she didn't have it in her to stand up.

"Wh-what do you want from me?" Risk found herself asking.

Mazzulah's feminine lips curled in amusement and sick delight. Her golden eyes glowed with power mortals could not even begin to comprehend. On her shoulder, Alpis perched.

Traitor, Risk thought the word in his direction.

"It is not his fault that he must do as I command. He is your hope. I had to see if you could make it without that."

Risk narrowed her eyes at the god. The blood moon shining down on them made Mazzulah's dark gray skin appear a dark red. The gold insignia on her forehead shined brighter, and those onyx horns that Risk also possessed, seemed both maleficent and powerful.

"What do you want from me?" Risk repeated, her voice stronger this time. Steadier. She lifted her shoulders off the ground, and they protested greatly, but she refused to just lay there in the presence of this god.

She had to try.

"I told you already. I am training you to your ascension," Mazzulah said, tilting her head in a way that sent a pang through Risk's heart.

"But I don't know what that means," Risk said, pausing only to push herself up further—so that she sat back with her knees and shins pressed to the floor. She was still below the god, kneeling, but it was something. "How are you going to train me?"

Mazzulah didn't answer at first. Instead, she stared.

She stared for so long that Risk began to fidget. While she wasn't in her male form, the inscrutable gaze of a god was not to be taken lightly.

Just when Risk began to think the god would not answer, Mazzulah said, "Quinn has done a good job with you. She took you from being a meek little mouse and taught you what it meant to have teeth and claws. She helped you heal from the horrors of your childhood. Without what she did, my training would mean nothing. It would do nothing, because without her, I would break you." Mazzulah stood, and Risk's heart began to gallop. Her shoulders shook, and she knew with great certainty that it was because of fear. "I won't lie to you, little bird. I will break you either way. It is only once you've been broken and rebuilt that you can be what I need you to be. Quinn taught you how to fight. She taught you how to be strong. She had a beast tamer teach you how to control your magic. That is good—because I won't teach you that."

Mazzulah knelt in front of Risk, her greater height still putting her over a head taller.

"What will you teach me?" Risk asked, hardly a breath.

When the god lifted her fingers to Risk's cheek, she shuddered and tried to pull away. Mazzulah curled her hand, pinching Risk's chin between her forefinger and thumb as she forced her to lift her head.

"What you crave above all else," the god said simply. "When you are thankful to your sister for what she has done, but can't stop the envy that grows in your heart. When you are lying in bed and the night-mares come and you burn with anger and hatred and even fear. When your inner beast seeks release . . . it is not strength that you crave, my girl. It is power. I will teach you what it means to be powerful, and then some. I will train you to be a god among those men. And when we are done here, no one will ever be able to harm you again—unless you let them."

Inside her, something responded to those words.

A yearning that was greater than the fear she felt for the god. Greater than the feeling of being trapped once more. Greater than the exhaustion that plagued her.

Risk lifted her head of her own volition and stopped trying to pull away.

"I'm listening," she said softly.

The smile that Mazzulah gave her . . . it was cold and cruel, and above all, it was full of promise.

"Let's begin."

CHAPTER 9
DREAMS FROM BEYOND

"The funny thing about guilt is that in running away from it,
you tend to also run toward it."
— Draeven Adelmar, rage thief, left-hand to the mad King of
Norcasta

D raeven drifted in that place between wakefulness and sleep. It was his favorite place to be. Where the nightmares hadn't yet come, but peace existed. When he was awake, it was only anger and guilt, but here, those dark thoughts couldn't touch him. Taint him.

All too soon he found himself slipping down the slope of consciousness. The fuzziness ceased as a black void expanded beyond him.

He sighed. At least this nightmare came in the form of isolation . . .

Or so he thought.

"Lord Sunshine," a voice said. Draeven's back went straight as a rod. He blinked.

"This isn't real," he whispered to himself as a reminder. She wasn't real. She was just a nightmare. A manifestation of his guilt conjured to torture him every night. Though, if she were real, Draeven suspected she would find great amusement in the fact that she was the source of his nightmares.

"I can assure you, my Lord Idiot, that I am quite real. It's unfortunate that Lorraine is a null. I would have rather gone to her, all things considered, but you'll do."

Draeven clenched his fists, willing himself not to turn and look at her as he chanted under his breath.

A wisp of black smoke drifted over him, paralyzing him with fear.

And then, the woman herself stood there. As if conjured from the smoke, her pale body appeared. In his dream, her hair was still lavender and tied back in the braid she preferred. Her leathers were missing, though.

Instead, she wore nothing.

Draeven swallowed hard. His dreams had taken many forms over the months, but never this.

"Put some clothes on," he uttered, looking away.

"Really, Draeven? I come back from the dead and

it's my nakedness that bothers you? You really are a bore."

Draeven squeezed his eyes shut because now he understood. Instead of replaying the night she died, or his ascension, or even the night his own sister died —his mind had turned to a new torture.

It was enough to make him wonder if perhaps Quinn found a way to haunt him from death. That would be very much like her, to elicit fear even when she no longer existed in this world.

Cold scales slithered over his skin. Draeven jumped to his feet.

"Stop—" he said. The snake wound itself over his shoulders and refused to be shaken. Draeven froze.

"You're still afraid of him? Hm. Well, at least there's that. You two are going to be close companions for the next little while until I can return."

"Stop," Draeven said again. "You're not real. You can't be. I saw what was left of your body. You are dead. We burned you. We mourned for you, but this —this is my own mind. I didn't mean to get you killed. I never thought—"

"You didn't kill me, Draeven. Neither did Lazarus, though I'm sure the fool doesn't see it himself. If anything, I got myself killed."

Draeven paused in his ramblings, and then he looked. He *really* looked.

Her eyes were crystal clear as ever, and just as cruel as they'd always been. Her cheekbones were sharper, as if cut from glass, and on her lips, a wicked grin sat. She'd clothed herself, but not in the leathers he remembered. Instead, she donned two black pieces of fabric. One for each of her shoulders. On her waist, a silver belt held them in place.

"I-I don't know what to say. I can't see how you're possibly alive, but . . . I don't see how you could come from my mind either."

One corner of Quinn's mouth twisted. She lifted her hand and extended a single slip of parchment toward him.

"I can prove it, Draeven. And while I don't have time to explain the details—I am back. Not alive, per se . . . but not dead either. Risk walked into the dark realm and made a deal with Mazzulah. We both did. I have to see that through, and then I will return."

Draeven opened and closed his mouth. He didn't know what to say, but he took the letter between his hands, the parchment rough against his fingers.

"If you're real, why did you come to me? Why not Lazarus?" he demanded of her.

The smirk dropped from her lips and her face became unreadable.

"Because he can't know that I've returned. Not yet. But he does need to know that N'skara has turned against him. They've allied with Triene. I will handle my homeland, but you need to prepare. Triene is making moves for war—and you might be the hand that feeds—but I am not there, which means you also need to become the hand that strikes."

"Quinn . . ." Draeven started. "Even if this is true —Lazarus is not what you remember. He is not *who* you remember because you died. He doesn't trust me. He doesn't trust anyone."

"He doesn't need to," Quinn replied. "He just needs to be ready because we *have* to win this war. Failure is not an option, Draeven. Prepare yourself. Talk to Lorraine. But do *not* let this get back to him. I am coming home, but he can't be distracted by my absence right now."

"What part of he doesn't trust anyone do you not understand—"

"Figure it out," she replied, her voice clipped. "We all have a role to play here. You're feeling guilty about my death? Make it up to me and be sure that the Ciseans and the Ilvans have not also turned. Find out about Bangratas and Jibreal. And for the love of Forseya, stop being a *neuken*."

The subtle way in which she called him an idiot in his own native language made Draeven think. If he wouldn't be surprised to find out she found a way to torture him from the afterlife, perhaps she really did find a way to come back.

Perhaps this was real.

"How long until you return?" Draeven asked.

"Soon," she answered, reaching out to stroke the head of the serpent on his shoulder. "I will communicate with you through Neiss and dreams where I can. You need to keep him hidden from Lazarus. If the king finds him . . . from what you've said, I have no doubts he will act irrationally."

The dream began to fade. Quinn's voice grew distorted. Draeven was waking up.

He reached out and grasped her hand. It was cold to the touch. Colder than it had ever been.

With time running out, Draeven told her the only thing he could and hoped—prayed that this wasn't a nightmare.

"Hurry," he said, stressing the urgency.

Quinn smiled, and her body disintegrated into smoke.

The black void vanished. Draeven sat up, his eyes flying wide open. He gasped.

The red walls of his quarters and sound of banging on his chamber doors bringing him back to awareness.

"The carriages are ready, my lord," his head guard called through the door.

"Thank you," Draeven called back. The banging ceased. "Please notify our stewardess. I'll be out shortly."

Footsteps sounded as the guard walked away. Draeven's shoulders uncoiled. Tension easing until he realized there was a weight there that was very real.

And a letter between his fingers that he hadn't fallen asleep holding.

His lips parted, equal parts shock, relief, and dread.

It was real.

Quinn was back. She was back . . . and Lazarus didn't know.

Lazarus couldn't know.

His mouth snapped shut, and his jaw tensed as he unfolded the parchment.

He wasn't sure what she would write after all she said.

Perhaps an explanation or a plan . . . but her written words were neither.

You thought you could get rid of me, didn't you?
Unfortunately for you, I am back, and I am coming home.
Prepare them for war, Lord Sunshine.
I've told Neiss he could sleep with you. He wanted to eat you.
But I have no desire to be the hand that feeds.

His Right-Hand

DRAEVEN SAT BACK, AND NEISS SLITHERED DOWN HIS shoulder to curl up at the end of the bed. His hand fell to his side, the letter sliding from his fingers.

A quiet knock came at the door.

"Draeven?" Lorraine asked once.

"Come in," he replied just loud enough for her to hear.

The door opened softly, and the stewardess slipped in, closing it behind her. She turned to speak to him and stopped in her tracks.

Lorraine's eyes went wide as she took in the mauve-colored serpent at his feet. Her thin lips parted, and he could see his own emotions play through her features.

"She's back," he whispered, lifting the note from his bedside for her to see.

She approached him slowly, her eyes flicking between him, the basilisk, and the letter.

Her frail fingers snatched it from him once she was in range. He watched her as she read it, and unlike him, Lorraine didn't doubt. She didn't ask how or why or what.

She smiled for the first time in two months.

"We can't tell Lazarus," he warned. Her smile didn't dim.

She simply said, "Then we have a lot of work to do."

CHAPTER 10
UNLIKELY SAVIOR

Silence hung in the air like an omen.

In hindsight, perhaps the soldiers and the N'skari that survived would realize that it is when the day and night are quietest that you should listen the most.

Because some would. Quinn was neither vain enough nor idealistic to think she could kill all the rats. Just enough so that when she was done, N'skara would no longer be a country. The N'skari no longer a people. They would be myths and legends, and one day, nothing at all.

"It's time," she said softly. Her voice carried over the hundred or so men that had packed into the small makeshift tavern. As one they bowed their heads and filed out.

Quinn leaned against the bar, watching them go. Every soldier had a different location, but not a different order. They marched into the streets in their purple and gold uniforms. Most of them went to the docks. Some, however, went deeper into the city.

Night was not here, but it was upon them.

And when the sun sank below the horizon, it would begin.

A creak from a wooden step pulled at Quinn's attention. She waited until the last of the soldiers were gone to speak.

"I told you to wait until they left," she said without raising her voice. After a long pause, there was another squeak before a quiet voice answered.

"You sent them out," Trissa said. Quinn turned toward the staircase as the girl came around the corner. "You sent them to kill."

Quinn tilted her head. "Does that bother you?"

Trissa frowned. Her nose scrunched as she considered it. "I don't know," she answered honestly.

Quinn nodded. "They were bad men. I sent them to kill other bad men."

And traitors, Quinn thought silently.

"My mother used to say that two bad things don't make a good one," Trissa said.

"She's right."

Trissa frowned again. "Then why did you do it?"

Quinn considered that. "Because I don't care about good or bad. Those men were my enemies, and if I didn't destroy them now, then I would pay for that decision when I had to face them again."

"And the temples? The statues? Were those your enemies too?" the girl asked.

Quinn smiled. "Not in this life. Those were messages. Warnings."

"What are you warning them against?"

"N'skara is a bad place, and it's filled with bad people, but they're not the worst people. I am. I'm showing them what happens when they anger the wrong people."

"But I'm not bad," Trissa said, completely overlooking most of the statement.

Quinn shrugged. "Nothing is all bad or all good, and even things that are bad can be good. Just as things that are supposedly good can also be very bad. Perhaps if the N'skari had learned that lesson, I wouldn't need to teach them this one."

The girl went silent, and Quinn wasn't sure which part she was stuck on, only that something about it clearly bothered her. Another thump from upstairs made Quinn raise her eyebrows. Trissa looked at her sheepishly.

"Come down," she sighed.

Quietly, seven other pairs of footsteps shuffled down the steps. It occurred to Quinn that Axe was louder than these eight kids by herself. More unruly. More . . . difficult. The last child she'd spent any amount of time with had been raised by pirates, this group would be a lovely break by comparison. At least she hoped.

They lined up in front of her. A mix of five girls and three boys. They ranged in height from her waist to her chin and all dressed in the same scraps of gray that signified their status as lowborn. Quinn shook her head.

"Tonight, the city of Liph and every ship in its harbor will burn." To their credit, not a single child gasped or said a word. "I am journeying south, and I'm willing to take any of you that wish to survive with me. You will be expected to hunt. Make no mistake that the journey will be difficult—but there are worse things."

"Will we be slaves?" one of the girls asked. She was older, likely twelve or thirteen. She had thin lips and hard eyes.

"No," Quinn said. "I cannot promise what will become of you, but where I am taking those that choose to come with, none of you will be slaves. I can guarantee that much."

"Will there be other N'skari?" one of the boys asked.

Quinn shook her head. "I have been to six of the seven countries on this continent, and not once have I ever encountered an N'skari beyond our own lands. Our country was the smallest nation, and our people are the most recognizable. When you leave these borders, it's unlikely you'll ever see them again. Your customs, your cultures, your past—all that remains here if you leave with me. But I will make sure you don't starve, and I will get you somewhere you will be safe. You will learn a new language, new customs, and make for yourself a new future. But only if you choose to."

The children were quiet. Several of them looking between each other, trying to silently weigh their options. There were only two that didn't look at anyone at all.

Trissa and a boy. He appeared to be the youngest, and he wore a somber expression that would give Dominicus a run for his coins.

"I will join you," the little boy said.

"So will I," Trissa said.

"Me too," said the girl with thin lips.

Three of the five remaining children looked between each other with wary expressions.

Quinn motioned to the door. "If you don't want to come, I won't make you. If you think that you're better off here fighting for scraps against grown men and fending off the cold—be my guest. You would have been too weak to make the journey anyway."

At her words, one of the three girls stilled, though the other two shuffled out the front door. She gave them another minute to decide before she flipped open the trunk underneath the bar. Rations that the previous owner had been serving were already wrapped. She pulled them out and started piling them on the counter.

"First, we are going to eat. What we eat now we don't have to carry. Then we are going to round up as many cloaks and boots as we can so that you don't freeze to death in the wilds. Lastly, you'll need weapons." Quinn unwrapped the first cloth and then broke the loaf of bread in half and handed a piece to two of them.

"Why do we need weapons if you can do that thing you did to the soldiers?" another boy asked as Quinn continued to hand out the loaves.

"Because this is temporary. I'm not your protector. I'm not your mother. I'm not even alive, and if you want to make it in this world, you'll find that you're better off being able to make it on your own without needing anyone."

"But," one of the girls started, "we're just children. We sweep floors and fold clothes and do what we're told—"

"That's a great way to die," Quinn said, folding her arms over her chest. "Only doing what you're told. Being unable to think for yourself. N'skara has taught you that you're nothing more than a servant, and maybe that's true—but from this moment moving forward, you are not lowborn. You're simply boys and girls. Everything past that is for you to decide."

They looked thoughtful as they ate, if not more than a little scared. Well, all but the one boy. The one who declared first that he'd be joining her. Quinn stood off to the side, dividing up the remainders for who would carry what, watching him out of the corner of her eye.

He looked just like the other children.

He didn't act like them though. Something about him was . . . different.

Familiar even.

Quinn wasn't sure what to think about that.

The sound of a boom coming from the docks made them jump. The children, all but the one little boy, stared ahead with fear on their faces and terror in their hearts.

"What was that?" Trissa asked.

"The beginning," Quinn said, smiling to herself. "And the end. Now hurry up and eat, we need to be gone within the next hour."

"Without hitting our lowest point, we might never reach our highest."
— *Mariska "Risk" Darkova, beast tamer, Mazzulah's heir*

Mazzulah said she would make her powerful.

She said that she would be a god among men.

That no one would ever harm her again.

But as the raksasa before her beat her bloody and blue—Risk couldn't help thinking that she'd been a fool.

Mazzulah lied.

"Precious heir," the beast cooed. His long black talons raked the front of her shirt. Risk's head thudded back, hitting the dense black sand beneath her. Particles drifted in the air, making her choke.

"Pretty heir," he continued, trailing one bloodied talon down the side of her cheek. Risk closed her eyes and turned her face. Tears welled, and she tried, but failed, to stop them from running down her cheeks.

"Pathetic heir," he snapped. She felt the clawed fist coming for her face. With her eyes screwed shut, she prepared herself for her own end.

Except . . . the fist never made contact.

She opened her eyes.

His black horns curled away from his forehead. Sweat ran from the thick locks of dark hair, down his forehead, dripping onto her prone form. Blue streaks smeared across his chest, but it wasn't his blood. It was hers.

He'd won the fight by all means.

Just like every raksasa that came before him.

And yet . . . he sat there, hovered above her, his open hand clenching around empty air as he restrained himself from what surely would be the death blow.

"Rise, Dartan," the god commanded. A dark sun covered the battle grounds in violet light. Risk squinted against the shifting sands as the raksasa stood and stepped away from her.

Stands made of obsidian stone, marble chunks, and purple quartz surrounded the black desert. They were not tall, not compared to the colosseum in Vusut where she and Quinn had been gladiators for a time. But they were packed to the brim, nonetheless.

Men and women and raksasa all cheered and jested. It wasn't them that Risk watched. Her time in the dark realm had taught her that they were inconsequential when the dark god spoke, as he did then.

Slowly, Risk sat up.

"Mariska Darkova, heir of mine . . ." Mazzulah began. Her arms shook as she tried to stand, but she was unable. "You are a disappointment."

Risk stopped trying and simply stared.

She knew it in her heart. She'd felt those golden eyes on her with each failure. She wasn't sure what the dark god wanted or how to achieve it. Risk was only half-raksasa. While she had the ability to survive in this terrible land without food or water, she was not as strong as Mazzulah's children. She was not as fast. She could summon claws, but what good did claws do when theirs were stronger? She could summon wings, but these beasts had wings themselves. Ones that flew higher and further and faster than her own.

Risk lacked in every way, and yet Mazzulah continued to put her in these death matches, letting her be beaten to a pulp.

Risk's hands curled into fists. Her own baby talons piercing her skin. The pain did not bring her clarity, though. The blood flowing from her veins did not slow her rapidly beating pulse.

She'd known that she was the weaker Darkova all her life.

She'd known that she wasn't cut out like Quinn.

She'd known that she was a disappointment, and yet she couldn't escape it.

She came here to right the wrong she committed. To save her sister from the fate she had condemned her to. And in doing so, she locked herself in a prison of her own making.

Tears burned in her eyes. The granules of sand stung as she blinked rapidly, trying and failing to get rid of them.

"I have waited such a long time for this opportunity, for dark Maji to be born that could win this war. Neiss and Beliphor have contributed amply. Saltira didn't even choose a Maji, but instead chose a child with a heart for war—and even that child is more useful than you." Mazzulah sneered, and for once, he didn't seem all that insane. There was a clarity in his eyes that Risk seldom saw. While he might be madness incarnate, he wasn't all gone. "I am the exiled king of gods and it is my heir that will lose me my freedom. *My heir* that will fail us."

Alpis perched on his shoulder. No matter how many times she'd called to him, the bird never came to her. Not anymore.

It occurred to Risk, not for the first time, that she was truly alone here.

Quinn could not save her.

Hope did not come to her.

And Risk? She was tired. Tire of fighting. Tired of merely surviving. Tired of being a pawn. A tool. An heir.

If she could end it all, she would. But Risk was too weak, even for that. Too scared.

And the cold, hard, inescapable truth was that she hated herself for it.

"Kill me," she said. It was hardly more than a whisper, but the crowd quieted instantly and Mazzulah narrowed his eyes. "Kill me," Risk said again, louder this time. "If I am such a disappointment—such a failure—then end me. Find a new heir. Win your own war."

His lips pulled back into a snarl of disgust.

"I think not," the god said. "But if you want to give up so easily, perhaps I should just let my raksasa do as they will with you. Maybe if you're good, you'll convince one of them to kill you."

Panic shot through her. She surged forward and lifted a single hand, reaching for him though he was too far away. "Wait!" she called, as Mazzulah stood and turned away.

The dark god laughed with condescension, and Risk froze.

That panic gave way to anger. To rage.

"She's yours, Dartan," Mazzulah said before vanishing in a cloud of smoke and taking hope with him.

The raksasa moved and all that Risk could process was fury.

Mazzulah had lied. He wasn't going to train her.

He was giving her to his demigod children.

To play with. To use. To destroy.

Red tinted her vision for the second time in her life, and while Risk was weaker in almost every way, she refused to be treated that way again.

The raksasa reached for her with talon-tipped fingers. Silver eyes with flecks of violet narrowed.

Risk darted to the side, but she was too slow. His hand wrapped around her throat. The sharp points of his claws bit into her neck.

She tasted blood on her tongue as he threw her to the ground.

A plume of black sand blocked out the sky and stands as he came down on top of her.

But while she was willing to give up for the promise of death, she wouldn't stop with the threat of *this*.

He reached for the shredded remains for her burlap tunic. It was three sizes too large and hung on her frame at the best of times. The raksasa raked a hand down the front, splitting it open.

Terror seized her chest. Her heart constricted as it tried to escape the cage of bone that enclosed it. Her throat closed as emotion too great to speak made her swallow.

And then she felt it, that little itch inside her.

Her magic desperately wanted to get out, and while it hadn't saved her any of the other times she'd tried, Risk would do anything to stop this from happening.

Hope was gone.

Quinn was gone.

Mazzulah was gone.

No one would save her.

For the first time, Risk would save herself.

Magic was all around her in this land of dark gods and demon children and dead souls, but there was other magic too. Magic inside of her.

And it was that magic that had finally woken up.

"Get. Off. Me."

The raksasa stopped. His hand uncurled from her throat, and his body moved. The creature's face blanked as he obeyed her command.

Risk sat up and pulled at the scraps of fabric, covering her front. She held them tightly over her chest and embraced the scent of blood and dark magic in the air.

She might not be fear or death or even war.

She was a beast.

And she would not be violated.

"Kneel," she commanded. Magic suffused her voice. Power thrummed in the air, hanging like a musical note that didn't want to end.

The raksasa bent his knee, but he was not alone.

From the surrounding stands, a great clap sounded as every master and slave obeyed her command.

Then a slow clapping began.

Risk blinked, confusion diluting her pull on the magic as the rage drained away. She turned in a circle, searching for the source. Not a single being moved though. Not a single soul had even breathed in the time she commanded them.

She frowned and then glanced at the dark throne.

Mazzulah appeared in a burst of black feathers, with Alpis on his shoulder. His eyes shined with pride and the power of the gods as he said, "I was beginning to think I chose wrong."

A trickle of anger leaked through as she said in disbelief, "This was all a test?"

Mazzulah laughed, and it was horrible. "Of course. I told you from the very beginning, I would break you to remake you."

She took a step forward, narrowing her eyes, and the dark god snapped his fingers.

The black desert and its stands disappeared in an instant.

Risk swallowed hard.

In front of her, the great staircase loomed.

"What is this?" she asked.

No one answered. Risk turned and looked at the door behind her. The place it led to was better and worse than this. She wanted to take it. To leave . . .

And yet something stopped her.

She'd told them to kneel, and they did.

She hated herself and Mazzulah for what happened, but for one single blissful moment Risk knew what it was like to have power. To have control.

And she would do anything to taste it again.

Even climb the forsaken staircase.

CHAPTER 12
LIVING DEATH

*"It is when we're at our worst that our demons seem like friends
and our friends seem like demons."*
— Lazarus Fierté, soul eater, the mad King of Norcasta

The scent of damp petals and midnight weeds called to him.

Lazarus rolled, tossing and turning in his sleep.

For so long, he never dreamed. The beasts had always consumed him in nightmares. It was the price of his magic, a price he willingly paid. But since he'd surrendered to those same creatures, he found a peace in sleep that he'd never had before.

Because it was only in the darkness that he could still see her.

Smell her.

In his dreams, they fought and fucked and conquered like the beasts they were. Her wicked smile made his heart race, and her cold eyes made his length stiffen. In this particular dream, she sat on his throne while he feasted between her thighs.

His entire court was in attendance and something within him wanted to roar with pride. She was his, and they knew it, he knew it, and most importantly, *she* knew it.

Quinn's head fell back as he sucked her sensitive flesh between his teeth. Lazarus' own desire riding him as the scent of her magic perfumed the air.

"Say it," he growled, not lifting his head.

Her head fell forward. A flush crept through her pale cheeks and dampness lined her forehead as she grinned and replied, "Say what, Your Grace?"

Lazarus clenched his fists.

He both loved and hated when she toyed with him.

"Say that you're *mine*. That you'll always be mine. That you'll never leave."

Quinn slowly blinked. "I'm yours as much as I can be, Your Grace."

Lazarus shook his head. "That's not enough anymore."

She opened her mouth to say something, but he roughly pushed two fingers inside her and all that came out was a moan. He circled his thumb over the tiny bundle of nerves. Quinn writhed against his hand. Her fingers curled around the iron and wood armrests as she arched her back and spread her legs wider.

"Say it," Lazarus ground out again.

"I'm yours," she said, chasing the release he would give her.

"And?" he prompted, his voice as hard as his shaft.

Breathy moans and little pants left her as her entire body convulsed. Her channel clenched and wetness covered his hand. "I'll never leave," she vowed.

Lazarus growled in satisfaction, but that pleasure was overwhelmed by an impending sense of dread.

This was Quinn. The woman who fought for her freedom. The woman who defied him at every turn. The woman, who no matter how much he gave, would never say those words.

She'd never promise to be his.

She'd never swear not to leave.

Quinn was many things, cold and cruel and callous above all—but she didn't lie to him when it came to matters between them. And that promise, it had been a lie.

Because Quinn belonged to no one but herself.

The scene shattered before him like glass. His eyes opened, and in the darkness he could make out the faint outline of his tent. Seconds passed and the scent of fresh snow left him, but instead of taking with it that painful clarity, that's all it left behind.

In a bed that was large enough to fit three men his size, Lazarus lay alone.

While summer was nearing its end, the sheets were painfully cold in their emptiness.

Lazarus clenched his hands into fists. The souls bound to him fed his fury, but he couldn't escape them anymore than he could the darkness.

It had been his home once, and now it simply served as a reminder of what he no longer had.

Lazarus shoved the covers aside and sat up. He got out of bed, barely noticing the plush rug beneath his bare feet or how sticks prodded him when he stepped outside. No soldiers guarded his tent. Only the kuras and the wraith. They stayed there, remaining vigilant as he walked out into the night.

Leviathan's eye was high in the sky and smoke sifted through the wind. The leftover remnants of a fire and food. The rest of his house that had come with were somewhere else, further away. That suited him just fine as he walked into the woods.

Echoes of a dark, sultry chuckle haunted him.

Memories of lavender hair drifted in the corners of his vision.

He knew they weren't real.

That his dreams weren't real.

That the things he saw and the occasional scent of her magic wasn't real.

But it felt more real than anything else.

Lazarus knew he hadn't lost his mind yet. Not

entirely. But it was coming. He was aware enough to know that if he couldn't dance with Quinn that he'd dance with Mazzulah instead. He wasn't so far gone as to not see the writing on the wall. Every dark Maji struggled with sanity. For him, he never realized how much he had, until a certain fear twister got under his skin and brought him clarity. She gave him life . . . and then she took it away.

He was nearing his own edge, but he wouldn't step over the side. There was still one thing to be done. One war to win. One debt to be repaid.

Lazarus stood there in the dark forest in the middle of nowhere and held on.

He took that grief and he held it close through the night. Letting it give way to the anger and the rage. Because fury was easier to handle and hold than the emptiness that filled him in her absence.

He felt nothing before he found her. She stoked a fire in him he thought long buried.

He might not be able to have that fire anymore.

But the fire that burned for revenge was close enough.

"Darkness does not equate to evil, just as light does not equate to virtue."
— Quinn Darkova, fear twister, walker of realms, reluctant protector of children

The sounds of screaming chased them from N'skara.

It was only when they stopped to make camp late that night that the echoes finally faded, and silence settled in. But there were other things that didn't leave them so easily. The smell of burning flesh and timber mixed with sulfur in the air. Smoke drifted in the winds, and it was only after three days that the muskiness it left behind faded too.

Three of the six children had a horrible cough that was slowing them down.

Rations were dwindling, and while Quinn didn't need food to survive, the rest of them would die without it.

While the cold was but a gentle wind on her skin, she took note of the way they shivered. Their teeth chattered. All six of them had blue fingertips and two had lost feeling in their toes.

They didn't complain for the most part. N'skaran children, particularly those that were lowborn, were used to the harsh conditions of life. Quinn knew that the hardships were getting to them. The cold, the wet, the lack of breaks, food, and water.

It was affecting all of them, and not for the first time Quinn wondered if it would have been kinder to leave them there. While most of the city and every ship would have burned, they might have been able to make something of it.

But what was done was done. She wasn't turning back, which meant the only way to go was onward.

In front of her, one of the girls stumbled. Her tiny hands were wrapped tight around the cloak that covered her shoulders. Exhaustion weighed down her shoulders, and she wasn't paying attention to the roots. Her body careened forward.

Quinn took two quick steps and grabbed her shoulder, halting the fall.

They were moving slow now, the last thing anyone needed was one of them to get hurt and make them even slower.

"Careful," Quinn chided, pulling her back into a standing position.

The girl turned her head and nodded once with her eyes downcast. "Thank you," she mumbled.

"Pay attention. I know it's hard and your body is weak, but if your will is strong, you'll make it. There are worse journeys than this."

Quinn's fingers dropped from her shoulder as she stepped around her and continued onward. Her field of vision kept track of the six of them regardless of where she was. She used that to her advantage as she quickly overhauled the front of the group and started to take a better look at her surroundings.

They'd made it off the coast and into the mountains, but they hadn't escaped the never-ending N'skaran winter just yet. Snow still dotted the forest floor and many of the creatures that lived here were either burrowed or dead.

She needed to find somewhere dry and flat, ideally. Sleeping in the slush was only going to make those who were sick, sicker. Quinn tempered her own frustration while casting her fear net wider. The inky black tendrils crawled along the rocks and slithered over the trees.

"That'll do," she breathed.

"Do you feel them too?" a voice asked beside her. She turned to look over her shoulder.

It was the boy. One that was different, though she hadn't figured out how just yet. She hadn't made a point to learn any other names after Trissa, but for some reason, he was set aside in her mind as *other*. Somehow.

"Feel what?" she asked him.

He looked away and didn't answer. Quinn narrowed her eyes, but the pants and soft crying behind her took precedence over her curiosity. At least for the moment.

"Listen up," she said, pivoting on her borrowed boot to address them. "I think there are some caves not far from here. We'll stop there for the night. The faster we get there, the more time off your feet you have."

A couple of nods were the best she got in terms of responses, but that was good enough for Quinn. Seconds ticked by, turning to minutes as they continued and only the sounds of desperation trailed them. The boy kept up beside her, holding pace despite his shorter legs, but still not speaking.

The sky darkened further, and it was only Leviathan's eye and the snow on the ground that illuminated the way as Quinn followed what the tendrils had shown her.

The clearing was small, but dry. The snow

stopped just short of the cave entrance and soft snoring could be heard from within.

Quinn lifted her hand in silent command for them to wait, but as she stepped forward, she wasn't alone.

The boy was there.

Quinn frowned. "Go back with the others," she said quietly, as she approached the front of the cave.

"He is old," the child said. "Tired. He wants to sleep and not be alone anymore."

Quinn paused. *Is he . . .*

"How do you know that?" Quinn asked.

"I *feel* it."

Feel. Not hear. That was an important distinction, though Quinn didn't know why.

He stepped forward in his boots that were too small and too worn. His cloak billowed in the wind. His youthful face was . . . expressionless. It wasn't as serene as her sister appeared when she approached an animal. It was without any emotion at all.

She should have stopped him. She easily could have, but her curiosity got the better of her. Her desire to know if her hunch was right outweighed any risk.

The little boy lifted his hand.

The snoring stopped, and from her vantage point, two glowing red eyes opened in the dark.

The beast moved. It couldn't spread its wings, but that didn't stop it from standing and then crouching as the child walked into the cave alone.

"What are you doing?" another voice asked her. It was Trissa.

"Shh," she chided, not looking away from the scene in front of her.

"He's going to—"

She never finished the sentence because the beast opened its jaws and let out a roar. The ground quaked and small pebbles tumbled from the rocky mountain side above.

But the little boy . . .

He didn't cower or run.

Quinn couldn't see his face, but she didn't need to.

The beast charged, and just when she was starting to ask herself if she should have stopped him, the impossible happened.

He touched the firedrake.

And it died.

The creature collapsed to the side. The ruby color of its eyes dulling instantly. And the little boy, he spoke.

"Shhhh," he whispered. "I'm here now. I'll be your friend."

Except he wasn't talking to the dead monster. He was talking to the one that slipped into his skin.

When the little boy turned back, his pale blue eyes were a fraction darker. A flash of scales rippled over his fingertips before disappearing beneath the tattered remains of his robe.

Now she knew why he seemed familiar.

There was a darkness in him.

Like calls to like, she thought to herself as he stepped out of the cave.

It wasn't a child that stared back at her, but a soul eater.

CHAPTER 14
WAVERING RESOLVE

*"Where does it stop when the lines between right and wrong are
already blurred? At what point do the lies we tell ourselves
catch up?"*
— *Draeven Adelmar, rage thief, left-hand to the mad King of
Norcasta, guilty liar*

"**Y**ou look like piss," Dominicus said.

Draeven let his hand fall away from the tent
flap as he stepped inside, his face grim and without
amusement. "I feel like it," Draeven replied, sitting on
the dusty cushion next to the weapons master. "You
might too if you weren't sleeping."

"Whose fault is that?" Lorraine commented
without looking at him. She stood with her back to

both of them. In her hand, two dead rats hung by their tails.

Draeven fought the urge to gag as he glanced between her and the pot of stew to her left.

"They're for the basilisk," Dominicus said, nodding toward Neiss. The other man's lips curled upward in mild amusement at seeing Draeven's disgust.

"Why is she feeding the beast?" Draeven asked. "And where's our food? The soldiers have already eaten—"

"Then you should have eaten with them. I don't have the time to feed you two specially when there's a whole camp that must eat," Lorraine cut in, still not looking at either of them. "And as for why I'm feeding him. Quinn doesn't want her presence known. Lazarus can scent and taste magic. If Neiss is off hunting in the wilds, there are decent odds His Grace will find him."

Draeven closed his eyes, wishing for the hundredth time that he hadn't taken that letter. That he hadn't let Lorraine in. He should have gone straight to Lazarus when Quinn came to him.

"We should tell him—" Draeven started.

"No," the stewardess replied. Her voice was ice cold, so similar to another woman that used to sit among them. "We've been over this."

"He's already half-mad, Lorraine. Maybe if he knew Quinn was back—"

"But she's not," she said, feeding the basilisk another rat. "At least not yet. Furthermore, she asked for you not to tell him."

"Last I checked, Quinn isn't who you serve," Draeven snapped, regretting the words immediately. "Lorraine, I—"

"Who invited that Norcastan *whore* into our court? Which hand told Lazarus to give peace and not war? Which hand urged him to bring the very people who led to her death into our home?"

Draeven swallowed hard.

But it was Dominicus who said, "That's not fair, Raine."

"Life isn't fair. That girl protected us with her own life. She didn't sit in my tent and begrudge life for being difficult. She didn't *avoid* her problems like a coward." Lorraine turned and faced Draeven then, crossing her arms over her chest. "She faced them. Now she's done the impossible. She's come back to us, and she asked for only two things. Prepare for war and don't tell Lazarus."

"I have been preparing them for war," Draeven said through gritted teeth. "Ever since she died, I've been doing the job of two hands and the king, because ours isn't exactly present, apart from the odd beheading."

He wanted to stop himself. Even as that guilt mounted, so did the anger. And Draeven hated being angry. He hated the way his Maji mark burned and his chest tightened. He hated the visceral response to lash out, and right now when he was hungry and exhausted—that's what he did.

And he hated it.

"Quinn serves Lazarus, just as I do. Everything she does is for that purpose."

"But do you know that?" Draeven asked her. "Do you *really* know that?"

"If not for Lazarus, what else has she returned for?" Lorraine replied. "She got her revenge in N'skara. She freed her sister. Slavery is now outlawed in Norcasta, and it's certainly not your charming personality that brought her back here. So, tell me, Draeven, since you can talk to her but instead choose to hide—why else would she return? Better yet, why don't you ask her if you're uncertain."

Lorraine turned and lifted a wicker basket to the edge of the table. The basilisk hissed as he slithered inside. Only when he was completely within did Lorraine cover the basket with a cloth, give Draeven one last withering stare, and then leave. The tent cloth swished behind her.

Dominicus let out a sigh at her exit. "You could have handled that worse, but not by much."

"Lazarus is fraying," Draeven said. "You two might not be able to see it, but I do. He calls her name in his sleep. He's restless. He goes into the forest for hours every night because he's haunted. If he knew she'd returned—"

"He wouldn't be focusing on war," Dominicus said. "He'd be focusing on her. From everything you've said, she's trying to help you ready for war. Those are different things, and if Triene really has infiltrated and taken N'skara, now more than ever he needs to be focused on his revenge."

Draeven regarded Dominicus. While Lorraine was biased by her own grief, the weapons master was not. He'd never particularly cared for Quinn. He was loyal to Lazarus, and what's more—he had a clear head that wasn't clouded by guilt.

"You think Lorraine is right?" Draeven asked.

"I think either way she believes she is and won't be dissuaded. She does have a good argument. If not for him, why else would Quinn return? Why would she come to you and tell you what she's seen?" Dominicus shook his head, his cold blue eyes focused on where Lorraine had disappeared. "At a certain point, nothing else makes sense. That girl may be bad to her core, but she was more than loyal to him. I'll never understand it myself, but in her own messed up way, I think she loved him as much as he clearly loved her."

Draeven sighed. "She did, but that doesn't change that our loyalty is to him and not her. She might be working in his best interest, but to go around him . . . that was always the right-hand's job. Not the left."

"True." Dominicus nodded slowly. "But even if you did tell him, you don't know where she is or how to find her. If anything, you'll just be inciting those beasts of his, and if Quinn really has returned, she'll find us. If she could find her way out of the dark realm, she could find anything. Focus on what you can fix, Draeven. From one member of House Fierté to another. We can't handle him going completely insane right now. She can—but she's not here yet. Do what's best for the house."

"And what is it you think is best for the house? Me lying?" Draeven asked.

Footsteps approached the tent and Dominicus moved to stand. "Omitting the truth is different than lying." Draeven didn't agree, but he didn't argue as Dominicus continued. "Make nice with Lorraine if you can find it in you. Tell her I agreed with her. I'm tired of being exiled to another tent, and Dumas is still days away. I might be able to find you some breakfast if you do."

Draeven put his head in his hand. The incessant buzzing in his temple, driving him mad. "I'll see what I can do," he muttered.

"Likewise," Dominicus replied.

Prick.

*"Survival is strength by another name. The ability to withstand
and endure is the true marker of the fittest."*
*— Quinn Darkova, fear twister, walker of realms, reluctant
protector of children*

Quinn's fingers touched the bottom of the
satchel. There was a quill and parchment.
She'd stored ink in a small vial and stopped
it shut with a cork. But the bread she'd been slowly
dolling out the past week, along with the remaining
meat from the firedrake's body—was gone.

Only crumbs remained.

"*Potes,*" she cursed under her breath, taking a look
over her shoulder.

The two girls that she wasn't sure would come

with were now severely ill. Trissa was holding in there, but she had better boots and a thicker cloak than most of the others. She and the boy were the only ones that rationed their food properly. The others had run out days ago and relied on the stores Quinn carried on her own back. If not for the firedrake, they'd probably be dead altogether.

The firedrake . . . she thought to herself, staring too hard at the boy she now knew possessed the rarest black magic that existed.

Mazzulah had taught her that dark Maji weren't as uncommon as the world thought. Most of them were just too weak for the magic they held. They fell prey to the madness or the despair, and if those didn't get them, the ascension usually did.

This one, though . . . she had a feeling he might make it. Maybe.

He was one of the youngest, but he'd managed the best. He didn't complain. He didn't boast of his magic. He didn't steal food from the other kids, though she knew if he tried, they'd let him. The others were scared of him. All but Trissa.

Quinn had suspicions about her as well.

But unlike him, she didn't think the girl had magic.

She was fairly sure she repelled it.

To be a null and live in N'skara . . . Quinn shook her head. It made sense that the two of them had held out this long and done better than the others. They were used to things being a little harder.

"How much longer?" one of the other boys asked. His body shook and the blue tint had spread from his fingers to his palms. He was having trouble opening and closing his hands. Most of them were. It was making the whole hunting aspect more difficult when only two of the six could even attempt to pull their weight.

"I'm not sure," Quinn murmured. They'd been going for a week. The worst of the weather was past, but that didn't mean they were out of trouble. High in the mountains it was still cold, but without the snow to use as water when they ran out.

Quinn suspected she'd lose the two girls if they didn't find the Ciseans soon.

She also knew better than anyone, they wouldn't find them until they wanted to be found. She just hoped that she looked like she used to so that they would recognize her. She still wasn't sure how long she'd been in the dark realm, but if she could get the kids to the Ciseans, she might be able to dreamwalk long enough to get an answer out of Draeven.

As it was the bastard barely slept, and the few times she'd tried to contact him, she hadn't been able to. Neiss suspected he was avoiding her intentionally and Quinn had to agree, but as long as Lord Sunshine did his job that was what mattered.

That and keeping her return to the world of the living from Lazarus.

Behind her, there was a thump followed by a muffled cry. Quinn didn't need to look to know what had happened. Still, she turned.

"Get up," she said softly.

The little girl looked up. Her skin was sunken in and her eyes bloodshot, yet dull. Any shine her silver hair might have had faded in the week they'd been traveling.

"I . . ." The child tried to answer, but the water gathering at her lids said more than the words. Quinn grit her teeth. She might be cold-hearted and cruel, but this was not a suffering she could revel in.

Not when she understood all too well.

"Get up," Quinn said again. "You have to."

None of the other children said anything, but their gazes were somber. They'd all lived in N'skara. They knew the signs of frostbite, exhaustion, and starvation. It was a deadly combination, and when water was also limited, it was all but certain. The only question was how long they all truly had.

"I-I'm . . . sorry," the girl breathed. Her full lips were chapped. Quinn pressed her own together as she watched the girl tremble on her knees in the woods.

Without saying anything, she walked back and picked her up, hooking one arm around her back and one underneath her knees. The shaking didn't stop, but they had to keep going.

All of them except Quinn would fall to the wilderness eventually if they didn't find the Cisean tribes.

Quinn carried the girl up the mountain all day. Leviticus' eye rose and descended, but she didn't stop and neither did the children she led. They'd reached a point where it was easier to keep going because whenever they did stop, it was harder to start again. Quinn adjusted her pace and kept at it.

The trees thinned the further they went. So did the air.

The chittering of animals started somewhere around late afternoon, signaling to her just how far they'd truly gone.

But it was only when she heard the softest of roars that Quinn paused and took notice.

Water.

Running water.

She took a sharp turn right, deeper into the woods, where the sounds of squirrels and cawing from the birds grew quiet once more. But the roar from the water grew loud.

The children following in her wake picked up speed, seeming to have finally realized what she heard and where they were headed.

She moved around a boulder that had fallen from the rock face and saw it.

A stream no wider than three feet, running over rocks with crisp, clear water.

The children moved to run for it.

And that's when they descended.

Quinn felt it only moments before they dropped down from the overhang.

Like shadows, they emerged in a dark blur. Men the size of beasts landed quietly as the rustling of leaves despite their size. Quinn didn't move, and neither did the children. Their eyes grew round as they took in the leathers and cloaks made from the pelts of dead animals.

They still wore masks of skulls with the jaws unhinged and carried spears as tall as her.

"*Eum chaka riek faerr mar.*"

You have trespassed on our borders.

Last time she heard that, she didn't know what it meant. Now she did.

"*Hayr chaka vurd kaeverkn,*" she called out.

I come as a friend to the tribes.

It was the same thing Lazarus had said. She hoped that hadn't changed. The truth of the matter was that Quinn came here because it was either here or Ilvas, and she figured between the two that Thorne would be more likely to take the kids and not exploit them as Imogen might. Assuming there was still a treaty. Still peace. That the man she once served and planned to return to was still allies with this tribe.

Quinn waited as the chanting she hadn't noticed this time stopped.

The layers of men peeled back as one in particular came forward.

He stopped in front of Quinn and raised his hand to the wolf skull he wore, removing it from his head. It dropped to the ground, the only sound in the silence.

Quinn's lips parted.

"Vaughn?" she asked in surprise. A strange warmth ran through her chest at seeing the mountain man once more. He didn't say anything, but instead drew her to his chest, even as she held the girl between them.

"You came back," he said in Norcastan, his voice thick with emotion.

"As it turns out, there are ways around death if you try hard enough," Quinn answered vaguely.

He smelled of mint and the mountain air. She breathed it in, and her chest tightened, thinking of another man that she wanted to see. To embrace.

Both Draeven and Vaughn were shaken to their core at seeing her, and not for the first time, she wondered if Lazarus would be too.

When Vaughn released her, the shock had faded in his face. A somberness took its place.

"Much has happened," he said solemnly.

She nodded. "More than you probably know. We have a lot of catching up to do. Am I still welcome among your people?"

A light entered his eyes, despite the heavy words.

"The she-wolf will always be welcome in Cisea."

Internally, Quinn breathed a small sigh of relief, though it was short-lived.

She might be welcome, which meant the alliance hadn't dissolved . . . but that still left the question on what exactly Vaughn was doing back here when he'd been an emissary to Lazarus. War was coming and Lazarus would need them.

Quinn took in the short growth of his beard and the youthfulness still present in his face. He still had an innocence about him despite being older than her. At least he was before her time in the dark realm . . .

"Vaughn, I have to ask. How long has it been since I died?"

He looked at her not with pity, but with sadness. "Seventy-three days."

Quinn tilted her head back to the sky so that they wouldn't see her expression.

Seventy-three days. Hardly any time at all had passed here, but in the dark realm it had been years. She hadn't thought to count it because she never thought she'd be leaving. Quinn came to terms with her death. She'd accepted it.

And then Risk came for her and made a deal.

Seventy-three days . . . while it felt as if no time had passed since she left Mazzulah's side, she also knew that for Risk it would be a lifetime. It bothered her now that she walked away. That she left her there. It needed to be done for so many reasons, and yet

Quinn couldn't help the sliver of guilt that her sister would not be the same when she came back out.

All she could hope was that it would be for the better.

Or perhaps the worst.

In some ways, they were the same.

CHAPTER 16

PERFECT STORM

"Suffering is not strong, but strength can come from suffering."
— *Mariska "Risk" Darkova, beast tamer, Mazzulah's heir*

A fire burned in her belly as she took the final step.

This time she did not collapse to her knees, though she wanted to.

She didn't scream or yell or cry, though she'd done plenty of it in the weeks it took her to ascend the stairway again.

Risk stood there, panting heavily as she tried to finally catch her breath. She wasn't sure when she'd be able to catch it again. If she'd learned anything in her time in the dark realm, it was that Mazzulah's mercurialness made her sister appear steady and level-headed. Something which, Quinn, most definitely was not.

"You were faster that time," the god mused in their female form. She still wore the strips of clothing that revealed enough skin to make Risk decidedly uncomfortable. That was probably the last thing she should be worried about, given the situation she was in.

When Risk didn't respond and instead focused on her breathing, all while glaring at the god, Mazzulah continued to say, "Louder too. Some of your curses were quite clever. They'd give Quinn a run for her money—if she had any." The dark god chuckled as if this were so funny.

"You wanted to prove a point. I chose to be here, and I want to be powerful. Point made," Risk said briskly.

"No," Mazzulah mused, tilting her head in a way that Quinn would have. Golden eyes that burned with immortal power focused on Risk. "I don't think it has been. You focus too much on the wrong things. Too little on the right."

Risk scowled, hunching her shoulders to pull at the burlap shirt that she still hadn't been able to replace. Risk didn't own any other clothes. She hadn't brought any with her, and it now seemed like an unwise choice given her front was largely on display.

Mazzulah snorted at the action.

"Like I said, you focus on the wrong things. How

you look, how little you have covered or not covered —it will not protect you. You wear men's clothing so that men don't look at you, but if a man wanted to do those things that they once did to your body—they would. It doesn't matter what you're wearing because it's not about your body. It's about power," Mazzulah said, that intense, steady gaze never lifting. It unsettled Risk, but she couldn't look away as the dark god sighed, "Or lack thereof."

"I wear men's clothes because they make me comfortable. I cover myself because I don't wish to show the world—" Risk stopped short. The words *what I am* stilling on her tongue.

Mazzulah smiled knowingly.

"You're still running from your past. Hiding in hopes that the world won't notice you and won't hurt you. But the world doesn't pick and choose who to hurt, little bird. Not usually. It just does, and the only one that can stop it is you. You have strength, but you're only just discovering what it means to have power. To make someone stop when you say stop."

Risk's breathing grew slow as her heart calmed. The sweat perspiring on her skin dried in the frigid air. The feeling of her lungs burning as they tried and failed to take in enough subsided. She tasted copper and dark magic on her lips.

"If I am so weak, why did you choose me?" Risk asked. "You have a thousand other children in the raksasa, and they are all stronger and faster than me.

Beast tamers are not so uncommon either. Surely you could pick one that's ascended and has already proven their worth to the gods. So why me? If I am weak and—"

"I never said you were weak," Mazzulah corrected, her voice sharpening.

Risk swallowed hard, a hint of fear entering her. She might be angry, but she still had enough sense to recognize the god as a threat—and herself as disposable if she pushed too far.

"I've said you're a disappointment, and you are. After having Quinn for so long, you're so frail by comparison." Mazzulah waved her hand in a bored manner, as if she hadn't just used her words like the sharpest knife on Risk's heart. "I've said that you would fail me, but I'm still holding out hope that all my hard work hasn't gone to waste. In all the years that I've been playing this game, never have I been so close to victory. Neiss crafted the perfect heir, and Beliphor's is near perfect. Saltira is still in the process, but I'm beginning to see why she chose the girl. Leviathan's and Tikkoh's are adequate. But you—you have yet to prove what you will be."

"Then why me?" Risk asked again, because after the months she'd spent here, that was the question she returned to every time.

"Do you know why the raksasa cannot be my heir? Or anyone's heir, for that matter?" Mazzulah said, pivoting in the conversation.

"No," Risk said, holding in her frustration. As her nails turned to talons, she fisted her hands in her shirt, still holding it closed as much as she could.

"Because the raksasa have no true power. Not in a world of gods. They have our speed, our strength, they are near impossible to kill, and they live immortal as we do . . . but we gods are beings made of magic, and the raksasa cannot even harness it. They are our children, mine and all the other gods, light and dark —though the light gods would not have you believe it. They're children we've had with each other, and with humans . . . when the mood was right." Mazzulah smiled deviously, and Risk's stomach turned, though there was no food for it to turn.

"We could pit the raksasa together for an eternity and it would be the same as smashing rocks together until one of them yields." The god did that thing again, where she waved her hand as if what she spoke about was as inconsequential as the weather.

And while Risk was no lover of the raksasa, it didn't sit right with her that the god cared so little for them. That Mazzulah would equate them to rocks and not people.

"Thousands of years ago, we created the Maji by picking people who had traits that we valued and whose soul could withstand our magic. We took a piece of ourselves and each of us gifted it to one person. Our first champions." Mazzulah leaned forward and then stood. Her height matching that of her throne. Her sable hair hung in long, wild locks that blew in the wind.

Risk locked her spine and her knees, forcing herself to remain on her feet this time.

"You said the champions of the dark were too weak," Risk said.

"They were. In the beginning, they held up well. Long enough to have children and wage war, but the madness crept in. Our power was too strong for their wills, and most of the children down those lines. It was only after hundreds of years and just as many heirs that we started to see a pattern. Those that suffered before the magic grew were the strongest at withstanding its seductive call." Mazzulah smiled, and it reminded Risk of another whose eyes were also cruel.

"You, my girl, my little bird . . . are a perfect storm. You have enough strength from your raksasa blood to not fall to the madness. You can control the magic because you are Maji. What's more, you've suffered more than any other beast tamer—and you are stronger for it."

Risk blinked, her lips parting. "If the madness is a problem, how is it that Quinn is perfection to you?"

Mazzulah chuckled. "With time, it might have been an issue before. But Quinn died. She is frozen in her most powerful state. The madness can't reach her anymore than it already does, and with her, the dark king will learn to navigate it."

"I don't see how me being raksasa exempts me from this," Risk said.

"You care for them. You care for all living things." Mazzulah looked at her with pity, and it was a strange thing to see on a god's face. Stranger still when she walked forward and ran her gentle claws down Risk's cheek. "You have the strength that runs in a god. Your soul is made of magic, the same as mine. But unlike the raksasa, you also have my power. You're as close to a god as a mortal can be. In truth, I don't even know if you're truly mortal. While I am old and have seen much, I haven't ever seen this. You're one of a kind, and that's what makes you so special. That's why you are my heir, and not the raksasa or another beast tamer. You are a true heir, one that could remake this world and any other if you wished."

"I don't want to remake anything," Risk said. "I just want to return to Quinn."

"Liar," Mazzulah barked and then laughed, pulling away. "You may want to return to her, but that's not all you want. You wouldn't have climbed the staircase if it were. Somewhere in you, you want power, Mariska. I said you're my true heir, and I meant it. In every way, you are the one I've been waiting for, even if you're not the one I want."

The bitter aftertaste of her compliment stung. "If I'm you 'true heir,' why do you insist on breaking me?"

"Because only in breaking you can I reshape you,"

Mazzulah said as if it were so simple. "Answer me this, do you know why Quinn is powerful? Even for a fear twister, she is extraordinary." This talk of her sister was beginning to wear on Risk. She loved her.

She loved her more than anything.

But she was so tired of existing in this shadow that Quinn cast.

It was larger than life or death and she couldn't escape it in either realm.

"No," Risk sighed. "I don't know why Quinn is so powerful."

Mazzulah grinned as if she could taste the bitterness in Risk's voice.

"She wasn't born that way. None of you are necessarily born that much greater or lesser. It's the beauty of humans and why the game is fun. Your power is determined by your strength of will. Quinn is powerful because she demands it of the world. She suffered, and now she makes it suffer."

"I don't want to make the world suffer," Risk said.

"No," Mazzulah nodded. Her black horns gleamed in the blood moonlight. "You don't. You have no real desire for revenge, no lust to exert yourself over others. Despite all that's happened to you, you're still innocent in some ways."

"I—I don't understand," Risk said. "You just said that suffering is what made her so strong."

"You have suffered, but you forget—you're gray. You don't have to be good or bad, little bird. You will never desire to make the world suffer as she does. Spite will not be enough to pull you through the ascension."

"Then why do it?" Risk asked, raising her voice. "Why break me if I don't need to suffer? Why put me through—"

"Because," Mazzulah answered, her voice soft once more. "Only in being powerless will you find that thing that will carry *you* through. If you thought the black desert was bad, you aren't ready for what will happen when your magic drains away and it's only your strength of will to keep going that will bring it back to you. Quinn survived her ascension because she was too spiteful to die. The dark king survived his because of his craving for power overall. The rage thief held onto his fire and let that desire to make things right carry him. Everyone needs something, Mariska, and I'm going to break you until you find what is yours."

Risk stared at Mazzulah.

She stared and stared and when a laugh bubbled up in her throat and the dark god frowned, she only laughed more.

"If that's why you're doing this, then you've failed. I already found what carries me through. Quinn. Hope. The chance at a better future where I might one day learn what happiness is."

Mazzulah regarded her.

"Is that so?"

"Yes," Risk answered firmly, even as some small voice in the back of her mind told her she shouldn't be so sure.

"Very well, then," Mazzulah said. She waved her hand and the cold wind vanished. The thrones disappeared. While the blood moon and dark sky remained, the platform overlooking the entirety of the dark realm had been replaced by a single thing.

The staircase.

"Let me know if you feel so certain when you reach the top," Mazzulah said, smiling like a fiend as the golden circlet emblazoned on her forehead glowed.

Then she disappeared.

Risk fisted her hands in her shirt, letting out a strangled, infuriated roar.

She wanted to drop to her knees and scream in frustration. She wanted to curse and to cry as she did before.

None of that would do her any good though. Not here, where the only god to listen was the one who spoke in riddles and insisted on breaking her.

Swallowing down those feelings, Risk dropped her hands from her shirt and started to climb.

Again.

"Fire and smoke go hand in hand. Both dangerous on their own, and twice as much so together, but never to each other."
— Quinn Darkova, fear twister, walker of realms, reluctant protector of children

She stood on the plush red carpet, arms crossed over her chest.

Across from her, Thorne stared, open-mouthed.

Fear tinged with awe broke through the Cisean leader's expression as he slowly moved to his feet. "I didn't believe them when they said it was you."

Quinn inclined her head in a slight nod. "No one does right now. But I can assure you, I am me." She motioned to her body. "In the flesh . . . mostly."

"How is this possible?" Thorne asked, making no

move to touch or embrace her as he did with Lazarus last time they'd met. She didn't think much threw the leader of the tribes off-balance, but returning from the dead seemed to throw everyone.

She couldn't really blame them, though she was beginning to grow tired of explanations.

There were more important things to talk of than her time in the dark realm.

"I was dead, and now I'm not." Quinn shrugged, hoping he would leave it at that.

"But you're not alive either, are you?" he asked, drawing closer. His eyes searched her form, but not like the men she usually encountered. He was looking at something else that very few could see.

"I exist somewhere in-between," she said. Quinn lifted a hand and it evaporated into black smoke before reforming. "Neither dead nor alive. Somehow both."

Thorne stroked the braids of his beard. His red eyes keen with interest as he shook his head and turned to reseat himself on his throne.

"I told Lazarus when you left that you were unlike any other Maji. The power you hold supersedes anything we have in living memory." Quinn couldn't help but notice the strain in his face. The dark circles beneath his eyes.

"It wasn't only my power that allowed me out of the dark realm . . ." Quinn started, debating how much or how little to tell. "I made a deal with a god.

One I need to keep. Tell me, why is Vaughn here and not with Lazarus?"

Thorne regarded her for a moment, and then threw his head back and let out a boisterous laugh. "Only you would say and do something that's never been done, and act as if it's nothing. I assumed, given word hadn't spread that you're back, that this is only temporary. You've come through the mountains for a reason, yes?"

Begrudging that he didn't answer her question, Quinn nodded stiffly.

"Does it have to do with six N'skaran children?" he continued.

Quinn sighed. "When I returned to N'skara, I learned that my people had betrayed us."

"Yet, six of their children are with you?"

"I punished the city for its transgressions. The kids . . . they didn't do anything. They didn't ask for what I brought down on Liph. I needed to go south either way . . ." Quinn trailed off, the sounds of a roaring fire and tribal music in the distance pulling at her. They'd arrived during dinner time, but the right-hand of another king returning from the dead was not something that even Thorne wouldn't at least pause his dinner to see. "And I remembered how your people were last time I visited. They're not like most of the continent. Imogen would sell those kids to the highest bidders. Jibreal and Bangratas would likely enslave them."

"I'm assuming you're headed for Norcasta to be reunited with your king. Why not bring them there?" Thorne mused, leaning to one side of his chair.

"Norcasta is going to war," Quinn said.

"So is Cisea, if this letter from my old friend is to be believed," he said. "Lazarus has called a meeting with the leaders of his alliance. I'm supposed to leave for Dumas tomorrow."

"I'll be coming with."

Thorne snorted. "Obviously, but that still leaves the matter of the children. You brought them here and you have no intention of taking them to Norcasta. My country will be at war soon, along with yours. What's the real reason you won't take them the rest of the way?"

Quinn pressed her lips together, toying with an answer and what to say. She settled for honesty. "I'm not a mother. I'm not kind. I'm not patient, nor am I selfless—and I'm okay by that. When I return to Norcasta, it's for Lazarus. I'll be shepherding war. N'skari have a very difficult time in this world. Two of those children I brought are . . . gifted. I know that your people would care for them and train them and give them the best fighting chance possible. Something I will never do."

"That's oddly kind for someone who claims to not be, she-wolf."

"Someone who is not kind can still show kindness," Quinn said. "I enslaved the minds of the

Trienian soldiers and had them raze Liph to the ground. I gave them orders to pillage and burn, and when it was done, to walk into the bay and not walk out. Those kids would have died in a month, maybe two for the stronger ones. I felt it unfair to leave them, knowing what I was leaving them to."

Thorne nodded, seeming to consider what she said. "What are they?"

"One of the girls is a null," she said slowly.

Thorne tilted his head. "And the other?"

"The youngest boy . . . he's a soul eater."

His bushy red eyebrows rose. "A soul eater," he repeated. "And you think it better to leave him here? Lazarus—"

"Will ruin him," Quinn said. That shocked Thorne into silence. "I serve him, and I stand by him even in death because like calls to like. We are not good people. If anything, we're both far from it. Lazarus found me when I was ready to be found, but that boy . . . he might be strong, but he won't be strong enough to endure my king. Your people have always been kind, and they're more open-minded than most. You don't look down on the darker magics. He would do well here."

Seconds passed, turning to minutes. Leviathan's eye rose higher with every creeping moment. Eventually Thorne said, "Very well. I'll take them. Pair them with couples who have struggled to have children of their own. They'll be cared for and raised in our ways, and should they choose to leave when they are old enough—we won't stop them."

"Thank you," Quinn said, and she meant it. "That's all I can ask."

"As for your questioning regarding Vaughn," Thorne said, "my old friend has seen dark times, but I fear none like this. Lady Lorraine of your house sent both Vaughn and the emissary from Ilvas back to give their house time to grieve and prepare. I intend to take him with me tomorrow. With the grieving period passed and you returned . . ."

"You think Lazarus will go back to normal and welcome them back?"

Thorne shrugged. "If I had to guess, he never knew they left. Either way, I cannot remain outside Cisea forever. I still need an emissary to handle things for when I must return. Vaughn will be that, and you will make sure of it."

Quinn narrowed her eyes. A touch of bitter cold leaked into the air and Thorne shivered. "That's your price?" she asked.

Thorne nodded, his throat bobbing in response to the magic she used without trying.

"Very well." Quinn shrugged again. She didn't disagree, and of all the people to send, she rather liked Vaughn. He was her friend. She just didn't like being ordered. Then again, she did show up with half a dozen starved and dying N'skari children. Relatively speaking, they were on equal footing right now. "Is that all?" Quinn was tired after her journey, but more than anything she just wanted to be alone. Perhaps with a hot bath. She might see if she could reach Draeven once more.

"Actually," Thorne said. She paused, mid-turn.

"Yes?"

"I've lived a good life. Longer than some. I hope to live longer still. In the end, though, most of us that exist in the gray don't know where we'll truly end up . . ."

His red eyes gleamed, and she knew what he wanted. What he was asking.

"You want to know what it's like in the dark realm." It wasn't a question, but still he motioned with his hand for her to continue. "I wish that I had a good answer for you, but I'm afraid that it's different for everyone. I never had any doubts about where I was going when I died. I always knew that it was darkness that awaited me. I didn't fear it . . . but I also didn't expect what I found. I died being crushed to death, and I opened my eyes to find myself on my knees before the dark god." Quinn recalled her awakening into the realm and smiled faintly. It felt like an old memory from years gone by.

"You saw Mazzulah?" he asked, and while there was a slight tinge of anxiousness in the air, it was mostly fascination.

Quinn chuckled darkly. "You could say that."

"What did you do? When you found yourself kneeling before them?"

"I stood up," Quinn said simply. "Apparently that's not a thing that happens often. The god took a liking to me. Even more so when one of their raksasa tried to stop me from standing and I kicked him off the edge of the great staircase. Raksasa can handle a great deal, especially in the dark realm, but I never saw that one again, and not a single raksasa touched me after that."

Quinn smiled to herself, and Thorne roared with laughter.

"You kicked a demon." He shook his head in mild disbelief. "I can see why it is that both Lazarus and the dark god have taken a liking to you. There was a time I thought you'd be happy here, in the mountains. Free. I can see now that I was wrong."

"Oh?" Quinn prompted.

"Any woman that can ensnare a king and a god—that can die and find her way back—that can defy the very order of things—well, I see now that you don't need freedom. No one is strong enough to hold you down." Moonlight leaked through the windows and the light drapes stirred in the breeze. "The entire world, perhaps more than this one, could not even stop you. What's more, you don't seek to rule it. Lazarus is a lucky man to have found someone who suited him so perfectly."

Quinn nodded, more to herself than anything.

"Let's both hope he sees it that way when he learns that I've returned."

The emotion leached from Thorne's face. "He doesn't know?" he asked quietly.

"No," Quinn said. "And for both our sakes, you shouldn't tell him. I'll be with your party tomorrow, and we'll journey to this war council together."

Thorne cursed under his breath. "You toy with fire, woman."

Quinn smiled to herself. "I suppose it's a good thing I'm smoke. The fire can't burn me anymore."

"But it can burn me," Thorne said, more solemn than before.

Quinn turned for the door in the floor and said over her shoulder, "Keep my return to yourself and I'll keep you and yours safe. See you in the morning, Thorne."

The only answer she received was another curse, and then Quinn slipped into the night.

CHAPTER 18

GRAVE MISTAKE

"NO COST IS TOO GREAT FOR PERFECTION."

— Nero, Emperor of Triene, God among men

A haunting, terrible lullaby played in the background as Nero took his tea. He tilted his head, listening for the slightest misstep. It would only take one, and the musician who was playing had been doing so for hours.

Sweat dotted the lower man's brow as he played endlessly for Nero's enjoyment. The real reason the emperor brought in musicians was not simply to hear them perform, however, but to hear them fail.

He loved when they made a mistake.

It was always their last.

A knock at the door made him frown. The man playing didn't falter for a single note. He was almost as good as the rumors claimed. But he would falter eventually. They always did.

"Enter," Nero said.

The heavy wooden door pushed open. One of his vassals entered, along with his head apothecary. Nero watched them approach. Their steps timid and eyes downcast the whole way. They walked like kicked dogs.

Nero smiled to himself because he'd trained them well.

"What do you want?"

"Your Excellency," the apothecary said, as they stopped several feet away, heads still bowed. "The incantation is ready. We must act now or risk waiting for the next moonless night."

Nero started tapping his foot lightly against the marbled flooring. He took another sip of his tea and the plate clinked when he set the cup back down.

The musician kept playing. Never slowing.

His lullaby carried the notes with such beauty it almost moved the great emperor.

Almost.

"Very well. The timing is right. It should only be another fortnight before the head of my messenger arrives."

Both the apothecary and his vassal shared a look.

"The head?" the vassal asked, unable to help himself. "You sent him a traitor's head." His cheeks heated immediately, and a ruddy flush swept up from his collar, coloring his pale complexion. Nero liked pale vassals. Had them imported specifically. The marks he left looked so beautiful on their skin . . .

"Yes, and my brother's temper will have gotten the better of him. He'll be assembling for war now. Making moves . . . preparing. We can't have that." Nero inclined his head, looking up at the singular portrait on the wall.

It was a painting he had created by a great artist.

Of him and Lazarus.

His brother had left when they were still young men, but this particular artist was quite skilled. Before Nero killed him.

He had a gift so great he couldn't bear to share. That was before he learned how to keep them. Before he learned that there were ways to perfect their imperfections.

In the portrait, he and his brother stood. Their scars nearly matched, but it was only Nero's left eye that was blind. Shoulder to shoulder, Lazarus was half a foot taller. His expression as menacing as it had ever been before he left. They both wore the purple and gold of Triene, but it was Nero who wore the crown. Nero, whose guiding hand rested on his little brother's shoulder. Nero that was the master to the monster.

They would get back to that.

When the game was won and his brother had nothing and no one, he would return to him. And Nero would welcome him with open arms.

The musician slipped.

Exhaustion had finally caught up and his posture had fallen, merely an inch, but an inch was all it took and the guide of the bow over strings was a single octave too high.

That note resonated. Thrumming in the air as the musician stopped playing.

He knew the rules, after all.

When the emperor invited you to play, you couldn't say no.

You couldn't fumble.

Because if you did . . . the emperor did love collecting things.

Nero picked up his teacup again and smiled into the hot liquid.

Then he brought it down upon the table. The cup broke, half of it fracturing and falling away, leaving behind jagged edges.

Nero stood from the gold-lined table. His bad leg locking in place. He leaned forward, and a scuffle drew his attention. The musician was trying to run.

Using his good foot, he kicked back the chair, and it blocked the path just long enough for him to turn and swing. The razor-sharp edges of the cup broke the flesh of the man's neck. His lifeblood poured down his white linen shirt that had been otherwise soaked with sweat. His thin lips opened and closed as he began to drown in his own blood. The gurgling sound was sweet music to Nero's ears.

"Will this be enough blood for the incantation?" Nero asked.

"Yes, Your Excellency," the apothecary said. Neither he nor the vassal had moved.

"Then do it and bring me his body when you're done. I have plans for this one."

CHAPTER 19
CHEAP THRILLS

"Death is only an adventure if you choose to live. Without
purpose, existence is also meaningless."
— Quinn Darkova, fear twister, walker of realms, in desperate
need of a bath

Quinn groaned in delight.

Her head fell back against the rock ledge as the hot water of the springs eased the tension in her muscles. While she might not need food or water or even sleep like the rest of them, a hot bath was always something to cherish. Her life as a slave had taught her that. Having gone so long without the luxury, to have an endless supply of hot water and a chunk of juniper soap to scrub her skin clean—it was

147

as close to perfection as could be found in the human realm.

The cold from the dark realm never truly left her. While she wasn't freezing, it was in the hot spring that she felt warm for the first time since coming back. And she reveled in it.

As far as things to revel in, Quinn thought she was doing pretty good.

In the time since she had returned, she'd already tortured a few men, burned a city down, destroyed a good portion of the Trienian armada, saved six N'skari children, and had a hot bath. It was the bath that most excited her. The rest of it were just things that needed to be done.

But she was good at that. Better than most at doing the hard thing. Making the difficult choice. Truth be told, she took a certain pride in that trait even though it was one most people would find horrible. Once upon a time her family had hated her for it. They hated the honesty. The bluntness. The brutal side of her that both Mazzulah and Lazarus seemed to find beautiful. That was one of the things she rather liked about being back. In the dark realm, Quinn was simply allowed to exist, and if she wanted to, wreak havoc. There was no urgency. No real chessboard. She got a little thrill out of playing games with the dark god, but overall, the stakes were low when you were already dead and didn't have the ability to fear.

But here . . . there were games to be had, even more so with war on the horizon.

The game to end all games, Mazzulah had called it.

Quinn trailed her fingers over the top of the water, musing about all that and more. She thought about Lazarus and what he'd do when he saw her. If he'd kiss her or try to kill her.

Quinn smiled, neither option was particularly unwelcome, and while she was delaying him knowing for a very good reason, she couldn't help the little thrill that ran through her knowing she'd get to see the reaction on his face. It would be priceless.

She would return and they would win the war and then . . . well, Quinn wasn't sure. On one hand, it seemed odd to be thinking about what would happen after the war, on the other, after spending years in the dark realm only to find mere months had passed . . . she had to wonder.

It wasn't that she'd grown tired of Mazzulah, but the fire in Lazarus called to her more than the ice. Or at least, what she remembered of it. A small part of Quinn wondered; would she still feel that fascination? The desire to push and to pull until he came unhinged?

Would she yearn for his savagery? Would she quiver as she once did?

Quinn didn't know. So long had passed that she wondered at times if she'd gone a little mad. She had actually danced with Mazzulah. Was it possible that the memories of her past life weren't the sharp bite of flame she remembered?

While a certain thrill went through her when she shattered a man's mind or left Liph to burn, cheap thrills only lasted so long. Quinn needed that darkness, that desperateness that she recalled—because she wanted to live again. At least in some capacity. And when the war was over, assuming they won it, she would have to move on from razing cities to the ground, hunting assassins, and torturing whoever she felt like. Live out however long her immortal life would be.

Being whatever or whoever she chose to be.

For so long she lived for games. She loved the carefully crafted manipulations. But when she died . . . all of that fell away.

She couldn't help but ponder if it would again when it was all over.

She was addicted and destruction was her poison of choice.

Quinn never got enough of it, but at a certain point, she would have to.

"But at least I got a hot bath. That's worth something," Quinn said to herself. In the back of her mind, a whispered hiss made her open her eyes.

"*Mistress.*"

"We've been through this, Neiss," Quinn sighed. "It's either Quinn or fear twister. You can even call me 'walker of realms' if you're wanting a change. But leave the master and mistress stuff for the gods."

His presence slithered through her mind. "*He sleeps.*"

Quinn groaned, this time for a very different reason.

"Of course he does," she muttered. "Right when I finally get something I want." Quinn huffed, but turned to dreamwalking nonetheless. She sought him out by simply thinking it, and unlike the other times when he'd been trying to avoid her, his mind was open.

"It took you long enough," she snapped, appearing in front of him. Draeven jumped, his eyes going wide at the sight of her wet, bare flesh.

"Black Baac," he cursed. "Put some clothes on! Why are you naked every time I—"

Quinn rolled her eyes, summoning a robe. It wasn't real and given that she didn't dream like him, she wasn't pulled into the sensory detail of his mind. Her skin once again felt cold to the touch. "I've tried coming to you, but you've been avoiding me. If you hadn't done that, I wouldn't have had to come during my bath. We don't always get what we want, do we?"

Draeven pinched the bridge of his nose, closing his eyes tightly.

"Are you dressed yet?"

"In a fashion," Quinn replied. He cracked one eye

and sighed with relief that both her breasts and other assets were covered.

"I needed to speak with you," Draeven started slowly.

"Oh?" Quinn said. "But not in the last week that I've tried to contact you? It must really be important if you're actively trying to—"

"Why can't I tell Lazarus?" he interrupted. Quinn raised her eyebrows.

"We talked about this."

"No," he breathed. "You made a decision as you always do."

"Yes, well, one of us came back from the dead and the other helped put them there. Forgive me for not asking anyone's opinion while I plan how to best keep myself out of the dark realm again."

Draeven swallowed, and Quinn sighed. His guilt was eating him alive.

"I'm sorry. I never meant for—"

"For the love of Forseya, I don't care—I just need you to swallow your guilt a little longer. I'll be back soon." Quinn waved her hand vaguely, and Draeven narrowed his eyes.

"How soon is 'soon'?" he asked, and when she didn't answer, he cursed under his breath. "He's losing his mind, Quinn. Those damned beasts of his are eating our soldiers and he doesn't care. Not about them or his house or even the crown. All he cares about is revenge, and while both Lorraine and

Dominicus are more than happy to go along with this little plan of yours—I need to know why I'm lying."

"Do you care for him?" Quinn asked.

"Like a brother."

"And Lorraine? Do you care for her?" Quinn asked. Draeven frowned, and she continued. "What about Dominicus? Axe? Vaughn? Your soldiers? The thousands and thousands of people that would die when Triene invades and no one was paying attention? Would you care then? Would you feel guilty?"

Draeven leaned away, his lips parting before snapping closed as he locked his jaw. Quinn lifted an eyebrow. "All of that aside, I could tell him—but I can't physically be there yet. My dreamwalking lets me communicate, but I can't physically travel over half the continent in a single night, Draeven. Use that brain of yours that claims to think so much. If I can't physically be there, it'll only make the madness worse."

He looked away then, a slight flush creeping up his neck.

She hoped he felt like an idiot.

"Why were you wanting to contact me?" he asked quietly.

"To know where you are. I only get a sense of direction from Neiss, not an exact location."

He nodded, smoothing the wrinkles in his tunic. "Two days from Dumas. We're headed for Shallowyn. Lazarus has called a meeting of his alliance."

"I heard."

Draeven frowned. "If you heard, then why'd you ask? Also, how'd you 'hear' this?"

Quinn tsked. "I heard he called a meeting—not where. Secondly, I'm staying with friends—"

"Thorne or Imogen?" Draeven asked, cutting straight through the fluff. Quinn laughed.

"Doesn't matter. I'll be there soon, like I told you. Now you have a time frame for how long you have to watch over Neiss, if that makes you happy."

"Many things make me happy, watching that serpent is not one of them," he replied stiffly.

Quinn chuckled. "Well, that serpent isn't the fondest of watching you either . . ." Her voice trailed off as a flicker of fear reached her. It wasn't coming from Draeven.

"What is it?" he asked.

"I think," she murmured, "that someone or something has gone horribly wrong."

"What do you mean?"

"I'm not sure," she said quietly. Spreading out her senses. Her field of vision touched something just beyond her periphery of Draeven's dream, and a sense so deep and profound it could mean death pulled at her. "I need to go."

"Quinn—"

She didn't hear the rest of what he said.

When Quinn opened her eyes, she was back in the pool, but the water had gone cold.

There were no screams. No cries. None of the sounds that told of terror.

But she felt it, and that was all she needed.

Quinn evaporated as she slipped into the realm of death. Her body extinguished in a puff of black smoking tendrils that drifted on the wind. She moved from the cave, down the path, all the way to the tree huts of the tribes.

Nothing seemed out of the ordinary . . .

But still she felt it. Like a beacon of darkness, it called to her.

Quinn followed its signal, drawing near.

She moved as a shadow in the night, soundless and unseen.

But she wasn't the only shadow.

No. That evil that called to her soul . . . it was also shadow.

Neither dead nor alive.

A creature of dark magic and despair formed.

Quinn peered into the midnight forest where the wind had stopped, and no scent came. She looked at the parts that were too still. Too perfect.

And two red eyes looked back at her.

CHAPTER 20
BLOOD MAGIC

"The road to destruction is paved recklessness as much as it is arrogance."
— *Quinn Darkova, fear twister, walker of realms*

Quinn leapt forward, her shadowy form permeating the air with fear. The creature—unlike anything she'd seen in this realm or the dark one—narrowed its eyes.

They touched, and Quinn jerked away.

She was walking the realm of death, not the living, and yet . . . . the slight contact she'd had with it left her burned. Those red eyes backed away as a howl of pain that could have shattered mirrors rang through the air.

It appeared that she'd hurt it too.

Good, she thought. *Things were getting boring.*

Quinn took off after it, transitioning from vapor to her true form—but not the one of flesh. This creature was not of the living world. She wasn't sure if it were from the dead one either.

It moved through the winding trees on the forest floor without leaving footprints, and she followed in its wake. Whatever it was, it emitted an evil that called to her. So dark and potent that the only way to find it was to look where the night was broken by a void.

That pained cry fell silent.

In the not far distance, footsteps thundered on wooden planks.

It had woken the tribe.

She needed to act swift. Strike it down before others could intervene.

Quinn tilted her head. The cold of the dark realm settled inside her, bringing with it a sharp clarity. A touch of ice so deep in her veins it bordered on pain. She liked the pain. She embraced it as she sought the red-eyed creature.

One who didn't know better might think it a raksasa, but no raksasa could access their magic. No, this was either human or Maji.

Or god . . .

That was a troubling thought, but Quinn wasn't a fool. She was playing the game to end all games. Mazzulah released a soul from the dark realm. What was to stop the other gods from also toeing the line?

"Me," she whispered.

In the periphery of her vision something moved. It was slight. Hardly there and easily mistaken for a cloud covering the moon. But tonight, there was no moon.

Quinn whirled around, letting her body explode in a fog of black magic.

The creature that had been lunging for her tried to pull back. Its shadowed claws curled inward as it shrieked again.

Quinn felt the flame against her very soul as she enveloped it.

One of them would give out eventually.

She was determined it would not be her.

She'd only felt pain like this once before. It was the night she stepped into the spring. Back then the waters had dragged her under. Threatened to drown her. The cold had been too great . . . this time it was fire. Fire and ash and evil, and she was the cold. She was the winter winds sent by death.

Footsteps drew near. She sensed others, but until it made to escape, she hadn't realized the creature did too. Claws raked through the mist, and if Quinn could have winced, she would have.

The creature parted her soul and ran through it blindly, wildly seeking a reprieve.

Quinn could not see who approached in the darkness, only that this being was headed toward them.

She didn't know why it was here, only that it

couldn't mean anything good, and that was enough reason to give chase.

Chanting started. At first it was a lone voice and then there were more. Men grunted and stomped their feet. A flash of silver spun in the air and she recognized the glint of halberds.

What the Cisean warriors didn't realize was that weapons wouldn't help them against this foe. The red-eyed beast was both living and not, and while she understood the rules of her existence, she didn't know the rules of its.

Powerful haunches like that of an ape leapt several feet up the rock path. Its feet both touched the forest floor and didn't as it covered the distance quickly, barreling faster and faster toward the warrior who stood at the top.

Torches of fire outlined the men, but it was the one in the center who blocked the path that made Quinn surge forward.

Pale green eyes focused on the beast coming for them.

His face was set in grim determination, and Quinn didn't even have time to warn them before he and the beast collided head-on.

Sable threads that twined together to make both muscle and bone slithered over his bare chest, beneath his skin. Quinn expected the creature to pass through and that the contact would kill him. She was wrong.

Those pale green eyes bled to black, blotting out the white entirely.

Quinn rematerialized in front of Vaughn.

But it wasn't her friend that stared back at her.

He lunged forward, and Quinn ducked, slamming her head into his abdomen. She heard the air leave his lungs as her arms grabbed at his waist. Instead of picking him up, flinging her weight back, and driving his skull into the ground—she kept pushing forward.

The warriors at his back stepped away. In the darkness, it was hard to see what exactly was going on, but they clearly sensed something was wrong.

Vaughn's body hit the ground, Quinn still half on top of him.

She tried to pull her arms out from under him. Rough hands grabbed her hair, pulling upward. Quinn snarled an inhuman sound of rage.

That seemed to pull the Ciseans back to attention. Several of them went for him and the others went for her as they tried to pull them apart.

"Stop," she said in Cisean. "That's not Vaughn. He could—"

The beast wearing her friend's skin smiled.

Then it twisted. His fist came up, kicking one man in the head. He spun, flinging the other holding his arm at Quinn. While she had greater strength and speed than most men twice her size, she already had three holding her back and now a fourth thrown into her.

The wind left her lungs, and Quinn groaned.

"*Potes,*" she cursed.

Quinn evaporated once more and the men around her dropped to their knees. She wasn't trying to harm them. It wasn't intentional, but when pure fear touched them, humans couldn't help their response. They weren't built to handle it. Handle her.

While she'd been a force to be reckoned with when she was living . . .

She was something else dead.

Something more than they could even comprehend.

Quinn reformed in the flesh behind the creature wearing Vaughn's skin. He had turned on his final guard and grasped his head between two hands. His thumbs pushed into the eye sockets. Blood leaked from them and the other warrior screamed.

Quinn placed a well-aimed kick at his leg, swallowing down her discomfort at the act. This wasn't Vaughn, her friend. It was a beast. A monster. One that would kill without regard.

His knee popped. The demon grunted as it fell sideways, dropping the warrior's body. Vaughn hit the forest floor, and Quinn kicked him in the side before leaning down to turn him over. His hand flashed out, trying to strike, but Quinn was faster.

She grabbed his wrist and dropped down on top of him, her knee in his sternum and her other leg extended out, digging into his arm.

Quinn pressed her forearm into his neck and leaned in close.

"Be gone, beast."

He laughed, crimson coloring his teeth.

The creature spoke, and the only words she understood were "kill" and "him."

Her blood ran cold.

It might not have been meant to reveal anything, but its words alone did just that.

Whatever was inside him spoke Trienian.

Vaughn didn't.

Quinn grit her teeth.

She couldn't understand it even if she wanted. While she could interrogate, the words would be lost on her . . .

Quinn lowered her head and exhaled a breath of black smoke.

The demon thrashed beneath her, but she held tight.

Forcing it to feel her fear.

"If you will not leave, I will smoke you out," she promised.

Hate glimmered in its unnatural stygian eyes.

More footsteps came, but these did not try to remove her. They gathered around and a quiet hush fell over the Ciseans.

"What is that?" Thorne asked.

"I'm not entirely sure," she said. "I found a creature lurking beneath your hut. I attacked it, and it went inside Vaughn. I cannot kill it without killing him."

The beast let out another slew of words she largely didn't understand apart from the occasional curse. No one spoke, but a gasp of surprise rippled around them.

They recognized the language too, at least some of them.

"He's been cursed," one man said.

"We should kill him. It would be a mercy," another echoed.

"No," Quinn said. "I will find a way."

She peered deep into its black eyes as she released another breath of fear. The arms she held down fought against her. His chest attempted to rise, but Quinn pressed down harder.

"What way?" one to her left said.

"I'm not sure just yet," she said slowly. "But I tend to get what I want in the end."

"Too much fear will break him just as surely as death," Thorne said.

Quinn pressed her lips together. Sweat slicked her forehead. Her naked body was widely on display, but if she moved, the creature was free.

"Bind his arms," she commanded. The warriors moved with haste, securing rope around both wrists and ankles. "Two men to each rope. We'll need to secure them."

"We only have six," one of them said.

"It'll work," Thorne answered before she could. Quinn frowned because she wasn't sure it would.

"I'm going to move, and when I do, you must keep him here until we can tie him to something more permanent—" Quinn lifted herself off him, and his arms surged forward.

Just before his fingertips could make contact, the rope went taut, and his hands curled into fists. Another slew of Trienian curses coming from his lips.

Quinn stepped back.

"I've never heard of a Maji that could do this," Quinn said softly.

Thorne removed his cloak and extended it toward her. She wasn't cold, at least not from the weather, but she took it anyway and tired it around her naked shoulders.

"This was no Maji," Thorne said solemnly.

Quinn lifted a brow. "No?"

It only took one look at him to know that Thorne was very much aware of what they faced.

"This is blood magic," he said. "Of the darkest kind. Only our most ancient of incantations and spells even hint at power to this degree."

The creature pulled at its bindings again, but the six of them held true. With her and Thorne here as well, it was contained.

"What is *it*?"

"I don't know," the Cisean leader said, never lifting his own red eyes from the creature. "But I think the men might be right. Whatever this is, we don't understand it. Death would be kinder, Quinn. It's what Vaughn would want."

"I don't believe death will kill it," Quinn said. "Which means killing him would be for nothing, and it would likely enter someone else. It knows that without something to cling to, I *can* kill it."

Thorne mulled it over. His thick fingers trailing over his braided red beard. His expression was torn because there was no right answer.

Their moments of indecision were a mistake.

The creature within him seemed to sense that its future was being debated, even if he couldn't understand the words. His arms and legs went slack, granting the rope just enough give before he dove to one direction.

The Ciseans weren't expecting it when he rolled sideways. The rope got tangled and several men lost their footing. He dragged the closest one down beside him and wound one of the ropes around the man's neck.

Both Quinn and Thorne sprang forward, but it was too late.

Vaughn bit into the man's flesh, tearing a chunk from where his shoulder and throat met. Blood poured from the wound as he tossed him aside and backed up.

It was hard to tell where he looked exactly when

his eyes were solid black, but when his head turned a fraction and Quinn followed his line of sight . . .

There, standing in front of a discarded halberd, was the boy.

The soul eater child.

The demon lunged, for the weapon or the kid, Quinn wasn't sure, but she followed after him.

Her hand grasped one of the ropes still tied to his wrist. She pulled it taut, and his body jerked to a stop. Her shoulder protested the motion, and Quinn wound the rope around her wrist, pulling tighter. He wheeled around, and she was ready to strike.

She was prepared to end this if she truly had to, though she would do as much as she could to avoid that.

But in all her calculations of what to do, it never occurred to her that the boy would reach out. That he hadn't come because he was scared, but because he was drawn.

"Nobody hurts Quinn," he said.

And for all her great power . . .

For all that she could do and be and destroy, she wasn't able to stop him.

Vaughn's eyes went black, turning green once more, a glassy sheen covering them. His knees buckled. He stopped pulling.

Quinn's lips parted. The word "no" not coming out even as she screamed it inside her mind, unable to see past her own horror.

Vaughn was dead.

His soul, and the beast that corrupted him, had found a new master.

The corpse fell to the ground. Unmoving. Behind him, the little boy stood there, pale blue eyes narrowed on it. Beneath his skin shadows swirled. She knew that her friend was there, and fury rose within.

Quinn lifted her hand, red clouding her vision—

Warm, calloused fingers closed around her wrist.

"Don't," Thorne said, and as fast as her rage came to her, it drained away.

She turned to him, and he dropped her hand, stepping away. His red eyes flared brighter. His expression turned stoic, leaning on the verge of losing control.

"You stole my rage," she said.

"You would have killed him," Thorne said through gritted teeth. "The boy cannot help what he is any more than you can. He does not understand what he's done. He sought to protect you."

"I don't need protection," Quinn said.

"No, but in the mind of a child that clearly cares for you—you did." Thorne closed his eyes, and Quinn let him take a few breaths to steady himself.

"You don't understand," she said, her voice soft, not from anger or fear or threat, but from the deep, chilling realization of what had happened. "When a soul eater dies, they cease to exist, but the souls they carried belong to the dark realm. Souls that go there are slaves to their raksasa masters who can do whatever they want with them. I didn't want to kill him because it would have been a pointless death for a good man. But this?" Quinn looked at the boy again, and she couldn't help the small embers of anger and frustration that came to life again. "This is worse."

All around them, dead and unconscious Cisean warriors lay prone, but it was only the one that was eaten that concerned her.

"I will mourn for Vaughn. He's . . . my son. But he is not alone in our mourning, Quinn. Many have died tonight. Mothers and fathers, brothers and sisters have all lost someone—"

"We have to find a way to free him," Quinn said.

"If there is a way, I don't know it," Thorne answered.

"No, but we know someone who might."

Both Quinn and Thorne looked at the boy, and that heaviness she saw in the leader, it filled her then.

"Are you sure?" he asked. "You didn't want him. You know the tribe will care for him either way—"

"It doesn't matter what I want," Quinn said. "We both know who sent that creature. Triene was either sending you a message, or this was an assassination attempt. It's too convenient that Lazarus sends for a summit and then a blood-magicked creature is here. There's only one soul eater who might have an answer for how to at least free Vaughn, if not bring him back to life—"

"And if not?" Thorne asked. "If we take the boy to Norcasta and there is no way, what will you do with him, then?"

Quinn pressed her lips together. "I don't speak Trienian, but Lazarus does. We might be able to get answers out of that creature. Find out what—"

"What of the boy, Quinn?" He motioned to him, and she sighed. He was young, though she didn't know his age. While the darkness ran deep, the way he looked at her then wasn't the Maji in him, it was the child. She sighed.

"I don't know, Thorne. But I've been to the dark realm, and Vaughn . . . he doesn't deserve what'll await him there. I have a war to fight, and now a friend to save. Past that, we'll figure it out. But the boy is coming with."

Quinn walked forward and extended her hand.

The child looked between her and Thorne, who she sensed had great trepidation about releasing him to her after what just happened.

Still, the boy took her hand.

"Please don't hurt him, Quinn. Vaughn wouldn't want that."

But it wasn't her who answered. "Quinn only hurts people who hurt her first," the little boy said.

Quinn pressed her lips together because what he didn't realize is that he had.

He took away her friend. One of her only friends.

For once, she was beginning to see the burden of

what it meant to have a dark Maji for a child, and why those same qualities she saw in him now made her people hate her.

"He is safe with me," Quinn said.

"And from you?" Thorne asked.

It was that empathy—that ability to understand—that let her release her anger. There were few in the world who understood Quinn, and fewer still who she understood in return.

But this child, this horrible, awful child was one of them.

She had hurt people for the ones she loved as well.

"They're one and the same," she said. "We ride at dawn."

Now more than ever, she needed to get back to Lazarus.

Nero had taken something from her, and if she couldn't take it back . . .

There were worse fates than death.

Quinn would make sure of it.

CHAPTER 21
RAT WINTER

"One does not need to be good to be kind, but kindness is an
action and not an intention. Motivation matters not."
— Quinn Darkova, fear twister, walker of realms

Her forearms rested against the wooden railing. She leaned forward, narrowing her eyes on the traveling party below. Thorne was out in full force with a dozen Cisean warriors and the boy, all readying for the journey ahead. Somberness hung in the air. A palpable tension that wouldn't dissipate. While the men didn't appear to fear the boy outwardly, Quinn couldn't help but notice the way their eyes flicked in his direction every few minutes—as if needing to reassure themselves where he was.

They did the same with her, looking up onto the

wooden bridge where she stood. Quinn donned the leathers of the Cisean people once more, but not the cloaks. She preferred being able to move, and in truth, any clothing constricted that now. She understood their desire for her to be at least somewhat covered.

"He cares for you," a voice said, approaching her.

Quinn didn't turn as she replied, "I know, but for the life of me I can't understand why."

"You saved him," Siva said, coming to stand beside her. The Cisean woman leaned forward, resting against the railing as well.

"Only because I doomed them to begin with. Had I not condemned a city to be burnt to the ground, I wouldn't have brought anyone, certainly not children. They only slowed me down."

"True," she mused. "But to a child, you saved him. The reasons why matter not. He feels a"—she paused to search for a word—"kinship with you."

Quinn sighed. "I feel the same with him, but not because he 'saved' me."

"You relate to the darkness in him," Siva said.

"I do."

"I think he is the same," Siva continued. "The other children are grateful, but they will not miss you. Except Trissa. She's a strong one. Quiet strength, but strong."

Quinn heard an admiration in Siva's tone at the mention of the girl. "You're going to take her, aren't you? For you and Thorne to raise."

Siva nodded. "We are. Our son is gone now. And Trissa . . . she speaks to me. She needs the right hands to guide her. A null has a gift many don't understand. She'll do well here."

Quinn nodded in agreement. Something inside her felt content knowing that the girl would be with them. The sun peeked over the mountain tops and birds began to sing. The cold ebbed, if only a little. "And the others?" Quinn asked quietly.

"They'll recover," Siva said. "Their bodies are strong, built for a colder winter than we have here. Their minds worry me more."

"We live in a hard world. It's better that they learn that young. They'll be more prepared for what's to come."

"They'll be safe here. Even if war comes, it's unlikely the southern men will make it up the mountain. Not with winter upon us."

"Yes, but winter isn't permanent," Quinn said. "Not yours, anyway."

"With any luck, this won't last longer than winter," Siva countered.

Quinn let out a dark chuckle. "I don't believe in luck. Good or bad, I make my own future. The gods are too fickle to be trusted with it anyhow."

When Siva didn't say anything, Quinn finally glanced sideways.

Her long blonde hair had been woven into thick braids and pulled away from her face with a leather tie. The crinkles around her eyes had grown more pronounced in the year that had passed since Quinn last saw her. She still dressed in leathers and carried her head like a queen—but there was a tiredness alongside the wisdom now.

Her eyes were focused on the men below her, and fear bubbled up.

"I'd like to think that they are benevolent beings, but with all I've seen, I don't think it's possible." It was only then that Quinn noticed the pale green flecks in her hazel eyes. Red marks lined her lids, the skin irritated as if it had been rubbed at too much. "We look to them the same way a horse looks to us, and while some of us are kind to our horses, not all are. The horse is a means of carrying things. They are little more than a slave, but happy in their ignorance because they don't realize it. I think we are the same —and it's easier to be ignorant and hope than to face the truth."

"There's more truth to that than you probably want to know," Quinn said.

"Probably," Siva agreed.

Silence spread between them, but it wasn't strained or tenuous. Unlike the somber tensions pervading the tribes this early morning—this silence was soft. Welcoming, like sleep that pulls you under after the worst of days. There was a small comfort in it.

Quinn turned back to the party; they were near

ready now. The horses were loaded, and the wagon filled with provisions. The morning light was nearly over the mountains. It was almost time.

"I have to ask . . ." Siva said, as if sensing it as well. "After all I've lost, I can't put my faith in gods, but you are close enough. Will you—"

"I'll protect him," Quinn said softly. "I can't promise you that nothing will happen. That wouldn't be fair to either of us. I can tell you that I'll try my best to make sure Thorne comes back to you."

"Thank you," Siva said, and while it was simple, those two words held so much emotion that Quinn felt her gratitude.

Thorne looked up to the platform and motioned with his hand.

Time to go.

They made their way down together, but before they reached the group, Quinn looked over at Siva. "I'm going to do my best to bring Vaughn back too— and if I can't, I'll try to make sure that wherever he goes isn't worse than here."

Siva paused, taking a slow breath. She looked up at Quinn, who stared back knowingly.

"He was a good man, my son. He deserves more than to live as a shadow of himself."

Quinn noticed how she talked as if he were dead while still acknowledging that wasn't completely the case.

"He is a good man," Quinn agreed. "And a good friend. I'm going to do my best by him."

"Then do your best by the boy," Siva said. Quinn stopped beside her. They were only a few feet away from the men, but the look in the Cisean woman's eyes was also knowing in its own right. "I understand how hard it is to be kind when someone hurts you. If you're going to take the boy and my son with him—then do your best there too. Raise him right, as Vaughn would. Teach him if not right and wrong, then at least how to survive and how to treat those beneath you—teach him so that he treats Vaughn that way. The legends say soul eaters can live forever, forever is a long time for my only child to be trapped."

Quinn didn't look away even though she wanted to. She didn't fidget under the intensity as some might, but instead lifted her head to the challenge.

It was a lot to ask. Some might say too much. But Quinn was loyal to those who were loyal to her, and Vaughn was most loyal of them all.

"I will," Quinn vowed.

She and Siva did not embrace, but there was an understanding between them. One that Quinn would honor.

The other woman nodded, and they approached the party, breaking off. Siva went to her husband, and Quinn went to the boy. He sat on the back of the wagon, legs crossed, staring off into the distance.

She took a seat next to him.

"What's your name?" She hadn't asked him in the time they'd been together, partly because she hadn't been planning on any of them sticking around, and partly because she preferred the distance. She didn't like anything relying on her, least of all someone else's children.

"*Wogat*," he answered. It was the N'skaran word for rat. "*Wogat Stieg.*"

Either his parents were unkind or his caretaker was, because they gave him an orphan's name—and not even a decent one. Rat Winter. It was the surname given to all orphans of the lower class in N'skara.

"Do you like being known as Wogat?" she asked him.

He shrugged. "It's a name. What I'm called doesn't change who I am."

Those words were wise for one so young.

"From here on out, your name is Kairick Fierté," Quinn said.

The wagon began to roll. The men mounted their horses, and Quinn stared at the treetops as they started their journey down the mountain, toward the east. To Dumas.

"Kairick means strong," the boy said.

"It does. And you are."

He seemed thoughtful. "What does Fierté mean?"

"Fire, in Trienian," she answered. Quinn wondered if it would be a mistake to give him Lazarus' name. Most of his house took it, though it was their choice. She wouldn't call him by the name of slaves. Her choice to change it was more for her than him, but true to her promise to Siva, the name she gave was kind. It was a name of power. One that would get him further in this world than that of an orphan.

The wheels of the cart turned, creaking over rocks and sticks and stones. The horses' hooves clomped, and the men didn't speak. She felt Thorne's eyes on her, on both of them, as she spoke to the boy in N'skaran.

"Am I that too?" Kairick asked.

"I don't know," Quinn said. "That's for you to decide."

After a few minutes, she moved to go lay down next to the sacks and see if she could contact Draeven. A small hand stopped her. It was warm to the touch.

Quinn looked at the boy.

He pressed his full mouth together. "Please stay. He likes it."

"He?" Quinn asked softly.

"The man," Kairick said, pointing to a space on his shoulder that was covered by the cloak. "He's happy when you're around. It makes him feel safe."

Vaughn, his name ran through her mind. *He's talking about Vaughn.*

Quinn wanted to curse. She didn't like the complicated emotions that twisted in her at his words, but instead, she simply said, "Alright. I'll stay here."

He smiled and let his hand drop away from her skin.

The wagon kept rolling, and Leviticus' eye moved across the sky, but Quinn didn't leave his side that day.

Nor any of the days after it.

"What makes the gods dangerous is not their power, but that they've lived so long they no longer empathize. How can they when they live outside of time?"
— *Mariska "Risk" Darkova, beast tamer, Mazzulah's heir*

R isk climbed and climbed and climbed.

Her body wanted to give out.

She wanted to give up.

To scream and cry and roar.

But she refused to give the god of the dark realm that satisfaction. She refused to stop just because Mazzulah wanted to break her. She refused to let herself be beaten down.

She'd survived horrors that no child or woman or even beast should ever have to endure.

She knew what it was like to be used, and she would never let that happen again. Never. Not in this world or the next.

She had survived so much that should have ended her. Rape. Isolation. Imprisonment. Starvation. Sickness. Dehydration.

And despite it all, she was here climbing. Ascending, because no one was taking this away from her. She'd walked into the dark realm for her sister, for love, and for guilt. She'd come here to prove something to herself as if her life were defined by what she could do for another. And in some ways it was. Risk cared so much for those she loved. She cared, and she hurt, and at a certain point they felt the same. Risk simply felt too much.

But that strength to love despite what had been done to her. The ability to hold on to hope, to hold on to whatever it was she wanted—that choice to persevere and actually do it—that wasn't exactly why she came here, but it still showed her the truth.

Risk reached the top of the steps and this time she didn't stop to gasp for breath. She didn't double over or pant or pause.

"Has your answer changed?" Mazzulah asked. The god was in her female form, her back to Risk, facing the blood moon.

"Yes and no," Risk answered, coming to stand beside her of her own volition.

"Oh?" Mazzulah tilted her head and turned her cheek. Gold eyes settled on her face.

"When I came here, I thought I was running toward something, but instead I was running from it. The world beat me down and then demanded I apologize . . . and I did. For so long, I defined myself by how others saw me. First the N'skari, then Quinn and her house. Now you . . ." Mazzulah didn't comment, instead letting her speak. On the god's shoulder, Alpis perched, watching her with the same golden eyes. "I came here because I wanted to prove to myself that I wasn't useless. That I could save the person that meant everything to me—and she does. I love my sister more than anyone, even myself. I've proven that, but it wasn't enough."

"What isn't enough?" the god asked softly, a haunting lilt in her voice. The madness was never far, but if you danced with it, perhaps it wasn't so unwelcome either.

"Saving her. I know I'm not useless, and I *hate* myself for ever thinking I was. I hate myself because these stupid thoughts of inadequacy hold me down. I hate myself because I want more out of life than chasing Quinn's heels and running from the world. She's a beautiful, brilliant, awful person. But I'm not her—I'm me, and I want to accept that without conflict. I want to ascend, but for me—not her. I want to meet the person I've always wanted to be . . ."

Mazzulah smiled, the gesture appearing both pleased and amused, and still—more than a little cruel. "You've learned," she said. "Good. Now the real training can begin."

Risk's face blanched. "The real training?"

"Mmm," was Mazzulah's hummed reply. She waved a hand, her obsidian claws reflecting the red sheen of the moon. The platform disappeared. The howling winds becoming a beast in the distance. The sides of her torn open shirt stirred in the softer, yet colder breeze.

Instead of looming staircases or black sands, the ground beneath her was a grass so blue that it appeared black. Trees with dark wood, crimson leaves, and giant purple flowers surrounded her.

"What is this place?" Risk asked, turning in a circle to see everything, but not sure where to look.

"The dark realm," Mazzulah said, lifting her hand to one of the flowers. A golden beetle with wings dropped down. The god examined the creature, her face not quite thoughtful, but contemplative still.

"Where in the dark realm?" Risk asked.

"The forgotten forest," the god said, then she ate the beetle.

Risk winced. Gold liquid dribbled down the corner of Mazzulah's dark lips as she grinned cruelly.

"Why is it forgotten?"

"Because those that are weak and try to escape

their masters flee here, thinking they can survive. The forest is dangerous, though, even to the dead." A shiver ran through her as Mazzulah spoke. "This part of the dark realm is the source of all life and death. It's the bridge between all worlds. Monsters worse than my raksasa prowl these lands, and no one that goes in comes out. It is called the forgotten forest because that's what you'll become if you enter it."

"What are we doing here?" Risk asked slowly. Dread thickened in her gut. She had a strong suspicion where the conversation was going, not comforted by Mazzulah's taunting smile.

"All gods are born in this forest. It was here that I found my familiar. The reason I became the king of the gods. I was able to lead us out, and from there we found the worlds, one by one, and conquered them." Mazzulah lifted her hand and a bird on shadowed wings dropped from the sky. Alpis. "You'll find your familiar here too."

"But—" Risk scrambled for words. "I thought . . . I thought Alpis might be mine."

The god laughed softly. "Alpis has been my companion for as long as time has existed. I sent him to you and Quinn. To lead you here. He is not the one for you."

"How do you know that my familiar is here?" Risk asked, eyes narrowed. Her heart beat frantically at the idea of being trapped in a forest, in a land where she couldn't die.

Mazzulah shrugged. "You're my heir."

Then the god disappeared in an explosion of black feathers, and Risk was alone once more.

Her breath came fast. Her magic reached for the surface, responding to Risk's volatile emotions. Talons pricked at her palms. White air plumed in front of her face as the moon began its descent.

She looked around every which way around her, but all she saw was forest no matter which way she turned.

A frustrated growl rose within and she clamped down on it hard, remembering her lessons. They'd been brief, but lasting. When both she and the magic were riled, bad things happened. They fed on each other, making her the worst she could be.

Risk worked to slow her breathing and erratic heart.

She focused on being calm and sensing the forest around her. Slowly but surely, she connected with the creatures there. She followed their paths, further and further from where she stood, expanding her field of vision—until Risk was no longer panicked because she was in control.

Mazzulah said she had to find her familiar. The god hadn't told her how to get out, which meant it was up to her to find a way.

This was a test like any other.

One that Risk refused to fail.

She had been weak all her life. She'd let people

convince her she was weak, but Risk knew the truth. She was strong. Strong enough to take her power back.

Strong enough to survive the forest.

Strong enough to find her familiar and ascend.

CHAPTER 23

GRIM LETTERS ON SULFUR WINDS

"The problem with lies is that no matter how many we tell, the truth is like the past—and it will always catch up to us."
— Draeven Adelmar, rage thief, left-hand to the mad King of Norcasta

Something had gone wrong.

Terribly. Horribly. Wrong.

Draeven simply didn't know what. Every night he slept, trying to reach Quinn, trying to learn what had happened. And every night he failed.

The mere fact that she hadn't contacted him, and that the basilisk wouldn't deign to answer his queries, said enough.

Whatever it was, he hoped it wouldn't affect her journey to Dumas. They'd arrived several nights prior at Shallowyn Manor, at which point Lazarus disappeared to his chambers and hadn't been seen or heard from since—apart from the beasts that now openly roamed the halls.

The kuras and the wraith were his ever-present guards, and the firedrake and windwyvern both owned the skies overhead. The elemental creatures brought on the cold chill of an errant wind from a winter that wasn't yet upon them, and they killed every being that dared get close to the manor if it was not a proven friend.

From the ground, his bloodlion roamed, scavenging any beasts the great birds killed with their deadly feathers. He dragged their carcasses back to share with the other beast, and then it was upon Draeven and his men to clean it up.

His stomach turned at the thought of the last creature they'd brought home and feasted on. Two fawns. It wasn't the filling that bothered him. It was the remains.

Those beasts hunted with a brutality that non-magical creatures had no chance of surviving.

There was only one creature that he knew Lazarus owned that had yet to make an appearance.

The troll.

It didn't take much for Draeven to guess why that was. Of all his creatures, that one had killed Quinn. Draeven wondered if Lazarus kept him close as a sort of masochistic punishment for what the soul had done. He was smart enough not to ask.

Two knocks at his door made Draeven pause. His hand dropped away from the drapes he'd been holding back to watch the wyverns in the sky. To contemplate what they would kill today, and if he could pay some of the guards enough to dispose of it without him.

"Come in," Draeven called.

The doorknob turned, and the hinges squeaked as it swung open.

"Word has come from Ilvas," Dominicus said. Draeven turned to see his face, more solemn than usual. "The queen is dead."

Draeven froze.

That horrible, awful thing that he knew had happened but hadn't told anyone . . . that had to be it. That meant Quinn must have been with Imogen.

"And Axe?" Draeven prompted.

"Word has it she killed the attacker but isn't handling her mother's death well. There were some bids for her throne . . ." Dominicus said.

"And?" Draeven prompted.

"Petra Stoneskin took care of them. The funeral burning has already been held, and if the letter Lorraine received is still correct, Axe's coronation was this morning. She should be here within a week's time."

Draeven let out heavy exhale. "Any word of what caused the attack?"

"An assassin," Dominicus said. "But no one saw it other than Axe, and she won't speak on it."

Draeven nodded. "Has she kept Petra as her hand?"

"From what Petra has told us, yes."

"Good," Draeven said, feeling for the young girl losing her mother, and thankful she had enough of a head to keep the most useful asset to both of them. "Petra has a strong mind, and she's loyal. She'll teach her well."

"There's more," Dominicus said, closing the door behind him. It was telling that he hadn't done that before. "Bodies are washing up on the Ilvan shore. Reports say they wear Trienian colors. Is it her?"

"I would have to assume so," Draeven said softly. "She said she had things to take of, but in her usual flair, neglected to tell me what they were."

"That's not all that's washing up on the shores," Dominicus said. "Pieces of ships. Barrels of gunpowder. The letter said smoke has covered half of Ilvas, and the scent of sulfur drifts on the winds. If I didn't know better . . ." He let his voice trail, waiting for Draeven to finish his sentence.

"If bodies are washing up all along the shore, that's not one vessel. That would be a fleet. I have to assume that she handled N'skara the way she does anything or anyone that betrays her." Draeven lowered his eyes to the letter she'd given him through a dream. The one where she told him to prepare for war.

"I haven't been able to get scouts or spies into N'skara. They haven't been able to cross the borders, even with the alliance in place. Several days ago, one of my men got past the usual check points. I'm eager to know what he finds."

"My guess?" Draeven said, lifting Quinn's letter and putting the end of it to the flame of a candle like he should have a week ago. "Nothing. She's likely destroyed it."

"That's my suspicion as well," Dominicus said, watching the letter as it burned. Draeven waited until the flames were near his fingertips before waving it out and then stomping on the ash remains. "Have you received any word on her return?"

Outside, the winds of the wyvern quieted. Draeven only noticed because he'd gotten so used to the howls and screams that it was quiet without them. Too quiet. The kuras let loose a howl.

He sensed something approaching.

Both he and Dominicus shared a look.

"Axe won't be here for at least a week if her coronation was today," Draeven said.

Dominicus' eyes narrowed. He turned and threw the door open, taking off down the hallway, Draeven on his heels.

Is it possible there's another assassin? Draeven thought. *One meant for Lazarus . . .*

Lorraine stepped into the hallway in front of them, but she wasn't looking at Draeven or Dominicus. She was following the basilisk that slithered along the marble floors toward the entryway.

Draeven's chest tightened and eased all at once.

There were only two things that would bring the serpent out of hiding right now.

Either they were in grave danger . . . or Quinn had arrived.

CHAPTER 24
SAEVYANA

*"Love is as beautiful as it is horrible. It brings out the best and
the worst in all of us."*
— *Lazarus Fierté, soul eater, the mad King of Norcasta*

Midnight weeds. Damp petals. Fresh frost.

The scent of her magic overwhelmed him. He'd smelled traces of it before. Sensed it in the dark recesses of his mind. He ignored its call then, but this time it was too much to bear.

The windwyvern was the first to sense her outside of him. The creature taking note and ceasing the frigid gusts it rained down on Shallowyn. In its eyes, he saw a head of lavender hair riding in the back of a wagon.

Next, the firedrake took note. Once, not so long ago, she had used its quill to sign Lazarus' name into her skin. It only took one glance at his hand to know that contract was broken, but the beast still recognized her. It remembered the taste of her blood.

The bloodlion followed them from the trees. Lazarus knew it was her face from the creature's mind. She looked into the forest, seeming to see him despite the foliage. Her lips twisted in a knowing smile.

The others were taking note as Lazarus stormed from his chambers and down the hall. He wore only leather trousers and a linen shirt that hung off his frame where he'd unbuttoned it. Doors rattled as they slammed into their walls, but he paid no mind to them or the vassals around him.

That scent of dark magic was calling to him, taunting him, destroying him.

He had to have it.

He had to have her.

Lazarus threw the front door open and stood in the doorway as she made her way up the stairs. He blinked, not sure if he could believe his eyes. Knowing he shouldn't.

But her hair . . . it was the same shade of lavender before she'd left him.

Her eyes were every bit as cruel, though seemingly older, even as she appeared unaged.

Her shoulders were strong. Proud. She carried herself with confidence as she ascended the steps and stared at him without apology when she reached the top.

Lazarus took a step forward, his lips parting.

How is this possible? he thought.

The short answer was that it wasn't.

That realization hit him like a bucket of cold water dumped over his head. Lazarus paused in his advance. Quinn tilted her head, and it was *so* like her . . .

Lazarus nearly lost control there.

"I knew Nero was cruel," he said. "But I didn't realize he was capable of this."

The demon wearing her skin narrowed its crystalline eyes. A perfect match.

If it weren't so impossible, he might question if it were really her.

But it wasn't. It couldn't be.

"That's because he's not," she said, her voice the same biting tone it had been in life. "I'm here by my own will, and that of a god."

A god, he thought. Hadn't Nero's messenger called him a god among men?

Lazarus laughed, but it wasn't kind. Nor happy. Nor sane.

"You're such a good imitation, I'm almost tempted to keep you," he said softly.

The bloodlion trailed up the steps behind her, past the people she had come with. The wyverns landed on either side of her. They all seemed curious, if not reserved. They couldn't see past the mask he did. They thought with an animal's intelligence, and to them, this was their mate.

She smelled the same. She looked the same. She stared at them unafraid.

But he knew better. No one comes back from death, not even Quinn.

He strode toward her, thrusting his hand out.

His fingers closed around her throat. The maruda before him didn't move. She simply stood there and cocked an eyebrow in challenge.

Cold burned his skin. She was colder than she'd ever been, and he liked the pain as he started to squeeze.

"You're not her," Lazarus said, trying to convince himself.

"Can you really not see past your own madness anymore?" the woman asked. "Are you really that weak?"

Shock went through him. Lazarus paused. His thumb caressed the dip in her throat.

Could it be . . .

Lazarus leaned in and inhaled her scent. He couldn't stop himself from running his lips up her jaw and pausing at her temple.

Gods, she smelled right.

"You may have them fooled," he whispered. "But not me."

He closed his hand, but instead of crushing her throat as he intended, only black magic remained. A crushing fear swept over him, sending him to his knees. Black tendrils, tiny and thin, moved through the air like an inky fog that he could touch, but not hurt.

The fog dissipated, and a hand fisted in his hair, pulling it taut.

He felt her front press against his back, her head inclined forward over his shoulder.

"Animals are wiser than men. Beasts know when they face a greater monster than themselves, and they don't allow their hubris to get in the way. It's why the horses have always feared me."

Another trickle of doubt touched him . . .

Nero was good, but not that good.

"Don't be a fool. As hard as it is to believe, I'm back. Ask Lord Sunshine, he's at the door. Lorraine has been caring for Neiss. Even Dominicus saw the letter I sent through Draeven's dreams. The souls cannot go mad as you have. They're already dead. Trust them."

He yanked against her grip, and she let him go.

Lazarus got to his feet and turned. Behind her, Draeven, Lorraine, and Dominicus stood in the doorway. Only Draeven's face was lined with guilt, and he knew then . . . she wasn't lying.

Lazarus looked from them back to her, taking her in again. He didn't know what to feel. Betrayal for not coming to him? Relief so great that he felt like he could breathe again? Anger for letting it happen in the first place?

Or possessiveness because she now stood naked in front of all of them.

Rage clouded his gaze because the latter two were winning.

Footsteps came running from behind him. He turned to look, noticing how Quinn's face had gone blank of all expression as he did.

A little boy with silver hair and ice-blue eyes ran up the stairs.

Lazarus frowned, not registering the N'skari words the child was saying.

Though he did take note to Quinn's stern reply.

"Whose is he?" Lazarus asked, wheeling around. His dark eyes were wild. Feral with accusation.

"You're going to need to be more specific," Quinn said, switching back to Norcastan. The boy went around the animals and came to stand beside her, unperturbed by her nakedness.

"You died, and somehow—someway—you found your way back with an N'skari child. Who. Is. The. Boy's. Mother?"

Quinn blinked, understanding dawning on her.

"I don't know." She shrugged dismissively. "He was an orphan I picked up on my way."

Lazarus narrowed his gaze between the boy who grabbed her hand and Quinn herself. Behind them, a mauve-colored serpent slithered up and sunk under Quinn's bare calf. Its body twining around her leg, beneath the skin.

If Lazarus weren't convinced yet, he would have been then.

It was true. As impossible as it was, she came back.

Lazarus couldn't process what he thought about it, let alone how he felt. All he knew was one thing: *saevyana* had returned to him.

And he wanted her alone.

Lazarus strode forward, standing toe-to-toe with her.

He lifted his fingers to her cheek. Ice ran through him. She shivered beneath his touch. He curled one calloused finger under her chin to lift it and said, "Come with me. Now."

Lazarus stepped around her, grabbing her wrist as he did so, unwilling to release her for even a moment.

He strode toward the front door and his vassals stepped aside, heads bowed with what he hoped was shame. There would be consequences for their actions. Later.

"Leave the boy with them," he snapped.

Quinn murmured something in N'skaran, and the sound of her voice set his blood aflame. Anger coursed through him. Jealousy that she was even bothering with the child when he was before her.

The soft voice of the boy's answer made Lazarus growl and tug harder.

"Lorraine, take him and don't let anyone else near him."

Were Lazarus not coming to grips with the fact that *his cruel woman*, his fear twister, his right-hand had returned—he might have thought about that. Considered why Quinn had phrased it that way.

As it was, Lazarus did not care.

He dragged her down the hall and toward his wing of the manor. Beside him, her breathing was soft. Faint, even. Her steps were silent as always. Her eyes narrowed.

They entered his chambers, and the door slammed behind them.

Lazarus stopped, pivoting on his heel to face her.

He wanted to yell at her, to be angry, to say the things he should have said, to fall to his knees again—this time to worship her. But he didn't do any of that.

Lazarus lifted a hand to her hair, burying his fingers in the silky strands. He pulled her in, and their bodies collided. Their mouths fought for dominance, but Lazarus was winning that fight.

Some people kissed like they were dying, but that was nothing like kissing the woman that gave you life again. Lazarus released his hold on her wrist to run it down her back. It slid over her backside. He cupped her there and grabbed a handful, his nails biting into her supple skin as he lifted her.

Quinn fisted both her hands in his hair. Her lips waging war on him as she ground her body against his.

Lazarus walked them toward the bedroom. Her back hit the closed door roughly, and Quinn gasped. He pulled back just far enough to run his lips down the column of her throat. The hand in her hair tightened as he angled it to the side and inhaled deeply.

"Are you going to sniff me or are you going to fuck me?" Quinn demanded.

He nipped at the place where her neck and shoulder met, and she moaned.

"You died," Lazarus rasped against her skin, sucking on the flesh of her collar bone.

"I came back," she breathed. He growled again.

"You'll be lucky if I let you out of my sight ever again," he said huskily, pulling away to open the door.

Lazarus didn't close it as he strode toward the bed.

It was wrinkled because he'd barely slept since they arrived, but intact.

Lazarus removed his hand from her hair and all but threw her down before him.

Quinn sat up and reached for the laces and on his trousers, muttering, "You have no way to contain me even if you wanted."

Impatient as she'd always been, she pulled once

and the laces snapped, then unraveled. His length came free, thick and heavy.

Quinn repositioned herself, kneeling on all fours, and grasping his bare shaft in a tight grip. Lazarus could do little more than grab the wooden bed posts on either side of him as she took his head in her mouth. Saliva coated him, and that coldness he felt gave way to the warm heat of her mouth as she wrapped him tight.

Lazarus groaned, thrusting forward.

Ice-blue eyes peered up at him as he hit the back of her throat. She gagged, using the wetness of it to cover him more and pumping him with her fist.

He grabbed her by the hair and pulled her off of him, his shaft pounding with need between them.

He had to have her. Whatever else he might need to say, it could wait. His need for this terrible woman could not. Quinn continued to work him with her closed fist and Lazarus said, "Remove your hand from me."

"Make me," she challenged.

Lazarus reached down and grabbed both her wrists. He lifted them up over her head as he crawled onto the bed after her. His legs straddled her hips as he pushed her back. Her back touched the mattress, and Lazarus lowered his face to the vee between her breasts.

Quin arched upward. He changed his hold to lock her wrists in one fist and lowered the other hand between them to grasp her breast and push it up. Lazarus took her nipple between his teeth and bit softly before sucking.

Quinn bucked beneath him. Her sounds of pleasure guiding him to a new kind of madness.

Lazarus released her nipple and repeated the action with the other. He alternated both breasts, trying to push her into oblivion.

"I'm not going to fuck you," Lazarus said after releasing her breast with a pop. The pale pink skin now bloomed a deep shade of red for him.

"Oh?"

"I'm not going to make love to you," he continued, ignoring her.

Lazarus reached between them and ran two fingers through her wetness.

"I'm going to *own you*," Lazarus said in a husky rasp. Preparing to do just that.

Before he could thrust inside her, she disappeared beneath him in a puff of black smoke. This new trick of hers was something he wasn't sure if he was fond of as he inhaled her essence of fear, hardening even further.

"Nothing owns me, Lazarus. Not you. Not the gods. Nothing. I came back because I chose to. I *chose* you." Lazarus turned over on the bed and regarded the lavender-haired vixen that stood naked, hands on her pale hips.

This was really her.

His Quinn.

"I don't have to mark you to own you," he said, pushing forward off the bed and onto his bare feet. Lazarus towered over her though she was a tall woman.

"I don't have to bind you in contracts," he continued, running a single finger over her bare shoulder. Lazarus reached for her, and she didn't evaporate this time. Instead, she let him grasp her hips and lift her. She wrapped her legs around his waist and grasped his length between them, lining it up with her opening.

"I don't need the words, Quinn. You came back of your own will."

Lazarus thrust once, seating himself in her to the hilt. Quinn's body shuddered against him. She pushed her heels into him as she threw her head back in ecstasy.

Quinn's hips moved, trying to gain her friction. Lazarus held her there, reveling in the feel of her sheathing him once more. He never thought he'd have this again. Have her again.

"Just fuck me," Quinn panted. "You can worship the ground I walk on later."

Lazarus stepped back until his legs hit the bed. He sat on the edge, letting Quinn's legs straddle him on either side.

He released one hip and trailed his hand over the slight curve of her stomach. He cupped her breast, tweaking her nipple. A groan escaped her as she placed both hands on his shoulders, ripping his thin linen shirt in half.

Her breasts bobbed as she slid herself up and down his shaft. Her tight channel clenching him. Lazarus couldn't help moving that hand from her breasts to her throat. He held her there, lightly at first, and when her wetness coated his length, he slowly tightened his grip.

Lazarus looked deep into Quinn's eyes, and he found that darkness there.

She loved what he was doing to her. She loved the way he made her feel. And while she may never say it —she loved him. And he knew it.

He owned her heart, and it was black and shriveled as his own, but he cherished it more than anything in all the seven kingdoms.

"Say my name," she gasped with a possessive gleam in her eye. Her nails dug into the flesh of his shoulders. He felt her thighs quake. Her body shook with unchecked desire.

"Quinn," he growled, squeezing tight.

"Ah," she moaned. Her whole body seized up, and Lazarus flipped them. He kept his hold on her throat, using his other arm to hold the majority of his weight while he pounded into her. Her opening fluttered around him before seizing tight.

"Saevyana," he groaned, finding his own release.

Pleasure shot down his spine as his shaft hardened

further inside of her. Lazarus thrust shallowly, emptying himself into her warmth. When the final urge to claim her faded, at least for the moment, Lazarus didn't move. He lowered his head into the crook of her neck and sighed.

"Why was I the last to know you'd returned?"

*"Destiny is just a more ignorant term for being manipulated by
the gods."*
— *Quinn Darkova, fear twister, walker of realms*

Quinn didn't react. She'd known it was coming, whether before or after they'd lost themselves in each other was the only question.

She felt liquid gush down her thighs as Lazarus leaned up, bracing himself with both his forearms. He'd yet to move, and the proximity was both intoxicating and too much.

Quinn's memory hadn't done right by him. The fire she felt, the rush, the desire . . . it was more than she recalled. Those thoughts of warmth only a distant illusion from the real thing.

Her chest had eased from the first look, because throughout it all—the shock, the anger, the betrayal—nothing had changed between them. If anything, it was better than she ever remembered. But here, with him lying on top of her, asking her the harder questions—it was almost too much.

His dark eyes took her in. The scar over the left starker than ever before.

Quinn released a loose breath and stretched her arms high above her head. Her spine curved as she arched upward, stretching her pleasantly sore muscles.

He glanced down, his gaze dropping from her face to the tips of her breasts as her nipples brushed against his chest and hardened. Lazarus pressed his lips together, as if to keep himself from licking them, as she was certain he wanted to.

"I asked you a question, Quinn."

"I was deciding how to answer, *Your Highness*," she replied in an equally terse tone of voice.

"Let's start with the truth," he prompted.

Quinn disintegrated as she stepped out of the living realm and into death's. Her body reformed as flesh, several feet away. She strolled over toward the wingback chairs, taking note of the furnishings.

"No spirits?" she asked, noting the distinct lack of a crystalline decanter.

"You're avoiding," Lazarus said in a hard breath.

"I'm curious," she shot back. "Since when did you stop drinking?"

He rolled over, then sat up, and she felt his eyes on her back as she looked at the roaring fire instead.

"Since you died," he said, as if it were so simple. "I have enough demons of my own plaguing me, and I couldn't face any more."

Quinn wasn't sure how to respond to that. So she didn't.

"You were the last to know because you care the most," Quinn said softly. "If you knew I was alive, you would have followed me to the ends of this world. I couldn't have that. You couldn't have that. I needed you here, making war."

The bed creaked under his weight as he shifted.

"If I knew you were alive—" He started then stopped. She was right, they both knew it. "Why does it matter if I chase you or our enemies?"

It was a better question. A smarter one. One that Quinn had to handle . . . carefully.

"One doesn't simply walk out of the dark realm, not without Mazzulah's permission. I am no different in that," Quinn said.

"What did you promise the dark god?" Lazarus asked. His madness must be clearing if he was falling back into their old rhythm.

It pleased Quinn because he was going to need that edge about him. He couldn't fall into grief and lose himself. There was too much to be done.

"*I* only made one promise. Risk made the other. She is half-raksasa. It allowed her to enter the door and ascend the steps. She wanted to bring me back. Mazzulah said that if she stayed there until her ascension that I could return . . ."

"And?" Lazarus prompted. The mattress creaked once more. His footsteps padded across the stone floors.

Quinn stared at the red flickering flames as he sat in the wingback chair beside her. He leaned back, placing his arms on the wooden rests, and steepled his fingers together.

"We are to go to war and win," she said. "The gods have been playing games since the beginning of time, and their favorite is when they play with us. They choose heirs and guide them through this world. Invisible hands that we call destiny moving things aside or putting them in the way."

"To what end?"

"Why do we play games?" she asked.

Lazarus inclined his head. "They toy with us for amusement."

"Partially," she said, her voice turning distant. "The gods are in a never-ending power struggle, and the games they play using us decide the winner. We go to war because that's how Mazzulah wins—and us by extension."

"And if we don't?"

Quinn looked away. This one small aspect was

what made her . . . uncomfortable. And she was loathed to admit it.

"If we lose, Mazzulah takes me back and kills you all."

She didn't want to look at him, but she sensed his mood darkening.

"Why not kill you as well?"

"Well, I'm not exactly alive as it is," Quinn mused, trying to steer the conversation into clearer waters. Ones she felt sure she could navigate. "I walked out, or more accurately, was carried out. I now exist in all realms at once. If I die again, that's it."

"From what the legends say, soul eaters are the same," Lazarus said, his voice deceptively quiet. Controlled.

"They're true," she mused. "You and I are the same in that now."

"Then why are we killed, and you returned?"

"Because that's Mazzulah's price," she said, avoiding the answer still. The truth that the dark god had taken a liking toward her. More than a liking. They were obsessed with her. A fascination, similar to his own.

And while Quinn never acted on it . . . she didn't exactly shy away either.

Her body was her own. Her mind her own. She was dead, and at the time had no way of knowing that there was even a chance of coming back.

Quinn hadn't made promises. She didn't owe Lazarus anything.

Yet, she couldn't help the unease.

She loved to toy with him in front of others. Leave them with lingering touches. But Mazzulah was a god, one who had been playing games far longer than them.

"Why does the god of the dark realm want you?" he asked, seeming to piece together what she tried not to say.

"Everyone wants what they can't have," she said flippantly.

Hands nearly hot as the fire grabbed her hips and pulled her onto his lap. Her back pressed against his chest. His shaft throbbed against her backside.

"Not everyone," he said quietly, his lips skimming the hollow of her ear.

Quinn parted her legs so that his were in between hers. Her breath quickened. This feeling . . . this heat that blazed through her . . . she never wanted it to stop.

This was what it meant to be alive, and in his arms she no longer felt so cold the dark realm would rip her away.

"Did Mazzulah touch you this way?" he asked, sliding a rough palm over her stomach and through the patch of curls at the apex of her thighs. His fingers slid between her folds, toying with her.

"No," she breathed.

"Mmm," he hummed, slipping two fingers in her. His palm pressed into her clit, and she threw her head back against his shoulder and groaned. Her legs opened wider on their own accord. "And this way?"

"Never," she panted.

Lazarus used her free hand to grasp her chin and turn her face. His lips brushed over hers, and Quinn shuddered, rocking into him.

"What about these?" He ran his thumb over her lips. Quinn's half-hooded eyes opened, and her silence spoke the truth.

Lazarus' face hardened.

But he didn't reprimand her. He didn't scold her. He didn't make outlandish claims. While he always sought to control her, he didn't cross that line as much as she wondered he might.

Lazarus removed the hand from between her thighs, and Quinn growled. Lazarus snarled right back as he dropped both hands to her hips once more.

"Hands on my knees," he commanded.

Curious about where this was going, Quinn obeyed.

He lifted her several inches, and it was only her hands gripped tightly on her knees that kept Quinn from careening forward. His tip brushed against her entrance.

Then her body came down.

Quinn gasped as Lazarus filled her in one go.

"I don't care what you did with Mazzulah. You're

here now. You're *mine,*" he snapped, lifting her once more to slide up and down his shaft.

"I'm no one's," Quinn replied harshly as they settled into a rhythm. "And that's a lie if there ever was one."

Their skin slapped together as Lazarus sped up, pounding into her with a brutality meant to punish.

"You're right," he said through gritted teeth. "I do care. I'm seething inside that you let someone else touch you. I'm furious that you contacted Draeven before me. I'm *burning* with the need to tie you to my bed and win this war myself—so that I don't lose you." His voice turned hoarse as emotion clogged it, but not something sweet or kind. This was a dark possession that sought to own.

"I'm already dead," Quinn reminded him, breathing heavier.

"I know. Not only do I get a second chance—you won't age or die either. I wanted five years, then I lost you and now forever is in my grasp."

"Lazarus," she moaned, both a reprimand and a plea.

One of his hands slid around to her front. Two blunt fingers whorled around her clit, sending Quinn into a frenzied state. Her toes touched the ground and her muscles strained as she worked herself up and down his shaft.

Pain ripped through her shoulder as Lazarus bit down there. She knew without looking that he'd drawn blood. Lazarus groaned beneath her, and Quinn let out a garbled cry as her channel trembled. Lights exploded behind her eyes as everything went black. Quinn's body twitched and shuddered under Lazarus' control, and those two fingers continued to stroke her even after it turned from pleasurable to painfully too much.

Lazarus wrapped an arm around her waist, lifting her entirely as he stood. A few long strides and the soft mattresses pillowed her front as he positioned her on the edge of the bed.

"I should have let you go when I found you, but we're both so far gone beyond that now. I don't love you, Quinn. Love is too weak of an emotion for this clawing *need* in my chest."

He shoved back inside her, and Quinn moaned into the feather bedding.

All her life she'd fought feeling too deeply. Too strongly. Feelings were for weaker men who couldn't survive without. Somewhere along the way Quinn lost that. Perhaps it burned up with the heat inside her when he was near, but she couldn't keep her distance. While she would never allow someone to own her, neither a god nor a man, Quinn couldn't stop herself from craving this—whatever it was.

Call it love. Call it hate. Obsession. Compulsion. Infatuation.

She didn't care.

No one in her life nor her death made her feel as

Lazarus did. No one understood her so acutely. No one else wanted her with such a fervor, not even Mazzulah.

Quinn had told him once that she was his in all the ways that mattered, and despite her years in the dark realm—nothing had changed.

She and Lazarus were more than fate or destiny.

They were inevitable.

CHAPTER 26
MYSTERIOUS ORIGINS

"If one doesn't understand, then they're asking the wrong
questions. Knowledge is the bane of ignorance."
— Draeven Adelmar, rage thief, left-hand to the hopefully less
mad King of Norcasta, slightly less guilty liar

"You sense it too?" Dominicus said, coming to stand beside him. Draeven crossed his arms and leaned against the doorway.

"Quinn doesn't just bring orphans home," Draeven said by way of answer. He watched Lorraine in the kitchen with the boy. While none of them could understand them, the boy seemed to know at least a couple Norcastan words. The first one after Quinn leaving being "hungry". Lorraine had acquiesced and had taken him to the kitchens.

"You think she's lying?" Dominicus asked. Distrusting of the child simply because who he came with.

"About not being the mother?"

Dominicus nodded.

"No," Draeven shook his head. "She's only been gone two and a half months."

Lorraine diced up a dappa fruit and placed the chunks on a wooden plate along with a slice of cheese and a piece of fresh bread. His bright blue gaze went wide as she set the plate down in front of him.

He started to devour it. The ferocity reminding Draeven of how Quinn was with food when she first joined them.

"We don't know anything about the dark realm or what happened there," Dominicus said, clearly not convinced as he, too, watched the child inhale his food.

"The child is N'skari, not raksasa," Lorraine's voice cut in.

"And you think there aren't plenty of N'skari in the dark realm? After what we saw?" Dominicus said. Lorraine narrowed her eyes in his direction as she leaned against the clay tiled counter. The boy didn't pay them or their conversation any mind.

"You think Quinn would sleep with them?" Lorraine replied. Draeven had to give her that. If there were any people she truly hated, it was her own.

"And beyond that, do you really believe her the type to have a child?"

Dominicus lifted his hands in surrender, not wanting to anger the woman. "All I'm saying is it's unlikely that they have the moon tonic in the dark realm, and Quinn isn't exactly the most modest female. If she thought she was never coming back . . ." The other man trailed off, causing Lorraine to scowl.

"She might be rash, but she'd never be that reckless. She wouldn't risk it," Lorraine said. "Beyond that, she was dead. I doubt the dead can have children." Her lips twisted in a way that if she were the woman they spoke of, she likely would have called him a fool. As it was, she settled for being correct and Dominicus muttering under his breath about things they don't understand.

"I don't think the child is Quinn's," Draeven said eventually, and Dominicus glared at him. "Lorraine is right that while Quinn is rash, she wouldn't put herself in a position to have one. She has no desire to be a mother. Thankfully."

Lorraine gave him a sharp look for his last comment, but Draeven shrugged. "You can care for her all you want, but even you must see she'd be a horrible mother, Lorraine."

The older woman didn't respond, and that was telling enough.

"If not her child, then what other reason does she

have for bringing him here?" Dominicus asked, stepping into the kitchen. He wandered close to the boy before Lorraine stepped in his path.

"I'm not going to hurt him—" he started.

"She asked that no one touch him except me," Lorraine said.

"Which is curious by itself," Draeven said softly. He stepped into the kitchen as well and let the door swing shut behind him. "Why would she ask that? If she knows we're not a danger to him . . ."

An idea occurred to him, and he didn't like it. Not one bit.

There was only one reason she'd give that command in the few seconds she had before Lazarus dragged her away. Either she worried for the boy's safety . . . or she worried for theirs.

"He's a Maji," Draeven said.

"How do you know?" Dominicus said, turning away from Lorraine to look at him.

"I don't." Draeven shrugged. "But I think he is. Quinn knows Lorraine is a null. That's the only reason I can see her saying for only Lorraine to touch him."

All three of them looked over. Red dappa juice ran from the corner of his mouth as he stuffed slices in faster than he could chew. The silver head of hair hung over his eyes as he kept his head downcast.

"It's possible," Lorraine said eventually. "But she has no need for a Maji child." She turned her back on them to wipe his face with a damp cloth. It came away smeared crimson and brown. "A dirty one at that."

"Maybe it's what he can do," Dominicus pointed out. Lorraine tilted her head to the side, looking back over her shoulder.

"He's a boy. Even Quinn wouldn't send a child into war," she scoffed. Draeven had a feeling Dominicus would be sleeping alone once more if he kept it up, even if he weren't wrong. "And neither would Thorne for that matter," she added.

The Cisean leader had been shown to his quarters along with his guards and they hadn't seen them since.

"It's not like Thorne would get a say. She came back from the dead; what would he do to stop her?" Dominicus said. Lorraine reeled around and dropped the dirty rag on the counter. Her brown and gray hair was pulled back in a tight braid, but thin strands had slipped free and were forming little curls around her face. Her eyes were severe as she stared at her partner and lifted an eyebrow.

"You didn't care for her in life. I thought perhaps you might learn when to let it be in her death. Apparently not."

The other man stepped back as if he'd been slapped. Draeven looked away, suddenly feeling the urge to go check on Thorne, or his guards, or really anything.

"Raine," Dominicus started.

"Don't 'Raine' me, Dominicus Alexander Stone," she snapped. Lorraine untied the apron at her waist and tossed it on the counter as well before holding her hand out to the boy. He took it without question, and they strode through the kitchen and out the door. It swung shut behind them with a clap of wood on wood.

"That went poorly," Draeven said.

"You think?" Dominicus sneered, before shaking his head and walking out. Draeven hoped he had enough sense to not go after her right now. It wouldn't do any good. Like it or not, Lorraine cared for Quinn as if she were her own child, and she protected her just as fiercely.

Even from assumptions and accusations that Quinn herself would likely not care about.

Draeven sighed and exited the kitchen. He knew that someone should greet Thorne, and that Lazarus was being exceptionally rude in not doing so. However, it wasn't every day that a love lost comes back from the dead.

If only she hadn't come back alone . . .

Not for the first time, Draeven found himself wondering about Risk. Where she went. Why she wasn't there. He had to think she had something to do with the fear twister's return, but it didn't answer where she was or why she hadn't returned.

He planned to ask Quinn that. Whenever she and

Lazarus surfaced. Although, that might be awhile if the sudden way the creatures retreated to his quarters were anything to go by. They'd followed them from the entryway and stood guard outside the king's wing, even more protective than they'd been before.

Draeven steered away from both Lazarus' wing and the one Thorne was being kept in. He was questioning whether he'd still be the left-hand now that Lazarus knew of his betrayal. He wasn't sure if Quinn's return would soften him there or not, and it pained Draeven that the reality of it would likely come down to that. He wasn't going to risk the king's anger further by speaking to Thorne without him.

Footsteps clambered down the hall. Draeven turned as one of his guards came around the corner.

"My Lord, Lady Lorraine sent for you."

He started in the direction of her rooms without needing further information. His boots were heavy against the wooden floors. Draeven sighed, hoping desperately that Lorraine wouldn't attempt to drag him into her and Dominicus' quarrel, or even worse, that he would be berated for his own line of questioning. While pissing off Quinn came with the concern of waking up to snakes in one's bed or being haunted in his dreams, pissing off Lorraine would land him burnt dinner and no one to clean his tunics for weeks.

He wasn't sure which was worse as he approached her door.

The handle jiggled as he went to turn it. The door

creaked as it swung open, and Draeven stepped inside.

But what he saw was possibly the last thing he ever expected.

In the center of Lorraine's quarters, a large metal tub was filled with water. The boy sat in the middle. His silver hair dripping wet. Shadows moved beneath his skin, and Draeven knew what they were with a single look, but it wasn't the shadows that made him pause.

Vaughn sat in front of the tub, playing a game with the boy.

They clapped hands and bumped fists while the child hummed a song under his breath they couldn't understand.

"I think I know why Quinn brought him home," Lorraine said softly, several feet away from them. Her eyes were sad because she'd realized what Draeven was only now coming to.

This child was a soul eater.

And he'd devoured Vaughn.

CHAPTER 27
WAR COUNCIL

"To win the game, you must be more than a piece on the board.
Even a queen, while powerful, is still a pawn when controlled
by another."
— *Quinn Darkova, fear twister, walker of realms*

Quinn trailed through Lazarus' chambers as sunlight peaked through the windows.

Lazarus had been insistent last night. He'd fall asleep and wake when she tried to get out of bed, only to take her again. In between their couplings, he questioned her about the dark realm, the time she spent there, and the deal she made. Yet, he took care to not make demands.

Quinn thought that perhaps, in her death, he'd finally learned that she would be free at all costs, and that trying to bind her wouldn't end well. He was smart enough to not demand another contract. Quinn wouldn't sign it.

She wasn't a pawn to be used. She moved her own piece on the board and decided for herself who she would fight for. While it would be him until they both ceased to exist—she wouldn't be forced into it.

A soft knock made her pause.

Quinn took a robe that was hanging off the chair to her right and slipped her arms through it. She tied it loosely at the waist before padding across the cool floors.

She cracked the door open and peered out. A messy head of silver hair greeted her at waist height. Quinn sighed and stepped into the hall, closing it firmly behind her. The bloodlion and the kuras watched them through slitted eyes. Quinn took it as a good sign that neither had attacked the boy, but instead seemed interested in him.

"Why aren't you with Lorraine?" she asked, ignoring the souls.

Kairick tilted his head back and swallowed hard. "She's nervous around me."

"Did you show her the souls?" Quinn asked him pointedly.

"The man wanted to come out, and I was bored." The lack of apology in his voice intrigued her. While Quinn wasn't maternal by any means, it was curious to see how a dark Maji child acted. While all children weren't the most empathetic, he was both more and less. He could feel and speak to beasts, but he didn't empathize with them necessarily. He used them as a crutch for his own sadness.

"You shouldn't have done that," Quinn sighed again. Sometimes she missed being able to sleep. While her dreams were usually nightmares, it was often its own kind of reprieve. At least the way she remembered sleep. It had been several years, and the closest she could come to it now was the meditative dreamwalking state she used to contact Draeven.

However, that wasn't a reprieve.

Quinn wished she could now, watching Kairick frown as he tried to understand why what he did was problematic. She'd learned he was seven on their journey to Shallowyn. He was small for his age. Likely the lack of nourishment. No child that young could truly understand the complexities of what it meant to be a dark Maji, or why it made others nervous.

"I'm sorry, Quinn," he apologized.

Quinn blinked, not sure what to do with that.

"Try not to do it again without me around," she said, glancing down the hall as a flustered Lorraine started toward them. Quinn's lips twitched in amusement.

"I'm sorry about—" Lorraine started.

"It's fine," Quinn said, as the older woman stopped before her. Lorraine's expression softened as she looked at Quinn before wrapping her arms around her shoulders.

Quinn embraced her back, surprised at the warmth that spread through her chest.

"I missed you," Lorraine said softly.

"I missed you too," Quinn said, releasing her after a moment. Lorraine stepped back and brushed her hands down the front of her night dress, her fingers fidgeting nervously. A habit she had when she was overwhelmed by emotion. Quinn didn't comment on it.

"He must have snuck out while I was sleeping," Lorraine said.

"I gathered as much. He has a tendency to pop up places when you don't expect . . ." Quinn let her voice trail off as she thought of that night where he'd appeared and then consumed Vaughn. He shouldn't have been there. If he hadn't, she wasn't sure if Vaughn would be dead or alive, but either was better than being trapped.

"He's a soul eater," Lorraine said, not like a question. "Why did you bring him here?"

Lorraine had judged her when they first met, but over time that judgement faded into acceptance. This wasn't any different. She spoke with some trepidation, but Quinn could tell she hadn't jumped to conclusions.

The door behind her swung open. The hinge screeched in the near-empty hallway.

She didn't have to look to see that Lazarus stood at her back. She could feel that dark gaze on her, making her skin tingle. Palpable tension thickened.

"That's a question I'd like to know the answer to as well."

Quinn rolled her eyes and a hiss of anger came from behind her. She leaned over, putting her face-to-face with Kairick.

"Tell the man to come out," she said. He looked at her with round eyes, but obeyed, nonetheless. His hand didn't even twitch before Vaughn came forward and reformed in front of them. His eyes were still black; whatever had been done by the blood magic still afflicting him.

She stood and turned around, arms crossed over her chest and eyebrows lifted.

Lazarus' face didn't reveal a single emotion as he said, "Why are his eyes black?"

"Blood magic," Quinn replied, watching carefully as a tremor went through him. Not a physical one, but one of fear. "Or so Thorne believes."

"Thorne knows of this?" Lorraine asked, horror bleeding into her tone.

"He was there when it happened. We both were. Kairick consumed Vaughn thinking he was protecting me, and now him and that creature are bound inside him."

Lazarus appeared troubled, which made Quinn

all the more curious when he said, "Tell me everything."

DRAEVEN PACED BACK AND FORTH, THREATENING TO wear a path into the stone floor. Lorraine was deeply troubled. Dominicus was traditionally stoic and reserved. Thorne appeared mostly tired at this point. His own reservations and concern depleted by how long he had to think on the road down.

It was only Lazarus that seemed to be a cumulation of things.

Quinn leaned back in her chair, lifting her boots to the edge of the round table before her as she did so.

"I know you're all-powerful, but really, Quinn, must you do that?" Lorraine said. Quinn pressed her lips together, more amused than annoyed that even with everything going on, Lorraine still had time to criticize her manners.

"I'll wipe off the table myself," she said.

Lorraine didn't look pleased, but let it go.

"I thought soul eaters were rare?" Draven said. "Legendary even?"

"They are," Quinn said, crossing her arms over her chest. "Because dark magic is too much for most to hold. The instability that comes with it tends to corrupt. Most dark Maji children are killed or kill themselves. That's what makes them rare."

"He doesn't seem particularly unstable," Dominicus said. "But he still consumed Vaughn."

"Kairick is a product of his environment," Quinn said. "He was raised as an orphan, and it's likely that whoever did so didn't realize what he was, or he would have been drowned in the ocean by the N'skari Council. He turns to the souls for companionship because he's lonely."

"You sound like you care about him," Draeven remarked. Quinn shrugged.

"I understand him. He and I were bred in the same pit. While I was highborn and beaten for my differences, I can't imagine his life was easier. Siva believes he clings to me because I saved him. I don't know if that's true, but he consumed Vaughn and the creature that was in him because of me."

"My wife is a smart woman," Thorne said. "Insightful. We'd do well to listen to her."

"The child presents a risk," Dominicus argued. "Arguably one too great for us to let him stay here."

"There's a reason I said for none of you to touch him," Quinn said. Her sharp blue gaze riveted on the weapons master.

"He could consume any of us if he perceives us as a threat to you, and if he can't control it, he could even consume *you*," Dominicus said, unwilling to yield. She respected it in a sense. "Lazarus, you must see that this is a problem—"

"He holds Vaughn's soul," Quinn snapped, losing some of her already waning patience. "Regardless of the risk, we need to find a way to remove it and the blood magic creature attached to it."

"That's easier for you to say, but the gods don't favor all of us," Dominicus replied. His eyes flashing.

"Enough," Lazarus commanded. He didn't slam his hands on the table or even move to lift his gaze from the wooden pieces spread out over a map of the Sirian continent. "There's no way to remove Vaughn, not until the boy comes of age and enters the ascension. It might be possible in the Cisean springs with the right stone, like Quinn and the basilisk, but the odds of killing all of them increase tenfold. I will not enter the waters for a child, and neither will Quinn."

"You do not command me—" Quinn started.

"You exist as a soul that transitions between worlds. You don't even have a body to anchor you. If you entered the pool, you'd be consumed as you are and then both you and Vaughn would die. On the off chance you both survived, you'd be trapped."

"He's right," Thorne said, sighing deeply.

Lazarus didn't say more, but he didn't need to. Quinn pressed her lips together and looked away. Not even for her friend would she risk being enslaved. They all had lines they wouldn't cross, not even for each other, and that was Quinn's.

"Is there a way to remove the malevolent force within him?" Lorraine asked in earnest.

"Possibly," Lazarus said. "But it would be dangerous, and if the boy miscalculates, he'd damage them both. Vaughn would be in incredible pain."

"He might already be in pain," Quinn retorted.

"Not like this," Lazarus said, the tone in his voice warning her to listen. "He's bound to the child like Neiss is to you, but what do you think it would feel like if you were ripped in half but couldn't die?"

Quinn opened and then closed her mouth. "Mazzulah let some of the raksasa torture some particularly terrible souls that way as entertainment. In the dark realm they can't die from it, but they also can't heal." She trailed her fingers over her leather pants, scraping her nail over the tiny specs of dirt that stuck to them. "It was brutal, but effective."

Draeven cursed under his breath and turned away. Dominicus' eyes hardened, and Thorne let out a deep chuckle.

"It's no wonder that the dark god took a liking to you," he said, red eyes amused despite the heaviness that was dragging him down. Lazarus' jaw clenched.

"So, there's no way to free him? He's stuck?" Lorraine asked.

The king shook his head. "Once a soul is consumed, there's no giving it back. It entwines with our own and takes a piece of us for itself. That's why soul eaters have to take care with how powerful the beasts are that we consume."

Silence filled the room as the stark truth settled in.

There was no way to save him. He would die and be sent to the dark realm. Quinn didn't grit her teeth or show her anger, but instead let the unnatural cold settle around her.

She lifted her head, and when she spoke, her voice was cutting and without emotion. "Then we need to question the creature in him. Learn how it came to be and how to prevent it from happening again. The boy will be raised here and taught how to control himself. Vaughn's a slave either way, but we can shape his master."

"You can't be serious," Dominicus said.

"Completely," Quinn replied, letting her boots drop to the ground once more. She leaned forward, elbows braced on the table.

"While you might not fear what it or he can do, some of us remember what happens when Maji are allowed to roam these halls unchecked—"

Faster than he could react, Quinn stood, slamming her hands down. She jumped up and kicked her legs through the opening between her arms and the table. Her body slid eight feet across the smooth surface, knocking the wooden figurines away as she slowed to a stop right in front of Dominicus.

Quinn reached out and grabbed him by the throat, lifting him from the chair with little effort.

"Of course I don't fear him. I fear nothing. I am fear itself. Neiss' chosen heir for the war to come. Something you'd do well to remember before reminding me of my untimely death like I'm a common skeev." Quinn leaned forward, black smoke coming from her nostrils. She could feel Dominicus' fear rising even as he tried desperately to control his reaction.

"Quinn—" Draeven started.

"She's right," Lazarus said, cutting him off. "You've made your thoughts quite clear, Dominicus, but the boy is staying. If Nero has recruited the Maji from N'skara, we're going to need every advantage." Quinn opened her hand and let Dominicus slip from her grasp. She lifted her eyebrow in challenge as he gasped for air, looking from Quinn to Lazarus and then Lorraine.

The stewardess met his flinty gaze with a hard one of her own.

He looked away first, and one corner of Quinn's mouth curled up cruelly as she slid off the table and walked back around it to retake her seat.

"There's something more we need to discuss than the future of the young soul eater," Draeven said cautiously, his gait slowing. Quinn narrowed her eyes as she sensed nervousness waft from him like perfume.

"What?" Lazarus replied, his tone like ice. Bitter and cold.

"Imogen is dead," the left-hand replied without emotion.

Lazarus' eyes darkened. The bloodlion hissed at Draeven from the corner and the kuras let out a howl from wherever it was in the manor. Lazarus clenched his fists.

"The Queen of Ilvas died, and you didn't think to tell me?" he asked softly. Quinn tilted her head. She sensed anger rising in him. Rage.

"I only found out about it moments before Quinn arrived yesterday," Draeven said. His words were steady. But there was a tremor within him that she detected.

He was lying, but not outwardly.

She wondered if Lazarus noticed.

He loosed a breath, and his hands unclenched. She decided not. If he realized his left-hand was lying to him, she didn't think he'd let the offense go by. After the favor Lord Sunshine paid her in keeping her return to the living a secret, Quinn didn't breathe a word.

"How? When?" Lazarus said harshly, as if single syllables were all he could manage right now.

"Assassination one week ago. I believe it was the same night that Quinn and Thorne encountered a creature in Cisea," Draeven said.

Lazarus went still. Utterly immovable for a moment.

"Did her heir survive?" he asked, softly but not

kind. Not gentle. The souls were rallying. Rioting. The bloodlion paced furiously, narrowing its yellow cat eyes at everyone but Quinn.

"Axelle killed the assassin and was coronated yesterday. We were told to expect her in the coming week. She's named Petra as her hand."

"Good," Lazarus said, relaxing a fraction. "I want scouts placed along the path between here and Tritol."

"Already done," Draeven said. "I've asked the northern lords to rally their bannermen and prepare for war. The southern ones have already gathered and are awaiting orders."

"Keep them there for now. We need the Ilvan Queen here to make final arrangements. Thorne, will you be able to remain until then?"

"My wife has told me that I can't come home until I bring her the head of the man who took our son," Thorne said. "I'm afraid I'll be imposing on your hospitality for a while yet, old friend."

He smiled, but it was sad.

"She believes Nero is at fault?" Draeven asked.

"The creature spoke Trienian. Who else would send a demon that speaks that language?" Thorne asked.

"If blood magic is at play, I have no doubts it's Nero. I'll be questioning the creature shortly. Is there anything else that I haven't been made aware of?" He looked at his vassals—Draeven, Dominicus, and

Lorraine. Quinn sensed some broken trust there. But it was broken on both ends and would take time to repair. Time and action.

When none of them spoke, Lazarus dipped his head. "Very well. Draeven, begin combing our ranks for Maji soldiers. Man or woman. Offer them twice the pay if they're willing to fight. Dominicus, start inquiring with your spies in Triene. Lorraine, follow up with Bangratas and Jibreal to see what happened there." The others began moving toward the door, and Quinn stood to join them. "Where are you going?" Lazarus asked.

Quinn peered over her shoulder. "To begin Kairick's training. No one else is comfortable enough to do it, and you've work to do with preparations."

Lazarus' brow furrowed, but he didn't argue. "Don't go too far. I'll find you when I'm done."

Quinn inclined her head and then turned on her heel. The kuras fell into step behind her, a silent shadow sent by her king. She allowed it, for now.

After all, Quinn reveled in the power she held over him, as much as she fought the control he attempted to exert over her. Even in death, that hadn't changed, and it was still her favorite game to play.

"One is either a player in the game or a piece on the board. To try and be both is suicide by another name."
— Lazarus Fierté, soul eater, the still mad King of Norcasta

His hands curled around the railing. In the last week, an unnatural cold had settled over Shallowyn Manor, and Lazarus strongly suspected it was Quinn. Her very presence leaked the essence of death and darkness. He loved it. The scent of her magic had grown more potent than before. The ashen steps in her wake were visible for all to see, not that she seemed to notice.

The beasts within were less feral since her return, but twice as protective. They didn't like anything being within several feet of her, except him. Certainly not the soul eater child she was sparring with in the training field below.

Her lavender hair shined almost silver in the bright sun. Dead leaves drifted all around them, kicked up from their boots and the inept use of a dagger. Quinn had insisted he be given a real one, so that he learned early what it meant to hold a weapon. Lazarus acquiesced, but it didn't make him more comfortable with the boy being around her.

The only thing the child had going for himself was that he adored Quinn. Lazarus was near certain he'd never attempt to actually hurt her. Still, he tried to oversee every training he could, and the times he wasn't physically there, the kuras and firedrake were for him.

Part of him was fascinated, watching her with a child. If he'd ever wanted heirs, it would have been with her. The rest of him couldn't stop clenching his fists in jealousy. He was thankful she didn't want children at all, if she could even have them, because he didn't want to share her more than he had to.

Despite her proclamation that she didn't understand maternal feelings, she did seem fond of the boy. As much as Quinn could be fond of someone. She exhibited a greater patience than she usually had, something that perplexed Lazarus even more. She was hard on the boy and didn't shy away from leaving nicks and scrapes and bruises, but nothing permanent. Nothing truly cruel.

It beguiled him, and he didn't like it.

A single knock at the door in his chambers drew his attention.

"Enter," he called, still watching the training below.

Draeven walked in. His dark blonde hair unkempt and circles under his eyes. "Axelle is within a day's ride. Our scouts reported that she's traveling with a moderate party to prioritize swiftness. I'm having Lorraine ready her quarters."

Lazarus watched the boy attempt to aim the knife upward, as if stabbing through Quinn's ribs. She blocked it easily, and he lost his grip. The silver dagger tumbling several feet away. She pointed at him and told him to pick it up. No room for argument. No sympathy. He did so without complaint, and they carried on.

"Is that all?" Lazarus said.

Draeven shifted some, clearly uncomfortable.

"Will Quinn be returning as your right-hand?" Draeven asked. Lazarus was mildly surprised he finally had the balls to do it.

"No," he answered.

"Why not?"

Lazarus turned and lifted a brow, but his left-hand didn't continue. "Quinn doesn't wish to be bound by a contract again, and having her under one makes her more susceptible to Nero's schemes. I'd rather she not have any official ties to me in writing."

Draeven blinked slowly. "You're trying to protect her?" The words came out shocked.

"Partially," Lazarus said, trying not to grit his teeth. He still hadn't forgiven Draeven for being dishonest with him, even if Quinn had been the one telling him to do it.

"What are you not telling us?" Draeven asked slowly.

"Lord Adelmar, I don't have to tell you anything."

Draeven's lips twitched. His face drawn tight with stress. He sighed. "If this is because I didn't tell you she'd returned—"

"It's not," Lazarus said shortly. "Although, while we're on the subject, I wouldn't suggest you do that again if you'd like to remain my left-hand."

"Apparently I'm your only hand, though you won't tell me why," Draeven smarted back. He was clearly as much at his end with Lazarus as Lazarus was with him.

"Just as we have spies, so does Nero," Lazarus said.

"If you really thought I was a spy, I'd already be dead. Be honest with yourself, Lazarus. This is because I kept her existence a secret." Draeven stood several feet away and seemed to instill himself with the spine to keep going. "I won't ask your forgiveness for it because I'm not sorry I did it. You lost yourself in your grief, and someone had to make the hard calls. I needed you to focus on the war efforts. She needed you to focus on the war efforts. As it turns out, all our lives are on the line if we don't win. I can't—no—I won't apologize for what I did because that's what a hand should do when the king is indisposed."

"You're right," Lazarus said.

"What?" Draeven's face dropped in shock. His lips parted before shaking his head.

"I'm not repeating myself," Lazarus said, and that seemed to snap his left-hand out of it. "I am angry with you for withholding the truth, but it doesn't change that it needed to be done. Quinn has convinced me of that, and it's the reason you are still my hand. That does not mean that I'm giving you permission to do it again, however." Draeven lowered his eyes at that.

"If that's not the reason you're not telling me, then why?"

Lazarus sighed. "I questioned the creature inside of Vaughn. It's one of Nero's. As long as he's using blood magic, I can't risk all of my plans being with any one of you, except possibly Quinn."

"Because she can fight it off?" Draeven asked.

"Yes," Lazarus said, turning on the balcony to look down at the woman in question. She wielded black tendrils in the form of a person to face off against the boy, giving him the chance to actually stab something. She seemed to do this almost lazily, half her attention on the boy and half aimed toward the balcony. Her shrewd gaze met his, and she flashed a wicked grin.

His length stiffened, but Lazarus reined in the urge, turning back to Draeven.

"Is there no way to protect ourselves against blood magic?"

"Not this kind," Lazarus said. "Nero isn't taking any chances. It's clear he's trying to remove our allies. When that doesn't work, he'll turn to the members of my house. I doubt word has reached him of Quinn's return yet, but it won't be long."

"Then what?" Draeven said. "We can't hide. We can't protect ourselves. What are you proposing we do?"

"Prepare," Lazarus said. "Dominicus reported that Nero's army is starting its march north. We need to be ready for when they reach us. How goes the search for Maji?"

"Decent," Draeven said. Lazarus could tell he wasn't pleased with the answer he'd given, but he also didn't want to let on what he and Quinn were planning. "I've gathered a hundred Maji, mostly light and gray, but a few darker ones as well."

"Any fear twisters or soul eaters?"

"No," Draeven said. "A good number of beast tamers and healers, though."

"I'll speak with Quinn on training them," Lazarus said.

Draeven frowned. "I assumed—"

"You'd be training them?" Lazarus supplied.

"Yes," Draeven said, more hesitant than before.

"You're too soft," Lazarus replied. Draeven's frown deepened, and a red glint entered his eyes as anger surfaced.

"I'm too soft to train them, but not the skeevs is what you're saying?"

Lazarus appraised the man he once considered his closest and only friend.

"You can't train everyone, and Quinn will likely go too far with skeevs. She holds too much prejudice, and she's too powerful to risk losing her temper with them. You're more flexible in this, and she's more prepared to push the Maji to their edge than you are. She might not be my right-hand in name, but she's choosing to act as such still." Lazarus stepped inside his quarters and went to pour a glass of water from the crystal decanter that used to contain spirits. He still struggled with how deep in himself he'd gone for over two months, but slowly was working his way back because he needed to. Quinn had come back, and they were going to crush their enemies together. Revenge would never taste so sweet as it would with her by his side.

He needed to be level-headed for that.

Calculating. Cautious. Above all, present of mind.

"I see," his left-hand said, still slightly bitter but less offended than he'd been.

"Draeven, I'm only going to say this once for both

you and Dominicus. I'm choosing to overlook your transgressions because you believed you were doing the right thing, and you're the type of man that will always do what he thinks is right. I've always known this, and until Quinn, you always trusted that what I was doing was right. If not in the immediate, then in the end . . ."

"What are you saying?" Draeven asked.

Lazarus took a long draw from his glass and swallowed before setting the glass aside and looking Draeven in the eye.

"Don't get in my way again. Don't lie to me again. Don't withhold information again. I am king, and I will not be made a fool or live to see my plans ruined because you thought you knew better than me. You are my left because you're not easily swayed. I can forgive Lorraine's transgressions easier because I understand her love for Quinn. You and Dominicus, however, you chose to play king, and I won't stand for it. Be my left-hand, or no hand at all."

Draeven opened then closed his mouth, then nodded once.

"I understand," he said. He lowered his eyes, and Lazarus didn't know what was going through his mind, he just hoped that he'd come to his senses soon.

"Good. Relay that to Dominicus when you see him. I'm tired of the brooding, and it isn't going to help him with Lorraine."

Draeven opened his mouth as if to comment, and then he paused and said, "Very well."

Lazarus waited for him to let himself out before returning to the balcony.

There was much to do, but just like before, Quinn was an obsession he couldn't rid himself of. A fascination that never lessened.

Both him and the dark god had that in common.

The difference was Mazzulah let her go in favor of winning the game.

Lazarus had lived without her once, and he was never letting her go again.

Not for his crown.

Not for his country.

Not even for the whole Sirian continent.

He'd sooner let them all die than lose her, but he was playing a game where winner takes all. Losing anything was not an option.

CHAPTER 29
QUEEN OF MOURNING

"The truth can either break someone or make them stronger, and only that person decides which."
— *Quinn Darkova, fear twister, walker of realms, the hussy*

The black carriage, pulled by four steeds, sent an interesting message.

Quinn stood at the top of the staircase next to Lorraine as she watched it roll down the long dirt drive. Kairick stood on her other side, dressed like a noble boy. He wasn't watching the carriage, though. He was watching the skies.

His firedrake wanted to come out. However, Lazarus wasn't keen on sharing anything. If not for the fact that he held Vaughn's soul, Quinn might have been willing to let him return with Thorne when this was all over. Two soul eaters under the same roof was going to present problems. Quinn was choosing to take things in stride and pressure Lazarus only when needed.

Today he was tense. She thought it best not to poke the barely contained soul eater when he was stirring restlessly. Thorne stood at one of his sides, and Draeven at the other as the carriage slowed to a halt. Several horses came to a stop behind it. Ilvan guards dressed in black and gold. Quinn wondered if the change to their house colors would be permanent with Axe in charge, or if it were simply mourning.

The front man jumped off the side and went to open the door, but it opened on its own before he got there. A fiery red head of hair popped out first. Axe jumped down, brushed her black shirt off, and then lifted her head.

None of the amusement or childlike innocence she'd had was there now.

There was pain, lots of it, mostly repressed beneath an even greater amount of anger. Her eyes were red around the edges, if dry now. She wore no crown even though golden embellishments lined her clothing, and an axe was strapped to both hips.

"Queen Axelle—"

"Where is Vaughn?" the young girl said, cutting straight through Draeven's pleasantries. Behind her, Petra exited the carriage. Her gaze was guarded and her hair more grayed than it had been the last time

Quinn saw her. Similar to Axe, she wore black and gold. Her expression that of sorrow.

Quinn and Lorraine shared a look of concern.

Draeven cringed, and Thorne looked away. Only Lazarus remained stoic.

Axe narrowed her eyes up at him.

"Where. Is. Vaughn?" she asked again, this time to the king directly.

"Quinn," Lazarus said once, his voice rumbling like depths of mountains.

The girl's eyes widened briefly in surprise as Quinn put a hand on Kairick's shoulder and started down the steps.

"I thought—"

"I was dead?" Quinn said, cutting her off. Draeven shot her a look, which Quinn chose to ignore. This was Axe. A sixteen-year-old pirate. She may be a queen now, but Quinn didn't care. She'd spoken to gods in the same manner.

"Aye," Axe said slowly, confusion taking over as her gaze dropped to Kairick. He didn't shift uncomfortably under her glare. He merely returned it without reproach.

"I still am, in a sense," Quinn said vaguely. "But that's a conversation for another time."

"I don't see Risk anywhere," Axe said, her sharp blue eyes sweeping the front of the mansion.

"She's not here," Quinn replied. "She's in the dark realm, training with Mazzulah."

Axe lifted both her eyebrows as if finding that difficult to believe.

"The dark realm?" the young queen asked.

Quinn nodded once as she stepped off the marble staircase and onto the compact dirt.

"Why is she there?" Axe asked, rolling with the knowledge that Quinn had returned and the dark realm was real, faster than most everyone else. Other than Quinn, Axe was the only one to have ever met a god. Perhaps after that, she realized there was very little outside the realm of possibility.

"She made a deal to get me out. She'll be back when she ascends," Quinn said. She sensed the judgement coming from Draeven. He'd made his thoughts clear on what they should and shouldn't tell the girl, but not only was she a queen, she was going to send men to fight and die for this war. Quinn wouldn't lie to her about it. Not when they gained nothing from lying other than sheltering someone who shouldn't be sheltered.

Axe pressed her lips together. "Where is Vaughn?" she asked again, this time tiredness leaked into her voice along with something else. Desperation.

"Kairick, let the man come out," Quinn commanded.

Axe's eyebrows drew together in confusion as the boy lifted his hand. A shadow moved forward and then detached from his skin. Vaughn formed with the stygian eyes of blood magic still affecting him.

Axe's expression shattered.

Her blue eyes seemed to fracture as understanding passed over her. Her lips parted in shock. Nearly half a minute passed that way before she asked in an apathetic voice, "Where is Vaughn?"

Quinn could sense the anger building within her, and it had nothing to do with being a fear twister. Axe knew, but didn't want to face it.

"He's right here," Quinn said slowly.

Axe started to shake her head. "No. No. That *thing* is just a black mass that looks like him—" she started.

"There was an incident. The same kind of creature that went after Imogen entered Vaughn," Draeven started.

"No," Axe repeated. She reached for one of the hatchets at her waist, and Quinn moved quick as a snake. Her pale fingers locked around Axe's wrist, stopping her from pulling the magical weapon.

"Let me go, you hussy," Axe demanded, struggling. Behind her, Petra did the same, moving to grab both of Axe's arms. Quinn released her, stepping back to stop Kairick who had lifted his hand in her defense and was inching toward Axe. His expression was dark.

Quinn cast a look down at Kairick that had him dropping his hand. Vaughn dematerialized and slipped back beneath his master's skin.

"Stop this, Axe," Petra said quietly, speaking in Ilvan.

"He killed him," the young woman snapped in a

half-growl, half-yell as she tried to lurch forward. Petra turned to stone, and Axe's rants became futile.

"He consumed him," Quinn replied. "Killing him would have been kinder, but he doesn't understand. With time, we're hoping to separate the blood beast from Vaughn, but until then—"

"I'll kill him," she threatened. Quinn shook her head.

Perhaps Draeven had been right that telling her all of it up front would be too much on her.

"Then you'll kill Vaughn too," Lorraine said, stepping forward. She descended the steps and strode past Quinn and the others to stand in front of Axe. "It's a tragedy what happened to him, and there's a small chance that in time we can fix it. But right now, the person who caused this—the real person, not Quinn, not the boy, but the man that sent those things after him and your mother—he's still out there. *He* is our enemy." Axe stopped struggling as Lorraine spoke. "You're a queen now. You can choose to be a sullen child and let Petra and your advisors decide everything, or you can be the queen your mother would have wanted. Would she have stood here and thrown a fit?"

Lorraine lifted an eyebrow, and Axe's lip quivered a little as she said, "No."

"No," Lorraine agreed. "She would have slit the throat of the man who did it and dumped his body in the ocean as an offering to Myori."

Axe's breathing slowed a fraction as it sunk in. She looked past Lorraine to Kairick, and her eyes hardened, but she stopped fighting. Petra released her slowly, and she didn't reach for the axes. She just looked to Lorraine and said, "You lot asked me here because you want my men and my armada. You have it, but I get to kill the git when it comes time."

Then she strode past Lorraine and Quinn and Kairick and all of House Fierté. She ascended the steps with her back to them and didn't turn around.

Petra flashed them a tight smile and followed after.

It was only when all of her guards had either entered behind her or pulled around to the stables that Quinn finally said, "Did any of you see the mark on her forehead before she left?"

Lorraine shook her head. As did Draeven.

But Lazarus' gaze burned as he said, "I did."

"What was it?" Draeven asked.

Quinn stared up the steps to where the young queen had gone, wondering not for the first time how great a hand the gods chose to play in shaping their champion's.

"It was Saltira's symbol. The mark of the Goddess of War."

*"Only when you lose sight of who you thought you were can you
find who you truly are."*
— Mariska "Risk" Darkova, beast tamer, Mazzulah's heir

S he wasn't sure how long had passed before the
frenzy set in. The madness. The desperation.

Lost. She was lost in the forgotten forest.

And if she didn't find a way out, she'd fail.

Quinn would lose the war.

Everyone would die.

And once more, Risk would be the weak link.

Risk fisted her hands in her hair, pulling hard. Her
arms had scars from her scratching down them. Her
body was thin once more, painfully so. But this cursed

realm kept her alive all the same because the raksasa blood that ran through her veins.

Risk's breathing turned harsh.

She dropped to her knees, letting her legs sink into the muddy forest floor. Shadows and light drifted over her as she lowered her head to the ground, screaming in frustration.

Weeks. Months. It could have been years already for all she knew.

Years surviving but never really living in these forsaken woods.

Anger heated her, and that age-old rage she held close to her chest blossomed.

Risk wanted to give up so badly. She wanted to give in and just die.

But she also didn't, and it was her anger toward the dark god that made her pick her head back up. It was that rage that made her pull herself up and start to rise.

It was her determination to get out of this forest and show Mazzulah and everyone that she was more than they wrote her off to be—that drive that made her stand and begin to walk once more.

Her magic was now out all the time. It listened to the sounds of the forest and felt the beasts call within. They came to her often, but none of them was the one she thought.

Her familiar.

She needed to find it.

Somehow.

Risk continued onward, walking almost aimlessly. If the blood moon rose and descended, she never knew it from how thick the foliage had grown. She'd be thankful to see any sky right now, even a dark one. All she saw instead were luminescent insects and flowers on creeping vines and black trees. It was beautiful in a sense. Chaotic, and yet serene.

But she hated it.

She hated this forest so much because it never seemed to end.

The trickling water made Risk lift her head. She'd found it before, but the beasts in it had worried her. They were stronger than anything she'd controlled before. Wild and untamable. She'd kept moving because of it, but now . . . she was just frenzied enough to not care.

The sound of water made her thirsty. She stumbled forward, pushing past giant plum-colored leaves. This stream was smaller than the one she'd found before. Only several feet wide instead of several dozen. It glowed a pearlescent blue, the rocks at the bottom visible.

Risk's lips parted as she came to a stop in front of it. Her magic had already searched for animals, but the ones that were near were tamable. Easy for her to master.

She didn't sense the sleeping giants that had been near the water before.

Risk dropped onto all fours and dipped her hands into the stream. Water flowed over them, washing the dirt away. She cupped her fingers and lifted a tiny pool of it to her lips.

Bliss.

It overwhelmed her.

She drank and drank, and when there was no more, she cupped her hands and did it again.

It never occurred to her to stop.

She never wondered why it was this stream filled her with utter relief.

Not even as she tumbled into it in her haze.

The water rushed over her head, and part of her brain started to worry. But even as she choked, she drank. The water filled her with that bliss, drowning out all worries just as it drowned her.

Risk's eyes started to close.

She felt herself falling once more, but this time it was into darkness. True darkness. A deceptive warmth wrapped around her that should have told her this wasn't right.

The dark realm was cold.

Eternally frigid.

The last thing she should have felt was warmth.

But she did.

Soon the warmth started to ache, and then burn. It started in her chest and spread through her limbs like fire. Immense pain overwhelmed her.

Risk's eyes flew open. Her body lurched upward as the water she'd drank tried to expel itself from her system. She gagged, spewing liquid everywhere that no longer looked beautiful and clean, but black and oily.

On the other side of the substance, two giant paws stood.

Risk bared her teeth at the creature even as dizziness threatened to take her. A pounding started in her head that was mirrored by the beat of her heart. Her eyelashes fluttered.

"Leave me," Risk commanded, the words slurring from her lips.

She clenched her hands in the dirt, feeling it squish beneath her palms.

"*Never*," came the reply.

Her eyes flew open for one long second.

The creature was almost twice her height. The body was shaped like a cat. Black fur the color of the void made it darker than any shadow. Its eyes were blue.

Brilliant, piercing, unnatural blue.

Just like hers.

Risk lifted one hand because that was the only action she had the strength to do.

The beast lowered its head. Its jaw was large enough to eat her arm in a single bite, but the creature didn't attack her. It pressed its forehead into her palm.

A shock went through her, as if she'd been struck by lightning.

Her fingers tightened once more, this time feeling damp fur. A sound like thunder boomed through the sky, but it wasn't a storm.

It was her familiar.

"*Rainier*," she whispered.

A second one followed, and she felt a distinct trill of pleasure that was not her own. This creature knew her. It recognized Risk as *hers* by scent alone, and the bond between them solidified with a single touch.

"*You cannot die*," the creature told her. "*I have waited too long.*"

"I'm weak," Risk said, releasing a bitter laugh that rang hollow. "You chose wrong."

"*You're strong. Stronger than all of them. So strong I could not find you because your magic was everywhere. Only now with it draining away could I see.*"

Risk careened forward, but instead of landing in the puddle of bile, a wet nose held her up. She panted softly. Not understanding what was going on.

Even at her weakest in the temple, she'd never felt like this.

"*You cannot die,*" Rainier said again. "*You must ascend.*"

Her heart jumped. Risk moaned softly. A wet tongue lapped at her, and Risk fell to the side. Half of her face pressed into soft moss. The scents of dirt and magic and darkness swirled in the air around her, all while her heart thundered.

She was scared. So scared that this might be the end.

That she would truly never see Quinn again.

That she would never return to the Sirian continent.

That she would fail and doom all of her friends and only family.

"*Ascend*," Rainier said again, repeating it over and over and over again in her mind.

Mazzulah had told her that she would not survive unless she found something to give her the will to live. Her fear of failure was not enough. It was failure that held her back. That made her believe she was not good enough, or strong enough, or pure enough.

But if not failure . . .

Risk opened her eyes and looked straight into Rainier's.

"I will ascend," Risk said, and she meant it.

"*You will ascend*," her familiar repeated back to her.

Holding her through the worst of it and grounding her even as death threatened to tear her apart.

Hope wasn't strong enough.

But an unrelenting tempest . . .

She was going to be that storm. A force of nature.

It was that thought that Risk held onto as the last of her magic drained from her.

She was both Maji and raksasa. A being that was made of magic, and a woman that could harness it.

Both left her, and that brief but beautiful connection with Rainier fizzled out.

If she were any weaker of will, she would have lost then and let the darkness take her. She would have surrendered to the warmth she so desperately wanted to feel.

But Risk was not made to be warm.

She was a woman of two worlds.

She was a storm of ice and fury. A tamer of beasts. The heir to the rightful king of the gods.

And she would not let anyone, or anything, contain her any longer.

Not even the ascension.

She might not get to rewrite the past, but she had the power to change her future—if only she took it.

Magic flooded her veins.

She screamed in agony and triumph as her heart turned so cold it froze.

The thumping ceased.

Thunder rolled.

And when Risk Darkova lifted her head, she had no intention of ever bowing it again.

CHAPTER 31
PAIN AND PLEASURE

"True perfection is possible, but only if you kill the flaws first."
— Nero, Emperor of Triene, God among men

Music trilled through his tent as the whore on his lap bounced up and down. Her wet cunt coated his stiff length. Perky breasts greeted him with every sway of her hips. The makeup on her face had been expertly painted to make her more to his liking, not that Nero cared to look at her face all that often.

The flap to his tent swished aside, but the musician kept playing. His nimble fingers might have slipped once, but never again. Nero hummed along to the melody as his captain of the guard stepped inside.

"Your Excellency," the beast of a man said, dropping to one knee.

He had golden hair like a lion, and tan skin, a flaw that Nero accepted because he was just that good at his job. Almost as good as Lazarus would be, but Nero stowed that thought for another time.

"Report, Lord Zairaynas," Nero said softly. The woman on his lap moaned wantonly, in a way meant to entice him.

The lord was careful to not look at the girl even once, even though Nero could see a bulge forming in his trousers. A cruel smirk formed on his lips.

"The armada has been deployed. Our forces march north on your command."

"And our allies?" Nero asked, toying with a lock of the woman's pretty brown hair. He liked long hair on women. Dark hair. It made things so much more . . . fun.

"En route to Dumas already, as you *requested*," the captain said, swallowing hard when the whore spread her legs wider, pushing herself harder to bring Nero to release.

Stupid girl, he thought, though it amused him that she tried.

Her pleasure would never give him that.

"Very well," Nero sighed, growing bored with this conversation already. "Is that all, Lord Zairaynas?"

"Y-yes, Your Excellency," the captain said. His tongue darted out to lick his lower lip as the whore's fine backside danced in his view. Nero could tell she was putting on a show for him, for both of them.

The knowledge gave him an idea. Instead of dismissing the captain, he said, "Do you like what you see?"

For a brief second, Zairaynas' eyes dropped to the junction where their bodies met. His eyes dilated, and Nero knew the rumors he'd heard about this particular guard were true. Though, he never thought to indulge in them before now, not when he had so many fancies.

"It would be uncouth of me to say, Your Excellency," the captain answered.

Nero reached around to fondle the firm globes of her ass, watching as the captain swallowed hard.

"I asked you a question. I expect an answer," the emperor replied. It was the only warning his captain of the guard would get.

After all, they were all replaceable. Save one person.

"I like what I see," Zairaynas said thickly, coming to his senses.

Nero released his grip on her ass and slapped one cheek hard. The woman jumped, and for the first time since she'd began, he hardened further.

"How long has it been since you had a woman to warm your bed?" Nero asked, already knowing the answer.

"Too long, Your Excellency."

Yes, Nero had heard as much. He'd married into a wealthier family with a pretty daughter, but the thing about pretty flowers is they wilted when taken out of the sun. Rumors ran abound in the capital that he was too rough with her. Liked to leave bruises. Marks.

Nero liked those things too.

Except, unlike Lord Zairaynas, Nero's pretty flowers didn't get to run back to the sun when they decided it was too much.

"Would you like to taste her too?" the emperor asked, and the girl on his lap faltered for a second. Her heartbeat quickened in fear. Her skin grew flushed, and it had nothing to do with her ministrations.

"If Your Excellency is offering, I would not decline . . ." the good captain said, licking his lips again as his control started to slip and he drank in her pale form.

"Up," Nero commanded once more, slapping her backside again. The girl slowed, as if dazed, though he knew that wasn't the case. She slowly lifted herself off him and stumbled back a step.

"Your Excellency," she murmured in a submissive and frightened tone.

His length twitched, and Nero smiled.

"Show your appreciation to Lord Zairaynas. His wife has been gone for quite a long time. Offer him your ass to use as he likes," Nero said.

His thumb brushed across his bottom lip as he narrowed his eyes on the girl. Her cheeks went pink, and the pulse in her neck fluttered like a little bird.

She didn't want to. Nero could tell that easily by the way she fumbled over her words.

She was a virgin there. She'd been a virgin everywhere before he'd paid for her.

Nero liked them young and inexperienced.

There were no bad habits he had to break, though he did love doing it.

"My lord," she began. "Would you like my ass?" Her cherry red mouth trembled.

"I would," he growled roughly.

"No bed," Nero chided as she started to move toward it. "Turn around and give it to him where you are."

Her legs were stiff as she turned around and bent at the waist. There was nothing in front of her to grab but Nero's knees, and even she was not so foolish as to try that.

Behind her, Zairaynas unlaced his trousers and pulled his length free.

"Hold your cheeks open for him," Nero commanded, his own shaft stiffening further as her eyes started to water. She reached around with shaking hands and grasped her pale flesh, pulling it to either side.

The lord loomed behind her, and when he began to push in, the tears fell. She pressed her lips together, trying not to openly sob. Zairaynas was not a small man.

When he was seated firmly, her hips started to

careen forth, but he grabbed them and began to pound into her. Nero paid little attention to how roughly he took her beyond the sheen of crimson that covered the other man's length. Her tears were what interested him. They painted her face prettier than the makeup ever could.

"Ask him to finish inside you," Nero said, relishing the way she was powerless.

"P-please finish inside me," she said, choking on the words.

It was only a few more moments before Zairaynas groaned. His hips jerked. The movements stilling.

Overall, the whole ordeal had only been a minute or two.

But Nero was harder than he'd been in the previous twenty.

The girl's eyes fractured like glass as Zairaynas pulled out of her. Blood and seed dripped down her legs as he laced himself back up.

"Thank you, Your Excellency," the captain said to Nero, without regard for the girl he'd used.

"Leave us," Nero said. He'd served his purpose, and now Nero would enjoy the spoils.

He didn't lift his eyes from the girl as Zairaynas exited the tent. The musician still played, never missing a note.

"Now," he said, with a savage grin. "Where were we?"

Her eyes went wide as Nero motioned to the

ground in front of him. She stepped forward and then hesitantly dropped to her knees. When her hand went to wipe the tears from her face, Nero grabbed it, stopping her.

"Leave them," he commanded. He used his free hand to run down her cheek, almost gently. She leaned into the soft touch until he curled his fingers around her jaw and pressed inward. Her mouth popped open, and he guided her head to his shaft.

Panic flared in her eyes, but she didn't dare argue. The mistress of her brothel had at least trained her in this. She knew what was to be expected of her, and she adjusted, taking him into her warm mouth openly, if not eagerly.

Nero ran both his hands through her hair as she sucked on him.

His nails scraped against her scalp as he said, "Deeper."

She moved in, pressing her face closer to his groin, though not close enough to take all of it. Nero's hand turned to fists as he dragged her forward. His tip touched the back of her throat, and she gagged. He liked that.

Fresh tears spilled down her cheeks as he started to thrust deeper.

Her skin turned red and then purple as he didn't let up, instead taking his pleasure at her expense.

The pain was what he wanted.

She started to struggle after another moment

passed, trying to fight him off. He released her hair to wrap that hand around her throat and squeezed.

She choked again, her mouth opening wide in an attempt to get air.

Nero rocked into her, thrusting hard.

When her eyes turned glassy and blank, pleasure shot down his spine.

He released into her and then cast her aside. Seed spilled out of the corner of her mouth as her head hit the floor.

Dead.

He laced up his trousers and stood to pour himself a glass of spirits, sighing deeply into the music. His eyes lingered on her form.

She was pretty. Not quite exquisite, but few women were. She'd keep Zairaynas loyal.

Nero mulled over her worth as he finished his drink, and when it was empty, he set the glass aside and kneeled beside her.

One calloused finger brushed down her dry cheek, the salty tear stains so visible against that skin . . .

It was that thought that made him reach toward her chest. His fingers brushed against her sternum and white tendrils jumped from him to her.

She gasped. Life coming back to her in an instant. Nero stood up and went for another drink, his bad leg stiffer than it was before.

"Don't speak," he told the girl. Her mouth snapped shut, though questions burned in her eyes.

"Get dressed and go find Lord Zairaynas' tent. Tell him he can do what he wishes with you. You belong to him now."

Her cheeks were still an unnatural shade of white. Her heart hadn't restarted. Blood did not pump in her veins, but she lived all the same, which meant she felt pain all the same.

Zairaynas would enjoy breaking her and would be too busy to betray Nero.

At least, that was Nero's plan because there was still so much to do before he came face-to-face with his brother once more.

CHAPTER 32
BRUTAL HONESTY

*"Lies are for the weak. Those who do not fear the consequences
have honesty in everything."*
— *Quinn Darkova, fear twister, walker of realms*

Quinn stared at the wooden figurines, her eyes narrowed in concentration.

"Check mate," Lazarus declared. Moving his piece to solidify the kill.

Quinn's hand swept across the board, knocking all the pieces aside in frustration.

"Black baac," she muttered, standing to stride across the room and stand before the fire. She extended her hands toward it, close enough that were she not dead, it might have burned. Instead the warmth suffused her, relaxing that terrible, dreadful cold within that clawed to get out.

"You never look far enough ahead," Lazarus said, moving to stand beside her. "You always go for the kills, even when they're bait."

"That's because in real life, even if they're bait, I would simply kill them all. I wouldn't stand to protect a useless king whose whole purpose is to dally around the board attempting not to be killed. Pathetic."

Lazarus chuckled, the sound similar to the boom of thunder. Beside her, the kuras brushed up against her barely clad hip. The feathers smooth and soft against her skin.

"Never change, saevyana," he murmured over her shoulder. A thick arm wrapped around her waist from behind, his calloused hand coming to rest over her abdomen.

"Couldn't even if I wanted to," Quinn said.

"Does being dead bother you?" Lazarus asked. Quinn mulled over the answer as her fingers brushed against the edge of the flame. It was hot, but the burn felt good.

"Not really," she answered. "I'm stronger than I was. Stronger than any Maji, I reckon. I can change my form and fight the blood creatures Nero might send after us. The cold has always been in me to some degree, it's just more exaggerated now . . . I'm more myself than I've ever been."

"You won't change, though. You won't age or grow or bear children, even if you change your mind in a thousand years. Your only options will be this or a true death."

Quinn shrugged, not all that bothered. "The moon tonic Lorraine made was disgusting. I'm happy to not have to take it anymore, and whether it's now or in a thousand years, I'll never be any less cruel. If anything, time tends to jade people . . . I'm fine by that. And if one day I'm not, then I'll end it."

His hand tightened around her waist. "Sometimes I forget how honest you are, despite your wickedness. It's both refreshing and disconcerting."

"It's a product of not knowing true fear," Quinn said. "I can't feel what you and others do. I'm incapable of it, and therefore I'm incapable of all things associated with it. If I were to die a true death tomorrow, I wouldn't be pleased, but I'd be dead. It's not as if I'd exist in some capacity afterwards. The concept of death holds very little meaning to me after all I've seen."

"Speaking of death," Lazarus said, releasing the arm around her waist to move to stand beside her. "I need you to not kill the Maji you're meant to be training."

"I'd never *try* to kill them," Quinn scoffed.

"Yes, well, how about you *try* not to," he said pointedly, punctuating his statement with a lift of a masculine eyebrow. Quinn snorted.

"They will be fine," she said, waving him off as

she turned for the balcony. "And if they aren't, they weren't fit for your army to begin with."

"Quinn," Lazarus groaned. Not in pleasure, to her annoyance.

"All will be fine, Lazarus. I will handle the Maji, Draeven will handle the skeevs. Axe will listen to Petra for how to go about deploying the Ilvan armada. Thorne's warriors are attempting to form a barricade through the mountain passage. It's all going according to plan."

She stepped outside, and for any other woman, what she was wearing would be considered scandalous. Given she was just as happy naked as she was in leathers, the sheer negligee at least covered her more intimate areas, even if it left just as much on display.

"That's what I'm worried about," Lazarus said.

"Nero will not stand a chance, and once word comes back on what's happening in Jibreal and Bangratas, we can try to bring them into the fold. With six countries united, this war will end before it begins."

Lazarus didn't say anything, and his lack of reply made her turn her face and narrow her eyes. "Unless you're still keeping secrets and have reason to believe he can overpower us."

"No," he sighed. "I just know him. He wouldn't be moving for war if he weren't certain he could win. He clearly knows of my alliances, which means he also knows that one of his abominations failed to kill Thorne. Yet he still marches. Something isn't adding up."

Quinn looked up at the half-moon. It covered the forests surrounding Shallowyn in shadows and night. The firedrakes lit up the sky as they circled overhead but kept their distance from each other.

"It's been a long time since you've seen him," she said eventually.

"A person like him . . . they only change for the worse. He's like us, and he believes I wronged him. I underestimated Amelia and paid for it dearly. I won't do the same here."

Quinn turned and leaned back against the railing, crossing her arms over her chest.

"How did you get the scar over your eye?" she asked him.

"You mean how did he?" he replied.

Quinn shrugged. "They're the same scar. It's likely the same story."

"Not always," Lazarus said. "Perspective makes a great deal of difference. I imagine Nero fancies himself the hero of his own story."

"Is he?" Quinn asked.

"No more than you or me," came his reply.

Quinn left the balcony, evening musings in the form of deep conversations calling to her instead. The double doors shut behind her, guided by black tendrils. She took a seat in one of the wingback chairs and gestured for Lazarus to do the same.

"Then tell me," she said. "How did you get it?"

Lazarus sighed deeply before taking the chair across from her. She might have poured him a drink under other circumstances, but he'd all but banned spirits from being in any of the rooms he frequented. Her king might fear very little, but he feared his own loss of control under their guidance.

"Nero and I aren't brothers in blood; at least we weren't. We were both orphans living on the streets of Iamont when we found each other. I was seven at the time, and he was nine. We became friends quickly. Easily. Something that wasn't the norm for either of us because we were both Maji—and in Triene, all magic had been outlawed. Light or dark."

"That seems a bit simpleminded," Quinn said.

"The emperor was not well-liked," Lazarus said, reaching for the water, likely more out of habit than anything. "Which helped us at the time. Nero was a great speaker, and even better manipulator. Over the next few years, our group of orphans grew. We went from pickpocketing street vendors to taking out guards, and when Imogen ransacked the royal coffers, it was Nero and I that helped her do it. We got her into the palace, and she gave us a portion of the profits. That's when things really started to change. The old emperor was losing power, and Nero was gaining popularity with the people. They didn't see past what he wanted them to, though. That was reserved for me."

"And what was that?" Quinn prompted, leaning forward to rest her elbows on her knees.

"Greed. Nero always suffered from it, but something began to change around that time. The more power he had, the more power he wanted. The more money he stole, the more aggressive he became in stealing it. Nothing was ever enough."

"Well, he's emperor now, so I can see where this is leading."

"Perhaps," Lazarus nodded. "But not where it began. He was born a healer, and he was always powerful, but he hungered for more. He wanted gifts like mine or yours. Things that he deemed 'useful.' That's when he started practicing with blood magic. He recruited scholars and apothecaries in his quest for power, and eventually, one of them found the answer."

"This," Lazarus motioned to his scarred eye, "is the result of it."

"How?" Quinn asked, narrowing her eyes.

"On a blood moon, there is a way to make a sacrifice to the gods in hopes that they'll endow you with more power," Lazarus answered in a clipped tone. She wondered if he realized the detachment that entered his voice. "This was said to change skeevs into new Maji with gifts that had never been. Nero heard the stories and knew this was his chance. I was only fifteen at the time, and while I was starting to question some of his methods, it wasn't until that night that I truly saw him for who and what he was."

"What was the sacrifice?" Quinn asked, the curiosity was gone from her voice, and an unsettling note had entered it. A dark gleam in her eye.

"When the moon was highest, we were to slit a newborn's throat as an offering to the gods, and then use the same knife to blind ourselves in one eye as proof of our determination."

Quinn sat back, silence settling heavily between them.

She had questions, so many questions, but it was a statement that made it to her lips.

"You didn't do it."

"What?"

"You didn't blind yourself," she said. "But he did."

She recalled the vision she'd had of the man with a cane and only one eye.

Lazarus lowered his head. "I couldn't do it. I tried to back out when he brought the child. He used his own son, thinking the gods would endow him with even more magic for the added sacrifice. While I didn't know the babe . . . I couldn't slit its throat, and I couldn't blind myself. He was enraged by it, but refused to miss his chance. After seeing him kill his own son without a second thought . . ."

"You knew he'd give up anything for power," Quinn surmised.

"Yes." Lazarus' eyes lifted, and she saw the shadows in them. The old haunts that he didn't want to relive, but he couldn't stop either.

"Did it work?" Quinn asked. Surprise flared in his gaze, and if he were shocked that she'd even think about it, he didn't say.

"I don't know," Lazarus replied. "I fled into the night while he was wounded. I raided our coffers and took everything I could carry. While I couldn't bring myself to kill him then, I also knew it was only a matter of time until he tried to find a way to use me. I wasn't going to let that happen."

"Hmm," Quinn murmured. "Curious . . ."

"What's curious?"

"You. Him. Why, after all this time, has he decided to go to war with you? If he wanted you dead, there are easier ways. Amelia certainly could have played her hand differently and it would have done the trick. So why war? Why now?" She steepled her fingers and rested her chin on top of them.

"If I had to guess, he either means to kill me personally, or keep me. Either way, it's all a show to prove his strength. Nothing more."

"Keep you?"

Lazarus flashed her a dark look. "Why do kings and emperors want people like us?" he asked her.

"Power," Quinn breathed. Lazarus nodded.

"I could never be a slave to another's will, and that's what I would be under him. I knew if he didn't find a way to take my own magic that he'd settle for owning me as a pet."

"That's horrible," she said. "And coming from me, that says a great deal."

Lazarus didn't respond at first, instead seeming to be stuck in his own mind, mulling over some thought she wasn't privy to. It was only when Quinn moved to stand that he spoke.

"Did you feel that way before? When you were under contract with me?"

Quinn paused, neither looking at him, nor the floor, though she stared in the general direction of them both. "In the beginning I did."

"What changed?" he asked. She noted that he never apologized for taking her or forcing her hand. Though he seemed to understand that she would never be a slave again.

"We did," Quinn said simply. Lifting her eyes to meet his. Dark irises burned with intensity. "We both did. We became more than simply master and weapon."

"You're still a weapon," Lazarus pointed out.

"Yes," Quinn grinned. "But not yours. Not anyone's, except my own."

Quinn stood, and her hands moved to the straps of her sheer negligee. She pushed them over the curve of her shoulders, one at a time. The fabric dropped to her feet.

Lazarus rumbled in approval, reaching to grasp

her waist.

Quinn let him, and it was her choice. It was always her choice, and in the end, that was the difference.

CHAPTER 33
OUT OF THE DARK

"When you have found who you are, you don't need others to tell you who to be."
— Mariska "Risk" Darkova, beast tamer, Mazzulah's heir

R ain battered her face. She clung to her familiar's back, but like her, the creature was not of the world of the living. Neither of them held any warmth. With her heart frozen and cold because of the magic she took from the dark realm during her ascension, Risk didn't need the heat anymore.

She embraced the storm and its bitter winds as Rainier's wings beat powerfully.

Risk's hands gripped the creature's damp fur, clinging to her as she flew through the dark sky. Below them the forest gave way to desert sands that hadn't seen rain in so many years they'd forgotten what it was like.

A single platform rose up from the black desert. A column of stone with a nearly never-ending suitcase. Rainier flew higher into the clouds where lightning raged, and thunder boomed. Risk did not flinch from the elements. She did not seek to hide as they flew through the worst of it.

She embraced it.

Became it.

The platform where the dark god awaited her came into sight.

Mazzulah stood before the twin thrones in her female form.

The blood moon turning the raindrops to crimson sheets as they rained down on the god. Mazzulah smiled up at the clouds as Rainier started to descend. Her black wings beating in slow, steady thrusts. Twenty feet from the stone, she tucked them in tight as she and Risk plummeted.

A crackling echo shot through the dark realm as Rainier landed on the platform. Risk released her familiar's fur, and flung her leg over the side, sliding down her back.

Mazzulah didn't greet her, and Risk had a feeling she was waiting to see what she would do.

"I'm leaving," Risk said, as she walked up to the god. She did not bow. She did not kneel. She did not cower even as Mazzulah reached a taloned finger for her and traced it over her cheek. Her blue eyes were steel and storms as she stared at Mazzulah and the dark phoenix she'd called Alpis.

The god continued to smile as Risk stood her ground. "Good," she purred after a moment. "You're ready."

Risk narrowed her eyes. "You're not going to stop me?" she asked.

Mazzulah dropped her hand and started circling her, then turned to Risk's familiar and did the same.

"I left you in the forgotten forest months ago, and you've returned with a night sphinx as your familiar. I thought these great beasts were extinct. It seems I was wrong."

"*Not extinct*," Rainier said. "*Waiting.*"

A cruel grin crept up Mazzulah's lips. "Yes," she murmured, reaching out a clawed hand to brush her fingers over the animal's snout. Rainier's mouth curled back in a snarl that reverberated through the dark realm. "I can see it. Only my true heir could claim such a creature."

"I upheld my end of the deal. I stayed till my ascension. I claimed my familiar. It's time for me to return."

"It is," Mazzulah agreed. "The war is brewing, and it nears its peak. They will need you to win. No other heir will be able to do what must be done. The glory to mine alone . . ." Her golden eyes turned distant, and the insignia on her forehead glowed, illuminating light into the dark shadows.

"What do you mean?" Risk asked, frowning.

"You'll see," Mazzulah said, briskly turning away. "I have said much, but there are still things I cannot say. Some rules must be followed. I cannot risk it . . ."

"Risk what?"

"You'll see," Mazzulah said again, returning to her throne.

"When the time comes, tell Quinn that she knows what to do if she wishes to win the game."

Risk clenched her teeth. "I don't suppose you'll tell me more than that?"

"No," Mazzulah shrugged. "I can't. I won't. The wheels are spinning. The board is set. All that's left is for the final cascade to begin, for the winner will take all."

The dark god ran her hands over the armrests of her throne. Red-tinted water dripped down her face, running in rivulets over her neck and between her cleavage. If not for Risk's makeshift shirt she'd created out of palm fronds and leaves of the forest, she would likely look the same.

"Then it's time," Risk said, turning away from the god. She reached the edge of the steps, and Rainier came up beside her. When she descended this time, it would be of her own volition.

"Actually," Mazzulah said. If Risk's heart had beat, it might have jumped at the inflection of the god's voice. Risk turned her head and narrowed her eyes. "There is one more thing . . ." Mazzulah said softly. Seductively. Her smile held a secret, and Risk knew that whatever this last thing could be, it was the real reason the dark god had kept her here.

CHAPTER 34
CHAMPIONS OF THE GODS

"Dark and light are as relative as good and evil."
— Quinn Darkova, fear twister, walker of realms, Neiss' heir

Draeven's foot tapping was driving Quinn insane.

"Can you stop that?" she snapped. He paused. His legs stilling as he looked up at her from across the mahogany table.

"Sorry," he mumbled. His violet eyes were bloodshot and tired. The weeks had been grueling in their preparations for the Trienian army, and while that was important, they could defeat the army itself and it would mean nothing if they couldn't find the light gods' heirs.

"Arguing amongst ourselves won't help us,"

Thorne pointed out, stroking a hand through his red beard. Quinn narrowed her eyes but didn't comment.

"The continent is full of people," Dominicus said, redirecting the conversation. "It's impossible to know who all the heirs are."

"I hate to say it," Draeven added, "but I agree with Dominicus. We don't even know for certain which one Nero is."

Quinn tsked under her breath, and the weapons master bristled while Draeven simply sighed.

"If you have a thought, just say it," Dominicus said in a hard voice.

Quinn leaned forward, staring at the wooden figures of the gods. She picked up Neiss' figurine, turning it over in her hand. "I am Neiss' chosen one." She set it down on the right side of her and picked up another. "Lazarus is Beliphor's." Quinn placed it beside the first. "I have a strong suspicion that Axe is Saltira's." At the mention of her name, the young queen simply cocked a brow. She was mercurial these days. More volatile, and prone to even greater mood swings. Quinn and the others let her be because they understood that grief was wild.

Next, she picked up Mazzulah's. "My sister Risk is Mazzulah's, though Mazzulah is considered a dark god because they were once king and then deposed. They control the dark realm, but that's because they are also the god of beasts. We consider beast tamers to be gray Maji. Perhaps the lines between light and dark are not as stark as they seem . . ." She twisted the figure between her palms. The wood carving was nothing like the actual god. Only a sad imitation.

"If Saltira chose a non-Maji for her heir, I would think that anything is possible," Lorraine said, sitting on Quinn's other side.

"Which only further shows that anyone could be an heir. Not just Maji," Dominicus argued, earning himself a sharp look from Lorraine that left him glaring at Quinn in turn.

"Yes . . ." Quinn mused. "But there's something that all of these gods have in common."

She placed Mazzulah's wooden carving beside the other three.

"What is that?" Thorne asked.

"They were all statues at the dark temple in N'skara. This place is the only gate to the dark realm on this continent, possibly in this world. It predates N'skara as we know it, which makes me believe they are the original gods, even if history has chosen otherwise."

"Were there other statues at the gate?" Lazarus asked, his voice soft but deep. He was facing away from the table and toward the window instead, seeming to watch something no one else could see.

"Yes," Quinn said. She picked up the statues of Tikkoh and Leviathan.

"God of Fire, and God of Moon and Shadows," Thorne said.

"Dominicus seems the most likely heir for Leviathan," Draeven said.

"I'm not so certain," Quinn replied. "Leviathan is the god that oversees the night. He's a friend to the shadows. The only light that truly coexists with the dark without overpowering it . . ." Quinn's eyes slowly lifted to look at Draeven. "I think his heir will be less obvious," she said. "And less surly."

Dominicus rolled his eyes, and Quinn set the figure aside.

"Tikkoh, however, I think is quite obvious," she said.

"Who?" Dominicus asked.

"Me," Draeven said, without Quinn needing to speak. She inclined her head toward him.

"His Maji mark is a ring of fire. It's the same symbol as Tikkoh's," Quinn said. "While not the strangest mark for a rage thief to bear, it's uncanny that you, much like I, were brought here by certain . . . . circumstances. With what I know of the gods, I believe that was him pushing you this way."

Lazarus seemed to sense where the conversation was going because he chose that moment to turn away from the window. "Who the dark heirs are matters less than the light, but if what you say is true, then it's possible the light heirs are from the gods' temple in N'skara as well." His dark eyes settled on her. "Do you remember whose were in front of the temple?"

"Yes," Quinn said, leaning back as she sat the final figure aside. She picked out six more from the dozen or so remaining on the table and placed them on her left.

"Ramiel, the God of Balance and Justice," she said, motioning to the figure that was slightly larger than the others and held a sword.

"Skadi, the Goddess of the Winter." This one wore a long flowing robe. The wooden face was blank, desolate.

"Leviticus, the God of Sun and Light." This figurine stood opposite of his twin, Leviathan.

"Telerah, the Goddess of Peace." She wore a flower crown and palms together in a motion of prayer. Quinn wrinkled her nose. She didn't pray to anyone, certainly not the gods.

"Vissilez, the God of Magic." He wore long robes similar to that of the N'skaran people. In his hand, some sort of artifact sat, though she couldn't tell what.

"And Myori, Goddess of the Sea." The stormy expression didn't really match the seashell clothing. Her trident was even taller than she, and it pointed threateningly in front of her as if she'd strike anyone down.

"What are the odds that one of these heirs died when you razed N'skara to the ground?" Draeven asked.

"Low." Quinn brushed a stray lock of lavender hair from her face, tucking it behind her ear. "Most of those left were lowborn. While Kairick is a soul eater, it's only because of his age he wasn't yet discovered. All the N'skaran highborn were taken to the Triene."

"They were a seafaring people. I suspect most of them will be placed on his armada," Lazarus said, narrowing his eyes at the board.

"Straitlaced gits or not, I'll end them if they're in league with that cock sucker."

"Axe," Lorraine chided softly. The pirate queen shrugged dismissively, and Lorraine muttered something about everyone losing their senses. Quinn cracked a grin.

"While knowing the gods is useful, it still tells us very little about who their champions are," Draeven said, redirecting the conversation just as Dominicus had done.

"Did Mazzulah specifically say they had to die?" Lorraine asked.

Quinn mulled over that answer, thinking over her times in the dark realm. Recalling the deal made. "Mazzulah said we had to win, but not what that meant or how."

"Defeating the army could win the war?" Lazarus said.

"Not necessarily," Quin said. "Talk of death and revenge was mixed in there, but you have to understand that Mazzulah isn't entirely sane. For a being in near isolation for that long, deity or not, it changes you."

"You speak like you know of it," Draeven said softly. Almost empathetically. Quinn could sense Lazarus awaiting her answer. While he'd questioned her much, there were still things she avoided. Topics she preferred not to talk of.

"I do," she answered. "While only months passed here, I was in the dark realm a very long time. Things are different there and I was adored by a god older than time itself. I spent more time with Mazzulah than I have with the rest of you several times over. It's a strange thing, and I can only imagine what it's like inside their mind." She trailed her fingers over the wooden image carved in the likeness of his male form. "I saw snippets of it sometimes. Fragments. The gods are not kind. They are not benevolent. They might have created us, but they made us for the purpose of toying with us. We're all but slaves to their wills as they decide what destiny and fate is. This game they've been playing ends with this war, and I can only assume that means taking out the pieces on the board. The army is important, but none of us will be free until we find the heirs and end them."

"Are you afraid of them?" Dominicus asked boldly.

Quinn snorted. "Never. I do not fear. However, I've spent enough time with one of them to know we shouldn't be stupid. The army is important, but it's foolish to focus on that alone."

A knock at the door made them all turn. It

cracked open, and a guard stepped inside. It was not one of Lazarus' however, but Thorne's.

"What is it, Nemiah?" the Cisean leader asked.

"We received word from the pass," he said.

"And? Spit it out, my boy, we haven't got all day."

The guard's face didn't twitch. The somberness in it not able to be lifted even by Thorne's easy nature. Quinn sensed his anxiousness. Fear was riding him. She cocked her head.

"Our men have been overrun. We've lost the passage through the mountains."

Shock went through those in the room that could understand Cisean.

"The army?" Quinn asked him. "It's already there?"

Impossible. That was far too fast for even the lowest numbers they'd heard reported.

"No," the guard said, shaking his head. "They didn't fly purple and gold."

"What colors were their banners?" Lazarus asked, his voice full of threat and fury.

"Green and silver," Nemiah said. "As well as red and white."

Bangratas and Jibreal.

They had questioned why no messages were ever sent back, why no spies seemed to return.

It was not because their messengers were inter-cepted. It was because they'd allied themselves with the other side.

"Those double-crossing bastards," Axe said, letting loose a string of curses.

"What's happened?" Lorraine asked.

"Bangratas and Jibreal have broken through the pass in the mountains and are marching for us as we speak," Quinn told the others who couldn't understand.

"Gods help us," Draeven said, running a hand through his dirty-blonde hair.

"Haven't you been listening?" Quinn asked him. "The gods are the last ones we should be praying to. We have to help ourselves."

As fighting broke out amongst them, Quinn noted how Lazarus only stared at her. His head tilted. Their eyes met. He nodded once, which meant it was time to start putting plans into motion.

"Prepare the men, ready the Maji. If they've indeed broken through the pass, we only have days before the full force of both countries will be upon us."

"Lazarus, are you certain we shouldn't be retreating for Dumas right now? Dumas has walls, the ocean. Shallowyn doesn't have the same defenses—"

"Yes," Lazarus said. "And that's exactly why we'll stay. This is only the beginning. They are the prequel for what's coming. We're going to need those walls and that ocean for Nero's army. Shallowyn can be rebuilt, but if we lose our strongest hold this early in the fighting, we won't last. Now leave me and make the arrangements."

The other vassals got to their feet and began preparations, but Quinn was no longer a vassal. She looked over the wooden figurines once more, thoughts of the other champions weighing heavily on her despite the coming battle. It was only in that second pass that she noticed something about Leviathan.

Something almost completely obscured, if not for the slight rounding of the wood with deeper indentations. In his hand, there was a small vial. Understanding dawned on her, but she tucked it away, watching as everyone left the room.

*"They say it's poor taste to kill the messenger, but that action is
sending a message too."*
— *Lazarus Fierté, soul eater, the less-mad King of Norcasta*

"She's come a long way," Lorraine said, walking beside him. He stood on the raised platform of Shallowyn overseeing the Maji training.

"She has," he agreed. Below them, Quinn stood with her back straight and shoulders proud as she instructed the Maji, having more patience than he thought she were capable of. Kairick was among them and progressing surprisingly fast under Quinn's tutelage. He was further along in his control over his magic than most of the grown men and women. "Are you here to give me a lesson on letting her train

Kairick with the rest of them?" he asked, turning to look at his stewardess.

"No," Lorraine said. Her brown eyes still settled on Quinn and the boy. A faint smile curled up her lips. "He listens to her more than anyone. If she tells him not to hurt them, he won't. Dominicus is just paranoid. His distrust of magic runs deep."

"He needs to get past it," Lazarus said. "We don't have time for that."

"I agree," Lorraine said. "But he's stubborn as an ox. Much like Quinn in that regard. Telling someone to get over something often doesn't make them do it. If anything, it tends to make it worse."

He watched Quinn pair them off, putting Kairick with a water weaver of greater skill. She walked around them in a circle as they began to spar. The water weaver pulled from the ground and sent a whip at the young boy. Kairick responded by calling on his firedrake. A spray of deadly quills shot down his arm that he flung toward the more advanced Maji.

If Draeven were in charge, he would have intervened.

But Draeven wasn't, and Quinn did not.

The weaver summoned a wall and turned it to ice when the quills were only inches from his face. They embedded deeply, their sharp ends pointed at him, but the weaver was unharmed.

"I'm assuming you've come out here for a

different reason if it wasn't to chastise me like the others?"

"I have," she said. Lorraine pulled a piece of parchment from her pocket and extended it. "Word from the south finally came. The soldiers from Leone intercepted the supply line behind the Trienian army." He took the paper from her. Its texture rough between his fingers as he opened it. "While the line was long, they couldn't get accurate estimates on the number of troops because every man and woman killed themselves before they could be questioned."

Lazarus' blood ran cold.

"All of them?"

"There were no survivors," Lorraine said. His eyes scanned the letter. Hundreds of men and women. They stabbed themselves and slit their own throats.

"Thank you for bringing me this," he said, a polite dismissal. Lorraine was usually the first to leave when he did, but this time she stayed. Hesitating.

"I realize I am only a stewardess and an apothecary. Both Draeven and Dominicus are more skilled in the arts of war, but if I may be so bold, something isn't right. Not even trained soldiers all fall on their swords when captured. These men and women were merchants, farmers, blacksmiths, and people too weak for the army to take." She brushed a stray gray hair back, tucking it into her braid before folding her hands over the front of her dress. "Something is amiss here, and I don't know if it's the gods or Nero himself, but I suspect foul play."

"You're not alone in that," Lazarus said. "It's why we aren't retreating to Dumas. Not yet. If Nero's army is even fifty thousand men, he has enough to block us in the city. He may not even push for a siege when he could starve us out. Both our and the Ilvan armada are transferring as much food as possible to the city as we speak. We need to cripple the other armies before falling back."

Lorraine bowed her head. "I understand, Your Grace."

She stepped back to leave, and Lazarus said, "Thank you, Lorraine. Let me know if you receive any more reports."

As Lorraine turned to leave, a shout came from the clearing below.

"Make way," a man on a horse yelled in brutish Norcastan. The soldiers near the far edge of the trees parted. He came out of the forest with his head high and waving the banner of Lazarus' enemies. He had blonde hair and wore a sash of red and white. Behind him, another rider followed, this one in green and silver.

Both the kuras and the bloodlion ran past him, coming up on either side of Quinn to flank her as the Maji parted.

"What is this?" he asked, projecting his voice over the training ground.

Whispers broke out, but with a single, sharp command from Quinn, they quieted.

"Silence," she snapped. The clomping of hooves as the intruders slowly made their way over the five hundred meters was a treacherous walk.

Only when they were within spitting distance of Quinn did they stop.

Lazarus had a feeling it had more to do with the growling kuras at her side than anything else. Cold winds drifted over Shallowyn as an unnatural frigid air settled over them. Quinn hadn't reached for the knives strapped to her waist or back yet, but that didn't mean she was calm.

It was quite the opposite. He sensed that darkness building in her at the very sight of them. Her lips pulled back in a snarl.

"His Majesty asked you a question, messengers." Her voice was filled with wrath held only by the greatest of restraint. The one closest to her swallowed, looking far less certain than when he'd stepped out of the forest.

"We come on behalf of King Elijah of Bangratas, and King Doran of Jibreal. They propose to negotiate the terms of your surrender."

The training grounds had gone utterly silent as Lazarus considered his answer. Before he could say a word, Quinn chose to speak.

"Surrender?" she asked quietly. "What a quaint

offer from your traitorous kings. Is that what they are calling the massacre they have planned?"

The messengers shared a look.

It was not the woman they were speaking to, but the fear twister they'd egged on and brought forth.

One of them coughed, shaking the tremble off that ran through him.

"How does Your Grace wish to proceed?" His voice shook from the building fear, and Lazarus wondered if Quinn realized she was doing it.

Still, he answered.

"There will be no surrender. Your kingdoms come at their own demise."

Their faces turned white. Ashen with the growing unease coming from the woman at the steps. The kuras whined a high-pitched sound. The bloodlion arched its back and hissed in their direction. They did not like these outsiders so close to her. They did not like the wrath they incurred or the threat they represented.

"Very well, we will deliver—"

"Not so fast," Quinn said, stepping forward. She lifted a hand, and Neiss slithered forth, dropping out of her skin and snaking down the compacted dirt, straight for the horse closest to him. "They sent two messengers, but only one of you is needed. I'd like to add to my king's response."

Neiss grew in size, becoming large enough that the horses started to spook. He was faster, though, winding himself around the first mare's legs, snaking upward and trapping it. The creature bucked, tossing its rider, and Neiss grew ever larger, then opened his gaping jaws to devour the horse entirely.

The rider hit the dirt, and the Maji surrounding him all stepped away. He scrambled to his feet, or at least tried to. "Show them how we treat traitors here," she commanded. Kairick stepped in front of her and his firedrake descended from the sky. A wild screech echoed through the valley as the great bird descended on the man. It snapped its jaws at his arms and crimson squirted. Neither the boy nor Quinn winced as the creature picked him apart piece by piece.

It was gory and horrifying and powerful.

When the beast went for the head, Quinn lifted her hand.

"Not that part. We'll send that back with this messenger so he can tell the others what awaits them."

Kairick whispered, and while Lazarus couldn't hear the words, the firedrake stopped its assault. It tossed the torso of the man up in the air and then jumped into the sky, snatching it before flying off. Little more than bits of severed limbs and a pool of blood remained.

But the head was intact.

"Neiss," Quinn said, with a lifted eyebrow. The snake seemed to sullenly release its would-be meal and returned to Quinn. A tendril of fear leapt from her hand, sending the heading flying. The remaining messenger trying to flee paused as it rolled toward him. His eyes were wide as Quinn grinned savagely at him. "Take that with you, and let Elijah and Doran know that I will be seeing to them *personally* when I get my hands on them. I don't like liars, and I don't respect traitors. I will burn both their lineages at the stake for what they've done."

As the messenger scrambled to pick up the fallen head, Lazarus saw Lorraine stiffen from the corner of his eye. She hadn't left as she'd intended, but instead heard as Quinn swore to kill Doran's lineage. He only had one heir. One that hadn't been seen or spoken of in over a decade.

Her son.

"Mazzulah had said that loving her was akin to loving destruction, and the god wasn't wrong about who or what she was. She wreaked havoc wherever she went, but only in earning her love and loyalty could one guarantee their own survival."
— *Quinn Darkova, fear twister, walker of realms*

The sun was nearing the horizon. In the distance, banners flew.

Green and silver.

Red and white.

Quinn turned away from the balcony and went to braid her hair away from her face. Lazarus had already gone with Draeven and Dominicus, readying what army they had. In his absence, she prepared herself for battle. Donning the red and gold armor he'd had made for her before her untimely death. She'd never had a chance to wear it. Now she did.

Quinn was just putting on the light chain mail when a knock made her pause. "Come in," she called. She couldn't sense who was in the hall, which meant it could only be one person.

Lorraine opened the door and stepped inside. Dark circles lined her eyes. The crinkles at the corners of them were more pronounced this morning. If Quinn had to guess, the other woman likely hadn't slept a wink. Neither had Lazarus, or most of Shallowyn.

"Need some help?" she offered.

"Alright," Quinn said, turning to lift the breastplate to her chest. There were decent odds she'd be naked before the battle even got truly underway if she needed to slip into the spirit realm, but wearing the metal pieces assuaged Lazarus' desires to control her. It didn't hurt that seeing her in his colors would present them as a united front.

"Word has it they've nearly a hundred thousand men," Lorraine said softly, securing the back plate to the front with the snaps on her shoulders.

Quinn let out a low whistle. "We've only got fifty thousand, including Dumas," she said. "We'll have to end this quickly to minimize casualties."

Next, they secured her arm pieces. Lorraine's

nimble fingers fastening the straps with quick efficiency.

"I have complete faith in you that you'll be victorious," Lorraine said. Quinn handed her the thigh pieces and stood taller as the other woman knelt to strap those on too.

"This is only the beginning. There is no other option but victory. If we lose too many now, we won't stand a chance with Nero's army."

Lorraine didn't say anything. There was a hum in the silence. A thickness in the air that had little to do with the damp morning, and more to do with the armies that would clash today. Quinn couldn't feel anxiety for it was just another form of fear. But she could sense trepidation in others, and even without the ability to read Lorraine, the worry that creased the stewardess' features was apparent.

"You will do what needs to be done. That's why you're the right-hand," she said softly.

"I'm not his hand anymore," Quinn said. "Though I choose to act it."

"I suppose that's true," she murmured, toying with a particularly tricky clasp. "You've chosen to act as a hand even though you scheme as much as he does."

Quinn gave her a wry grin. "You sound resigned."

"On the contrary, I find it refreshing. While you've always been unrefined, your cunning and brutality give you a mind for battle and war. You see beyond the obvious. You were always meant to be more than just a dog told to bite."

Lorraine sat back to admire her handiwork before giving the plating over her knee a sharp tug. When the piece only shifted a fraction but didn't slip, she gave it a pleased nod before standing.

"Where did you learn to put on armor?" Quinn asked her as she turned to pick up the helm. It was closer to a crown than anything. The golden head piece came up to form sharp spikes, twining metal that was red in color formed thorny brambles around the bottom of it. A thin gold base that came down and formed her face on either side kept the brambles from piercing her skin.

It was beautiful and terrifying.

Quinn loved it.

"My husband," Lorraine answered softly.

Quinn looked over at her, noticing then how she toyed with the edge of her dress, picking at nothing in particular. Her pulse fluttered. Her skin was clammy. Quinn knew the signs of fear and anxiety well.

"I didn't know you were married," Quinn said slowly.

"Once," Lorraine replied. "It was a long time ago."

"Is he who you were seeking asylum from?" Quinn asked, her eyes narrowing. She couldn't make sense of why Lorraine was nervous. *Was it the battle? Perhaps . . .*

"I was," she answered. "My husband . . . he was a very powerful man. No one would take me in and risk his ire. No one but Lazarus, that is."

"That's why you're so loyal to him," Quinn said slowly.

"It is," Lorraine nodded. "Listen—"

A horn sounded. The single note hung in the air. Long and low and forlorn.

It was time.

She and Lorraine exchanged a look. She was hiding something. Or rather, wanted to reveal something. Quinn could tell, but battle was calling.

"Afterwards," Lorraine said, dropping it. "Come find me afterwards when you've won. Then we'll talk."

Quinn scanned her features. If it were anyone else, she might have been wary. She might have started to question them. To wonder.

But not Lorraine.

"Afterwards," Quinn agreed. Lorraine tucked a stray lavender hair under the metal headpiece and smiled.

"Now you're ready."

She turned to look in the mirror, and the woman that looked back didn't look like a slave, or a hand, or even a queen—though Lazarus clearly modeled her head piece after a crown.

She looked like a god.

A deity so great that men would quake in fear as she walked.

Immortal and inhuman.

Powerful.

Then she smiled because Lorraine was right. She was ready.

Quinn strapped on her sword and donned her daggers. When she stepped out of Lazarus' quarters, the vassals stopped in their tracks and stared. Their heads bowed without her saying a word as she passed by. The sounds of fighting echoed in the distance, and Quinn picked up her pace. Her boots slapped against the hard marble as she stormed down the steps of Shallowyn and stopped before the line of horses waiting to be used to carry messengers back and forth swiftly.

She approached the first of them, extending her hand as Risk taught her.

But in dying, the fear that wafted off her very being had become all the more potent, and the creature wouldn't be calmed. She cast a frustrating look at the stable boy who jumped forward in an attempt to help her rein it in, but the stallion broke free and moved back, kicking up dust with its front legs.

"Myori's Wrath," Quinn coughed, waving it off. She stepped away, and the horse soothed immediately, much to her annoyance.

She needed to get to the front lines . . .

"Quinn!" a young voice called out. She looked up,

shielding her eyes from the sun. Kairick stood at the top of the steps. The firedrake he'd consumed beside him. "Ride Tarien," he said.

Quinn ran an appraising eye over the great bird. It could easily hold her weight, but she'd need to take care to avoid the deadly sharp feathers and their poisonous edges. The beast turned its head, one yellow eye staring straight at her.

Quinn found herself intrigued. Emboldened even. Death did that to her sometimes.

"Alright," she said, ascending the steps. The firedrake lowered itself, allowing her to walk over the top of its wing as she'd seen Kairick do a hundred times. It waited patiently for her to seat herself, placing her legs on either side of its neck.

He lifted his head and looked at Kairick.

But the N'skaran boy only had eyes for Quinn.

"Be safe," he said solemnly, slipping back into their home language even though he'd come a good way in learning Norcastan.

"The only ones who should be afraid are those who seek to hurt me," she said.

He swallowed and nodded once, and the firedrake lifted its wings.

In a single flap, they were airborne. The cold winds of winter's edge beat at her face as they rose over the treetops. Quinn fisted her hands in the softer, non-lethal down feathers where Tarien's neck met his sternum.

The battle came into sight.

The firedrake let out a screech that bordered on a roar.

A giddy sort of excitement filled her at what she was going to do.

It had been too long since she truly had let her power out to play.

Too long since she'd pushed herself to her edge and then toppled over into that sweet, sweet darkness.

Fear was what she lived for, and while the armies of Jibreal and Bangratas didn't know it yet—fear was what had come for them.

CHAPTER 37
FEAR UNLEASHED

*"Only true friends take the time to call you a fool while they're
dying, for it takes a fool to know a fool."*
— *Lazarus Fierté, soul eater, King of Norcasta*

L azarus' sword swung, metal meeting bone as he
beheaded another opponent when a vengeful
outcry rippled over the grassy valley.

Every man, woman, and soldier looked up.

A dark shadow flew across the sky, wings spread
wide to block out the sun. Red feathers glinted as the
firedrake turned to the side. On his back was a rider
dressed in golden armor.

Black tendrils snaked behind them, like scattered
ashes across the sky.

Her lavender hair a flag, waving in the wind.

Lazarus grinned viciously, turning to impale another soldier.

"She would ride a firedrake into battle," Draeven yelled over the clash of swords and singing of steel. He swung once, his violet eyes turning red. Channeling the power of a rage thief, he cut his opponent in half. The blade sliding through armor and flesh and bone as if it were butter. "Only someone who can't feel fear would ever get on one of those beasts."

The firedrake swooped low over his soldiers, heading straight for enemy lines. Its wingspan was easily twenty feet from tip to tip, and it carried its shadow over the battlefield. Quinn thrust her hand outward and a wave of black magic shot forth. Instead of inflicting harm upon the other army, they aimlessly swirled in the sky above.

"What in the dark realm is she doing?" Dominicus called, smoothly slitting another man's throat.

Lazarus titled his head to the side.

As the firedrake started to turn, the swirling mists gathered to form a giant number in the sky. Seven.

Seven?

Lazarus frowned as deadly feathers shot from the firedrake's wings.

While she was clearly trying to aim for the other army, there was no true way to discern who it would hit. Lazarus opened his mouth to give a command for them to get down when the unimaginable happened.

Water shot up from the battle lines like geysers

into the sky. They spread over the front of the Norcastan army, like thin pools that contorted light in the sky. The spread only stopped when each geyser of water touched at the edges. Just as the deadly feathers reached them, the wave above his men turned to ice —protecting his forces while allowing his enemies to perish.

The clang of metal gave way to screams. The sharp edges of the firedrake's feathers were so poisonous and sharp that any who had been harmed by one would be dead in less than a minute.

The ice melted and returned to the ground just as another number formed in the sky.

Three.

This time when the beast swept, it opened its gaping jaws and released a great breath of flame. Unnatural winds gathered that fire and kept it from crossing into Lazarus' army, instead sending it further into the Jibreal and Bangrati forces.

Those screams overpowered the sounds of battle.

"They're rotations," Lazarus said, both impressed and not entirely surprised. He twisted the longsword in his grip and funneled the strength of the troll to stab the metal straight through another man's breastplate. Blood leaked from his lips. Pain contorted his face, and then he was forgotten. Just another face in the endless onslaught as he thought of Quinn. "She taught them rotations for what to do on her command."

Another number appeared and Lazarus wished he would have focused more on what she was teaching them than on the woman herself. All those times he'd watched her training them, and he had no idea what it meant.

The ground shook.

"What does one mean?" Draeven yelled as massive sections of the ground itself lifted into the sky. Grass and dirt and rock, all shot upward to form a wall between the two armies. The sections came up one at a time, quivering as if the Maji controlling it were struggling to hold, and then settling as if resolve had kicked in. The sky darkened as black tendrils began to eclipse the sun. Terror filled his veins and that of every other soldier.

"I don't know," Lazarus said, the breath hissing between his teeth.

What he did know was that she was planning something big. There was no other reason for the separation between armies. Fear and trepidation bled into him, and they were not his own. He sensed her everywhere and nowhere at once. His own grief over her loss surfaced, still fresh even after the weeks he'd had with her. His paranoia blossomed. His anxiety began to claw.

He lifted his hand and called forth his firedrake.

The beast came without delay and shot into the sky.

Lazarus focused on what the creature was seeing as it overcame the wall, but he was not prepared for it.

Not as he thought.

Quinn slid from the firedrake's back and fell forty feet through the air. Her braid whipped up and her arms spread wide. Not a single trace of fear touched her face as she plummeted, and Lazarus' chest tightened for a brief, suspenseful moment.

"What's going on over the wall?" someone called, whether it was Draeven or Dominicus he wasn't sure. All of his attention was on Quinn as she landed on one knee, fist planted into the ground. A shockwave went through the battlefield, strong enough that the walls of dirt began to crumble, straining against her raw power.

She lifted her head, and a shudder went through him.

Not a spec of blue was in her gaze.

Her eyes had gone wholly and utterly black. The veins around her face darkened. Her skin paled even further.

She looked like death incarnate.

A reaper of destruction.

Fear given form.

His vision on her cut out as something slammed into him. Lazarus stumbled backwards and lifted his sword, then paused.

It was Draeven.

Blood covered his armor. Lazarus didn't realize at

first whose blood it was. Not until he noticed the sharp blade that had been rammed through his hand's shoulder. He'd pushed Lazarus out of the way and had taken what might have been a killing blow, given their difference in height.

Lazarus surged as Draeven disarmed the soldier, then stabbed him through the neck, before dropping his sword. He swayed on his feet, and Lazarus was there before he could fall.

"You need to get back to Shallowyn," Lazarus said.

"But then who would protect you from making stupid mistakes for that woman?" Draeven answered through gritted teeth. "She was right, you know. All those times she called you a fool. You are. You're a fool."

Lazarus pressed his lips together as he looped Draeven's good arm over his neck. He carried half his weight and battled off the stray soldier with his other. "We can discuss you thinking I'm a fool after you've seen the healers—"

"There is no discussion. You're a fool to be in love with Quinn, but love isn't logical. Otherwise you'd know she doesn't need your help or your worry. She's the most dangerous one on the field right now."

As if to prove his point, another pulse of power shot from the other side of the wall and the dirt crumbled entirely.

Shouts rang out. But they didn't come from the

other side as the wall collapsed. A mound of dirt only a few feet high remained, but it was short enough and close enough that he could see with his own eyes why none of the opposing army had scattered.

The Jibreal and Bangrati armies were fighting *each other.*

Their faces were contorted in pain as soldier hacked soldier apart. Brother killing brother. They were vicious in their assaults. Removing limbs one by one, swing by swing, before ending it.

Even horribly injured, Draeven managed to give him a wry look, weariness not far beneath it.

Lazarus scowled and continued dragging him through the line of men. Overhead, the firedrakes both screeched and rained flame upon their enemies.

They might have been facing an army with a hundred thousand men, but as Quinn had proven time and time again, men were little more than pawns when she chose to play the game.

They could not fight her fear any more than they could the fire, and quickly, the enemy numbers began to dwindle.

"You need to stay," Draeven said in a strained voice.

"We can't. You're gushing blood—"

"I didn't say we," Draeven groaned. "You. You need to stay."

Draeven lifted his head. A sheen of sweat and dirt covered his face. His cheeks were flushed. But his eyes, those were wise. Despite the rage that may have coursed through his system, Draeven was holding onto himself.

"She will win this battle, but her rage—if I cannot be here to dampen it when the killing ends then someone must. She came back from the dead for you. I have to hope she can stop the killing for you too." Every word was dragged from his lips. Exhaustion and blood loss getting to him.

He could stop any soldier he wanted and command them to take Draeven back in his stead, but he did not trust any other to get him back in time. Not when his life was already waning . . . but there was one. One who was strong enough to carry his hand. One who could run near as fast as a horse.

Lazarus took a breath and then released the troll.

The shadow of its soul slipped forward and cemented. A beast nine feet tall with skin hard as leather. He looked similar to men, but there was no mistaking what he was. Not with the height and the misshapen face.

Lazarus looked at the beast he hadn't dared let out since Quinn's death, but he was the only one that could do this.

"You take him to Lorraine and stand guard at Shallowyn. If he dies, so do you."

Draeven's eyes fluttered, a brief look of surprise, but not alarm.

"You said you'd never forgive me for what

happened to her," Draeven rasped as the troll leaned down and lifted him as if he were a mere child and not a man.

"I don't have to forgive you to not want you dead," Lazarus replied. True and yet, not the whole truth.

"Be safe—" Draeven's rasp of a warning cut off as blood tinged his lips.

"Take him. Now," Lazarus commanded. The troll nodded once and turned, running the opposite way of the battle and toward the manor. Toward Shallowyn.

Soldiers cleared the way, stepping aside at the mere sight of the beast.

Lazarus pushed aside the worry that tugged him. Draeven would make it. He was strong. But the fight for his life was his own now. His and Lorraine's.

Lazarus feared Draeven was right. Quinn . . . she was just getting started.

CHAPTER 38
EDGE OF DARKNESS

"When we are nearest to the end, it is the things we want most that we cling to."
— *Draeven Adelmar, rage thief, left-hand to the King of Norcasta, dying*

Draeven hissed in pain as the troll ran, unintentionally jostling his wound.

It was bad. He knew it was bad, but he couldn't die now.

He wouldn't. Not when they were so close.

Not when there was a beast tamer he was waiting to see again.

Draeven didn't notice how he was fading. Nor did he realize when Shallowyn came into view. It was only when shouting started once more that he even tried to stir and found it difficult.

Panic started to set in as he tried and failed to open his eyes.

His chest felt like it was on fire.

"Get me a healer," a strained, curt voice commanded. He knew that voice, though he couldn't place it. Not with the pain consuming him.

He didn't notice when they laid him down. There was no relief when the breastplate was pried from him, followed by the chainmail. The burning, though, that worsened as the tunic beneath his armor was cut away.

Voices drifted in and out.

Darkness was closing in.

And the barest touch of cold reached for him.

But a face swam into view. A face he dreamed of often. Gray skin the color of winter skies. Obsidian horns and a head full of silver hair. Blue eyes brighter than the sky and more piercing than the sharpest sword.

A keen intelligence shone through them. Her strong will conveyed in the set of her brow. But it was her lips, so full, that made her an open book to read. They showed her kindness and compassion, even when her haunting, piercing eyes could not.

Draeven thought of her face, and he held on.

Even as the burning lessened and the cold creeped closer and closer.

He thought of her and a warmth stirred inside him, battling off that chill.

A fire raged inside him.

Rage that she had left without so much as a word.

Longing, because he missed her.

While their time together had been brief, something in him called to her. Understood her. And felt it calling in return.

It was that call, that desire, that burning that fueled him.

He needed to see that face again before it was all over and the dark realm claimed him.

And so Draeven held on.

He held onto that light though the darkness threatened to claim him, but when he opened his eyes, it was not that face that looked at him.

Cast in shadows with only candlelight to show her features, a very tired Lorraine sat beside him. Her eyebrows drawn together in concern. Her shoulders heavy with the weight of silence. He noticed then that the fighting had stopped. There was no clash of metal. No ringing in the distance.

"Did we—" he started, his voice cracking. He didn't know how long had passed. Only that he'd made it and the fighting was over.

Lorraine nodded. "We won," she said simply. Curtly.

Relief filled him, but it was followed by uncertainty.

If they'd won, why did Lorraine look worried?

"A wise woman once said that if you love someone,
bring them the heads of their enemies."
— *Quinn Darkova, fear twister, walker of realms, torturer of
traitors, slayer of kings*

The battle had lasted from sunup to sundown.

As Leviticus' eye slipped below the horizon, all was quiet, and all was loud.

There was a roaring in her ears that had overwhelmed the screams at some point, and it had blocked out little else than the desire to unleash herself upon the world.

She bathed in their blood as they ripped each other apart.

She was baptized in their deaths as the sheer magnitude of what she'd done overcame her.

They'd been facing an army of a hundred thousand men. While Lazarus and his army had fought, Quinn had annihilated.

Thousands upon thousands of deaths were on her hands. They were so stained red they actually appeared black in the low light of sunset.

But when there were no more to slaughter, when the colors of green and silver and red and white and gold all started to blur, Quinn took a deep breath. She inhaled the scent of copper and death. She savored the taste of blood on her lips and tilted her head back to smile at the sky as the clouds opened up. Rain poured down on the graveyard she'd made.

"It's over," said a deep, masculine voice that resonated like thunder.

"No," Quinn replied. "Not quite."

She lowered her head once more and looked Lazarus in the eyes. She knew what he saw. A fear twister that was more. A woman who was life and death wrapped into one. He didn't shy away from her cold, calculating gaze. She was on the edge of dancing with Mazzulah, but not quite there yet. There was one more thing, well, two, that needed her attention.

She peered past him to the two men that were placed on a wagon. Their hands had been tied behind their backs. Rags still soaked with some forgotten soldier's blood was pressed between their lips. They stared at her, fear and hatred in their eyes. She stared right back.

"I'm not sure if that's wise," Lazarus started, taking a step toward her. She moved to the side and strode forward, brushing him off.

"I made a deal with both of them. A deal they broke when they decided to ally with Triene behind our backs." She hissed the last word at them, and Elijah's eyes shuttered. "I promised vengeance on them and their lines because I don't like liars and traitors. I will deal with them."

Much of Lazarus' army had survived. They were picking over the field, searching for their own. To honor them for their service. At the tone in her voice every head within fifty yards lifted and then turned away as they all wandered further from her location. It was only the soldier at the front of the wagon, guiding the horses, that said, "Where would you like them, my lady?"

Lazarus didn't comment on the fact that his soldier had addressed her, asked her where they would go—and not him. Quinn knew it was because of what she'd done here. That while some men knew her from Leone, many had only heard the stories. What they'd just seen with their eyes was her saving them. Her ending the battle before it raged for days. Her saving their lives by flying a firedrake into the very center of the enemy and unleashing her deadly magic upon them.

Lazarus might be king, but she was something more to them.

She was a savior.

Quinn tsked, shaking her head, and then said, "The dungeons."

The soldier nodded once. Two others joined him, riding in the back beside the fallen kings. He made a sound with his mouth and snapped the reins once. The horses took off, the wagon with them, returning to Shallowyn.

"They look up to you," Lazarus said.

"They fear me. Fear us. We are gods to them, but benevolent ones, at least for the time being." Quinn started toward the wagon when a firedrake dropped out of the sky. It was Kairick's. The beast looked at her, as if to challenge her to ride him again.

"You slay tens of thousands of their enemies and ride a firedrake into battle. Of course, they fear you. They should."

"Does it bother you?" she asked, as she reached out a non-gloved hand to brush the very top of the bird's dangerous feathers. One wrong move, a slight ruffle from it, and she'd be dead. But the firedrake stood there, obedient to her almost as much as it was to its master.

While the horses may fear her, it seemed the monsters felt right at home.

"No," he said. She felt him come closer, to stand beside her. "It used to . . . but their fear will keep them in line, and their awe will keep them honest. If they look up to you, they won't turn on you."

She knew where his thoughts had gone. To a throne room where a crowd had turned on them. On her. She'd slaughtered them all, much like here. Except that battle hadn't ended so nicely for either of them.

"Probably not," she agreed. "But if they did, I'd kill them too. Their admiration for me keeps them safe, far more than it does me."

She lifted her hand, and the bird lowered its wings. Quinn walked across them, moving to seat herself behind its neck. Her legs straddling the softer, safer down feathers.

"It's been a long day. I won't tell you that you can't have them, but I urge you to wait. Celebrate with us first. Join me—"

"No," Quinn said sharply. "Nero's army draws near, and we are running out of time. Their deaths will be my celebration."

Lazarus stared at her, as if seeming to weigh his next words. Her mind still raced with aggression and war. She wasn't done. Not until she heard them sing. Not until she learned all they knew.

"Come find me when you're finished," Lazarus said at last. A blessing, not that she needed one.

Quinn nodded once and then the firedrake leapt into the sky.

It was a short ride this time. Not nearly as thrilling as it had been when she'd entered the battle. Shallowyn wasn't far. Just on the other side of the treeline.

The wagon was pulling up when they came into view.

The firedrake dropped down. A jolt rocked through her as its powerful haunches absorbed the impact and sent it straight through her spine. Tarien lowered himself and extended his wings, allowing for Quinn to lift her leg and shuffle to one side and then slide down its torso. Her boots touched the ground softly, only a crinkle of leaves giving her away. She strode past the soldiers that stopped and stared. They stepped aside for her, nodding and bowing and kneeling as she went.

Quinn ignored them, instead following the soldiers dragging the deposed kings through the halls. She trailed behind them as they descended deeper and deeper into Shallowyn. Taking a stairwell that went down the yard, leading to the catacombs, and just past them—the dungeon.

They tossed both men down in a cell and turned to Quinn. Before they could speak, she said, "Leave us."

They didn't need to be told twice.

Quinn didn't move from her spot until their footsteps faded. The heavy oak door slammed shut. When it was only the creaking of the metal gate stirring from a cold wind that blew through the cell window high above, the king called Elijah lifted his head.

"Get it over with, maruda," he spat. Quinn used to take offense to being called that. It was a wicked term for female Maji that went mad from the power. Hysteria, they called it.

Marudas murdered their husbands and sons in their beds while they slept.

They stole other women's husbands with their foul magic.

They were an old wives tale and a nasty slur, but of all the things to be called, Quinn didn't mind being a maruda. She hadn't in a long time.

"Calling me names won't make me go any faster," Quinn said softly. She was utterly silent as she strode forward. The cage they'd been placed in swung open, guided by an inky black tendril. "But I admire the attempt. You know who I am and what I do to people when I lose my temper. Unfortunately for you, I learned patience while I was dead."

Elijah shuddered. His dark blonde hair lank against his forehead. He'd once had tan skin, but it had turned quite pale over the last twelve hours. He almost looked as dead as her.

Quinn knelt before them and lifted a hand. Lazy wisps of black drifted off and brushed over both men.

Elijah began shaking in earnest, whereas Doran went still. His dark brown eyes narrowed in hatred.

"Now," Quinn murmured. "Tell me why you promised yourselves to Norcasta and then became an ally to our enemy."

Doran resisted, but Elijah didn't take much to sing like a little bird. She knew he wouldn't. He was the king of Bangratas. A softer king for a softer country. The mountains protected on one side, the ocean on the other. A desert separated them from most of Triene, and they and Jibreal had a very long, happy alliance.

"We were never friends," he growled. Her Bangrati was rough but passable enough to understand him.

"No?" she asked, sending more into him.

"Triene promised—"

"Don't speak. You know what the price will be," Doran warned.

Quinn tilted her head. "Oh?" she asked. He pressed his lips together, and she smiled.

It was a horrible, yet lovely thing.

Quinn reached for his throat, her bare skin touching his. "And what is that, Doran?"

His eyes narrowed into slits and the mere excess of her power bleeding into the air made Elijah piss himself. "Life," Doran ground out.

"Life?" That didn't make a great deal of sense. Death? Yes. But life . . .

"I didn't betray you for that reason," Doran said suddenly. Quinn knew he was trying to lead her away from this line of questioning. Of thinking. It wouldn't work. She'd get all the answers in the end, but she was curious what he had to say. "I betrayed you because your pathetic king stole my *wife*."

Quinn wasn't sure what he would say, but that hadn't been it.

Her face went blank. Doran grinned manically, taking her still features to mean he'd struck a nerve. Not understanding that it was when Quinn was quietest and most closed off that one should worry.

"Yes," he said. "My pretty little wife for his own. He'd visited us some ten years ago and then left with my wife and son." He sneered at her, and Quinn still didn't react. "When I saw you in the colosseum, I knew who you were. What you were. I picked you, preyed on you, learned all I could so that I knew the best way for Amelia to get under your skin." He grinned vilely. "I told Erwing of your raksasa sister for him to take an interest. I sent them to sow discord."

Anger, true anger, touched her then. He'd revealed a great deal to her already, and it wasn't even midnight.

"Lorraine was your wife," Quinn said.

"Is," he spat. "Marriage is eternal. She belonged to me then, and she belongs to me now."

Quinn's face hardened. "People don't belong to other people. We are not dogs."

He laughed then, the fear and his own madness bringing out the worst. She saw the monster beneath the skin. "That bitch might as well be. She tried to poison me, you know. I knew about it, though, and it didn't work, but when I sent my soldiers for her, she was already gone. She took my son with her. My *heir*."

"Lorraine might not always be a kind woman, but she is just. If she ran, there was a reason," Quinn murmured. "Let's find out the truth."

The black wisps changed shape, taking the form of spiders. They crawled over his clothes and across his skin, biting wherever they went. Quinn tasted his fear, and it was as potent as his evil. She reached forward and grabbed his jaw, prying his mouth open.

Doran started to beg. His eyes turning panicked and pleading.

Yes, he'd heard stories. Those tales were always a far cry from the reality. There was no way for them to convey the sheer inhumane methods Quinn used when she wanted the truth.

The spiders swarmed, entering his lips. Crawling down his throat. Pure fear filled him, and Quinn saw.

"You beat her," she snapped. "You raped *him*."

A child. His child. Disgust filled Quinn. Fury so cold it burned.

She saw Lorraine, young and beautiful and bruised. Oh, he'd picked her from hundreds of girls because she'd been nice to him when he was young. The youngest prince. The one so unlikely to get the throne that no ladies ever noticed him. He killed his brothers off one by one to take the throne, and her with it. Lorraine was a lord's daughter. She married him. She acted the beautiful wife, even when he was angry. Even when his slaps and backhands turned to fists. Bruises turned to broken bones.

Still, she dealt with it for years.

Until the night she caught him raping her son.

Doran was a special kind of twisted. He may have fucked her and loved her, but he was both jealous and obsessed with their son. His possessiveness knew no bounds. His depravity, the very worst sort. Quinn sorted through those memories, the twelve years he'd had Lorraine.

He'd even shared her with Elijah several times in their youth. But his son, what he did to him . . . no, Doran hadn't revealed that to anyone. Even he knew how horrible it made him.

It was the day after Lorraine caught him that she tried to poison him.

Lorraine, who dealt with so much. Who endured what she never should have had to endure because of his fascination with her. She snapped.

That was why she'd run to Lazarus. Asylum, she had called it.

Quinn shook her head, but she kept watching, seeing.

She was going to rake through his mind like a knife and leave it in tatters. Only when she'd broken him so well and true would Quinn surface.

"Did you know," she told them, "that I'm not truly

alive, but some sort of in-between. I don't eat unless I feel like it. I don't truly breathe; it's mostly out of habit. I also don't sleep. I can't." Quinn released his mouth, and he toppled to the side. She pulled a dagger out of her belt, and then she started to carve. Piece by piece. Strip by strip. She was careful. Never too much or too fast. Alternate the pain and the fear. Too much of either would break them too fast, and Quinn . . . she didn't need sleep. She needed blood. "This is going to be a very, very long night for you both," she whispered, finally yielding the rest of her mind to the dance.

Insanity, some called it.

She felt she was coming home to the sounds of their singing.

CHAPTER 40
BLOOD SOAKED

"There is nothing so thrilling or intense as loving a dangerous woman. When you don't know if she will kiss you or try to kill you, it's a love that weak men do not survive, and strong men would give anything to hold on to."
— *Lazarus Fierté, soul eater, King of Norcasta*

The council chambers were silent.

Shallowyn was silent.

Three days had passed since the battle in the valley. Three days since Quinn had descended into the dungeons. She still hadn't returned.

That first night, the celebrations were loud. Fifty thousand men had gone on up against an army twice their size and won. Less than two thousand men were lost that day because of her.

Fear's Massacre. That's what the soldiers were calling it.

They'd partied in and around Shallowyn till dawn. The sounds of music and merriment so loud it drowned out the other things going on at his manor. It was only on the second day, when the men had finally passed out drunk and the partying had stalled, when the music had quieted . . .that they heard.

Screaming. Bone-chilling, fear-induced screaming.

It came from the dungeons, and all knew who those screams belonged to.

It continued throughout the day, never stopping. Never ending.

It was only when night came once more that the screams started to fizzle out.

But Quinn hadn't surfaced.

It was last night that Shallowyn had gone silent and the sounds of death still hadn't lifted from the manor. No one dared speak in more than a whisper, and while they still revered her, the sounds of two dying kings was enough to make his soldiers fear her more.

Today was the third day.

Lazarus stood around the mostly empty council chamber. His house stood with him, as did the boy, Kairick. Axe had already been sent on before the battle even began to ready her armada and begin preparations in Dumas. Thorne was absent as well. He and his warriors, what remained of them, had left a week ago to try to aid with the supply lines coming in and out of the city.

Half of the army had left that day, and the remaining half would be well on their way soon. Nero's forces had reached the pass in the mountains that morning. They had days at most before he would be upon them. A week at most, if Lady Fortuna was kind. But Lazarus didn't put much stock into the goddess' favor. Leaving things to chance was a great way to end up dead.

"We need to leave," Dominicus said. "It's not safe here, and—"

"We wait for Quinn," Lazarus replied. They'd had this conversation a dozen times in the last two days.

"It's been three days," Dominicus argued. He'd grown more impatient over the evening. More agitated. Lazarus wondered if that was because Lorraine had refused his visits since he and Quinn got into it in the council chambers. Perhaps it was her fear that she used so forcefully in the dungeon below, leaking into the air, slowly driving the other man to the edge. The most likely possibility was that he simply didn't like her or care to wait.

"We wait for Quinn," Lazarus repeated, unmoving in this.

Dominicus shook his head in frustration but didn't press a third time. While Lazarus' patience had returned with the fear twister, he was still king and did not let his vassals rule him. Except for one, though she wasn't a vassal any longer.

Seated beside an unreadable seven-year-old and a troubled Draeven whose chest was bandaged heavily, was Lorraine. His stewardess' lips were pressed tightly together. Her thin fingers gripping each other where they laced together on top of the table.

Tension drew every muscle in her body taut from the moment Quinn had returned three days ago.

He didn't have to guess why. Quinn didn't look kindly on liars and traitors, and Lorraine had never really told her where she came from, who she was. Even through all they'd been through, she kept those secrets buried from all but Lazarus.

Ten years ago, he'd smuggled her and her son out of Vusut, the capital of Jibreal.

They'd changed the boy's name and sent him to a school for lordlings. One outside the large cities, in a place that his father would never find him. While Doran was a powerful man and a king, he wouldn't go to war over Lorraine and the boy. Not with Lazarus.

Not when he knew his secret, one that would disgust his nobles and dishonor his name. He might be king, but the things he did to his own son . . . rumors like that could stir rebellions.

So Doran let it go, or at least didn't act upon it.

Until now.

A heavy wooden door slammed shut. The metal

lining and frame banging together loud enough it echoed throughout Shallowyn.

Lorraine looked up, meeting his eyes.

He saw pain there. Unbearable pain and resignation for what she thought was to come.

They didn't hear Quinn as she walked down the halls, but Lazarus could feel her power as it drifted nearer. She walked with a slow steady gait, stopping outside the council room.

The brass handle clicked, and the door swung open.

Lazarus froze, his lips parting at the sight of her.

After the battle, she'd been covered in sweat and blood and dirt.

Now, blood had saturated her hair so thoroughly not a hint of lavender shown. It appeared the darkest red with only a tinge of brown—dry, and stiff—in the low light of the council room. Not an inch of her pale skin was clean. Splatters and drips and smudges covered her and her armor. Layer upon layer saturated so deep that it lined her eyelids and congealed on the lashes.

Only her eyes were a color other than crimson .

The black had drained away from them, and instead they were the lightest shade of blue. Almost translucent as they looked over the room and settled on Lorraine.

She knew.

Quinn walked forward, stygian magic and flakes of dried blood left in her wake.

Lorraine stood, her expression guarded as Quinn approached her.

The fear twister's face was unreadable and not even Lazarus knew what she felt.

She stopped.

Only a foot apart they stood, eye to eye.

Seconds passed as Quinn stared at her and Lorraine searched her face in return.

"Quinn, I—" Lorraine started. She didn't get to finish before Quinn lifted her arms and wrapped them around the other woman's shoulders. She embraced her fiercely, and those crystalline eyes met Lazarus' own over Lorraine's shoulder.

There was something unnamable in her expression. Something he would decipher later as she said, "He will never, ever hurt you or your son again."

Three days' worth of tension drained away from the woman he'd known for a decade. Her shoulders eased, and she hugged Quinn back, squeezing her tightly around the middle.

"I tried to tell you before the battle," Lorraine murmured, her voice thick with emotion.

"I know."

"I'm sorry I—"

"Don't apologize," Quinn said sharply, pulling back just enough to cup both Lorraine's cheeks. Her blood-crusted eyebrows drew together. "You did what you needed to do. You protected him as a parent should. I wish my mother had been as strong as you. Never apologize for what you did. Never apologize for not telling me. We all have secrets, Lorraine. They don't make you a liar or a traitor."

Lorraine's lip quivered, but she held that emotion in and nodded, bringing her own hands up over Quinn's. "Thank you," she whispered.

Quinn nodded once, and they shared one last look. If Draeven and Dominicus were confused, they didn't show it.

"Why are you covered in blood, Quinn?" Kairick asked. Lazarus had nearly forgotten him. The boy had an uncanny way to disappear in the silence, much like Quinn. He had a feeling it had to do with the pit they were forged in, or so Quinn would say.

She turned to the boy and without kneeling said, "Some bad men hurt people I care about."

Lazarus noticed Draeven's frown. He doubted his left-hand thought it was acceptable to be as blatant with the child as she was.

"So you hurt them back?" Kairick asked, his N'skaran accent thick but his Norcastan vocabulary growing every day.

"I did," Quinn said. The boy nodded once and mumbled something he couldn't make out, slipping into his mother tongue. Whatever it was must have pleased Quinn given the corner of her mouth curved up. It was the first hint of something on her face since she'd surfaced, and while he hadn't been the cause of it, he'd take it.

Just as fast as that amusement crossed her features, it disappeared. Solemnness took over once more, and he knew that Lorraine's past wasn't the only thing that had weighed her down these past days.

"What is it?" Lazarus asked. Her eyes drifted downward. She ran a dark red hand over Kairick's head.

"Go find a vassal and help them run a bath for me in the king's chambers," she told the boy. He nodded once, and without hesitation, he turned for the hall. Her eyes were haunted, staring at nothing in particular as she waited for the door to click shut behind him.

Only when it did, she spoke.

"They allied with Nero out of fear," she said slowly. "He contacted them before I ever met them and kept their alliance secret. He used them to watch me to know how best to play the Reinharts. Erwing's interest in Risk . . . it wasn't coincidence."

Draeven cursed, his expression darkening.

Quinn didn't even seem to notice.

"Neither was Amelia's interest in Lazarus. Every move they played, it was because of what Doran and Elijah learned from *me*. The night I died is more my own fault—my own arrogance—than anything else."

"What did you see?" Lazarus asked quietly, knowing that wasn't it. There was more.

"I was wrong," she said, the mists suddenly clearing from her face. Her expression turned sharp as she regarded him. "You warned me that he was not like my other opponents. You told me to take care, but that same arrogance blinded me to the possibility that he could truly rival us." She laughed once, and it was bitter. "All this planning, all this power," she lifted a hand, and it evaporated into smoke before their eyes. "It may have been for nothing."

"What. Did. You. See?" he repeated.

"Elijah and Doran didn't fear him because he could have them killed," Quinn said softly. "They feared him because he has the power to bring them back."

CHAPTER 41
BATTLE OF WILLS

*"The line between recklessness and fearlessness is
thinner than one may think."*
— *Quinn Darkova, fear twister, walker of realms, would-be
assassin*

L azarus' face didn't change. It was only a twitch
in his jaw that told her he was disturbed. Few
others had her ability to mask their emotions, and the
man she called king was one of them.

"That's not possible," Draeven said. "No one can
bring people back from the dead."

"I came back," Quinn said quietly.

"You bargained with a god," Draeven replied.

Quinn nodded. "I did, but who is to say he didn't

also bargain with one . . ." Thoughts turned in her mind. The things she'd seen.

Elijah and Doran had met with Nero years ago. They'd seen firsthand as he killed one of his vassals and brought them back. They'd watched as the young man, dead but not, rose from the pool of blood. Whatever magic Nero used to bring him back also gave him complete and utter control. He commanded the vassal to rip himself apart.

Sobbing, pleading, and utterly destroyed—he did.

Piece by piece.

There was only a pile left when he was done.

Both Jibreal and Bangratas had allied with Triene because he was better to have as an ally than an enemy.

Quinn shook her head, her stiff braid swinging over one shoulder.

"Is that possible?" Draeven asked. "To bargain with a god for power?"

She met Lazarus' heavy gaze from across the table.

"Yes," they said at the same time.

Draeven cursed again.

"Even if he can bring them back, our numbers estimate his army is larger than any we've ever seen on this continent. He can't bring them all back," Dominicus said.

"What makes you think they're all living to begin

with?" Quinn asked him. Dominicus narrowed his eyes and then looked away, letting out a heavy breath.

"You think the Trienian army is dead?" Draeven asked.

"No," Quinn said. "Not completely, but I think that if the numbers are even partially right, that we'd be fools to think they're all living."

"Does bringing them back give him power over them?" Lorraine asked softly.

Quinn tilted her head, angling it toward the other woman. "Yes," she said slowly.

Lorraine nodded as if she now understood something. "The army in Leone cut off the supply lines in the desert, but they weren't able to question them. Every man and woman killed themselves."

"They weren't living to begin with," Quinn said, following where she was going.

"It makes sense," Lorraine continued. "Do they need food and water when he raises them again?"

Quinn pulled the metal headpiece from her hair. It snagged in her dry strands, snapping some of the thinner ones as she tore it off and plonked it on the table. She used one bloodstained hand to brush the wiry strays back again as she said, "I don't know. The demonstration he gave them . . . the vassal didn't survive it."

"What do you mean?" Draeven asked sharply.

"He commanded the boy to rip himself apart."

Draeven swallowed and didn't ask further. For a

rage thief who knew how to fight and kill, he had quite the aversion to the darker side of murder. He might know rage, but he didn't know depravity. Not as Quinn did.

"This changes nothing," Lazarus said after a moment. Dominicus opened his mouth to argue, and Lazarus cut him off with a sharp look. "Whether he can bring them back or not, an army still marches for us. We need to retreat into Dumas and warn both Thorne and Axe. If the vassal in his demonstration didn't survive, it means there is still a way to kill them."

Quinn narrowed her eyes.

"We can kill a great number of the army, but if he's as strong as me, he'll simply bring them back," she argued.

"As much as I hate to say it, she's right," Dominicus added. "The army is a problem, but even if we kill all of them, without dealing with him, it may be for nothing."

"I agree," Draeven added.

"As do I," Lorraine murmured.

Quinn lifted an eyebrow in challenge to Lazarus, and he scowled back.

"He's a problem we can't deal with yet," her king said through gritted teeth.

"He was," she replied. "But things have changed."

"Nothing has changed."

"I feel like you're both talking of something the

rest of us don't know about," Draeven chimed in almost idly. Lazarus sent him a sharp glare, and Draeven looked away, but he didn't refute the statement.

"There's a way to deal with Nero. We've known since the beginning, but we've been delaying in favor of trying to draw out the other light heirs—"

"Quinn," Lazarus said sharply. It was an order to be quiet.

"We have days before that army reaches us. If we make the wrong choice, you and I aren't the only ones to pay the price," Quinn replied in a hard voice.

His gaze was fire and ashes. Smoke and wind. He stared at her with an intensity that she had little doubt what would happen when they returned to his suite, but now wasn't the time for such things.

"I am King," Lazarus said through gritted teeth.

"And I am not your vassal," she replied in the same manner. "This isn't your decision. If anything, it's mine."

The muscle in his jaw ticked. "I implore you as your king and your . . . partner, that you reconsider and wait."

"I don't think I can," Quinn said, leaning forward to place both hands on the round oak table. "Not with what I know now. He needs to be dealt with, light heirs be damned."

"What were you just saying about your arrogance?" Lazarus replied, raising his voice. His body mimicked her actions, leaning forward. "This is an arrogant, foolish decision."

"It takes a fool to know a fool," Quinn snapped, baring her teeth.

"Myori's wrath," Draeven muttered. "Just what exactly are you planning to do, Quinn?"

She held Lazarus' stare as she said, "Dreamwalk."

"Come again?" Draeven said, his eyebrows drawing together in her periphery.

"What she does in the dreamstate happens in the living realm," Lorraine said, picking it up faster. "She plans to assassinate the emperor in his sleep."

Quinn inclined her head.

"No," Lazarus growled.

"It's not your decision to make," Quinn replied.

"Not that it matters what I think here, but I feel like this plan is rash. Borderline insane," Draeven said.

"Exactly," Lazarus started, but Draeven continued, cutting him off.

"However, I also think it's the best shot we have and the only thing that might work."

Lazarus scowled at his left-hand, who shrugged and then winced at the movement. Quinn frowned, only then noticing the bandages around his right shoulder and chest.

"I agree," Dominicus said. He sat stiffly in his chair, staring at the map in the center of the table.

"And you?" Lazarus said to Lorraine. "Are you

going to convince her to do something that might kill her for good this time as well?"

The stewardess gave Lazarus a steady look, and said, "It doesn't matter what I think. She's already made up her mind for herself."

Quinn's lips curled slightly at the corners. Lazarus' scowl deepened.

"I don't like this," he said.

"You don't have to," Quinn replied. "There's a reason you picked me for your right-hand. I do what needs to be done. What no one else can or will do."

"You're not my hand anymore," Lazarus told her. His voice was like gravel. Deep and dark. Her blood heated a fraction.

"No," Quinn said with a wicked grin. "I'm not. Which means there's no contract that will let you stop me from doing this."

The look he gave her was nothing short of menacing, but Quinn wouldn't give in. She couldn't.

"We'll see about that."

CHAPTER 42
RAMIEL'S GIFT

"We all have good and evil inside of us, but to give either too much power is just another form of slavery."
— *Quinn Darkova, fear twister, walker of realms, willful assassin*

Quinn had barely settled into her bath when Lazarus joined her. He cleaned her skin and then took her twice before pulling her from the tub. That was when the knock came.

The carriages were ready. They were departing for Dumas immediately.

Quinn narrowed her eyes but didn't argue it.

She knew the game he played at. Lazarus couldn't physically stop her, so he was going to distract her from entering the dream state as long as possible. He should have known it wouldn't work. Nothing and no one could stop Quinn when she set her mind to something.

Not the gods. Not death. Certainly, not a man.

But she played along, for now.

They sat opposite of each other in the carriage. It would take a full day minimum for them to reach the city walls. With nowhere to go and nothing but road, she smiled into the dark carriage as he started to drift.

Lazarus, for all his intelligence, either didn't consider that he'd eventually need to sleep or simply chose to ignore that he was inevitably putting her off but unable to stop her. Either way, Quinn waited as Leviathan's eye moved across the night sky. Lazarus' eyes grew hooded and then closed. She gave it a few more minutes, letting him fall deeper before she leaned back against the shuddering windowpane. She turned to the side and kicked her feet up on top of the low bench and crossed her arms over her chest.

Slipping into the dream realm was as easy as cutting a string. She didn't so much as feel her body leave the physical realm, but instead felt the sleeping minds of hundreds, thousands, pulling her in different directions. Without Lazarus and his own connection to Nero, she might have found it impossible to actually pull this off. Finding one sleeping mind among many was difficult, but she knew enough to let herself be tugged further away from the carriage. She drifted through the remainders of their army. Most of the Maji had gone, and none carried in them the distinct tint of darkness that she sought. She drifted further, traveling to the very edge of the country where she felt the pull strongest.

There were so many sleeping souls.

So many Maji.

Quinn had to steel herself as she started to walk through them, one by one, drifting through their dreams like a wraith did the land. Most of them were either dreamless or nightmares. Very few had good dreams, and even then, good was subjective. She passed by them with little more than a thought, drawing closer to the one she felt calling.

She could see him. His location. He shone like a brilliant star in an endless night. His light magic blinding in its intensity. But the undercurrent of his dreams . . . they were just as dark as hers. Darker even.

Quinn smiled to herself, walking into them without regard.

She didn't expect to see Lazarus there. Albeit, a younger, more haunted version.

Blood spilled from a cut over his eye. The moon was red and full. They stood at the edge of the continent, looking into the void where one had gone. Behind them, great monstrosities of buildings loomed over the river's edge.

Crimson pooled on the dock, dripping between the wooden boards.

Quinn didn't look away from the swaddled bundle that saturated red. It had been covered, as if someone couldn't bear to see it.

"You're weak," a voice hissed in Trienian. She'd been practicing with Lazarus these past weeks. Learning the one tongue she did not know from the Sirian continent. This voice was not endless night skies, shadows, or smoke.

It was not death. It was not fear.

It was light, beautiful even, in its melody. It enticed her with its very sound, and it was so many times worse than any she'd ever heard.

"This is a gamble," the younger Lazarus said gruffly. He gripped the knife tight in his fist. "We don't know if it will truly—"

"Excuses," the other voice said. He stepped out of the shadows, and Quinn recognized him immediately. He had no scar yet. There was no cane. His face was more beautiful than any man she'd ever looked upon. He was perfection, but his eyes . . . they were evil. True evil that surpassed light or dark. Black or white. "You're weak, my brother. Give me the knife. If you won't do it, I will."

Lazarus clenched his fist and then said, "No."

Quinn tilted her head. This was not how he'd told the story. Not quite.

"I will not waste the death of my first and only son. Now do as you're told and *give me the knife*." His voice never hardened. It never turned dark and delicious. It stayed soft, coaxing, despite the words coming from it.

"You don't deserve the power of gods," Lazarus replied. Nero's expression didn't change as he trailed forward.

"I will take it from you if I must," he said. Lazarus went wholly still as Nero lifted a hand and cupped his cheek like a brother . . . or a lover? Quinn wasn't sure. Lazarus' gaze strayed to that hand as if he were also realizing that. "I gave them my son. A worthy sacrifice. If you are going to stand in my way, though, perhaps it is a sign. They ask me to give them someone I love."

"You wouldn't . . ." Lazarus said. The look on his face wasn't so certain. Neither was Nero's as he seemed to consider this.

"Give me the knife," he said at last. "I will not ask again."

Lazarus' hand trembled as he lifted it, as if he were going to hand it over.

Then he twisted and slammed it into the side of Nero's thigh, raking downward.

Shock reverberated through Nero's face. Not pain. Not fear. Not even when Lazarus pulled the knife from it and dropped it on the planks. It thudded once and blood gushed from the wound. Nero didn't fight him as Lazarus shoved him off of the dock and into the dark waters.

He didn't flail or scream as he went under. Lazarus paced for a moment, waiting to see if he came back up. His hands twisted. She could sense uneasiness in him as he glanced at the water every few seconds.

A group of men drunkenly started down the street in the distance, coming toward them.

"Hey you!" they called. "What are you doing out there?"

Lazarus turned, and with a single look back at the thrashing waters, he ran.

Quinn didn't follow him, though. This was not his dream. His memory. She stayed on the docks, a sick feeling in her gut telling her where this was going.

As she suspected, the waters parted as Nero came up, spluttering for air. His breath hissed between his teeth as he reached up and dragged himself from the warm yet turbulent waves of the southern sea.

Instead of bandaging his leg or trying to save it, he lifted his head and started to crawl for the knife. Blood and seawater mixed as he pulled himself the ten feet toward it.

Without hesitation, he lifted the blade and blinded himself.

Not a sound of pain left him as he lay there beneath the blood moon.

"You should have died that night," Quinn murmured.

"I should have," that same beautiful, melodic voice said. It didn't come from the Nero before her that lay underneath the sky, but from the one behind her that stepped out of the shadows.

Quinn turned, crossing her arms over her chest. "How long have you been standing there?"

"Since I sensed you walking through my mind, fear twister," he replied. His eyes raked over her, hungry, but she didn't think it was for her body. "I will admit, I'm surprised to see you. Not much surprises me these days."

"You had me killed."

"I did." He licked his lips. "You were an unknown. Something I hadn't planned for. I sent the Reinharts for *you*. Yet, here you stand, in my dreams."

"How did you survive?" Quinn asked him, looking between the dying man and the one before her.

"I didn't," he grinned.

Quinn narrowed her eyes.

"I died for a second. A single second. But I died in sacrifice to the gods of light." As he spoke, six figures appeared before the docks.

They glowed with the light of stars. Their skin harder than diamonds. Long flowing hair shaded in the pinks and oranges of dusk cascaded down their backs. They wore strips of cloth like Mazzulah had, but theirs were white, the purest form of the color she'd ever seen. They truly looked like the gods of light.

Especially their ancient, terrible eyes.

They didn't speak as they watched him, those eyes weighing his destiny. His fate.

When Nero died, it was indeed a single second.

Then each god extended their hands and one drop of that brilliant light floated from each of them and into him. It sunk into his chest, right to his heart.

The Nero of the past gasped, opening his eyes. The gods surrounded him, floating in the night sky.

"The game has changed," one of them murmured. Her icy blue eyes and blue-tinted skin made Quinn think she was Skadi, the Goddess of Winter.

"The end approaches," another said. His eyes were every color and none. His hair a mane of pearlescent locks that changed tint in the shifting winds.

"Why do you call on us?" the one in the center asked. The crown upon his brow marked him as Ramiel, God of Balance and Justice.

"I long for power," Nero said, his voice never wavering.

"The power to do what?" Ramiel asked.

"Everything," the younger Nero said. "I will remake the world as emperor of all, and temples will be built to you in every city."

"You would conquer the world?" another goddess

asked. Her voice as serene as still water. Telerah, Goddess of Peace. "Bring war to it?"

"Only through war can there be true peace," Nero said solemnly. She regarded him with shrewd eyes.

"He will not play nice with the other heirs," the third goddess spoke. She wore seashells and seaweed. Myori, Goddess of the Sea.

"Perhaps we don't need him to," Telerah spoke.

"Perhaps," all six of them said at once.

Ramiel floated down, descending onto the docks. His eyes flicked to the dead baby, still swaddled in bloody rags before regarding Nero once more.

Nero, who did not bow.

"You want for the power of gods. You seek that which you feel you deserve," the god said.

"Have I not proven my devotion?" Nero asked, his eyes narrowing even if his words were smooth as honey.

"Your devotion to power, yes. But you are not the only one who seeks power. Why should we give it to you?"

Nero didn't hesitate when he said, "Because I am the most devoted. I will go the furthest, bleed the most, do *anything* for it."

When Ramiel smiled, it was blinding with its beauty. So much so it hurt, but Nero didn't look away.

"We each have an heir whom we endow with power and guidance. You were born weak, weaker than most. Almost human. But your will . . . it might just be strong enough. Find the other heirs. Only in defeating our champions will you truly be worthy."

The light that emitted from him grew brighter and brighter until Nero had to look away. Until the light was so bright there was nothing but white.

Then it ended, and the night was dark once more.

Quinn looked away from the young Nero to the older one that stood before her, studying her with those cold eyes.

"This night changed my life," he said softly. He stepped forward, and she noticed that he still limped, even here. That leg that Lazarus had cut so deep . . . it was healed, but not whole. The gods had saved him but didn't take away the reminder that he was still mortal.

"Did you find them?" Quinn asked, her fingers itching to reach for the blade strapped to her side. Could she truly be this lucky? Could they?

"Of course," he replied, arrogant if not charming. "It took me a decade to do it, but I found them one by one. They were scattered across the continent, but blood magic . . . if you offer the magic enough, it can do almost anything." He sounded proud of himself, but also calculating. While he gave her answers, she had little doubt that it was thoughtless. He did not feel fear within her presence.

"And the gods," Quinn mused, pacing herself.

They moved in circles, getting closer and closer. "Did they hold true to what they said?"

He grinned at her as if it were their secret. "Come to me and I'll tell you."

Quinn lifted an eyebrow. "You had me killed once, lest I remind you."

"But you found your way back, at my brother's side again, I'm sure. I've never met another who could defy death itself. That's too rare to throw away again. I would keep you and together we——"

"Could kill Lazarus?" she asked him, then laughed outright. "Do you really think I would turn on him? I came back from death for him, why would I ever——"

"I don't wish to kill him," Nero said. "I wish to keep him. And you. The three of us, we could have such *fun* together."

"I've seen your ideas of fun," Quinn said solemnly, recalling the piles of human flesh.

"I've heard of yours," he replied. "I think we would be well matched."

They circled again, getting closer and closer.

They were only a hairsbreadth away when they both stopped, chests heaving. The scent of the ocean, steel, and the first bite of winter touched her.

"Surely, you've heard other things about me," she murmured. Drawing her dagger and pressing it to his throat in the same breath. He didn't flinch away as the steel kissed his skin. His good eye staring at her with an intensity she was growing accustomed to. "Such as my ability to hold a grudge. I murdered my parents for what they did. Do you really think I wouldn't kill you? If not for killing me, then because it's demanded as *my price* to pay for the deal *I made*."

Her throat stung. A sliver of pain running through her. Nero lifted his hand slowly and touched his fingers to her skin. They came away as red as the blood that welled against her blade.

Quinn frowned as Nero grinned, licking the blood from his fingers.

"Your deal means nothing to me. When I win the war, my gods will give me whatever I want. Even you."

Quinn stepped away, and his hand moved fast as a viper to wrap around her wrist holding the blade.

"What kind of magic is this?" she demanded. Looking from her blade to his neck to his fingers where her blood had touched, and then feeling the wound on her own neck to solidify what she was seeing.

"Ramiel's gift," he said, his tongue darting out to lick his lip once more. "Any harm done unto me shall have the same done back to you. An eye for an eye, if you will."

They cheated, Mazzulah had said. It wasn't cheating in the rules, but in the intent. The gods knew that this time it would be the end, and both sides planned for it.

"You are Neiss' champion. Born for greatness," Nero said the word with envy and lust. "I was no one's, but I became them all. I can do what no Maji can, not even Lazarus. You are both as dark as me, and whether you choose me or not, I have the power to take you. I will own you by the end of this war, Quinn Darkova."

"No man owns me," Quinn spat as she tore her arm away.

"I am more than any man. I'm the champion of six gods. A god among men, and no one defies me. I look forward to breaking you, Quinn."

Nero smiled at her, and then he woke up.

"Both pride and confidence stem from the same grain of truth."
— Lazarus Fierté, soul eater, King of Norcasta

He'd woken when the carriage jolted, and he realized his mistake.

Eyes closed, arms crossed over her chest, she wasn't sleeping. She couldn't, not anymore. Which meant she was dreamwalking.

Lazarus lunged forward and grabbed for her arms, attempting to wake her. His hands passed right through her, hitting the cushion back of the wood bench. His fingers curled into fists as panic and anger coursed through him.

"Quinn," he said. When she didn't stir, he said it again, and again, and again.

Leviathan's eye descended into the horizon, and only at the first inklings of a new dawn did she change.

His blood ran cold as a thin line of crimson traced her neck.

He reached for her once more, and this time, she gasped.

Her eyes flew open and her form became corporeal. It took her all of a second to calm and him all of a second to become enraged.

"He hurt you," Lazarus said, his dark eyes zeroing in on the cut. "He *marked* you."

"I hurt myself," she said, lifting a hand to the line. She seemed absentminded and unaware of his anger.

"Did you kill him?"

He waited for her answer. Eager but uncertain. He'd started this war. He'd vowed to kill his only brother. He wanted him dead . . . but something loosened and tightened in his chest when she said, "No."

Quinn looked away, and Lazarus frowned.

"No?" he repeated. "You didn't kill him?"

Instead of answering him, Quinn said, "You didn't tell me you tried to kill him that night. That you stabbed him and then threw him into the ocean."

Lazarus stilled, and while the carriage rocked, the windowpanes shuddered, neither of them moved.

"He told you that?" Lazarus asked quietly.

"No," Quinn replied, watching him carefully. "I saw it."

"Saw it?"

"In his dream." She unfolded her arms and dropped her legs away from the bench, turning to face him fully. "He was dreaming of that night when he killed his son and made the offering. I saw your fight and how he threatened to sacrifice you."

"And me stabbing him," Lazarus added, flatly.

"And then trying to drown him," she continued. "You left after that. Ran. I saw what happened then too. Did you know?"

Lazarus' eyebrows drew together. "Know?"

"He died, Lazarus. Just like me. Except his soul hadn't left the realm yet before the gods decided to step in."

He opened and then closed his mouth. He certainly didn't know.

Lazarus ran that night and only looked back to be sure he wasn't followed. He never returned to Triene after that. The edge of Norcasta and Bangratas had become the edge of his world as far as he was concerned. That was before Nero had Quinn killed.

"He made a deal with the gods?" Lazarus asked, his eyes dropping from her shrewd face.

"Not just any deal," Quinn said. "They saved him from death, and he bargained for power. They gave him the means to become each of their heirs. Do you know what this means? There are no other light heirs. He is *all* of them."

Lazarus shook his head. "Every god has one champion. You said—"

"Yes, one champion," Quinn said. "There's nothing in the rules that says they can't all choose the same champion. It's never happened before, and it won't ever happen again. This is the end. They knew that. They've always known that it would end with you and me and him. The dark heirs never made it so far in the past, and the light heirs were never strong enough. But if he is all of them . . ."

"He's stronger than any Maji," Lazarus said.

God among men, the title ran through his mind.

Isn't that what the messenger had said?

He thought it was pure hubris. Arrogance. He hadn't thought, ritual or not, that Nero truly could rival any of them. All of them.

He was just a healer . . . that could now bring back the dead.

Lazarus cursed.

"How did you get the mark?" he asked, turning over this information in his mind. There was more. There had to be more. Quinn was all powerful in dreams. She was a true nightmare that only waking could extinguish.

"I held my blade to his throat, and it cut both of us."

Lazarus froze and lifted his head. Their eyes met, and he saw the terrible truth there.

An eye for an eye, the same messenger had said.

Nero loved games as much as Quinn, and that single head had been all the clues he needed.

"Any harm done to him will also be done to the one who causes it," Quinn continued softly. "I don't fear death . . . but I hesitated. I went to kill him, not to die as well."

Lazarus laughed, and it was harsh and grating and swaying that dangerous line he liked to walk, as if straddling the edge of a blade. "Not only can he bring back the dead, but he's unkillable unless the person doing it is also willing to die." He shook his head, anger and sorrow fighting for dominance. This was the game to win all games.

Winner takes all.

He couldn't afford to lose.

Except, who else if not him or Quinn, could truly get close to the man?

Who else could end this?

Who else could die in both their steads?

His heart pounded and the ratcheting of the carriage along the road was like the pounding in his mind. They only had days to come up with a solution.

Not weeks.

Not months.

Not years.

Days.

They had to win an unwinnable war against an army that was larger than the continent had ever seen, and as if that weren't enough, then someone had to kill him and die themselves.

"Could you tell where he was at?" Lazarus asked quietly.

"The pass," she said. "They'd already crossed into Norcasta."

He lowered his head. If they were slow, it would be five days.

If not . . .

Lazarus thumped the side of the carriage and the driver cracked the window latching and stuck his head through. "Yes, Your Grace?"

"Speed up, and do not stop or slow until we are at Dumas gates', is that understood?"

The vassal whom he didn't recognize swallowed hard.

"Yes, Your Grace," he said, bowing his head at an angle that seemed uncomfortable. His eyes flitted nervously to Quinn before he seemed to realize what he was doing and leaned back, closing the window firmly.

The carriage lurched, and the thumping grew faster. Quinn bounced as the wheels turned faster, flying down the dirt road. She extended both hands to either side of the carriage to brace herself, and he reached out and grasped her chin, putting their faces inches apart.

"You do not get to die," he told her firmly.

"Neither do you," she said stiffly, her eyes burning in those icy depths.

"I have no intentions of it. Dying means leaving you and my crown, just when I had both in my grasp . . ." He released her chin to brush a stray lock of her lavender hair back.

"But someone has to die," she said softly.

"I know."

They didn't talk for the rest of the journey, both of them clearly stuck in their thoughts.

Someone had to die, but more than that, they had to get through the army he built first.

CHAPTER 44
DARKEST HOUR

"The truest testament of men is what they've said, and how they've acted in their darkest hour."
— Quinn Darkova, fear twister, walker of realms, failed
assassin

When the carriage finally slowed, it was late afternoon. She heard the creaking of gates and sounds of men as they entered the city.

She hadn't been here since the very beginning.

It felt like a lifetime ago when she beat a man in the square for whipping his slave. Bloodlust called to her just as much now as it had then, the only difference was that now she was free.

Free of her past, free of her inhibitions, free of those invisible chains that once bound her.

As the jolting smoothed slightly when the wheels met cobblestone, Quinn asked, "Are you going to tell them?"

Lazarus didn't answer her at first, and they were most of the way to the palace when he did. "I don't know."

"They're going to want to know why he's not dead."

"I know. That doesn't mean I care."

"If we fail, they fail too—"

"I know, Quinn," he snapped.

She lifted an eyebrow, giving him a sharp look. "Which one?"

He gave her a cautious glance. "Which one what?"

"Which poor fool are you considering sacrificing and not telling that they're walking to their death?" Lazarus didn't look away; she'd give him that. Most men would have the decency to be ashamed. Not him.

"I hadn't decided, but we have thousands of troops. What is one? I could set their family up for a good life. They'd never know."

Quinn shook her head. "I hope you're right," she murmured as the carriage came to a stop. "But if there's anything I've learned, it's that the gods won't make this easy for us."

There was a shuffling outside before the door opened. The vassal was smart enough not to offer his hand as she stood and stepped out of the carriage, not bothering with the stepping block he held in his hand. Dust bloomed as her boots hit the dirty streets.

She didn't wait for Lazarus before ascending the sandstone steps. At the top, both Axe and Thorne waited. Petra stood beside her young queen. A few scattered Cisean warriors hung back by the double doors.

"Word reached us of the battle two days ago," Petra said. "Fear's Massacre." She grinned, her yellow and gold teeth reflecting the sunlight. "It's all the men have been able to speak of." Axe elbowed her aunt.

"I'm sure it wasn't *that* great," the young girl muttered.

"Oh, it was," Draeven said, coming up the steps beside Lazarus. "She rode a bloody firedrake into battle."

Axe's mouth popped open, and she ran an appraising gaze up and down Quinn's form before sniffing once. "Hm."

Thorne chuckled as Quinn rolled her eyes. Even grieving and on the brink of true war, Axe was still Axe, no matter the crown she wore on her head.

"Come, we have much to discuss," Lazarus said. The tone of his voice brought the smiles and grins to a halt. His allies started to head indoors, but Quinn hung back and met that heavy gaze.

Something charged passed between them.

"I need time to think," he said quietly as the others filtered inside.

"We have no time. It's out. We couldn't even send for reinforcements and have them arrive before he takes Dumas if we wanted to," Quinn argued.

"You are strong. I am strong. We will find a way," Lazarus said, striding forward. She stood her ground and hit his shoulder with hers as he tried to pass, stopping him in his tracks.

"Strength is not enough. If it were, Mazzulah never would have lost. The dark heirs have always been stronger." Their breath mingled as he faced her.

"We are different."

"So is *he*."

A cough at the double doors made them both pause and look to Draeven.

"Your Grace," the left-hand said somewhat awkwardly. His shoulder and chest were still bound in bandages, but he seemed to be moving better, Quinn noticed. She wondered what happened in the battle for him to be as injured as he was.

Lazarus started to walk away when Quinn said, "If you don't tell them, I will."

"And if he sends another creature made of blood magic after them? To learn any plans we might make?"

"Then he does, but if we only have days, so does he. They're willing to die for you, Lazarus. They deserve the truth."

"If we tell them, they'll panic."

"Axe asked you for a promise that she could kill him. That was her terms for entering this, and she deserves to know. Petra is one of the most steady women I've ever met. Thorne does not *panic,* and he already knows half of the story. Invite your allies, but not the lords. Tell them the truth of this. They deserve to know."

"Why are you so insistent on the truth?" he asked her, ire entering his tone.

"We are not the only heirs. I have to think there's a reason for that. He's stronger than any Maji alone. He has an army that's estimated at half a million. By all accounts, we should lose . . . but I don't feel fear. I can't. I'm incapable of it. So instead, I'm focusing on what I know. They cannot even do that if they don't have the full picture. Eight minds are better than two."

Quinn waited a moment, until he said, "Very well."

She hoped this feeling in her gut was not a mistake.

"THAT WENT HORRIBLY," DRAEVEN SIGHED.

Quinn leaned back in the wooden chair, crossing her arms over her chest. They'd told the other leaders the truth, and it had been utter chaos. Axe lost her temper and took out two chairs and a centuries old mahogany table in the center of the room before Petra managed to drag her away. Thorne had been calm, as usual, but left shortly after to write to his wife. Quinn had never seen the Cisean leader so desolate, not even when his son had been consumed by Kairick. The planning was swift. The actions they could take limited.

The Ilvans would handle the bay. The Ciseans and Norcastans would protect the city.

They had walls and weapons and magic . . . but no one truly believed it would be enough.

Not against five hundred thousand men.

She still couldn't believe it, the sheer size. Quinn never indulged in spirits, but for once, she considered it.

"How many deserters do you think we'll have by morning?" Dominicus asked.

Quinn scowled, her gaze darting to Lazarus. He wasn't looking at them, any of them, but instead staring out the window to the sleeping city below. It was well past the midnight hour when all others but House Fierté had retreated to their quarters.

"Hundreds," Draeven said. "Maybe thousands, assuming either of them tell their men what we're actually facing."

"I don't think they will," Quinn murmured. "Axe might be angry, but she's not pulling out of the war. If Nero wins, he'll be coming for her next. Ilvas can't handle them alone. None of us can. Thorne might warn his generals, but the Ciseans have more honor than any other kingdom. They won't leave, not in our darkest hour."

"Even if no man leaves, the odds are impossible as long as Nero lives," Dominicus said.

"Not impossible," Quinn corrected. "Just difficult."

Draeven snorted, but it wasn't amused. "There's never been an army this size before in all of the history of the Sirian continent."

"Just because it hasn't happened before doesn't mean it's impossible. Many things that were not thought possible became so," Quinn reminded him quietly. Draeven nodded, but it didn't reach his eyes.

"Have you heard from Risk?" he asked. She wondered if the others noticed the slight change in his voice.

"No," Quinn answered, and it bothered her. Mazzulah had said Risk was her heir. She was only supposed to stay there until her ascension. Quinn knew better than anyone how time did not pass in the dark realm as it did here. It gnawed at her that Risk hadn't returned yet, not even a whisper of her.

She hoped that when she did, it wasn't too late.

"We're down an heir. We don't know who the last one is. We're fighting unwinnable odds—" Dominicus started.

"Just say it a little louder, that might make it more

probable," Quinn quipped. Dominicus' expression darkened.

"Are you trying to be funny?"

"No, I'm pointing out that complaining doesn't change it. Restating the facts we already know doesn't alter them. We have no choice but to try. It's try or die, at least for you and most of the continent."

The weapons master glowered. His chair legs scraped the ground as he pushed it back and stood. "I'm going to bed," he said. No one bid him a good night.

Quinn muttered, "bastard," when the door closed behind him.

"He's not wrong," Draeven said.

"That doesn't make him not a bastard," Quinn replied. "And it doesn't make him entirely right either. Complaining didn't get me out of N'skara or the dark realm. Doing something did. Rally your skeevs and tell them to remember Fear's Massacre. Maybe they'll be less inclined to desert."

"It would probably help if you didn't call them skeevs," Draeven muttered. Quinn shrugged.

"It's what they are," she said, even if a small part of her did twinge. She didn't care for them, but something had changed over the weeks in the way they looked at her. There was still fear, but the awe, the admiration that had grown and then blossomed at the battle in Shallowyn. While Quinn had always known what it was like to be feared, she'd never known an admiration like this. Only lust or derision.

It was a new feeling. She still wasn't sure if she liked it.

Draeven sighed, moving to stand. He winced in pain, but no one commented on it.

"I'm also going to bed. The next few days will be long."

As he made his way toward the door, Quinn looked to Lazarus. He'd yet to weigh in since they left. Neither had Lorraine, for that matter. She appraised them both.

"I'm going to check on Kairick, and then the patrols," Quinn said, getting to her feet. Neither of them moved, and she had this distinct feeling they were waiting for something.

"I'll come find you soon," Lazarus finally said, and her suspicions doubled.

She made a show of going to the door and closing it firmly behind her. Part of her wanted to listen. To press her ear to the door and see what they were saying, but the rest of her said she should move on. Continue walking. Whatever they wished to discuss, they wanted the room for a reason, though they didn't ask for it.

Quinn turned down the hall, and right when she was near the end, she heard a snippet of conversation that carried on the stale air to her heightened Maji hearing.

". . . terrible acts must be committed for the greater good . . ." Lorraine's voice drifted toward her. It was hardly a whisper, and she didn't catch Lazarus' reply as she continued walking.

Quinn wasn't sure what they were talking about, but she had a suspicion she'd find out in three days.

CHAPTER 45
FOR THE ENDS

The sun peeked over the horizon.

Quinn stood at the edge of the wall, looking off into the distance. She was already dressed in her armor. A beacon of red and gold that shone like a living flame. Her brow was set, and her lips pressed together in a hard line as figures appeared at the farthest reaches of her line of sight.

She gripped a dagger in each hand, her knuckles showing white as death.

The battle drums started within their walls. In the distance, there was no war march, no rallying, no sound—just the endless marching. They moved as one over the crest of the outermost hill. The sound of their boots hitting the ground echoed like thunder.

Draeven cursed as Leviticus' eye rose higher, and the lines of men never dwindled.

"How many do you count?" Lazarus asked.

"Two hundred thousand," Dominicus said.

"Two fifty," Draeven corrected, his sharper eyesight seeing further.

"They're still coming," Quinn murmured as they approached the three hundred thousand mark and continued past it.

"The estimates did say five hundred," Dominicus said softly.

They watched in silence, waiting for the break in troops. The reprieve in men. When it came just short of the expected five hundred thousand, Draeven sighed in relief. It was short-lived.

Beasts five horses tall approached. Their tusks were long, sharp, and deadly. They carried trees in their trunks, cut off at either end to form battering rams.

"Myori's wrath," Quinn murmured as Draeven said, "Woolly mammoths." She'd seen them in Bangratas, but only from a distance. They were rare and prized creatures, but ten of them now descended the tallest hill, coming straight for Dumas. A ripple of unease spread through the cavalry below them. They might have stood a chance against men on horses, but mammoths . . .

they'd be obliterated by a single swing of those rams or a swipe of a tusk.

On their backs, carriages were held in place, holding people, though Quinn couldn't tell how many.

"Archers or Maji?" Dominicus asked, his blue eyes narrowed on the same thing.

"Probably both," Draeven said. His sandy blonde hair settled in his eyes, and he pushed it back with a rake of his gloved hands.

They waited at the edge of the forward-most wall as the mammoths came closer and closer. It was only when the front of the army was nearly upon them that figures appeared once more.

Ice thickened in her veins, and the temperature over Dumas dropped several degrees as Quinn realized that wasn't all the army.

What little odds they had started to crumble as line after line appeared on that horizon. So many so, that they were still coming. It was a sea of purple and gold banners as far as the eye could see.

When the front line finally reached them, they stopped, several hundred yards away. The four-thousand-man calvary seemed measly compared to the might of Triene. Pitiful and hopeless.

"By the gods . . ." Draeven turned away, putting a hand over his mouth. Dominicus looked to the sky, his fists clenching at his side.

"It's not over yet," Lazarus said calmly.

"These are impossible odds," Quinn murmured.

He cut her a sharp look sideways. "Weren't you the one that told them that even the impossible is possible?"

"We could have five times as many men as we do, and this would still feel unwinnable. You saw the ships in the bay this morning. We're outnumbered on all fronts."

His dark gaze focused on her, making the hairs on her spine stand on end as he said, "What do you propose we do, then?"

"Fight," Quinn said without hesitation. "Their numbers do not change that. We fight or die, and while we will probably die anyway—that's not a reason to give up."

At the very edges where even her better eyesight blurred, a horn sounded.

It was a command. A single, forlorn note that told both sides to prepare.

When it ended, the Trienian army marched once more. They did not run. They did not hesitate. They started for the calvary and did not stop. On the walls and in the city streets, soldiers stood at attention, waiting for Lazarus' command.

"Why haven't you opened the gates?" Quinn asked quietly.

Lazarus did not answer as the two sides met in a clash of swords and pikes. Blood covered the front lines in seconds and a steady melancholy entered the city as the Trienian army held their own, despite the horses.

"They need reinforcements," Quinn said. "Without them, they'll be—"

"Slaughtered," Lazarus said, his eyes not lifting from the field. "I'm aware."

"I just said we are going to die either way, but—"

"We're not going to die," Lazarus said quietly. "Their sacrifice will be remembered."

Quinn watched, something cold and angry igniting in her chest. She knew the emotion, but not why she felt it. She'd killed thousands without regard, and her hands weren't even stained by these deaths, yet they bothered her. Quinn seethed.

"What are you playing at?" she asked him.

The corner of Lazarus' lips curled upward, a cruel grin if there ever was one.

"You'll see."

The sun drifted higher in the sky and the Norcastan forces dwindled.

It couldn't have been more than an hour when they were at the gates.

Quinn's patience reached the end of its rope, and she stepped up onto the stone wall battlement. A warm, calloused hand grabbing her own was the only thing that stopped her from daring the jump and destroying what enemy she could.

"They are at the gates," Quinn snapped. "You let those men die *uselessly* while we cowered behind our walls. If this was a game we could win by hiding, I'd understand, but they will breach these walls long before they starve us—"

"Look," he said. A single, hard word.

Her eyes cut to the grassy plains now stained crimson.

Soldiers were stumbling over each other. Gaps in the lines appeared. That unbreakable wall of purple and gold shattered as men dropped to their knees and then toppled sideways.

"I don't understand . . ." Quinn turned to look at Lazarus but found herself staring at another.

Standing in front of a wall of soldiers that looked on with grim faces was Lorraine. Her hands were clasped over the pleat of her skirt. Her brown and gray hair braided back. She didn't stare at the enemy army that was falling, failing, without reason. She looked at Quinn, and there was knowledge in her eyes.

A black crescent moon formed on her forehead. A mark of the gods.

A declaration from Leviathan, the God of Moon and Shadows.

She poisoned her husband then ran . . .

Terrible acts must be committed for the greater good . . .

"What did you do?" Quinn asked, her voice hardly more than a whisper.

"What we needed to do to even the odds."

CHAPTER 46
POISONED ODDS

Nero sat atop his mount, his mouth twisted into a feral sort of grin.

The walls of the city were still far, but not so far that he didn't see that gleaming armor of red and gold. She stepped up to the battlement as if to challenge him, and Nero's length thickened.

There would be enough time for that later.

Once he'd taken the city and shackled both her and Lazarus to him.

Nero licked his lips and snapped his fingers. The musician started to play, that sweet lullaby filling him, easing him, carrying him away as blood stained the grassy plains.

He didn't once lose focus, watching the front lines from atop the hill as his forces attempted to siege the wall.

That was when it happened.

As surely as his victory had been guaranteed in might, something was amiss. Soldiers began dropping like flies. They'd stumble, then fall, their bodies nothing more than shaking husks by the time the next row of soldiers stepped on them and kept marching.

A barked order from one of his generals had the emperor's personal guard parting ways. Lord Zairaynas approached, his large hand fisted in a younger soldier's hair, dragging him before Nero.

The boy's eyelids were half-closed, his mouth bobbing aimlessly like an inexperienced whore as Zairaynas tossed him in front of Nero's horse.

"What is this?" Nero asked.

"A problem," the lord replied.

The battle continued on, the scent of copper and a sickly rot perfuming the air. It only took a few moments before the boy soldier's eyes turned red and then began leaking blood. Splotches of maroon dotted the visible skin of his face and neck.

Nero narrowed his eyes when the skin weakened

and then broke apart as if acid had eaten away at it. The soldier screamed as his eyes melted and then dripped from his face. A faint hissing sound was all that was left when the emaciated corpse sagged to the ground. There was not muscle or flesh left to bring back.

Only a pile of bones barely held together by stretched skin and a rancid smell.

Anger licked through him. A fire lighting in his veins.

"He was poisoned," Nero said.

"Many of them have been," Zairaynas said. "Troops are dropping left and right, Your Excellency."

"What is the source?" Nero asked.

"We're still trying to determine—"

Nero snapped his fingers, and the steed that had once been a living, breathing creature lowered itself to the grass without hesitation. Nero kicked his good leg over one side and pulled the cane out of one of the many side holsters. Zairaynas fumbled, dropping to both knees as Nero walked toward him.

Nero cracked the cane over the lord's skull. Blood splattered Nero's face as Zairaynas collapsed beside the boy. He didn't bother to see whether he was dead or alive. The lord had served his purpose in getting them here, but he failed when he let the army be poisoned.

His head apothecary and other vassals all lowered their eyes from the sidelines where they stood. "Well?" Nero demanded, starting toward them. "Does anyone know what caused this?"

"Your Grace——" a vassal said. There was only a brief flash as he swung the cane again and struck her.

"I am your Emperor," he seethed. "Kings are beneath me."

"Your *Excellency*," the apothecary said, making sure to exaggerate the title. "The soldiers would have needed to consume it. There is no way for a simple poison to reach so many unless it came from a shared source."

"What are you saying?"

The apothecary's expression was grave, fearful. Nero appraised him as he said, "Either somehow they poisoned our supplies . . . or they poisoned the river."

They'd been having supply problems for weeks. If it weren't for so much of the army already being dead, they might not have actually made it to the city walls.

But this . . . this would not do.

He did not come this far to lose.

"No soldier is to be given food or water until we breach those walls," Nero commanded. Not a single vassal or captain or general dared to protest, though the light in their eyes turned bleak.

Men could only live so long without provisions, particularly men who fought.

Nero didn't need them to be living to fight.

No, he had other means.

The harmony of the violinist faded as he turned his attentions to the battle. His power sought the dead and dying like a bloodlion to scent. Much of his army had perished. Too many to count. This was a crippling blow that could spell the end if he were weaker.

But he was Nero.

Emperor of Triene.

God among men.

The chosen champion of all six light gods.

Raiser of the dead and beholder of Ramiel's gift.

He would not be defeated by a simple poison.

Nero tossed his cane aside and got to his knees.

He bowed his head to the grass and breathed deeply, sinking deeper into the depths of that music. He did not dance with Mazzulah in his mind's eye, for Nero was too far gone to simply dance.

The scent of grass and dirt and copper and the sickly sweetness of the most brilliant of all light magics mixed together as he funneled deep into himself.

His bad leg twinged in pain, but Nero ignored both it and the burning from his blind eye. He offered himself to the power bestowed on him.

His sacrifice.

Both the gods and his light magic listened.

Fire ignited in his veins. A scream threatened to tear itself from his lips, but he would not utter it. Not a single sound. He died in silence, and he would live in silence as the power of life itself washed over him.

And the dead rose.

CHAPTER 47
HERALD OF LIFE

"Desperation breeds the best and the worst in us. For when there is no choice but to try, you will give it everything. For better or for worse."
— Lazarus Fierté, soul eater, King of Norcasta, Beliphor's heir, lover of Fear

She was ice and wind and death as she shook off his hand and jumped from the battlement.

Quinn descended on the incoming army as fear incarnate.

Wings of black smoke sprouted from her back to slow her descent. She landed and then rolled, and those stygian feathers exploded, killing the soldiers nearest to her instantly.

Lazarus had been right when he looked at her all those moons ago and saw a weapon.

What he didn't understand was that he would not be the hand to guide her. She belonged to no one but herself and would be wielded by no one but herself.

The chains of the gate clanked as the soldiers below tried to rapidly open it. Lazarus, not one for patience, released the firedrake from his skin. The great bird burst forth and then held steady in the air as Lazarus reached up and curled his hand around one of those deadly talons.

The creature batted its wings fiercely to hold both their weight as it descended over the wall and dropped him ten feet from Quinn. She barely seemed to notice as she engaged soldier after soldier, never faltering. Never hesitating.

Lazarus fell into a rhythm, keeping pace with her but not interfering as he took out soldier after soldier himself. The purple and gold gave way to crimson as he soaked himself in the blood of his enemies. The fighting became a repetition of sorts.

Dodge. Stab. Side-step. Swing.

Again. Again. Again.

His own heartbeat pounded in his ears, drowning out all sound. He called on the troll, the bloodlion, the windwyvern, the wraith, the kuras. He called on his souls. His companions.

And he unleashed them on the world.

Norcastan soldiers swarmed at his back as the gate

finally opened and the mass of his army flooded through.

Quinn fired off commands in the sky and magic rained down on their enemies.

They could do this. They could truly win and end it all.

Hope was a dangerous thing, and just as it started to form, so too, did it crumble.

Something snagged at his boot. He pulled away, and it caught again.

Lazarus frowned, only daring to look when he cut down the three men in front of him. Dirty fingers grasped at his feet, trying to pull him down . . . or pull itself up.

He stepped away, and another hand grasped. Then another. Then another.

The ground itself shook violently as light exploded from the farthest vantage point. It was blinding in its intensity. Lazarus threw his arm in front of his gaze, trying to shield himself as the light of a star ignited so bright that all of the Sirian continent had to have seen it.

The ground shook further. Crevices appeared as hands clawed for them. Fingers and bones reached for the sky, reached for that light, and Lazarus knew that once more he'd underestimated his brother.

"He's controlling them!" Quinn yelled. A tidal wave of black magic shot through the battlefield, flinging men out of the way as if they were nothing.

Quinn walked through the wake she'd made, crossing the dying trenches to get to him. "They feel fear, but I can't control them. Even as they lose their minds, they still do as he commands."

Lazarus looked back to the unnatural glow.

They had to stop him to get through the army.

They had to get through the army to stop him.

And at the end of it, someone had to die.

A nameless, faceless soldier . . . they'd never get close enough.

"I've got an idea," Lazarus said. His eyes narrowed, and he pointed at the other end of the valley. The firedrake and windwyvern both took notice as he silently bid them onward.

The cold winds of winter swept through the valley, followed by the flaming heat of the firedrake's breath. They attacked the soldiers with wind and flame. Destroying all that they could in their rampage.

Nero might be able to control men, but these beasts, they were his and his alone.

"You don't know if this will kill you or not," Quinn murmured. Her eyes were focused on the sky, and they both watched as the great birds ate up the distance to the woolly mammoths.

"It's our best shot," Lazarus said as a volley of arrows shot through the sky. The windwyvern darted to the side, barely missing the lethal projectiles. The firedrake twisted, facing the hard feathers toward the archers in the carriages atop the mammoths. The arrows pinged off, unable to break through.

But in defending from one set of archers, the firedrake opened itself up to another attack.

The woolly mammoth on the other side swung its head. That giant tree still in its trunk as it slammed into the firedrake.

A keening screech filled the skies and Lazarus felt his connection with the bird waver. The firedrake plummeted.

Falling. Flailing. Fizzling.

He felt the dread, the fear, the panic as the bird crashed. Then silence.

"Is it dead?" Quinn asked quietly, just loud enough to be heard over the shouts and screams. She twirled periodically, moving quick as a viper to unarm and slit the throats of their enemies.

"Yes," Lazarus said, not looking away as the windwyvern avoided that same swinging trunk. It was almost out of their reach when a different kind of trap sprang.

Archers shot arrows attached to rope. They burrowed in the other mammoth and ground, but the purpose of them wasn't to hit the windwyvern. It was to stop it.

It dove right then left, trying to skate between the gaps in the rope.

"It's not going to make it," Quinn said. "You need to pull out."

"You can't control the dead, and our forces aren't strong enough to stop them," he replied. "We have to take risks. I cannot lose—"

He didn't get to finish the sentence before a pike with a foot-long metal arrowhead was thrown from the top of one of the mammoths. The windwyvern tried to avoid it but ended up taking it in the wing.

Quinn growled under her breath and turned to stab a man in the eye with one of her daggers before casting Lazarus a vicious look as the bird fell, and the soldiers finished it off then.

Its dying screams haunted him.

This was it. They truly had no way to reach Nero and end this.

The armies would fight until only one stood.

Fear traced through him, and not the kind that made his heart pound. This wasn't Quinn's fear. This was his own.

Lazarus threw himself into the fight with a sort of desperation that only a man with everything to lose could feel. He didn't notice the skies darken as he cut down his enemies. He didn't see the flashes of lightning that reflected off his sword.

It was only when he heard the thunder that Lazarus lifted his head.

A storm was brewing over all of Norcasta.

Over the world.

And in the center of it, a giant winged beast flew with a rider on its back.

"What is that?" Lazarus said, nodding to the sky. Quinn lifted her head and then narrowed her eyes.

"I think . . ." She focused for a moment, and then her expression smoothed. Quinn smiled at the dark skies as the first drops of rain descended onto them. "Risk has ascended."

CHAPTER 48
A CHANGING TIDE

"Anyone can be broken, but each of us must choose if we will be remade from it. We must choose what we will become."
— *Mariska "Risk" Darkova, beast tamer, Mazzulah's heir*

W ind and rain battered at Rainier's wings. Risk lifted a claw-tipped hand and pulled her wet locks of white hair away from her face, peering down at the battlefield from the sky.

She hoped she wasn't too late.

Judging by the sheer number of soldiers and red swatches of color that painted the field . . . she was right on time.

On wings of night, she and her familiar dropped from the skies. She projected picture after picture of Quinn, Draeven, Lorraine, and Lazarus to the night sphinx. They combed the field up and down. Fear and worry tried to eat away at her heart, but it was frozen, solid as ice in her chest, and it no longer beat. She pushed past those dark feelings and the hopelessness that tried to sink in, and she circled the battlefield once more.

"*There*," Rainier said, tilting to one side to bank a hard right. Risk gripped her wet fur and squeezed her tired thighs. They'd been riding for weeks, crossing from the dark realm to the Sirian continent and then across it.

Risk didn't sleep as she once had, and it made the journey easier. Neither hunger nor exhaustion slowed them down. Still, Rainier could not fly forever, and Risk's body—while stronger than ever—still wasn't used to flying. Especially without a saddle of any sort.

They'd improvised in an attempt to get to Norcasta as soon as possible.

With her ascension, her powers had been amplified to incredible heights. She sensed Neiss across the continent and followed that connection to the serpent.

She didn't see him in battle now, but as Rainier moved closer and closer to the ground, she spotted Quinn.

She wore red and gold. Black magic drifted behind her in the wind like a dark cloak. Ashes fell from her skin with every twist and twirl of her blades. Her sister, pale with ethereal lavender hair and eyes of the lightest blue, wielded death and destruction.

But when she looked at Risk and saw her, it wasn't the fear twister that smiled.

It was Quinn. Her Quinn. The one she'd walked into the dark realm for.

Soldiers scrambled to get out of the way as Rainier snapped her wings in and they dropped to the ground. Risk unclenched her cramped hands and stood on the back of her familiar. Rainier's tail swished side to side in agitation at having people so close to her.

Like Risk, she preferred space, and a battlefield was anything but.

"Took you long enough," Quinn shouted.

Risk couldn't help but smile as she jumped down. Her boots hit the trampled grass with a thud.

"I came as fast as I could," Risk said. Spotted fur sprouted on her skin as she took on the speed of a cheetah. Her claws grew even longer, sharper. Her blue eyes narrowed into cat-like slits. Risk didn't carry daggers or knives. She had no shield.

But she didn't need one.

Not anymore.

As she leapt into battle, a feeling of rightness settled over her. Everything in their lives, both hers and Quinn's, had built to this. Two sisters once broken, now stronger than ever.

They spun in circles, protecting each other's backs. One would duck and the other swiped. Fear washed over her just from being so close in Quinn's presence, but it didn't hurt as it once had. She might not be fear, but she was the tamer of all beasts—her own sister included.

"You've gotten better," Quinn remarked, shooting a black tendril from her fingertips to stop a man dead in his tracks.

"I spent a long time in the dark realm," Risk said.

"I know," Quinn replied, ducking under her arm as Risk swung her claws toward someone's neck.

"I have something to tell you." Risk elbowed a soldier in the throat before turning and stabbing him through. Blood coated her hands and splattered her clothes. The gurgling chokes of his dying reminding her of the stream she almost died in before her ascension. Risk pressed her lips firmly together and then ripped his head clean from his body.

"We have a lot to talk about if we can stay alive long enough to win," Quinn told her, eyeing the head that hung from her closed fist. "Mazzulah really did do a number on you."

"You have no idea," Risk said, then corrected, "well, you might, but this can't wait. I brought a message back with me."

Quinn stopped fighting entirely. Her jawline hard and eyes glittering with darkness as she said, "What is it?"

"Mazzulah said you know what to do if you want to win the game."

It was only for a fraction of a second, but for that

brief pause in time, her sister's lips parted. She looked at the sky once and then back to Risk and nodded.

"You understand?" Risk asked slowly, sweeping her foot to the side to trip a man.

"I do," Quinn said. "But I need to get past this entire army to do it."

Not far off, beasts Risk had never seen before were closing in. There were ten of them, each as tall as ten horses, with long, deadly tusks, and trunks that held trees. On their backs, archers were clearing the way for them. Maji used elements and other tricks to make quick work of the Norcastan king's army.

Risk frowned. They weren't going to hold out long at this rate. Even with her and Rainier, who was enjoying pouncing on men and then tearing their limbs apart.

"I can deal with the army, but you'll need to be quick."

"How fast is 'quick'?" Quinn said, falling back into rhythm with her.

"Minutes. I can't say how many for certain," Risk replied. "But there's no way for me to discern one army from the other. My field of vision can't tell friend from foe."

Her sister nodded. "You'll have to subdue them all." Her gaze turned mildly concerned as she said, "Are you sure you can handle that? I had to die and relinquish my physical body to channel enough magic to put down thousands, and this army is *hundreds* of thousands."

Mazzulah's words washed over her.

Only their heir could do it.

This had to be it; what she was talking about.

"I can do it," Risk said, "but I'm going to need Rainier's help. She will ground me. I'll need someone to protect me . . . just in case."

She could tell from the expression that crossed her sister's face that Quinn really did not like that.

"I can do it," another voice said. Risk turned, and standing there before them, panting from exertion— was Draeven. "I'll protect you both."

Risk was overwhelmed with emotion, but it was different than the feeling of when she first saw Quinn. She swallowed hard, barely dodging another attack in time, before nodding.

She could process this feeling, whatever it was, when there weren't men with swords trying to kill them.

"Alright," Risk said.

"I'm going to need a way to get across . . ." Quinn murmured to herself, sending a wave of fear behind her without looking. A dozen men collapsed to the ground and began clawing at their own eyes. The ones who didn't, kept coming, and the king killed them.

"Quinn, I don't know what you're planning—" Lazarus started.

"To end this," she said, "to win." She turned to him, and Risk had to look away. There was a vulnerability in her expression that she never saw on her sister's face. "I know what I need to do," Quinn said.

"We can find another way," the king said in a growl.

"There is no other way, Mazzulah said so. This part . . . this has to be me."

Risk saw it out of the corner of her eye as they kissed. She would have blushed before, but with them both occupied, she didn't trust them enough not to get themselves stabbed.

Draeven seemed to think the same as he came up beside her.

Quinn pulled away and turned to Risk. "Wait for my signal," she said, before disappearing in the crowd and running in the opposite direction.

"Wait—" Risk called, but it was too late. "How will I know her signal?"

Draeven snorted and took Quinn's place at her back.

"You'll know."

CHAPTER 49
HEIR OF WAR

*"Hopelessness is just another form of surrender and it will kill
you faster than any blade."*
— *Axelle, Queen of Ilvas, Saltira's heir*

The salty air licked wounds as she swung from one ship to the next. Her grip on the rope eased, and she executed a perfect landing. In one swift move, she pivoted and swung one axe while throwing the other.

"Die, die, die," she grumbled, hacking away at the already rotten flesh.

Cannons boomed and the scent of sulfur filled the air.

The ship lurched before rocking with the waves.

Axe made a mad dash across it, jumping onto a crate and then the railing before she leapt from the side, grasping for another dangling rope. The sail rotated, and she rode it halfway around the ship before landing back on her own where she'd started.

The enemy ship began to sink rapidly. Powder kegs ignited as more and more cannonballs shot through the wooden hull. Axe rubbed at her nose with the back of her hand and then extended it outward. Her still flying axe careened through the air, returning firmly to her grip.

"How many ships have we lost?"

"A dozen or so," Petra answered.

Axe turned her hat, letting the dangling beads slide into her periphery. The hat had been her mother's. *Madara* . . .

She was gone. Vaughn was gone.

But Axe would make them proud.

She'd sink the undead N'skari bastards to the bottom of the sea, even if it meant joining them. There would be no surrender.

"Prepare *Imogen*," Axe said softly. "Have her readied for me."

The wind whipped her hair away from her face as she stared out over the bay. The dark water churned, threatening death to any pirate or sailor that went over the edge. Axe lifted her blue gaze from the water to the armada before them. A mass of purple and gold sails.

She wanted to see those sails burn.

She wanted their ships at the bottom of the ocean.

She wanted the rage inside her to be felt by all.

Axe wasn't sure how long had passed before Petra came up beside her and rested one hand on the railing. "She's ready."

Axe nodded, but as she turned away, she paused. "If I don't come back . . . Ilvas is yours."

"Axe," Petra said, reaching for her. Determination surged within her, and Axe ran. She climbed the stairs two at a time, pushing past her own men, and then vaulted over the side using the one hanging rope available. Petra's heavy footsteps thudded behind her. "AXE!" her aunt screamed as she swung onto *Imogen*'s deck.

The ship had been finished the day her madara died. It was meant to be the crowning jewel of the Ilvan fleet.

Instead, Axe planned to use it to end her enemies.

Her feet had barely touched the wet planks when Axe threw her hatchet, cutting the rope off before Petra could reach it. Her aunt screamed bloody murder. "Don't do this, Urchin! It's not what your madara would have wanted, girl . . ."

Axe ignored her as she ran up to the helm. Her hands wrapped around the newly finished wheel and turned it hard to the left. The ship glided across the treacherous waters as it maneuvered at her command.

She raced down the steps once more to unfurl the sails.

A gust of wind hit them as if the skies were on her side.

Imogen shot through the gap between the fleets, heading straight into the heart of enemy waters.

She threw open the doors that led below deck and climbed as fast as her feet would carry her. The cannons had been prepped, just as she'd requested. Their wicks were ready to be lit.

Axe grabbed a torch from the wall.

Firelight bathed her face. An explosion rocked the ship as the Trienian ships fired on her.

Not wasting time, Axe got to work, lighting each cannon.

She was at the end of the line when the first one started to go off.

Thuds from above deck made her narrow her eyes. She gripped the torch in her sweaty palm and a hatchet in the other as footsteps sounded. The doors to below slapped against the wooden sides. She waited for them to descend all the way, as many of them as possible.

Some looked more dead than others. All of their flesh rotted in various stages. There was no light in their eyes as they looked at her. No gleam of humanity as they charged.

Axe didn't hesitate to flip the lid off the nearest crate.

They didn't falter in their pursuit, and she wondered if they knew that it was gunpowder in the crates that lined the walls.

Were they so far gone they didn't feel fear?

Or like her, were they simply willing to die for a purpose?

Axe didn't know, and she didn't ask.

"For madara!" she shouted before lowering the torch. "And for Vaughn," she added softly, right before it touched the fine black powder.

The explosion that followed was instant. She didn't have time to process much beyond pain as the entire ship went up in flames and she was blown back.

Imogen exploded with enough gunpowder to destroy fifty ships.

Like her enemies, Axe should have been torn limb from limb by the blast, but she remained mostly intact as she fell into the churning black waters. Her consciousness wavered as that burning intensified. She didn't register that it was the inhalation of water. All she saw was black. All she felt was pain.

The symbol of two axes crossed at the hilts glowed on her forehead. A beacon.

The waves raged as Axe floated deep beneath the surface.

She didn't feel the shadowy hands grab her and pull her up. She didn't see the man drag her to the largest chunk of wood left from the explosion. She didn't feel it as he hauled her over the edge and began pounding onto her chest.

But she did hear him.

In those final moments before she sat up and coughed water, a voice drifted over her and said, "Live, little pirate. It is not your time."

"You don't have to like someone to respect them, nor do you need to be friends to become true allies."
— Quinn Darkova, fear twister, walker of realms

It seemed as if time itself was nipping at heels.

Quinn ran as fast as she could, jumping over bodies, squeezing between men, and ducking blows meant for her. She didn't stop to fight. She didn't pause to save anyone or give orders. As the storm brewed overhead, Quinn ran, and she didn't look back.

As she passed through the gates, she heard her name being called.

"Can't stop," she shouted back without turning her head, only answering because it was Dominicus.

Footsteps followed her, and she sensed him on her heels, but Quinn didn't dare slow until she reached the palace. Even then, she took the stairs as fast as she could. At her back, he yelled, "What's happened? Why are you leaving the front?"

If only it were a simple answer.

She gave the only one that might make him back off.

"To win the war," she shouted, and breezed past the soldiers and through the double doors. They bowed their heads respectfully, not a single one daring to deny her. That was good. The faster she found Kairick, the better.

Behind her, a string of curses told her that Dominicus hadn't actually let up in the slightest. Quinn shook her head as she headed for Lorraine's chambers, where Kairick was supposed to be. She reached the room, guarded again by two soldiers— not that they would be much help if the castle were taken. Draeven had insisted as a means to keep an eye on him so that no one and nothing went *missing*.

Quinn threw the doors open and stepped inside. The room was empty, but the doors to the balcony were open. The wind ruffled the long drapes. They writhed in the air, twisting and turning as gust after gust came through, making the glass-paned doors slam into the walls and shatter.

On the balcony, Kairick stood, hand in hand with Vaughn.

His eyes were still black, but something about his expression seemed familiar.

"I told you not to let them out without me," Quinn said as she approached.

Kairick grimaced. "She was going to die. He sensed it. He needed to help her."

Quinn paused several feet away and looked at him again. Really looked at him.

Was it possible that he was fighting against the parasite in him? That he'd somehow found a way around it?

"She?" Quinn asked.

"The little pirate," Kairick answered. The breath hissed between her teeth as she inhaled sharply. He was fighting.

But there wasn't time to explore that.

"I need you to bring out Tarien. I need to ride him again."

Kairick blinked up at her. His eyes big and blue. He didn't have the innocent expression most children seemed to. But he wasn't devious either. He lacked the empathy and understanding for both. "Okay," he said.

Lifting a small hand, he released the firedrake. The balcony wasn't large enough for it to perch, so it hovered mid-air instead.

"What are you doing?" Dominicus panted, finally having caught up.

Quinn and Kairick and Vaughn all turned.

His face blanched.

"I'm going after Nero," Quinn said. "Don't try to st—"

"I'm coming with," he said, striding forward.

Quinn frowned. "What?"

"I'm coming with. To go after Nero."

"But you're you, and—"

"I'm assuming you have a way to get past the army?" he asked, coming to stand toe-to-toe with her. Quinn's gaze slid sideways to the firedrake. Dominicus swallowed.

"Of course it's the damned firedrake," he said.

"You don't need to come with," Quinn replied. "In fact, I don't recall asking you."

Instead of arguing, Dominicus unlatched his cloak and let it drop to the ground before stepping around her and going right to the ledge. He looked at the giant bird and said, "Please don't drop me."

Quinn gaped as the bird shifted closer. Dominicus grabbed the railing and swung one leg over and then the other, perching on the edge. He looked back at her and said, "If you fail, someone has to do it."

It dawned on her then that this wasn't about not trusting her. It wasn't magic. It wasn't about how much they did not get along.

He was willing to ride the firedrake into battle alongside her, so that no matter what—Nero died.

Quinn nodded once. He turned back to the creature and jumped from the ledge.

His legs spread and the firedrake dropped several feet as Dom landed on its back and grasped at the soft but strong down feathers.

Quinn climbed over the ledge, eyeing how little room there was behind him. Dominicus wasn't a large man, at least compared to Lazarus, but he was a man. One that took up most of the room.

"What are you waiting for?" he asked through gritted teeth.

The firedrake beat its wings, lifting itself higher once more. The bird turned to give her a meaningful look and then flicked its eyes downward.

"He wants to carry you with his talons," Kairick said.

Quinn eyed them for a moment. "Give me your gloves," she said to Dominicus. He tugged them off and tossed them at her, hitting her in the chest. She pulled them over her hands, wrinkling her nose at the dampness. They were a little loose, but not too bad. She nodded to the bird after testing her grip, and Tarien picked up wind, shooting up five feet. She reached for his talons and wrapped each of her hands around one. When the gloves held, she nodded once at Kairick and the firedrake shot into the sky.

"We have to get across the field at all costs," she told the bird, hoping it understood, or that Kairick was listening and would guide it.

The wind battered at her body as it hung hundreds of feet over the ground.

A drop from this high would kill her instantly.

But Quinn felt no fear as she held on with everything she had. They neared the edge of the city, but it was only when they crossed that Quinn gave the signal.

A giant black skull made of smoke formed in the sky.

It opened its mouth, and a snake crawled out.

One second passed. Then two.

Lightning struck the ground in front of her like a bolt from the gods themselves.

But the power that answered her wasn't a god.

It was violent and feral and tinged with the same cold that came from the dark realm.

It was Risk.

CHAPTER 51
OF FURY AND FLAME

"The key to power is neither fear, nor fury, nor control. It is acceptance. Only in accepting ourselves for all that we are, both good and bad, can we become who we are meant to be."

— Draeven Adelmar, rage thief, left-hand to the King of Norcasta, Tikkoh's heir

They fought back-to-back until the skull appeared in the sky.

Draeven wasn't sure what he expected to happen. He knew that Risk would be powerful when she came into her own. However, not even in his wildest dreams could he have guessed how powerful.

The air was charged with something unnamable and foreign to him. The storm over them swirled round and round, the thick clouds blotting out all sunlight. Risk lifted a hand into the sky, her fingers tipped in claws.

Her blue eyes glowed with power.

Lightning struck where she stood, but she did not scream. She did not die.

The single flash was blinding, and the aftershock singed the air itself.

Thunder clapped when she closed her hand into a fist.

And all as one, the entire battlefield and beyond dropped to their knees.

The mammoths toppled over each other, their riders thrown from the carriages on their backs. Any horsemen were kicked off as those beasts knelt.

Not a single head remained unbowed as far as his eyes could see.

Not even Lazarus.

Draeven sucked in a tight breath of air because he was the only one standing, beside Risk herself, and her familiar from the dark realm.

Seconds ticked by. She didn't speak. The muscle of her jaw twitched, and he heard grinding. The vein in her temple seemed to throb as time passed.

Quinn and the firedrake cleared the mammoths without issue and continued forward, but Risk . . . she was holding the entire world at her feet to give her sister a chance. To give them all a chance.

Her breath grew harsh. Ragged.

Draeven faced her and took her other hand. She squeezed, and he nodded, accepting the punishing strength, helping her in any way he could so that she could hold on.

"Breathe," he said quietly.

In. Out. In. Out.

He did it with her, and every painful hiss from her was like a stab to the chest.

Blue liquid dripped from her nose.

Her hand that gripped him was shaking, shuddering, trembling.

He thought he'd seen power. He thought he knew what its burden was, but there was nothing in the world like this woman.

Her onyx horns quivered as her legs shook, threatening to give out.

He didn't look away to see where Quinn was, he just hoped that it was enough.

"Hang in there," he said, clenching her hand back. "You can do this."

Risk bared her teeth at him, a whine building in her throat. He continued breathing with her. In. Out. In. Out. He talked her through it as the minutes passed by, but he sensed her breaking point. She could bring the world to its knees, but to do so . . . blood now ran freely from her nose. Starbursts of blue lined her otherwise unblemished face. Vessels that had popped under exertion. Blood was just beginning to drip from her ears when she screamed, and all that power snapped back.

She fell to her knees, and Draeven released her hand.

Behind him, the horde had risen once more. Draeven turned to them and stood his ground. Nothing and no one was going to hurt her.

The old injury through his chest barely twinged as he—for the first time and only time—gave himself fully to the power of a rage thief.

With a battle cry that could rattle the mountains, he lunged into the fray. His vision stained red, and he felt the fury of a lifetime. His arms ignited in flame. It shot down his sword, turning the blade a gleaming red.

He didn't even truly register it as the sword cut through flesh and blood and metal and bone. The limbs cauterized instantly, and those bodies that didn't —they boiled, then exploded.

Copper coated his tongue as the minutes blurred together.

When there was nothing more than a pile of bodies, Draeven threw down his sword and turned back to Risk.

He looked at her familiar. Its body was that of a panther, sleek and black. Its eyes glowed blue as hers.

"We need to get her out of here," he told the creature, hoping it understood.

Draeven reached for her, and it growled, but he didn't back down. When she weakly accepted his help, the creature lowered its eyes in submission. Risk's head lolled as he grabbed her arm and threw it around his shoulder. He grabbed her by the waist, thankful for how tiny she was given he was still injured and probably just made it worse. It was hard to tell with the rage still coursing through his system.

He turned to haul her onto the giant predator's back when excruciating pain ran through him.

Draeven stumbled. He didn't even have time to swipe or protect his back before both he and Risk fell against the large cat. He looked down and shuddered at the stump where his foot should have been, blood gushing from the wound.

A hiss that was far too loud to be Risk jolted him from his stupor.

Draeven turned his head to see Neiss, easily fifty feet long and still growing. Anger and fear rippled through his body before surprise washed over him. Neiss coiled, rearing back to strike. But not at him. He snapped forward, grasping the solider that had attacked Draeven, and swallowed him whole.

The basilisk wrapped around the giant cat's body, forming a barrier with its own skin that neither sword nor magic could penetrate. He wasn't sure when or how Quinn had been able to send the serpent after him, but for once, he was grateful to see him.

Neiss looked to him, briefly nodding his head before turning and keeping watch. Draeven returned the gesture, unable to process that he just thanked a snake.

"Draeven," his name coming from Risk's lips startled him. Everything was so vibrant and yet not. It was loud, yet he struggled to hear. He had a feeling she'd been saying his name for a while now.

"You need to go," he said. "You're not strong enough to fight them all off, and I can't protect you." His vision was beginning to blur. Sound was becoming more and more distorted.

"I do," she agreed. "But you need to live." Risk pulled away from him, and he didn't know why until his own sword loomed in front of him.

"Wh-what are you doing?" he asked, struggling to stay awake.

"Trying to save you, now turn on the fire."

"I don't know how," he groaned, turning into the slick fur of the cat.

So soft . . .

"I said turn on the fire."

Power leaked from her command and Draeven, weak from the blood loss trying to claim him, was hopeless to resist. The last of his rage ignited once more. She extended the sword toward him.

"Take the sword and press the blade to the wound."

Unable to deny her, even as he felt himself slipping away, Draeven took the sword. He pressed the hot edge to his wound. The pain barely touched him as his consciousness started to wane once more, and not even Risk could hold him.

Draeven closed his eyes, but not before he saw her face bathed in firelight.

He promised himself then that if he lived through this, he was going after her.

Even if her sister was a nightmare.

She was worth it, and so much more.

CHAPTER 52
FEARLESS

"In the end, we must conquer ourselves. We are our own worst enemies."
— *Quinn Darkova, fear twister, walker of realms*

The wave of power that brought the world to its knees only lasted long enough for them to reach the end of the line. Quinn dropped from the firedrake's claws at the same moment the soldiers stood. They formed a semi-circle around the emperor who was keeled over in the dirt.

"Nero," Quinn said, by way of greeting. She didn't have forever to do this, and every precious second was another one that someone she cared about could die. Permanently.

The man in the grass turned his head. The scar

over his left eye looked grotesque. His skin appeared hard and leathery. The corner of his mouth curled up into a cruel grin. His good eye focused on Quinn.

"I was so certain it would be Lazarus and I in the end. I can't say that I'm truly disappointed it's you, however. He could never do what needed to be done when it was hard. But you—you understand. Don't you, Quinn?"

She narrowed her eyes on him as the firedrake touched down behind her.

It emitted a roar and breathed fire on the soldiers that would dare stop her.

"You don't know him," Quinn said. "Not truly. Just as you don't know me. You think you do. Everyone has lines that they won't cross. Good. Bad. Evil. Everyone but you. You would truly do anything for power. Kill anyone. Me? I kill when people hurt me. I play games. Lazarus also kills for power, but he doesn't kill those who are loyal. You have no regard for anyone or anything but yourself."

Quinn trailed closer to him. Nero didn't seem alarmed. He still thought Ramiel's gift would protect him. That he was invincible. Untouchable.

"My lack of empathy makes me supreme. Emotions are messy, complicated things. People would be better off without them," Nero said, slowly sitting up.

Quinn squatted in front of him. "That's the thing. Everyone feels something. Even if you can't understand others, you still have emotions." She reached out and ran a fingertip over his cheek. The magic he'd expended to bring so many back left him weak. Crippled.

"You're bold for one that knows killing me means their own death," he said, narrowing his eyes.

Quinn tsked. "I believe you said, 'any harm done unto me shall have the same done back to you.' They are not the same." Quinn grinned maniacally, and she swore that somewhere out there she heard a laugh, deep and dark and sultry. As if Mazzulah knew that they'd won.

"They *are*," Nero said.

"I can't feel fear. It does not touch me. I may die. I may not. Either way, you don't scare me—because while I might not feel fear, *you do*."

Quinn placed the palms of her hands on either side of his face.

Nero's good eye rounded, the pupil dilating. He reached for her with tendrils of light, but Quinn evaporated, taking her truest form.

In the death realm, she kissed his lips and surrendered both of them to the consequences.

Nero's eyes turned black, and his mouth opened as if to scream.

She peered in his mind and saw all his little wicked games. The terrible things he'd done. The even more horrendous things he would do.

And then, she showed him her darkness.

Ramiel's gift.

An eye for an eye.

Quinn had spent three days quietly thinking on it. What weapon could kill him and not her?

No blade.

No poison.

But when Risk brought her a message from the dark realm, she knew the answer for certain.

No other power would succeed except fear.

She could kill him with it and end this, but fear, it never harmed her. It was her truest friend and her oldest companion. It was where she felt safest.

If she feared the ends, it never would have worked. It would have eaten her alive as surely as it did him. But she didn't because Quinn was Neiss' true heir.

Mazzulah was right. She was the best and the worst.

She was Quinn Darkova.

Right-hand.

Survivor.

Fear twister.

Fear itself.

And she would end this.

Nero's heart shuddered, skipping a beat. His eye fractured under the weight of power, faster than most of her victims, in truth. His body shook, and scratchy rasps escaped his throat.

She didn't even need to send images into his

mind. She let it play all on its own because when all other emotions were stripped away, what was left of him was no god.

Nero, Emperor of Triene, was just a man. A horrible, awful man.

A mortal driven to slaughter for power because he feared what he was without it. He feared being small and meaningless. He feared powerlessness, and it was that fear that ultimately was his own destruction.

Not even the power of six gods could protect him from that.

As dusk settled, the game finally ended.

Nero—son of no one, loved by no one, mourned by no one—died.

Quinn could have sworn in that final moment before the light left his eye that a cold wind, not from this world, drifted over the continent to greet her.

The door to the dark realm opened, only for a moment.

Just long enough for the king of gods to whisper across the world, "*Thank you, my beauty. We are finally free.*"

"For some, death is the end, but for others, it is just an extension of living."
— *Mariska "Risk" Darkova, beast tamer, Mazzulah's heir*

One by one, hundreds of thousands of men fell dead in an instant.

Risk urged Rainier on, encouraging her to fly faster. As fast as she could.

The storm cleared, and the Leviticus' eye slipped below the horizon. Night was upon them when Risk spotted it, a massive darkness that could only be one person.

Rainier neared the ground, and Risk jumped from her back. She landed awkwardly on her ankle but pushed herself forward. The grass was dead. The men in the semi-circle along with them. Beside her sister's unconscious form lay two men.

The first was what Risk could only assume was the emperor. His skin had turned black. His eyes exploded. Nothing more than a husk that appeared to be black glass remained of him.

But the other . . .

Risk knelt between him and Quinn.

She searched her sister's form first. It wavered between the dead and living realms, unconscious but alive. At least in some capacity.

Her worry lessened as she turned to the other man.

He wasn't dead, but he was dying. Blood drenched his clothes and his breathing was abnormal.

"What happened here?" Risk asked him.

"They were given orders to kill her at all costs while she was distracted with Nero. It was an ambush. They had Maji. They had—" he coughed, and crimson dotted his lips. Risk tried not to grimace.

"Where's the firedrake?" she asked him. His eyes darted to the side where a mass grave lay. Bodies were piled one on top of the next. She couldn't make out the beast in it, but beside it, a faint black outline told her that what Dom said was true. They'd killed it; the beast was bound for the dark realm now.

"Return and be free," she whispered. Power emanated from those words. A blessing. An image of the firedrake appeared, and the beast bowed its head and then got swept away. The embers of its soul drifted back to the dark realm where it would continue onto the forgotten forest—where all beasts came from and where all returned.

Dominicus coughed again. Risk looked down and pressed her lips together.

She knew there was no saving him. She barely even knew him, but he'd saved her sister, and for that, she would stay with him until the end.

"You fought bravely," she told him.

"I'm going to die," he said. There was no sadness in his voice. No anguish. No pity. If anything, he was resigned.

Risk hesitantly took his hand and squeezed softly.

"Yes," she breathed. "Is there anything you want me to tell them?"

His eyes were unfocused, staring up at the great expanse that was the night sky. The stars were just starting to come out when he said, "Tell Lorraine that I love her, and I know she loved Quinn. I protected her, for her. And that wherever I'm going . . ." His voice started to wane. Words were becoming difficult. The end was near. "Tell her I'll wait for her."

The light in his eyes flickered, and he closed his eyes for the last time.

His spirit formed in front of her, and she whispered the only thanks she could truly give for a soul bound to her realm. "Return and be free."

Unable to resist the call of the dead, his soul drifted away along with so many others that were finally free. Risk gave a moment of silence for him with her head bowed, and then she turned and picked up Quinn and brought her home.

CHAPTER 54
FROM THE ASHES

Quinn turned on her side and settled into the pillows. It'd been so long since she'd been at rest. She hadn't been able to sleep since—

Quinn bolted upright. Her eyes flew open.

She blinked several times, simultaneously processing the dim lighting of candles with closed drapes and the sounds of battle that echoed from her memories. As it came pouring back into her, Quinn turned. Risk was there, sitting beside her in a chair. Her sister looked more at ease than she could ever recall. Her white hair was braided back in plaits that had to be Lorraine's work. She was dressed in leathers that fit her well for once, and her eyes—they glowed with power. Risk smiled.

"What happened? Why was I asleep?" Quinn asked, looking around once more. Lazarus was nowhere to be found.

"If I had to guess, I'd say because killing Nero the way you did launched you into a state in-between life and death. Fear can't truly kill you, but you exerted a great deal of power to do it and your body needed to heal." Risk shrugged.

"I don't have a body, not really."

"You still have a form, even if it's not always in this realm. Your magic and your soul are one. As far as I can tell, you used too much of yourself, and it scattered parts of you that needed time to come back together." Risk leaned forward, one clawed hand running across the silk sheets. While Lazarus wasn't there, they were in his chambers at the palace in Dumas.

"Where is—"

"Bathing," Risk said before she could even finish. "I brought you back here after the battle, and he refused to leave your side for several days. Lorraine finally convinced him he needed to bathe when I told them you'd be waking soon."

Something settled within her. Quinn leaned back against the headboard and blew out a breath. "We won," she said. "It's been so long that it's hard to believe."

Risk nodded slowly. "The game is over. Mazzulah returned to the realm of the gods immediately after you killed Nero. She took the other dark gods with her. It remains to be seen what will happen with the light ones . . . but I don't think they'll be bothering our world again."

Quinn narrowed her eyes and really looked at her sister.

"You've changed," she said after a long minute.

"So have you," Risk replied. "The dark realm does that to people."

Quinn nodded. "You were gone a little over a month and a half in this world."

"I know," Risk said. "After I brought you back, Lorraine and I had a very long talk. While it felt like years to me . . . not much time passed here at all. I'm not sure how I feel about that."

"I was the same," Quinn said. "It gets better."

Risk looked away, and while much time had passed for her, Quinn knew her sister's tells.

"What aren't you telling me?"

Risk took a deep breath, and Quinn noticed the

lack of a heartbeat coming from her. "I can't stay," she said. "Not permanently, at least. I have to go back."

"What? Why?"

Her sister caressed her cheek with a claw-tipped finger. "The real reason Mazzulah demanded I stay was because I had to ascend in the dark realm so that I could absorb some of its magic. I'm the heir they've been waiting for. I'm half raksasa, so I can actually survive without aging, but I'm also half beast tamer— so I have the magic to keep the raksasa in line. I bonded to the dark realm when I ascended there, so that I could take Mazzulah's place when we won the war."

Quinn opened and closed her mouth, for once caught off guard. "That's . . . Myori's wrath. That's insane. I'm not leaving you in that place—"

"You're not leaving anything," Risk said softly. "I love you, but this isn't your choice. I agreed to it, and in return, the gods will never return to our world. The game is over, and I'll be the guardian to the world of the dead."

Her eyes were earnest, as if begging Quinn to understand. Minutes passed by when Quinn finally said, "Is this what you want?"

"Yes, actually," Risk answered. "I never fit in with this world, and that's because half of me isn't from here. Now I can exist in both. I have my power and my own purpose outside of you."

Quinn threw her arms around her sister's shoulders and drew her into a crushing embrace. There was a time when Risk would have frozen and shied away from all contact, but she didn't do that. She wrapped her arms around Quinn in return and hugged her fiercely.

"All I ever wanted was for you to find your place," Quinn said. "Even if it's not with me."

"I will always have a place with you, but I needed to learn what it meant to be on my own. To survive on my own and find power on my own. I have, and the best part is that you can visit me anytime you want —since you technically exist in both realms."

A cough from the doorway made them pause.

Lazarus stood there, wearing nothing but a towel wrapped around his waist. Water dripped from his hair onto the marble floors. Quinn swallowed hard, and Risk pulled away.

"I'll give you some time . . ." Risk said, moving to stand.

Quinn grabbed her wrist. "You're not leaving yet, right?"

"No, I'll stay for a while. Come find me tomorrow and we can talk more."

Quinn nodded and let Risk step away. Lazarus moved aside so that she could leave.

The door closed behind him. Lazarus prowled closer, a predator like no other.

Quinn twisted her body, sliding her legs over the

edge of the bed, and let him come to stand between them.

His calloused hands grasped her thighs to widen them further. The towel dropped away.

Instead of taking her as she expected, he released his grip on her legs and wrapped his arms around her upper body, pressing them together skin to skin.

The scent of fire and ash soothed her. He inhaled deeply, a contented rumble coming from his chest.

"I thought I lost you."

"I'm not easy to kill these days," Quinn said.

He pulled away and cupped her face with both hands. Quinn shivered at his touch. He lowered his face so that they were inches from each other.

"I know better than to ask you to marry me. Telling you to stay safe will do nothing but push you away. Luckily for both of us, there are several countries that are now without leaders. Will you stay with me? Conquer with me? If not as my wife, then as my general and my lover?"

All her life, she'd had an itch she couldn't scratch. A nagging feeling that weighed her down. A clawing in her chest.

But for the first time, there was none of that. Only silence and a mild warmth.

She knew without asking that this was what it meant to be at peace.

To exist in a place where she was finally . . . happy.

Quinn smiled at him, and it was just as wicked as ever. Just as cruel.

"I'd love to," she purred. Lazarus groaned in turn.

They didn't speak after that.

CHAPTER 55
A NEW BEGINNING

*"Even a field burned to nothing but ash will eventually grow
again. The land may be scarred, but time finds a way to heal."*
— Mariska "Risk" Darkova, beast tamer, Mazzulah's heir,
guardian of the dark realm

R isk walked down the back hallways of the
palace, avoiding the most populated areas. She
weaved her way through them until she found the
king's garden, and in it, a sleeping Rainier.

Risk smiled faintly at her familiar and felt another
presence brush up against her magic.

"I've been looking for you," he said. Draeven
stepped out of the shadows. His violet eyes glowed
in the moonlight. He walked with a cane while he
was still adjusting to the wooden leg piece. His days

as a soldier were over now that he was missing a foot.

"I've been with Quinn," Risk said softly, not wanting to disturb Rainier. The night sphinx still needed sleep, even if Risk did not.

"Lorraine told me. How is she?"

"She's . . . Quinn." Risk shrugged. "Lazarus is with her now."

"Ahh," Draeven said. "I see." He moved to stand next to her, close but not touching.

"I'm sorry about your leg," Risk said awkwardly. "I'm sorry you got hurt defending me." She gnawed at her bottom lip, looking anywhere but at him when she felt his gaze on her face.

"I don't regret it. Not for a second," Draeven said.

Risk turned and then blinked slowly. He was standing much closer than she'd realized.

Their faces were only inches apart.

"Draeven, I—"

"I like you," he said. Risk started to step away, and he followed, but he didn't grab her or touch her. She backed up until her spine touched the hard wall behind her.

"I like you too," she started slowly. "I don't have many friends."

"No," he shook his head. "I *like* you. I like that you're compassionate and assertive and kind. I like that you care about other creatures for more than what they can offer you. I like how loyal you are to

Quinn, though I question sometimes if she deserves it. I like you for you, and I like you—*more* than a friend. Do you understand?"

Risk's lips parted. She opened then closed them twice before saying, "You know what I've been through, right?"

His jaw tightened, and he nodded once. "I do."

"Then you know that I might not ever be able to give you things—"

"I'm not asking for anything, Risk, well—that's not completely true. I want a chance to see."

Her nose scrunched as her eyebrows drew together. "A chance?" she asked slowly.

"To court you," he said.

"But I just said—"

"I know what you said," he interrupted. "But I'm serious. I'm not asking you to do anything you're uncomfortable with. Just . . . spend time with me. See where it goes."

Risk pressed her lips together and frowned. "I'll be returning to the dark realm in a few weeks."

The corner of his mouth turned up. "I don't mind waiting."

"Are you sure? I may be gone a long time," Risk said, lifting her eyebrows.

"I'm sure," he said, sounding amused. A light twinkled in his eyes that she hadn't seen before. "You're worth it."

"How do you know that? If you're not asking for anything . . ."

"I told you," he said quietly. "I like *you*. I like everything I know about you. I like who I am around you. Will you let me spend time with you?"

Risk stared at him, frozen to the spot. If her heart weren't ice, it would have been beating erratically. She didn't have her body to tell the warning signs anymore.

But she did have her magic.

Under any circumstances, when Risk felt unsafe, her magic leapt to the ready, prepared to defend her. Yet, with Draeven, it hadn't even bothered to tell her until he stood only feet away.

In his presence, she felt calm. Her magic was stable. It didn't try to attack. It didn't prowl around him, looking for weaknesses.

Then again, Risk felt safe around him. He was the only person other than Quinn that she trusted to protect her when she was so deep within the thralls of her power that she couldn't protect herself.

But was that enough? Was being safe enough? Was liking him enough?

Risk leaned forward, a thought taking shape in her mind.

"I want to try something," she whispered. "But I need you to not move, no matter what. Okay?"

Draeven didn't hesitate. "Okay," he breathed.

She stared at him. Their faces coming closer and closer together until she was becoming cross-eyed to hold his gaze. Draeven closed his eyes at the last possible second, but he didn't move—just as she'd asked.

He stood there, lips parted, and he let her make the decision.

Risk released her bottom lip and leaned in, crossing the last inch before she could change her mind. Their lips pressed together, and they were so soft.

So warm . . .

She tilted her head and deepened the kiss. Risk explored his mouth and this strange sensation running through her.

Her breath grew heavy. Her chest tightened with some kind of feeling.

Risk sighed softly against his lips before breaking away.

When Draeven opened his eyes, they glowed red as the raksasa, but Risk didn't feel afraid. Far from it.

"How was that?" he asked huskily. Draeven cleared his throat, and Risk tilted her head. She could tell that he was worried about her decision, which meant no matter what she decided, he would honor it.

"Meet me in the courtyard tomorrow night and we'll go flying," Risk said.

His eyes widened. "You're certain?"

Risk leaned away, frowning. "Is that not how this

'courting' goes?" she asked, feeling uncertain all of a sudden.

"No, that's not what I meant. Flying with you would be my honor—I don't want you to feel like you have to do this. If you need more time to think—"

Risk leaned in again, surer this time, and pressed her lips to his.

Draeven stopped talking. His lips moved against hers and it felt . . . incredible.

"Does that answer your question?" she whispered.

"Yes," he breathed.

EPILOGUE: 10 YEARS LATER

"Darkness means many things to many people. For some, it comforts, and for some, it terrifies. For those that truly live in the dark—it is home."
— *Quinn Darkova, fear twister, walker of realms*

Quinn and Lazarus stood arm in arm on one side. Lorraine, Kairick, and her son, Nathaniel, on the other. In front of them, Risk and Draeven locked hands as they swore their vows at the top of a hill on the first day of spring.

"Do you promise to love and *honor* this woman? Will you protect her at all costs? And buy her weapons on all holidays—"

"Axe," Lorraine chided under her breath. Axelle, now a twenty-six-year-old queen, rolled her one good eye. The other had been damaged by debris in the war, but instead of bemoaning the lack of an eye, she wore an eyepatch and claimed it made her 'look the part'. Quinn told Risk when she first announced their engagement that letting Axe of all people officiate it was a terrible idea. Risk hadn't exactly disagreed, but it was better than letting her plan it. The young queen was still as pompous as ever. She'd wanted a parade through the streets and cannons firing gold flakes beneath the sunset.

While some had changed over the last ten years, Quinn's sister had not.

She'd healed from the trauma of her past and embraced her role as guardian of the dark realm admirably—but she wasn't a people person. She never would be.

"I do," Draeven said firmly. He'd aged well, aided by Lorraine's potions. While it was inevitable that one day he would die, there were upsides in choosing to take the woman who ran the afterworld as your wife.

"Yes, but do you *promise* to buy her weapons because this is very important—"

"Axe," everyone groaned in unison. Risk's lips twitched, and Quinn sighed, still not seeing what her sister found so charming about the pirate girl. She might be a queen and a woman now, but she would always be a child in Quinn's mind.

"Yes, I promise to buy her weapons on all holidays," Draeven said.

"Thank you," Axe replied pointedly. "Mariska Darkova, do you promise to love and accept this man despite his faults? Will you forsake all the beautiful opportunities in favor of monogamy—"

"Myori's wrath," Quinn muttered. "Can you just say the damn vows?"

Axe narrowed her eyes and muttered, "hussy," under her breath. Quinn pursed her lips, and Lazarus patted her hand, which was looped through his arm.

"I've conquered five out of seven countries on a continent. You'd think she'd know better," Quinn huffed.

"We," Lazarus corrected.

"What?"

"*We* conquered," he said lightly, that hand stroking her own turning possessive.

"I suppose you helped," Quinn said with a grin. Dark delight flashed in his eyes, promising deliciously wicked things to come when they got back to the manor.

"Can we say our vows now?" Draeven interrupted.

"Be my guest, Lord Sunshine," Quinn quipped. He grumbled under his breath as Axe finished asking if monogamy was truly what Risk wanted. Unsurprisingly, she took after her mother when it came to relationships. While suitor after suitor came to Tritol to win her hand, Axe didn't believe in marriage any more than Quinn, but for different reasons. She had no desire to settle down or share her Queendom with anyone. Least of all a man who might try to put a stop to her shenanigans.

"I do," Risk said, smiling like the beautiful bride she was. She didn't wear a dress of white, but instead fine black tunic and linen trousers. Quinn had it on good authority they'd already consummated this marriage years ago, though Risk was very tight-lipped about it. Unlike Quinn, who would fuck Lazarus wherever it suited her, Risk was still uncomfortable with talking about any mentions of sex or affection.

Quinn wondered if she would always be that way, but forever was a long time, and there was no way to know. Given that Lord Sunshine was the person her sister picked, she imagined the prudish parts of her nature might stick around. Draeven also had no desire to talk about what went on between them behind closed doors.

"I now pronounce you husband and wife, you may kiss—or ya know—whatever it is you two do . . ."

Lorraine shot her a look, and Axe's jaw snapped shut. Risk leaned forward and gave him the most chaste peck on the lips that Quinn had ever seen, but she seemed happy and that was all that mattered to Quinn.

They turned and presented themselves as a couple, with the ribbon tying their hands together to signify their lives bound together. Quinn and the others clapped, and Rainier, who had been basking in the sun like a lazy cat, let out a tired roar. Neiss didn't even bother moving. Curled up on Rainier's back, he was enjoying some much-needed time in the sun. Hammocked in the basilisk's coils with her head hanging upside down was Talisa, a rotund and mischievous raccoon that Kairick had consumed after his firedrake perished.

Quinn walked over to her sister to congratulate her. Lazarus clapped Draeven on the back, and they fell into an easy rhythm.

"Where are you going for your honeymoon?" Quinn asked. Risk had left the planning to everyone else, and given she ran an entire realm on her own, no one had complained.

"Draeven arranged for us to go back to the Sari Sari Islands," Risk said. "What about you? Where are you and Lazarus off to next now that you've done your conquering for the next few decades?"

Quinn watched out of the corner of her eye as Vaughn appeared. Axe took off at a dead sprint, tackling him to the ground. "Kairick's ascension is close. We plan to take him to the springs to see if there's a way for Vaughn to ease his way out. Soul eaters . . . have a hard time ascending."

"He's come a long way," Risk said, watching them as well. "They both have." Axe hugged him fiercely, and he hugged her back. They were almost the same age now, but unlike Axe, Vaughn was forever frozen at the age he'd died. Like Quinn and Risk.

"Vaughn is able to control the urges leftover from

the blood magic, most of the time. He has occasional slips, but none while Axe is around," Quinn said quietly.

"If he doesn't survive Kairick ascending, you know I'll take care of him. He won't be tortured. I'll make sure of it," Risk told her. "Talisa as well."

"I know." Vaughn mussed Axe's hair like she was still a child, and she complained like one, though they all knew she lived for these visits.

"I'm still surprised he chose a raccoon," Risk said, looking over to the snoozing animals. Talisa's leg twitched, kicking Neiss.

Quinn shrugged. "He was lonely after Tarien died. He may not be a beast tamer, but he has an interesting bond with animals," she said, casting a glance at her sister. "She keeps Kairick and Vaughn company, and she keeps raiding the kitchen. It drives Draeven mad." Quinn grinned and chuckled to herself.

Risk muttered, "Yes, I've heard."

Lorraine stepped up on Quinn's other side. "Risk, dear, it's so nice to see you. You were gone longer this time."

Risk smiled at the other woman who now operated more as a regent in Norcasta than a stewardess. She and her son chose to remain in Dumas after the war. Nathaniel was everything his father wasn't, and when Lazarus offered to gift them any province they wanted, they chose to decline, instead ruling in

Lazarus' stead. Nathaniel had no real aspiration for power, and he focused on education. He loved knowledge, much like Lorraine, and took to studying in the libraries more than courting, much to his mother's chagrin. Lorraine loved to remind him she wasn't getting any younger and would love grandchildren, but he always reminded her that he was taking his time to find the right one. When he found someone who loved books the way he did, Lorraine would get her wish.

"I brought you something," Risk said, reaching inside her pocket. "It's from Dom."

She extended the letter to Lorraine, who tucked it away and thanked her quietly.

If Quinn were being honest, she didn't miss Dominicus, but she felt sorrow for Lorraine. Mazzulah bent the rules in letting Quinn out of the realm, but Quinn was also a fear twister. Her soul was accustomed to moving between realms before death. If anyone else were to try to leave, it would mean a true death. Instant. She couldn't bring back Lorraine's lost love, but she took love letters for them both ways every time she visited.

"How is he?" Lorraine asked.

"He's well. He plays chess with Imogen once a week and loses every time, but he keeps coming back. I'm starting to think he might be a masochist," Risk said.

Quinn snorted, and Lorraine smiled. A decade

had dulled the loss for her, Quinn could tell, but that didn't mean she didn't love and miss him. "He doesn't always know when to stop," Lorraine said.

"Yes, well, I think Imogen is quite enjoying the afterlife. She's made a harem with some raksasa . . ." Risk shuddered, and Quinn laughed.

"The more things change, the more they stay the same," Quinn said. She'd thought the same thing over a decade ago when she returned to her homeland for revenge.

She didn't find what she was looking for then. Only in death did she truly find life.

It was not the end for her. Not the end for any of them.

It was only the beginning.

And Quinn, she was looking forward to forever with Lazarus, and all the games they had yet to play.

The End.

MAGIC WARS: DEMONS OF NEW CHICAGO
BOOK ONE
TOUCHED BY
FIRE
USA TODAY BESTSELLING AUTHOR
KEL CARPENTER

For a decade, I've hated the supernaturals who owned my world.
I hunted them.
I killed them.

And now, in the most grand twist of fate—I am bonded to one of them.

Oh, the irony.

Being a supernatural bounty hunter isn't exactly a popular job. But after the magic wars, there aren't many things a human can do that will put food on the table.

Thankfully anything my right hook can't handle, my guns can.

Or so I thought.

When a demon summoning runs awry, the being that comes into this world changes everything.

I'm not sure if he's truly a demon or a god, but one thing I do know is that he's after me. I'd like to see him try.

I've got a promise to fulfill, and I'm not backing down.

The only way out of this is his death or mine, and I'll do anything to survive.

Even if that means making a deal with the devil.

—Get the Book Now!!!—

—Adult Reverse Harem Paranormal Romance—

A Demon's Guide to the Afterlife:

Dark Horse (Book One)

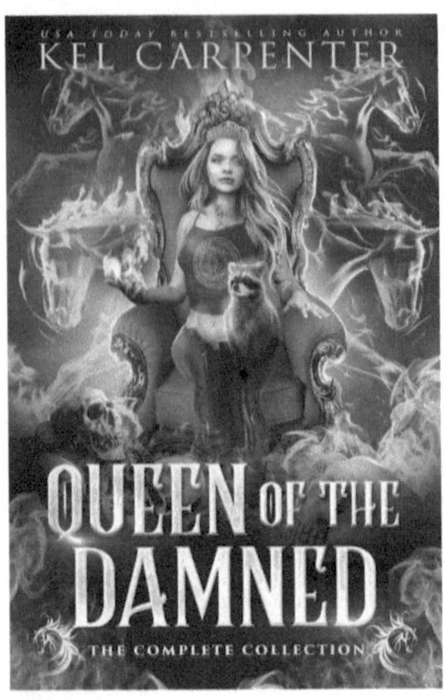

—Adult Reverse Harem Urban Fantasy—

Queen of the Damned Series:

Complete Series Boxset

—New Adult Urban Fantasy—

The Grimm Brotherhood Series:

Complete Series Boxset

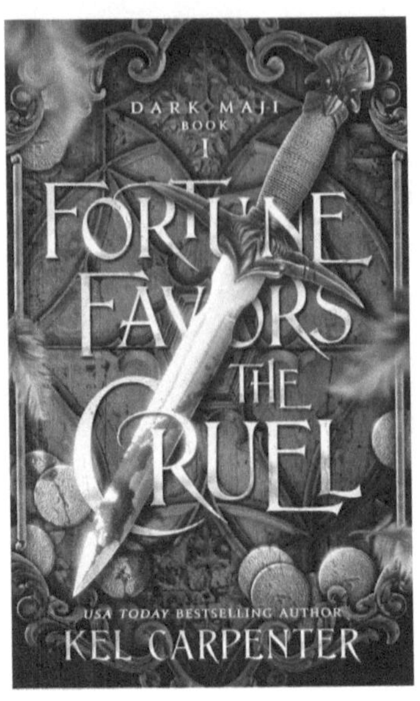

—Adult Dark Fantasy—

The Dark Maji Series:

Fortune Favors the Cruel (Book One)

Blessed be the Wicked (Book Two)

Twisted is the Crown (Book Three)

For King and Corruption (Book Four)

Long Live the Soulless (Book Five)

ABOUT KEL CARPENTER

Kel Carpenter is a master of werdz. When she's not reading or writing, she's traveling the world, lovingly pestering her editor, and spending time with her husband and fur-babies. She is always on the search for good tacos and the best pizza. She resides in Maryland and desperately tries to avoid the traffic.

Join Kel's Readers Group!

ACKNOWLEDGMENTS

I'm going to tell you a secret. This was the easiest ending I have ever written because it is the one I have enjoyed the most. It is also the ending I am most proud of.

Quinn and Lazarus have come so far, yet they remained true to themselves. Risk underwent a journey of healing that was very near to my heart. In some ways, it's sad for me to say goodbye. I've finally reached the place where I know they will be okay, though, and that they don't need me to write them anymore. It's a bittersweet moment finishing a series. I hope you loved it as much as I do.

Thank you to my team that has supported me to this point. Analisa, Graceley, Maegan, Courtney, and

Dom—you guys all helped make this story better in your own ways.

Thank you to my husband, Matt. Your never-ending patience, love, and support has made it possible for me to achieve my dreams.

And to you, dear reader, I thank you more than any of them. Without your support, I would not be able to write as I do. Crafting stories is my passion. It's one of my greatest joys, and it's because of you that I get to do it. Thank you for following Quinn and Lazarus to the end.

Long Live the Soulless!